'I think there is quite enough evidence to suggest that he may have been murdered, either for what he stood for or because of what he had found out about the Knights of the Cross. I am also convinced that neither the German Government nor the British Government want the truth to be known.'

'That makes it difficult for a journalist.'

Paget could see that I was preparing to leave. 'Using normal journalistic procedures, impossible ... I have an idea about how this can be done. I've discussed it with Gordon. But there is no need for you to be bothered with the details until you have decided whether or not you want to go ahead.' He took me towards the door. 'Given what happened to George, I cannot pretend that we can be certain that no danger would be involved. But if you were to uncover what I suspect is there, then you would perform a considerable service both to your friend and to your country. Indeed, it is not an exaggeration to say that it could affect the future course of the history of the world.'

Piers Paul Read is the author of thirteen novels and three works of non-fiction, including the international bestseller *Alive*. Past novels have won the Hawthornden Prize and the Geoffrey Faber, Somerset Maugham and James Tait Black Awards. He is married with four children and lives in London.

### *Also by Piers Paul Read*

#### FICTION

Game in Heaven with Tussy Marx
The Junkers
Monk Dawson
The Professor's Daughter
The Upstart
Polonaise
A Married Man
The Villa Golitsyn
The Free Frenchman
A Season in the West
On the Third Day
A Patriot in Berlin

#### NON—FICTION

Alive: The Story of the Andes Survivors
The Train Robbers
Ablaze: The Story of Chernobyl

Piers Paul Read

# *Knights of the Cross*

ORION

An Orion Paperback
First published in Great Britain by
Weidenfeld & Nicolson in 1997
This paperback edition published in 1997 by
Orion Books Ltd,
Orion House, 5 Upper St Martin's Lane,
London WC2H 9EA

A CIP catalogue record for this book
is available from the British Library.

ISBN: 0 75280 937 7

Typeset by Deltatype Ltd, Birkenhead, Merseyside

Printed and bound in Great Britain by
Clays Ltd, St Ives plc

The ridiculous is always so near to the sublime.
George Bernanos THE DIARY OF A COUNTRY PRIEST

*One*

## Saturday

*To have a woman.* The phrase has a manly ring to it. I imagine it being used by a soldier on leave from the front during World War I, or a French existentialist in St Germain-des-Prés in the 1950s. Imminent death or philosophical alienation detaches the act from the person.

If all goes as I anticipate this evening, I shall have a woman – the first in more than a year.

## Sunday

A mistake. As soon as I kissed her, I realised that she was not just a woman. She was Denise Trafford of the French team at the BBC Monitoring Service. I think she also had misgivings but we went through with it. Will it be awkward at Caversham tomorrow? We shall see.

## Monday

It was. Polite acknowledgement of our new intimacy but also an unspoken understanding that it would not happen again. Why do I not learn from past mistakes? Illusion, disillusion. The monotonous movements of the two-stroke engine that carries us through life. I thought I wanted a woman, then realised that no woman is just a woman, she is also a person. Was I dismayed that she was

3

not the person with whom I had shared my life for seven years? Not Ruth? A woman is a woman, I told myself, as I clasped her, felt her. But my senses told me she was different. Her odour: scent and secretions. Her sounds: forced. Perhaps faked. My body went ahead. My mind withdrew. To make love with detachment leads to disgust. Disgust at her. Disgust at oneself.

We had lunch today at the same table at the staff restaurant. Two others from her team sat beside us. We gossiped and complained. The status quo ante. Bill, today's duty editor, stopped as he was passing. 'Didn't you know George Harding at Cambridge?'

'No. Why?'

'He's disappeared.'

Why did I lie? Increasingly, I find that my reflex answer to any question is a lie. It buys me time to consider whether I want something about myself to be known. Why hide the fact that I was a friend of George at Cambridge? A close friend. One of his two closest friends. Because George is a success. So is the second, Gordon Taylor. George is a minister in the Government, Gordon editor of a national newspaper. Both are constantly in the public eye, while I am one of the public that watches them, paid modestly to monitor Russian-language broadcasts for the BBC. I translate and transcribe whatever comes over the airwaves from Moscow. Digests of what I write go to the researchers at the Foreign Office and to the foreign correspondents who brief George Harding and Gordon Taylor. I am the servant of the servants of my old friends.

## Tuesday

I lay awake last night comparing the bodies of Ruth and Denise. Ruth has longer legs and smaller breasts. Denise is in better proportion. Ruth's hair is black and straight. Denise's hair is wavy, brown and shoulder-length. Ruth bites her fingernails: Denise's are well-manicured. Ruth's skin is brown, Denise's white. I went on for some time, comparing and contrasting, concluding around four in the morning that their physical differences were superficial. Ruth was better in bed. Or so I remembered. At times. But Denise had not been put through her paces. She had not been given a chance to show what she could do. And possibly my memories of Ruth are distorted by retrospective illusion. When I am honest I remember that at times her open-mouthed ecstasy was in fact a yawn.

I awoke finally at six wondering if Denise was thinking in the same way about me. I had not been put through my paces. I had not shown her what I could do. While I write this, at breakfast, I hear on the radio that George is still missing.

## Friday

7.00 p.m. Alison questioned me closely this evening to find out whether I am being honest about myself in this journal. She considers it an important part of my therapy. I told her about my night with Denise, and what I had written about wanting 'a woman'. I could not see her (I lay back on her analyst's couch, she sat on a chair behind me) but I could sense that this aroused her interest. She did not ask for details of what happened, but probed the comparisons I had made between Denise and Ruth in an almost prurient fashion: this is apparently part of the technique of the proactive school of therapy to which she belongs. She pushed me to admit that the sight and smell of Denise without her clothes on actually provoked a sense of revulsion that I overcame only with an effort of will. I found myself saying that I had been taken aback by the sight of a great clump of dark pubic hair nestling between her white thighs.

Why? I could think of no explanation other than it seemed to me like a huge tarantula.

'But surely Ruth had pubic hair?'

'Less of it. And it was less evident against the cappuccino colour of her skin.'

There was a longer pause than usual as Alison made notes. When I left I noticed that she too has pale skin. Perhaps it is a mistake to go to a therapist who is a woman.

*Saturday*

The disappearance of George was the lead story on last night's *Newsnight* and takes up two columns on the front page of this morning's *Daily Telegraph*. It appears that last Thursday he went to Luxembourg for a meeting of second-ranking European ministers of defence. On the Friday evening, his civil servants flew back to England on the Luxair flight to Stansted. George remained in Luxembourg with his political adviser, Hugo Crook. They stayed at the Europa Hotel, which was close to the Kirchberg where the meeting had taken place. The two men dined together at the hotel restaurant, then retired to bed. George was to fly to Paris the next morning to join his wife for the weekend.

The next morning George had not appeared for breakfast. There was no answer from his telephone or to Crook's knock on his door. When Crook was eventually let into his minister's suite, he found that the bed had not been used. His belongings remained in his room. Inexplicably, Crook now assumed that George had taken an earlier flight to Paris. He himself flew back to London.

On the Saturday night, Patricia Harding had telephoned the ministry in London to find out why her husband had failed to turn up at the Crillon. The duty officer had referred her to Crook. Here the story becomes confusing. Although Crook could offer no explanation, he apparently assured Patricia that her husband's absence must be due to some misunderstanding. It was not until the Tuesday morning that the police were told that the minister was missing.

Jane telephoned just now to ask me to lunch tomorrow. I accepted and now regret it. Keeping this journal, which at first I resisted, has become absorbing; more interesting, at any rate, than the company of my sister and her bickering children. I must not become a recluse but going to a film with John and Anne tonight would have been enough. Denise hinted that she was free to come up to London but I said I was otherwise engaged. I made it sound as if I was sincerely sorry. I suspect that she was not convinced. Why did I pretend? Because I could hardly tell her about the tarantula.

Nor am I convinced that the tarantula is the correct explanation. Perhaps if I had brought Denise back to my flat in Fulham instead of going to hers in Henley our encounter would have been more of a success. Why did I dissuade her from coming to London even though I sensed she would have preferred it – a touch of glamour and excitement for only half an hour on a train? Because I did not want to make love to her on the bed that I had shared with Ruth. So we met at an Italian restaurant in Henley. She had gone back to her flat to take a shower and change. I came straight from Caversham. The food was good but the food was not the point. We both enjoyed that part of the evening, like two children playing truant from school. Then we went back to her flat in her car. She did not invite me. It was understood. It was a pleasant flat, but it was ... I search for the word. Dreary. Genteel. The furniture was modern apart from a small leather-topped repro desk. There were framed reproductions of Impressionist paintings on the walls, including Van Gogh's *Sunflowers*, and potted plants on the window-sill of the living room. Suddenly I saw a new dimension – her background, her class.

At Caversham, and even at the pub where we had gone for a drink on a number of occasions, she had seemed intelligent and amusing. She had told me about herself. She had been to a comprehensive school in Somerset, then went to York University. She had a taken a first-class degree. Attractive, intelligent, thirty-four years old. We would argue about the literature of our adopted nations: Tolstoy versus Flaubert, Stendhal versus Dostoevsky. But back in her flat there were no great writers to protect her, only paperback editions of their books. She was suddenly a middle-class spinster, daughter of a tax inspector, hard-pressed to pay the mortgage on this dingy flat. Even before I had sniffed her scent and secretions, I was repelled by the aroma of modest means. Ruth had been stylish. Ruth had been rich.

The Sunday papers, too, make George's disappearance their lead story but none has discovered anything that was not known before. They therefore fall back on speculation. The *Sunday Times* suggests that there may be a woman involved. Why else did Hugo Crook tell Patricia Harding on the Saturday night that his boss's failure to turn up at the Crillon must be the result of a misunderstanding? The leader in the *Gazette* predictably sees a political conspiracy: almost certainly, Gordon wrote it himself. Can it be a coincidence that George disappeared after a meeting of European defence ministers at which he vetoed a move to put a European Defence Force under a unitary command?

Last night, a film with John and Anne. Afterwards, at Pizza Express, we discussed snobbery. I did not tell them about Denise, but I raised the topic because yesterday's realisation that the physical aversion I felt for Denise had less to do with her body than her background had left me feeling ashamed. But seeing Anne and John outside the Odeon made me realise that their feelings about Denise would have been identical to mine. Indeed, Anne's would have been more pronounced. If Denise had been a Nigerian princess or an Eskimo author or an American painter, she might have seen a point. But a woman from our own middle class ... The thought of introducing Denise to Anne made me cringe.

Because of this, as we came out of the cinema, I felt angry with Anne, blaming her for the snobbery of which I now felt ashamed. When we were seated at a table in Pizza Express, I therefore said, apropos of the film we had just seen, that the vitality of Hollywood was the result of America's classless society in which everyone feels everything is possible, while the failure of our cinema reflected the atrophied condition of British society. We retain the social patterns and prejudices of the nineteenth century, and imagine that they are universally admired. In fact, where they are not ignored they are ridiculed, and where they are not ridiculed they are despised.

Anne looked bored. She loathes arguments. She only likes gossip. But John took up my gauntlet: like most barristers he likes to show off his eloquence to his friends. His argument went something like this: 'Of course we are snobs. It is part of our national identity and every attempt to change it has failed. The masses, the working classes, the common people, whatever you like to call them, have had every opportunity to get rid of the buttresses of privilege – the monarchy, the House of Lords, the public schools. Have they done so? No. Because they know that without its class distinctions, we would be a nation without qualities, as bland as the Dutch or the Swiss or the Swedes. The Europeans may be incredulous that, in the last decade of the twentieth century, we still have unelected members of our second chamber whose right to be there comes from their descent from Norman barons, Indian nabobs or war profiteers. But behind their ridicule there is envy because, for all our eccentricity, we are a nation with a clear sense of its own identity.'

Anne yawned. John continued. 'All human communities develop hierarchies of one kind or another. In the United States it is based simply on wealth. Anyone can rise but equally anyone can fall. This releases a certain energy, as you say, but it also leads to a great sense of insecurity. Everyone is competing with everyone else and, since there are inevitably more losers than winners, most people are discontented. Older societies like India, with its complex system of castes, are much happier despite their poverty because there people do not blame themselves for the wretchedness of their condition. In England, too, we have developed complex systems to compensate life's losers. We promote the myth through the media that the English gentleman is an anachronism – irrelevant, unreal. The reality, as we all know, is that a disproportionate number of the jobs worth having still go to those educated at Oxford and Cambridge and the public schools. Look at banking or the law or the higher civil service. Even politics. If you want to be a judge or a minister –'

'Talking of which,' interrupted Anne, 'what on earth do you think has happened to your friend, George Harding?'

*My friend, George Harding.* When I first heard that George had been made a minister, I was initially incredulous and then afraid. Until that moment, I had lived under the illusion that we were ruled by people who knew what they were doing: wise men, able men, responsible men. Now I was being ruled by George, and George, I knew, for all his fluency and charm, was a man of superficial learning and no judgement at all. George was a fool. George was a minister. Therefore, a minister could be a fool. And if one minister can be a fool, then several ministers can be fools; indeed, the entire cabinet can be fools. This understanding, I now appreciate, is part of growing up.

I telephone Jane to say that I have a hangover and so will not come to lunch. She does not believe me. Sisters can always tell when their brothers lie. But she also deceives. She pretends to be disappointed when almost certainly she only asked me out of a sense of duty. She thinks that I must be lonely without a wife.

I sit at my kitchen table writing this journal. Outside, sunshine, then clouds. When the sun shines, I am dazzled by its reflection on the yellow Formica top to the table. And on the white paper of my notebook. Every now and then, I look out at the backs of the houses in the next street. The dirty plates from my breakfast are in the dishwasher. The frying pan remains on the stove. In time, I shall make myself a tuna-fish and mayonnaise sandwich and drink a glass of skimmed milk. Tonight I shall watch television. Now, I must return to the questions that preoccupy me – Denise, Ruth, Anne, the tarantula, the potted plants in Denise's flat, George Harding.

Clearly, I could not pretend to Anne that I did not know George Harding because she used to meet him when she came to visit me at Cambridge. It is even likely that she had some kind of sexual encounter with George. She blushed when I once suggested it. 'Don't be absurd.' Anne, too, is a facile liar.

I remember that I was jealous. She was not my girlfriend, and did not come to Cambridge to audition for that role, but rather to meet other men through me. I was attracted to her but was too timid to make a pass and, anyway, felt that I knew her too well. It was clear as soon as she met him that Anne was attracted to George. Most girls were. I always thought that his face was too fleshy for him to be considered handsome, but men are rarely good judges of what appeals to women. George was rich, or at any rate richer than most of his friends. He had a car. He ate in restaurants. He also went to bed with women as a matter of course, while Gordon and I were inhibited by our sincerity and scruples.

Anne, though pretty, was not Gordon's type. He was already drawn to cosmopolitan types like Patricia, whom he eventually married – girls with Swiss fathers, South American mothers and flats in Eaton Square. Anne was an English rose. Her father was a retired brigadier. They lived in Avelscombe Manor in Somerset. My father was the rector in the same village. This meant little to George Harding. Little, but not nothing. At one point George asked me if it was true that Anne's father was chairman of his constituency's Conservative Association. I said he was not. George looked surprised. He said that Anne had led him to believe that he was. Determined women buy kisses with lies.

Gordon liked Anne but he did not know any better than I did how to handle women. Also, Gordon was an intellectual while Anne was not. When we sat in the Whim, a café on Trinity Street, Gordon would talk about Bagehot and the glory of the British constitution. Anne would pretend to listen. She once asked him to stay at Avelscombe for a hunt ball. She also invited George but George refused. I was one of the party. Gordon was in paradise. The crumbling old house, smelly Labradors, gumboots, fishing rods, dinner jackets – here before him was the English life that he had only dreamed of in his bedroom in The Cedars, Northcoate Close, Guildford, Surrey. Anne liked the way it impressed him. She flirted with class. But Gordon was too wiry, too bookish, and revealed by his unconcealed admiration for the English upper classes that he himself was not 'from the top drawer'.

Neither was I. The genius of the English system is that finally everyone is excluded so everyone aspires. Some

13

ferociously from the outer circles, like Irish terrorists or disgruntled blacks. Some obliquely, like authors and architects who pretend to be aloof, detached, *hors categorie*, until they are offered a decoration by the monarch whom they ridiculed in their youth – a knighthood, a peerage, an Order of Merit, a Companion-ship of Honour. From the very start, we aspire or our parents aspire for us. The best may be inaccessible but there is always something that will raise us a notch above someone else. In my case, the triumphs were always tarnished with the subsequent realisation that I had had to settle for second best: that my public school was a minor public school, my college in Cambridge a second-rate college. I was considered a success at Cambridge but there were always others who were more successful. In my last term I was elected Treasurer of the Union. Gordon was elected Secretary, George President. We were a triumvirate and held the reins of student power. We invited famous people to take part in our debates. They accepted because Cambridge retained its prestige. It was a good way for George to make the acquaintance of politicians: he had already decided upon a political career. Gordon dithered for a while between journalism and academic work, but already in his final year he was contributing articles to the *Spectator*, and he left Cam-bridge with the promise of a job as a leader-writer from the editor of the *Sunday Gazette*. Gordon had invited him to speak at the Cambridge Union against the motion that 'Britain is part of Europe'.

Dusk. I sit in the kitchen watching as the windows of the houses that back on to mine light up one by one. I pull down the blind, then move through to the sitting room. I note with satisfaction that it is tidy: living with one's own order or disorder is one of the pleasures of living alone. I look at my eighteenth-century English watercolours and pieces of antique furniture, all given to me by my mother, and again ask myself the question: if Denise had had original paintings on her walls instead of reproductions, would I have found her body more enticing? If so, what does that tell me about love?

## Monday

A dramatic day. In the middle of the morning, I noticed an unusual level of activity among the German monitors. Suddenly, the editor of the day appeared, then disappeared, then reappeared, then disappeared again. Nothing much was happening in our part of the world. I took a break, sauntered over to the Germans and asked what was going on.

'Harding's been found.'

'Where?'

'Floating in the Saar.'

This had been monitored on the German Press Agency. It was important to get the news to our masters at the Foreign Office before it reached them from some other source.

I went back to my work-station and called up the story on my screen. My old friend had been found by a fisherman near the town of Metlach. It seemed that his body had been in the water for several days. I went back to my desk. *Sic transit gloria mundi*. At lunch I sat with two colleagues. Denise joined us. We all wondered how George could have ended up in the Saar. Where was the Saar? One of the colleagues, Jan Tarnowski, said that it was in Luxembourg. Denise put him right. It rose in

France but flowed into the Mosel, which was a tributary of the Rhine. Jan blushed at his error. He is one of the half-dozen at Caversham who lust after Denise.

I believe that, of all those eating lunch in the staff restaurant, Denise was the most upset by the news about George – not because she cared about George but because it dominated the conversation and made it difficult for her to bring the conversation around from public to private matters. A number of my colleagues even seemed pleased. George's crude nationalism had not endeared him to the internationalist ethos that prevails at Caversham. But the dominant emotion was excitement. The death of a minister of the Crown in such bizarre circumstances set the scene for a drama that would unfold over the weeks to come. News has become an important source of entertainment. Nothing mitigates the ennui of everyday life better than a political scandal, except possibly a catastrophic famine or a good war. The Romans went to the Colosseum to watch gladiatorial combat; now satellite communications have made the whole world an arena. We watch the killing in Africa or the Balkans with horrified fascination. Best of all is a war like that over the Falkland Islands or Kuwait where we ourselves are in no danger but our own team takes part in the game. Even where Britain has no conceivable interest in the outcome, we can still support a team – the Tutsis against the Hutus, say, or the Muslims against the Serbs.

I get home in time for Channel Four news. George's corpse was fished out of the river at 9.48 this morning. Water in his lungs established that death was due to drowning. He was naked. Preliminary calculations suggested that he had been in the water for around a week.

16

*

I go to the kitchen and prepare a tandoori chicken curry for the microwave oven. As I poke holes in the white plastic covering with the point of a knife, I think of George. He is described in the *Evening Standard* as a man you either loved or hated. Was this true? At Cambridge I had loved him because he was confident, generous and amusing. He had overdrafts at his bank but at the Pitt Club or in restaurants he always paid the bill. He tipped the college porters for delivering messages, and in return they turned a blind eye if a girl spent a night in his rooms. He always kept a folded ten-pound note in his driving licence in case he was stopped by the police for speeding. When I read Nietzsche in my second year, I knew at once what he meant by the superman. George.

While my ready-cooked curry cools in its plastic matrix, I go to the living room to look up George in *People of Today*.

*Harding, George Anthony*: MP (C) Northvale West, 1985–; s. of Henry Denham Harding of The Old Rectory, Chillingworth, Wiltshire, and Christine Mary, née Malmsley; b. 9 March 1957; *educ*. Eton and Trinity College, Cambridge; m. 1982 Patricia Figuera-Ansbach, d. of Karl-Anton Figuera-Ansbach of Geneva, Switzerland; 2 s. (James Henry, b. 9 June 1983, Anthony Charles, b. 18 Sept 1985). *Career* research asst Conservative Central Office, 1978–80; director, Anglo-Oriental Holdings, 1981–84; Ansbach Enterprises (UK), 1984–; PA to Rt Hon. Hamish Griffield, MP, 1987; PPS to Rt Hon. Peter Trend, MP, PC, 1988–91; asst govt whip, 1992; parl. under-secretary of state, Welsh Office, 1993. *Clubs* White's, Pratt's, Beefsteak, Carlton. *Recreations* shooting, foreign travel. *Style*

George Harding Esq., 26 Queensland Street, Belgravia, London SW1.

This heavy book of reference was bought some years ago by Ruth and is still on my shelves because by the time she left me it was out of date: it was published before George's appointment as Under-Secretary of State for Defence. Ruth said that *People of Today* was essential for background briefing but its massive presence among our books also served as a mute rebuke. Even in 1991 there was an entry for both George and Gordon. There was none for me.

I told her that there should be a *People of Yesterday* as there was a *Who Was Who*. I composed my own entry:

*Latham, Michael Blaise*: s. of Rev. Richard Latham of Avelscombe Rectory, Avelscombe, Somerset, and Lavinia Jane, née Switherton, d. of Sir Henry Switherton, Bt.; b. 10 June 1958;
*educ.* Bradfield College and Selwyn College, Cambridge; m. Ruth Mayer, d. of Dr Samuel Mayer (*qv*) of Hampstead, London. *Career* graduate student, Univ. of Smolensk, 1981–3; research fellow, Institute of International Relations, London, 1984–7; freelance author and journalist, 1988–1990; subeditor, BBC Monitoring, 1991–5. *Publications*: *The Hammer and the Anvil* (unpublished). *Clubs* none. *Recreations* none. *Style* Michael Latham Esq., Flat 4, 22 Elm Park Grove, London SW10.

Ruth was not amused. She had assumed that by this stage I would be eminent and, if not rich, at least rich enough to enable her to work less at analysing investments and take the time to have a child. But history had played us a dirty trick. I had given up my position at the Institute of

18

International Relations to write the definitive book on the Communist Party of the Soviet Union. I had been promised an advance of £100,000 which had seemed a large sum when I signed the contract. I should have read it more closely. A quarter was to be paid on signature; a quarter on delivery and acceptance; a quarter on hardback publication; a quarter on paperback publication. With the first quarter, less agent's commission, viz. £22,500, I had to live for the two years it would take to write the book. Fortunately, there was Ruth's salary from Hoare Govett. She believed in equality between the sexes and so had no grounds to complain. She could also see that I worked hard; so hard, indeed, that the idea of having children was laid aside. But even as I reached the last chapters of my book, radical changes took place in the Soviet Union. Time and again, I had to revise what I had written, even alter what I had originally intended to say. The date for delivery came and went. The publishers did not seem to mind. Then came the breach in the Berlin Wall, the suspension of the Soviet Communist Party, finally the collapse of the Soviet Union. An awkward call from my agent informed me that the publishers had exercised their right to terminate the contract because of my failure to deliver on the specified date. There was a demand for the return of the first quarter of the advance.

Why do I recall this now as I eat microwaved curried chicken, my hand holding alternately a fork and a pen? Because it was at this moment that George Harding received his first job in government and Gordon was made deputy editor of the *Sunday Gazette*. Both men were still my friends. I was their expert on Soviet affairs. I contributed to George's speeches and wrote leaders for the *Gazette*. After the fall of Gorbachev and the rise of Yeltsin, my particular knowledge of the Soviet Communist Party was of less interest to them, just as it was of less interest to the public at large. Attempts to find another publisher for my book failed. My agent persuaded the first publisher to transfer the money I had already received to a new contract for another book that all parties knew would never be written. I abandoned my aspirations to be an author and tried to return to the life of an academic. But Soviet specialists were no longer in demand, and the posts that once would have been mine for the asking had either been abolished or would be abolished if any of the incumbents had been so foolhardy as to resign. I studied the advertisements every week in the *Times Educational Supplement* and the *Guardian* Creative and Media. I applied for many jobs and was offered only the one I still hold six years later, in BBC Monitoring at Caversham Park. It is a Band 7 job and earns me a salary of £20,000 a year.

*Newsnight*. Press conference in Saarbrücken. No one knows how George got into the river. Was he pushed or did he fall? Marks on his body but none suggests a disabling blow. Also, a clip of German detectives flying into Heathrow, presumably to interview Hugo Crook.

## Tuesday

Second press conference following the autopsy broadcast live. I call up the unedited transcript on my screen. Waterlogged lungs confirm that George drowned in the river Saar. From its state of decomposition, it is calculated that his body had been in the river since the previous Friday night or Saturday morning. There were marks on his body of a number of different kinds but none could be classified as a wound. Nor did the bruises suggest manhandling or a fatal blow. There was a high level of alcohol in his bloodstream. It was therefore possible that George Harding had fallen into the river, possibly in Saarbrücken itself, while under the influence of drink.

Then came the questions. What were the marks on his body? On his shoulder, shallow transverse lacerations. On his stomach, mild burns. On different parts of his body, the imprint of teeth, certainly human, probably a woman's. What could have made the burns? A travelling iron, perhaps, or curling tongs.

A question in English: 'Does this mean that he was tortured before he drowned?'

The answer in German: 'Taken with the traces of semen found in his urethra, it rather suggests sado-masochistic titillation.'

'Was someone else involved?'

'That is a plausible assumption.'

'Any theories as to who it might be?'

'None.'

The consensus at Caversham: *cherchez la femme*.

A session with Alison on my way home. Here, too, it is a matter of *cherchez la femme*. But which woman? To me the cause of my misfortunes is Ruth, who abandoned me when my fortunes and my morale were both at a low ebb. She marries me 'for better, for worse', then leaves me seven years later because I have not turned out a success.

Alison defends Ruth. She thinks that the real villain is

21

my mother. She thinks that I took out on Ruth the anger I felt at my mother for her lack of affection. She never hugged me as a child. I let that out in an early session. Alison thinks it significant. But today she struck gold. We returned to Denise and my ambivalent attitude towards her naked body, in particular towards the tarantula nestling between her thighs. Alison asked me if I could remember my attitude towards women's bodies as a child. Curiosity. Why do you say that? Because I remembered, one summer afternoon, when I was aged six or seven, peering into the private parts of the girl who lived on the farm next to the rectory.

'Was she older or younger?'

'Around the same age.'

'She let you?'

'Yes.'

'Was your curiosity satisfied?'

'The investigation was curtailed.'

'How?'

'We were in a barn. My mother found us.'

'Your mother found you?'

'Yes. *In flagrante delicto*.'

'What did she do?'

'She smacked me.'

A pause.

'And then?'

'She gripped my arm and took me home.'

'Did she say anything?'

'She said that I was never to do that again.'

A longer pause.

'Did you know why it was wrong?'

'No.'

'Did you do it again?'

'Not as a child.'

'What did you feel when your mother smacked you?'

'Shock.'

'Not pain?'

'No.'

'Or pleasure?'

'No.'

'Were you resentful?'

'Of what?'

'Of being punished for something you did not know was wrong?'

'It happened all the time.'

Jean-Jacques Rousseau's nursemaid used to birch his naked bottom until she saw that it excited him. Perhaps it was this that led Alison to ask if I enjoyed being smacked by my mother. I could sense that she was relieved when I said I was not. She is building me up as a sadist, not a masochist. An equally pointless hypothesis. I have never derived sexual pleasure from either inflicting or receiving pain. There was a decadent set when I was at Cambridge who read Huysmans and the Marquis de Sade while they listened to Wagner in darkened rooms, eating oysters and drinking champagne. It was all a pose. Or mostly a pose. I cannot answer for George. It was rumoured that some of the girls who came to visit him from London brought whips and rubber wet-suits. If one is not excited by such fetishes, it is difficult to believe it of anyone else, particularly a close friend. It did occur to me, but only some years later, that perhaps Anne's encounter with George had run into difficulties because he had asked her to do things that would have seemed obnoxious to an English rose.

It certainly seems unlikely that Anne goes in for anything particularly unconventional with John. One can never be sure. Practices that would have been thought perverse by our parents are now routine. Words like 'cunnilingus' and 'fellatio' suggested exquisite decadence to the would-be Oscar Wildes at Cambridge; now no one thinks twice about 'oral sex'. The only thing thought perverse today is abstinence: clearly, it was my not making love to Ruth over long periods of time that constitutes the cruelty Alison has in mind.

## Wednesday

Evidence in this morning's papers that the Government cannot decide how to respond to yesterday's press conference in Saarbrücken. It had hoped to exploit the public's sympathy but this is made difficult if it turns out that he died as the consequence of some perverse orgy. Anger in the anti-European broadsheets at the Germans' suggestion that the marks on his body came from 'sado-masochistic titillation'. 'As yet an unwarranted assumption,' says *The Times*.

I am beginning to regret telling everyone at Caversham that I had not known George at Cambridge. Was he titillated or tortured? Clearly, my reminiscences of George's student days would be of some relevance to the national debate. I remember, for example, that one of the girls who came to Cambridge to visit George was always dressed in black leather – black leather trousers, a black leather waistcoat, black leather shoes. Her black hair was shaped like a helmet; her features never moved to form an expression of any kind. She never spoke in our presence. I could imagine her tying George to a bedstead and brandishing a whip.

Ten years later, I found myself sitting next to this same

girl – now a woman – at a dinner party in Islington. She was married to a journalist on the *Guardian*. She talked to me about the problem they faced in choosing a secondary school for their children. They were both members of the Labour Party but their local comprehensive was among the worst schools in London. I was astonished by the contrast between the decadent *houri* of my youth and today's leftist bourgeoise. When I reminded her that we had met with George Harding at Cambridge ten years before, she said: 'Oh, yes. Isn't he doing well?'

'Do you ever see him?'

'God, no. He's so right-wing.'

'Wasn't he always?'

'I suppose he was.'

She did not seem to like being reminded of her liaison. It would have been awkward to ask her about George and whips.

Nietszche in *Thus Spake Zarathustra*: 'When you go to woman, do not forget your whip.' George admired Nietszche. He saw himself as an *Übermensch*. He may also have been glad to be reminded about the whip. Did he keep one in his rooms in Trinity in case his leather-clad girlfriend left hers in London?

*Thursday*
---

The discovery of the corpse 'of the British minister, Georgi Harding' reported today in the Russian media. Neither ITAR-TASS nor Ekho News Agency mention the marks on his body. Interfax alludes to 'unusual circumstances'. One forgets how prudish the Russians still are.

Unexpected feeling of elation on the 8.00 from Paddington to Reading. Should I mention this elation to Alison? She will think it signifies that therapy is working. I suspect it is simply because George Harding is dead.

Before I have a chance to mention it, Alison takes me back to the last years of my marriage to Ruth. Why had we so rarely made love?

'And what frequency is the norm?'

She ignores my counter-question. 'You were both physically quite well?'

'Yes.'

'Yet you did not make love for months at a time.'

'No.'

'Didn't you want to?'

'No.'

'Did she?'

'She thought we should.'

'Why?'

'She liked to conform to patterns of behaviour recommended in the colour magazines.'

'So when you did make love, it was because she thought you ought to?'

'Yes.'

'Did you feel that she enjoyed it?'

'Up to a point.'

'Did *you* enjoy it?'

'Up to a point.'

'What point?'

'It was not the same as before.'

'Not as good as before?'

'There was no sense of joy. Just physical release.'

'Can you say when you first started to grow indifferent to Ruth?'

'I was never indifferent: quite the contrary. It was not

what I felt about her but what I knew she felt about me that changed.'

'From what to what?'

'From love to disappointment.'

'Why?'

'She felt I had given up.'

'On what?'

'On life.'

'Why?'

'Because I was no longer ambitious. She thought the job at Caversham was a dead end.'

'Was it?'

'Not necessarily.'


BBC Monitoring at Caversham Park is a unique institution. People work there for different reasons. There are old anti-Communist *émigrés*, recruited at the time of the Cold War. There are bright young graduates who see it as a way into the BBC, or as a path to becoming a foreign correspondent. Some of these move on. Others marry and stay because they prefer the quality of life outside London. Two people doing the same job can have contrary attitudes. Denise sees herself as a success. I regard myself as a failure.

Ruth left me because I was depressed; I was depressed because I felt a failure; I felt a failure because I was stuck at Caversham in a dead-end job; but was it a dead-end job? Ruth thought so and urged me to do better.

Why? Did she think I was a failure because I thought I was a failure? Did my low self-esteem start to affect hers? Or did we consider my life dingy because we were continually comparing it with the lives of George and Gordon? Without them, we might both have decided that my job suited my talents. There were many advantages to working at Caversham – a pleasant ambiance, intelligent colleagues, a decent restaurant, sports facilities, a staff club, a crèche. It was bureaucratic, semi-secret, undemanding. At times it reminded me of my days in Smolensk.

But Ruth did not look back to Smolensk. She looked back to Cambridge. To George and Gordon. She wanted to be the woman behind a famous man – if not a minister or an editor, then Director-General of the BBC. She urged me on. For a time I pretended. I looked at the jobs advertised in *Ariel*, and went before a number of boards for positions in the Russian Service of the World Service at Bush House. I was boarded for one or two, but the selectors can always sniff out a man who is only going through the motions; after a year or two at Caversham, I abandoned the pretence.

But was this realism or resignation? Alison probes. It is important. She asks for a resumé of my explanation for the break-up of my marriage. Ruth was socially ambitious. When she first met me, I was a brilliant young Sovietologist with interesting friends like George Harding and Gordon Taylor. Eight years later, she finds herself married to a minor civil servant with no friends whatsoever. He is either too lazy or too cowardly to go for a higher salary or a better job. It is clear he will never provide her with the life he tacitly promised. Time is passing. The first wrinkles are to be seen around her eyes. Time to abandon ship and look for another man.

Alison is silent. Her silence tells me that she rejects this hypothesis. It is self-serving and so self-deluding. Her formula for health and happiness: know thyself! She asks me to recall the night before Ruth walked out.

It was the week of my thirty-fifth birthday. I had been

brooding on its significance as the half-way point between my birth and the biblically allotted life-span of three score years and ten. It was also the week in which it was announced that Gordon had been made editor of the *Sunday Gazette*.

I return from Caversham, tired after a late shift. Ruth suggests a party to celebrate my birthday. She has drawn up a list on her notebook computer of the people she means to ask. The list includes George and Patricia Harding, and Gordon and Delia Taylor. I say that I do not want a party. Reaching the age of thirty-five is no cause for celebration. Ruth insists. 'We never see anyone. For example, when did you last see Gordon or George?'

'I can't remember.'

'It must be four or five years.'

'Quite possibly.'

'Why don't you ring them?'

'I don't particularly want to see them.'

'You mean you haven't the nerve!'

My nerve had indeed failed me, but not in the way she supposed. Less than six months before I had summoned up the courage to ring my old friends. First George at the House of Commons, then Gordon at the *Gazette*. George's secretary thought I was someone from his constituency and put me through. It took him a moment to realise who I was. Then his tone was friendly enough. Only the other day, he told me, he had been dining with the Taylors and someone had asked what had become of me. I reminded him that I was working for BBC Monitoring. Of course, of course. I asked if he and Patricia could come to supper. Always difficult, you know, because of parliamentary business. What about lunch? Why not? He suggested a day five weeks ahead. On the morning of the day in question, his secretary telephoned to cancel. Pressing ministerial business. She said she would get back to me to make another appointment but never did.

Gordon was in a meeting when I telephoned but rang me back. He said quite candidly that he could never make supper because he so often worked late on the paper, and so felt duty bound to spend any spare evening with Delia and the children. Glancing through his diary, he also saw that he was tied up for lunch 'until kingdom come'. But he would definitely like to see me. It had been a long time. Hmmm … He leafed through his diary. What about this? On the following Tuesday, he had a spare hour between recording an interview in the South Bank Television Centre and lunch in the Savoy on the other side of the river. Why didn't we meet, say, for a late cup of coffee or an early drink in the cafeteria of the Royal Festival Hall? It was really quite pleasant. Much nicer than one might think.

I went. I rearranged my shift to be able to remain in London. Gordon kept our rendezvous. From where I sat in the cafeteria, I could see him climb out of a black chauffeur-driven Mercedes, and later stand at the entrance to the cafeteria, looking around with his usual expression of amiable perplexity, incongruous in the modern surroundings in his dark grey pin-striped suit.

He apologised for being late and warned me that he would have to leave early but, like the cafeteria, he was really quite pleasant, much nicer than one might think. He asked me what I was up to; knew all about BBC Monitoring; praised the World Service; assured me that the *Gazette* had always supported it, despite the cost to the taxpayer. He talked as fluently as he wrote and filled the time I had been allocated as precisely as he always fitted a thesis to a column of a thousand words.

I asked after Delia and the children. All were well. His brow furrowed. 'And how is …?'

30

'Ruth.'

'Ruth. Yes.'

'She's well.'

'Didn't she work for a bank?'

'Hoare Govett.'

'Children?'

'No. Not yet.'

'They change your life.'

'So I imagine.'

'I remember,' he said, 'that Ruth was very pretty.'

'Yes.'

'And Anne? Do you still see her?'

'From time to time.'

'She was great fun.'

He used the past tense, I think, not to suggest that Ruth was no longer pretty or Anne no longer fun, but to establish in his own mind, and perhaps in mine, that they were chapters from an earlier phase in his life. He looked at his watch. It was time to go. 'It *has* been good to see you,' he said as he stood. 'If only I had more time these days to keep up with my old friends.'

I told Alison about these encounters. I had never told Ruth. I had not told Ruth because they had left me feeling ashamed. Why ashamed? Because I was so passive, so humble, so obsequious, when dealing with my busy and celebrated friends. I feared that by seeing me through their eyes she would catch their contempt. It was one thing to have been ignored by George: he had never wasted his time on people he did not feel he could use. But Gordon had always purported to aspire to something more than worldly success. Both in conversation at Cambridge, and later in his columns, his line had been that 'It matters not if you win or lose but how you play the game.' As with the individual, so with the nation.

Time and again, he decried the Americans for their crude esteem of wealth, and the Germans and Japanese for their obsession with commerce. The genius of the British came from their respect for human qualities with no obvious utility – wit, style, curiosity, originality, learning. And loyalty. He always made much of loyalty. Not, it would seem, to old friends.

Because I had not told Ruth about my meeting with Gordon at the Royal Festival Hall, or about the cancelled lunch with George, I could not explain why it was impossible to ask them to the party, or that I was not to blame for the atrophied friendship. She therefore concluded that it was only my obtuseness that prevented her introducing these two luminaries to some of the colleagues she meant to invite from Hoare Govett. She went through into the bedroom and when later I joined her I saw from her face that she had wept. I lay down beside her and took her in my arms. She lay there like a sack, exhausted and dispirited. I suggested that, instead of having a party, we should have a child. She laughed. Or coughed. A laugh like a cough or a cough like a laugh. Whichever it was, there was no mirth. I moved to make love. She turned away. I persisted. The sack sagged beneath me. We made love – Ruth so removed from what she was doing that even her climax, which always came easily, might have been one that she had induced herself.

And because of her detachment, I too was detached and saw her body as if it was something apart – her legs bored, her breasts indifferent, her nipples deflated as if despairing of ever suckling a child.

*Friday*

At lunch in the staff restaurant, someone asks Pavel Kravchek why he is wearing a carnation in his button-hole. 'It is Margaret Thatcher's birthday.' No one knows whether he is being serious or can be bothered to find out.

Pavel is another of Denise's admirers. Clearly, in a confined community such as Caversham, a single woman in her mid-thirties is bound to be an object of male desire. It is also true that Denise is unquestionably the prettiest of the available women. Her face has a *fin-de-siècle* beauty, with plump lips, large eyes, an upturned nose. Her breasts, too, are of the kind you might see as part of the decoration on an art-deco Métro station in Paris, or the Grand Palais. Such looks are not fashionable: her bright eyes and healthy complexion contrast with the wan models in magazines. She has long legs, an elegant neck and a slim stomach, all of which appeal to my lecherous colleagues, particularly the Slavs.

*Saturday*

George Harding returned to Britain yesterday, in a coffin, flown from a British base in Germany to RAF Brize Norton. His funeral will be next Saturday in the parish church at Chillingworth. Only family and close friends are to attend.

Even the Sunday papers cannot spin gold out of straw. The continuing investigation in Germany merits no more than a mention on the inside pages. Only the *Gazette* continues with its line that George is the victim of a conspiracy of some kind. It castigates the Government for refusing to give him a state funeral in Westminster Abbey. 'He died while abroad on government business and died for his country almost as surely as any of those who fell fighting the Germans in the two world wars.'

Lunch with Jane at Clapham. Disastrous results. Mark is a wine snob, so there were four bottles of fancy claret. From boredom, I let him keep refilling my glass. Became benign with my nephews and nieces. Avoided joining them for a walk on the Common by pretending that I have to work. Returned to the flat, hoping to finish the Sunday papers.

A quarter of an hour after I get back, the telephone rings. It is Denise. She has been having lunch, or so she says, with friends in Chelsea. Could she drop in on her way back to Henley?

My befuddled mind can think of no pretext to put her off. Five minutes later, she is at my door. At first, I suspect that the lunch is an invention, but her flushed face at least confirms that she, too, has been drinking. She is wearing jeans, a T-shirt, a cashmere jersey, and adopts a jaunty, youthful manner as a matching accessory. 'So this is your lair,' she says, prowling uninvited from living room to kitchen to bedroom. She even looks into the bathroom and the cupboard by the front door. It is as if she means to make me an offer – for the flat or of herself.

34

I suggest making some coffee. We go to the kitchen. She leans against the sink as we wait for the kettle to boil. I glance at her face and wish she was not there; then at her thighs, enclosed by her tight-fitting jeans. I put the cafetière and two cups on a tray with a bowl of sugar and a small jug of milk. We go through to the living room. Denise sits back languorously on the sofa. I no longer look at her face, but only at her blue-denimed legs. The plunger of the cafetière stubbornly refuses to descend. I retract it and try again. This time, it slides into the glass jug as the designer intended. I wait before pouring the coffee into the cups. I glance again at her legs, then up into her eyes. Her eyes, not her face. They are not the eyes of Denise Trafford whose presence I resent, but of a woman who invites me to traverse the space between us that is covered by a kelim carpet and, after a few preliminary caresses, undo a button, unzip a zip and shake her out of her jeans. Tight-fitting, they drag her white knickers away from her pudenda: dreamily, she holds on to her knickers. The tarantula remains under wraps. She shifts on the sofa. I clamber over her and feel beneath the T-shirt and cashmere sweater. Is this pleasure? Then why do I feel rage? Because I know that the warm breasts belong to Denise Trafford whom I do not want to be there. I recall the words of St Paul, so often quoted from the pulpit by my father: 'I cannot understand my own behaviour. I fail to carry out the things I want to do, and I find myself doing the very things I hate.' The very things I hate with the very person I hate: in the tradition of the Fathers of the Church, I blame Denise for seducing me to act against my better judgement. The lair of the tarantula becomes the black hole of outer space, whose gravity inexorably draws all matter to its destruction. Helpless, I am sucked into the abyss. I rage against my fate. My gestures become rough. I shove the T-shirt and cashmere jersey over her face to obliterate her persona. If I have no will, then I am brute nature, and brutally I proceed with nature's task. She cries out. Pain or pleasure? No way of knowing. Her body moves. Is it rolling with the punches? Or undulating with the rhythm of rapturous sensation? Hard to tell. Now into my mind, befuddled with claret, comes the image of the marks on George's body. My teeth grip a fold of skin. I bite. A yelp. I yank back her head by her hair. She cries out again. I thrust and thrust again and then, with a final spasm of rage and disgust, drown the tarantula in its lair with my venomous sperm.

We both lie still. Sweaty. Drunk. Then, horror! I feel the soft tickle of a giant spider crawling across my back. I start. The spider's legs become fingers, then the fingers a hand that clamps me to the body beneath. 'Darling,' she whispers in my ear, 'that was wonderful.' A moment later. 'Well done.'

The coffee is cold. I take the tray back into the kitchen and make some tea. Denise follows, wearing only her T-shirt and knickers. Once again, she rests the small of her back against the sink. Silence. Then the growl of the kettle. I glance at her groin. A few black hairs protrude from the elastic, some stuck with sweat to her skin. Denise leaves her mooring at the sink and looks into the cupboards. For bread. Butter. Marmite. Honey. She makes herself at home.

Back in the living room, I wonder how long she will stay. She talks about this and that. The bagatelle of lovers. But we are not lovers. I am a hater. I hate her. I want her to go. I suspect that she knows this but it does not bother her. She is thinking: 'Post-coital *tristesse*.' Or: 'He is moody. How sweet.' Her face is fixed with the

36

smile of a woman's all-seeing, all-knowing intuition. 'You think you hate me but, in fact, as you have just demonstrated, you are powerless to resist nature and nature is on my side.'

She sits on the sofa, her naked legs tucked up beneath her. She munches toast. I switch on the television and watch *Songs of Praise*. Denise is puzzled. I explain. My father was a clergyman. I feel uneasy if a Sunday passes without some form of worship.

'But do you believe?' A chink of anxiety in her bland smile.

'No.'

She is relieved.

On the screen, healthy, radiant faces bawl out rousing hymns. This caterwauling has the intended effect. Denise puts on her jeans. 'I had better get back.' I rise to see her off to the sound of unctuous prayers and lusty singing. At the door, she gives me a soft kiss on my lips. '*À demain*.'

## Monday

To my surprise, Alison showed less interest this evening in the arachnophobic aspects of last night's encounter and returned instead to the words of St Paul. 'I find myself doing the very things I hate.' Where had I first heard them? From the pulpit. Spoken by whom? My father. Aha!

We have talked about my father before. Alison would like to build him up as an authoritarian figure but my conscious memories of him are of someone gentle, someone meek. 'Did you say meek or weak?' asked Alison.

'Is there a difference?'

'Blessed are the meek', as Nietzsche observed, consoles the losers in the struggle of life. It also justifies the passivity of people like my father who esteem peace and quiet. He never argued with his bishop or his archdeacon. If any of his congregation complained to him, he apologised even before the complaint was fully formulated. It was the same when it came to my mother. He had clearly decided from the start to let her have her way. I cannot remember him ever contradicting her on any question whatsoever.

'So it was your mother, not your father, who was the figure of authority in the family?'

'Yes.'

Alison was silent. I have become skilled at interpreting her silences and sensed now that she saw a piece of the puzzle falling into place. Her pencil scratched on the pad. I felt I could read what she was writing. 'Weak father, dominant mother, punished by mother for infantile sexual curiosity, fear of women and sex, *vagina dentalis*, suppressed sadism ...' And so on.

'The Catholics are right,' I said to her. 'The clergy should not marry.'

'Why do you say that?'

'Because the qualities the female of the species is programmed to look for in her mate are incompatible with those of a good priest.'

'You mean meekness?'

'Yes. The demands of natural selection ensure that women are attracted to strong men, and once married they continue to elicit that strength by nagging, complaining, arguing, provoking.'

'This is a description of your mother?'

'More or less.'

'And how should your father have reacted?'

'He should have told her to shut up.'

'What about your sister?'

'Jane?'

'Yes. How was she treated by your mother?'

'She was urged by my mother to learn from her mistakes.'

'What were these mistakes?'

'Forgoing a career to marry a clergyman.'

'Did your sister take her advice?'

'Up to a point.'

'Does she have a career?'

'No. But she married a banker.'

## Tuesday

The disadvantages of therapy: we begin to see all others through the prism of our own psyche and so lose any sense of their autonomous identity. Is Denise as dreadful as I perceive her to be, or are the features that elicit my disgust simply manifestations of neuroses inherited from my youth? Did I cross the kelim carpet to unbutton her jeans because I loved her or because I despised her? Does sex express affection or disgust? Do I resist her because I fear being emasculated by another mother? Or because I realise that she is not my type?

At work, I try to avoid her. I behave as if we have agreed that it would be better if we concealed our liaison from our colleagues. This would appear to eliminate the idea that among my motives in sleeping with her was a desire to triumph over my rivals.

Denise behaves as if she agrees. Yet every time she

comes across me in the Listening Room she gives me a quick look of *complicity*, which any other woman could interpret in a flash. It is as blatant as that fatal word 'darling' whispered in my ear. Fortunately, our shifts overlapped at lunch-time today but later, when she passed me in the corridor, she pursed her lips to signify a secret kiss.

## Wednesday

Therapy. Journals. Know thyself. What is the point? Better, surely, to live under the misapprehension that one is someone nice than face the truth that one is someone nasty.

## Thursday

I put this to Alison this afternoon. As always, she answers a question with another question. Did I think that I was nasty? Not nasty, perhaps, but hardly heroic. She answers: 'It is precisely in resolving this sense of inadequacy that the value of therapy lies.'

'But perhaps there is no resolution? Perhaps I am inadequate?'

Alison was silent for a moment. Then: 'Would it not be valuable to sort out your real failings from those that are illusory?'

'It might be preferable to go on believing that they are all illusory.'

'Then you can do nothing about them.'

Always, at the back of my mind, is the suspicion that Alison's advice is tempered by the thought of her fee.

Fifty minutes. Fifty pounds. No one is paid more for silence than the psychoanalyst. Thoughtful hesitations. Pregnant pauses. Except perhaps the barrister.

And what is the end product? The man who is 'cured'? Serene, mature, fulfilled – and bored! Compare him with the late George Harding. Riddled with complexes. Adrift in illusions. Powered by neurosis. Bogus patriot. Undisguised egoist. Did he stop to analyse the pleasure he felt as a woman cracked her whip? Or bit his skin? No. Like Achilles: better a short and glorious life than one that is long and dull. George relished the red meat of life while I count the calories in my muesli.

Alison never responds to challenges of this kind. Generously, one might say that she regards them as diversions that waste her time and my money. Ungenerously, one might say that she is afraid to expose her intellectual limitations by entering into discussions of a general kind. Far better to suggest fathomless wisdom with tentative silences, thoughtful hesitations, pregnant pauses, spiced with the occasional pinch of jargon.


## Friday

Gordon's campaign for a state funeral has failed. None of the daily papers took it up. George's funeral is to take place as announced at Chillingworth parish church at half past two tomorrow afternoon. Only his family and close friends are to attend.

## Saturday

Are old friends not close friends? This question met me as soon as I awoke this morning. It led to a decision over breakfast, to go to George's funeral. It is an impulse I have no time to analyse. A grey suit, a white shirt, a black tie. As I put them on, I think: Alison will approve of this self-assertion. The cowering ego sets forth from his fortress.

## Sunday

Why did I go? Was it to gloat as earth was shovelled on to his coffin? Was it to bolster my own self-esteem by mixing with the great and the good? Was it from sincere affection for a former friend? Or simple curiosity? How would Patricia regard my presence? Loyalty? Presumption? Would George's mother and father remember that I used to come and stay with them at Chillingworth during our Cambridge days? These were the questions that I asked myself as I drove down the motorway to Wiltshire.

I thought back to my first visit to Chillingworth. At first sight, George's circumstances were similar to our own. We lived in a rectory; they lived in an old rectory. But while Avelscombe was in Somerset, Chillingworth was in Wiltshire; and while Avelscombe was still largely inhabited by farmers and labourers and landowners like Anne's father, the Brigadier, whose families had lived there for several hundred years, Chillingworth had been colonised by affluent Londoners. Even the cottages had ruched curtains and BMWs at the door.

The contrast between the old and the new, the past

42

and the future, had been most marked when it came to the two rectories. My home was shabby, draughty, with brown patches on the bedroom ceilings where the roof had leaked a decade ago. George's, by contrast, had a level of comfort that my father would have thought hedonistic and my mother vulgar. There were fitted carpets with cushioned underlay, deep sofas with white damask covers, spotlit paintings, heavily lined chintz curtains, polished antique wardrobes and chests of drawers. There was a large television, concealed speakers, an internal telephone system and a heated swimming-pool beneath the rafters of a seventeenth-century barn. A Spaniard mowed the lawn and polished my shoes while his wife cooked the food and made our beds.

The money came from underwriting at Lloyd's. Both George's parents dressed in clothes so bright and well pressed that they must have been new or have come straight from the dry cleaner's. I never caught sight of George's mother without her face made up and her hair done. The father's face was pink; he smelt of gin and after-shave. The mother, of her scent and cosmetics. Both Gordon and I were treated by George's parents with a certain reserve, as if they felt that their brilliant son should have made some more significant friends. The most pleasant person I remember from those days was Lucia, the Spanish cook.

There was a manor house in Chillingworth but it had been divided up into flats. George's father, as resident of the most expensive property in the village, played the role of squire. There was cricket on the green, and jumble sales in the village hall. All the copywriters and merchant bankers with their wives and children joined in this rustic life. They could pretend for a weekend that there were no blacks or dossers or tower-blocks in

Britain. It was George's roots in this theme-park England that fed his political convictions and led to his later success.

I reached Chillingworth three-quarters of an hour before the funeral was due to begin. I parked my car at the far end of the village and walked from there to the church. Television cameras and photographers were already in position at the gate. Journalists looked to see if I was someone well known but, realising that I was a nonentity, went back to drinking coffee from the plastic tops of their Thermos flasks or talking on their mobile phones. Two policemen, looking for Irish assassins, studied me as I passed them. I wore a suit and a black tie: I was a plausible mourner. They let me pass.

The church was already half filled. I slipped into an empty pew on the far side and close to the back of the church. It was a position that abjured any claims to precedence, and also gave me a good view of others as they came in. I recognised one or two: journalists, members of parliament, then – as time grew shorter – two ministers from George's wing of the party. With the first, George's boss, the minister of defence, came Gordon and Delia Taylor: so august, I thought, is the editor of the *Sunday Gazette*. Then, another familiar face, a woman's – tanned, smiling as she passed Gordon, black hair swept back, a Nefertiti profile. Ruth!

Not Ruth alone but, a pace or two behind her, a tall curly-haired man, her current lover. I looked away, not to hide myself from her but to conceal from other members of the congregation the outrage I felt at her presence in the church. What possible right ... What tenuous connection ... The organ played the opening bars of 'Dear Lord and Father of Mankind ...' Patricia came in on the arm of her father-in-law; behind her two Etonian capons and George's mother.

The fury I felt at Ruth's presence smothered any other emotions that might have arisen at the sight of my former wife. What kind of reasoning could she have advanced in her devious mind to play the role of one of George Harding's close friends? She could not have seen him for more than five or six years, and in total on less than a dozen occasions. Unless ...

I looked around at the congregation and noticed at once a preponderance of women; sober dresses, elegant hats. How many of them had come to pay their last respects to a former lover? But surely not Ruth. I looked towards the aisle over the rim of my hymnbook as six men in black suits passed, carrying the coffin containing George. Behind them, I glimpsed Ruth. Her eyes were on the coffin. A tear trickled down her cheek. Then her eyes lifted and met mine. What was their expression? Impossible to analyse. But I knew.

When? After we separated, surely. But how? She no longer knew him. Or was it while we were married? When George was still my friend. I thought back to those dozen or so encounters, trying to recall the kind of detail that retrospectively would give them away. Opportunities? In abundance. Patricia often remained in the country: they could have had lunch and then returned to George's flat in Westminster. But why limit it to lunch? There were evenings when Ruth had worked late at Hoare Govett or when I had worked on a late shift at Caversham. Candlelit dinners. Then back to bed.

Would George have done it? Would he have seduced the wife of an old friend? No. Because his mind would have been on other things. But if she had offered herself to him? With no entanglements? George would not have hesitated. Ruth was beautiful, intelligent, safely married and certainly discreet.

Torment. The parson waffled on about judging not that ye be not judged – the closest he came to alluding to the circumstances of George's death – but as he spoke I judged and condemned. Gordon then climbed the steps to the pulpit to deliver the eulogy. I wanted to listen but the rage of retrospective jealousy filled my mind. Worst of all was the calm voice of reason, which suggested that this was all a red herring: that the tear might simply have been squeezed from Ruth's eye by the sentimentality that all women feel in the face of death. And that look over the coffin, which I had interpreted as an admission, had signified something quite different. Not 'I'm sorry, it's true, I had an affair with George', but 'I'm sorry, I would not have brought Joshua if I'd known you would be here.'

Was this the voice of common sense? Or cowardice? Alison claims that I always think the worst of women, particularly women I have loved; and now I was obliged to admit that the tear shed by Ruth, as the waterlogged corpse of George Harding passed her in the church, led me to envisage a tear running down the cheek of Denise Trafford when the turn came to be mine. No escape, even in death, from women's appropriating emotions. The male's inconsequential spasm of flesh transformed by the female of the species into an act of eternal commitment. A tear to show that he was once, and in a sense always will be, mine. Not a tarantula. A praying mantis.

Suddenly, I was distracted from this line of thought by the sound of my name, Michael Latham, spoken from the pulpit and echoing round the church. Gordon, in recalling George's Cambridge days, had mentioned me as one of the triumvirate that took control of the Union. Harding, Latham and Taylor. He spoke my name without any explanation as if those present should know who I was.

These few words improved my mood. They removed any doubts I might have had about my status as one of George Harding's old friends. No one could now say that my presence at the funeral was pushing the definition beyond the limits of common sense. My name had been spoken from the pulpit, there, in front of a cabinet minister. I was the third man.

The service continued. Sober hymns, solemn readings, invocations to a God in which few of those present believed; and who, if He did exist in the form suggested by the Christian religion, would most certainly have consigned the soul of George Harding to the fiery furnace where now and for ever he would be weeping and gnashing his teeth. His soul, not his body. No sounds came from the coffin as it was carried slowly out of the church. Behind it, once again, the father, the mother, the wife, the two sons. If there had been tears, the evidence had been erased by powder puffs and paper handkerchiefs.

After the cortège had left the church, a pause. The congregation was unsure as to whether it was expected to follow. Gordon and the two ministers took the lead, leaving their pews and walking down the aisle. The rest of us followed. We came out into the cool spring sunshine and made for the circle of people standing around the grave. All I could see was the back of the man in front of me, but I was close enough to hear the rumble of earth on the coffin and the vicar's words: 'From dust thou hast come and unto dust thou shalt return.'

A voice at my side asked softly: 'Are you going back to the house for the wake?' No need to turn my head: from its timbre, I knew that the voice belonged to Ruth.

'Of course.'

'Do you think I should go?'

'No.'

A short pause. Then: 'I think I'll go anyway. Josh can wait in the car.'

There was a movement in the crowd. The man in front of me stepped aside to make way for the chief mourners. I did the same. So did Ruth. Still stony-faced, Patricia followed her parents-in-law towards the Old Rectory. If she saw me, she did not recognise me, or if she recognised me she did not show it. Behind them came the two ministers; then Gordon, with Delia on his arm. As he drew level, our eyes met. He stopped. 'Michael. Good.' His glance moved to Ruth. For a moment he looked confused: the familiar furrowing of his brow. Then: 'And Ruth. Good.' He let go of his wife's arm and took hold of mine. 'You're coming to the house, aren't you? Patricia would want you to be there.' I let him lead me on. Ruth and Delia followed.

Did Patricia really want me to be there? She met me with a weak smile and feeble handshake, as if she might or might not know who I was: the practised greeting for constituents of a politician's wife. The parents, prompted by Gordon, remembered exactly and seemed glad to welcome a friend from the days when George was less of a statesman and more of a son. The father's mask slipped for a moment. A broken man. I almost felt sorry.

Most welcoming was the Spanish cook, Lucia, who stood at the dining-room table serving cold meats and salads. She remembered me well. As she greeted me, I was struck by how little she had changed. She was still middle-aged. Sixteen or seventeen years had passed, yet now she seemed no older. If she was now perhaps fifty-five, she must have been thirty-seven then – the age I was now. I felt as if this observation would lead me to some

48

important truth about life, but I was distracted by Ruth who, as she held out her empty plate to be loaded by Lucia, turned to me and said: 'I thought you might like to know that I'm pregnant.'

'Who's the father?'

'Who do you think?'

I shrugged. 'I don't know who you've been seeing.'

'I've been with Joshua for over six months. We're going to get married.'

'Good.' I said 'good' because I did not want to give her the satisfaction of seeing that the news made me feel bad. But she knew me too well.

'I'm sorry.'

'Just tell me one thing, before you begin your new life. Did you ever go to bed with George?'

'Don't be absurd.'

Did she blush? Hard to tell because of the dusky colour of her skin.

'Your parents must be happy.'

'About what?'

'That you're marrying a Jew.'

She turned down her mouth, raised her eyebrows and shrugged. This signified: 'I don't deny it.'

'After twenty years' wandering in the gentile wilderness, you're back in the promised land.'

'We didn't split up because you weren't a Jew,' said Ruth.

'It helped.'

This intimate conversation was carried on *sotto voce* as we stood together by the window, forking food into our mouths from our plates. I looked around for a way to escape. For all the bravado of my rejoinders, the conversation had brought me close to tears.

There were twenty or thirty people in the room. It was not difficult to establish which were family and which were friends. I strolled over to Gordon and Delia, who were talking to the minister of defence. Ruth followed. As we approached, they broke off their conversation. A glance from the minister was sufficient to inform him that I was not someone of significance. Nevertheless, Gordon introduced me in generous terms as a man who knew more about the former Soviet Union than anyone else in Britain. The minister showed no interest. He glanced at Ruth to assess her by different criteria and, deciding that she was not his type, used his empty plate as a pretext to walk away.

'A blackguard or a cretin,' said Gordon. 'I can't decide which.'

Behind us, Delia took Ruth by the arm and led her towards the french windows that opened on to the garden.

'At least he's here,' I said. 'He hasn't been frightened off by the scandal.'

'He knows the scandal is bogus.'

'If he knows, why doesn't he say so?'

'Because the Government don't want us to think that George was murdered.'

'What is their reason for covering it up?'

Gordon turned from the table, on which he had put down his plate, to scrutinise me as if a novel idea had suddenly formed in his head. 'Do you remember Paget?'

## Monday

Remained writing this journal last night until two in the morning. Hard to keep awake at my work-station. Persuade Kramer to swap shifts so that I will be free tomorrow. Denise suggested going to a film in Reading tonight: a 'sleep-over' in her flat was implicit in the offer.

I bought time by saying that Wednesday would suit me better.

Alison on the way home. She was interested in Saturday's encounter with Ruth. Why had I decided that she had been to bed with George Harding? I described the tear. She seemed unconvinced. I began to wish that I had not mentioned it. I had lost interest in Ruth. My mind is on tomorrow's lunch with Gordon at the Savoy.

## Tuesday

Apparently, because of its position on the river, the Savoy Grill is now used almost as a canteen by the senior people on the *Gazette*. They have a boat that whisks them up the Thames from the Isle of Dogs. Gordon told me this, I think, to make it clear that I should not feel flattered by the choice of such an expensive restaurant; and then, realising that I might in fact feel insulted by what he had said, spent twenty minutes describing how congestion in the streets would lead to a return to the days of Henry VIII, who had travelled to and fro between Greenwich and the Tower, Westminster and Hampton Court by boat.

Only when he had finished his asparagus did he turn to the topic that had led to the lunch. What did I remember of Paget? I told him what I have never told anyone before – that Paget had tried to recruit me into the secret service in my last year at Cambridge.

'You turned him down?'
'Yes.'
'Why?'
'I wanted to be a scholar, not a spy.'
'Couldn't you have been both?'

'I was high-minded.'

'I remember.'

'One usually repents of one's sins. I regret my acts of virtue.'

'Why?'

'The security services look after their own. If I had joined MI6, I would not have been sacked just because my expertise was redundant. I would have been switched to chasing terrorists or drug barons.'

'Would you rather be doing that than what you're doing now?'

'Monitoring Russian broadcasts is not particularly challenging.'

'What would you prefer to do?'

I shrugged. 'It's getting late to change profession.'

'Would you like to write?'

'Write what?'

'Features. Or even a book.'

'I did write a book.'

'I had in mind something less academic.'

'I'm open to suggestions.'

Gordon looked at the food on the plate set before him as if the bones of his grilled *poussin* would help him phrase a delicate or complex proposition. 'It seems to me that you might be the man to find out exactly what happened to George.'

Partridge. Brittle potato chips. I took a mouthful to buy time.

'You must have a dozen experienced investigative reporters.'

'They don't speak German.'

'What about your Bonn correspondent?'

Gordon shook his head. 'Too well-known.'

I picked up my partridge's slender leg and nibbled at the flesh.

Gordon leaned forward and spoke quietly, close to my ear. 'If only half of what Paget suggests is true, this could be the biggest story of the decade.' He leaned back. 'But it is not a story that will come out through conventional reporting and investigation. Someone will have to go undercover.' He paused. 'There could be risks.' Then: 'Do you want pudding?'

## Wednesday

I tell Denise that I feel a cold coming on and want an early night. She pretends to believe me, seeming sympathetic, biding her time. She reminds me that she has tickets for the opera on Saturday and extracts a promise that I will come. Of course, the opera is just a pretext for a night in London. She thinks she has me by the scrotum as surely as a farmer holds his bull by the ring in its nose. She may be right.

In the meantime, Paget.

*Paget, David*: OBE (1947); son of Herbert Edgar Paget (d. 1962), and Jennifer, née Gray (d. 1967); b. 23 Jan 1919; *educ.* Clifton College; Clare College, Cambridge (BA, MA). *Career* HM FO (war serv.) 1939–47; fellow, Clare College, 1950–53; tutor, Clare College, 1954–63; lecturer in history, 1947–67; director of studies, 1967–85. *Publications*: *The Genius of the British Constitution* (1968).

A worthless entry. Everything that is significant about Paget is left out. It does not take much cunning to realise that 'war service' in the Foreign Office means a role in intelligence, or that an OBE in 1947, when he was still under thirty years old, suggests that this role was of some importance.

Neither would anyone know from the bare job descriptions, 'lecturer in history' or 'director of studies', that Paget was the intellectual mentor of a whole generation of students at Cambridge, many of whom are now cabinet ministers, judges, permanent under-secretaries and one editor of a national newspaper, Gordon Taylor.

How to account for this influence? His *magnum opus* on the British constitution gives away little. More revealing are the book reviews published in *The Times*, the *Gazette*, the *Telegraph* and the *Spectator* in the late 1970s and early 1980s. What was significant about Paget was that, at a time of a collectivist, socialistic consensus, he was unambiguously individualist and right-wing. It is difficult to imagine, now, the beleaguered position at the time of such genuinely conservative thinkers as Hayek or Oakeshott. The moral superiority of the socialist stance was rarely questioned; and those who did question it were branded with the scarlet letter F for Fascist, and excluded from liberal circles in both academic and social life.

There is little doubt that, despite his brilliance, political prejudice might have prevented Paget winning a fellowship at Cambridge, had not it not been for his work during the war. His brilliance was undisputed: as an undergraduate in the late 1930s, he had dazzled his tutors and won a first-class degree. The fellowship at Clare was no more than his due. He had also been taken up by some in the circle around Keynes. He was considered handsome by the women. Beautiful by the men. It became part of the myth surrounding Paget that as an undergraduate he had been to bed with both E. M. Forster and Maynard Keynes. It was probably untrue.

There were no known homosexual liaisons after the war, but no certain heterosexual ones either. He remained a bachelor and kept no establishment other than his elegantly furnished rooms in Clare. He was said to visit foreign countesses in spas on the Continent during the long vacation, and to conduct discreet affairs with the wives of his friends during weekend house parties or in hotels in London.

The air of decadence that lingered around Paget enhanced his prestige among young undergraduates from middle-class backgrounds and minor public schools. Youths like George and Gordon. There was not as yet any necessary connection between right-wing radicalism and 'Victorian' moral values. Paget's philosophy of politics and history was essentially amoral, little more than Darwin's anthropology applied to human affairs. Look back and you see how the fittest have survived. Pointless to resist the inevitable: the aim in politics must be first to discern and then back the winners. 'Social justice' is a self-contradiction, a concept used by the weak to inhibit the strong. It was from Paget that George first heard of Nietzsche but to the ponderous utterances of Zarathustra Paget preferred the weary cynicism of Pascal. 'Since force cannot be made to submit to justice, men have made it just to submit to force, and since justice cannot be fortified, we justify force ...'

Impossible to appreciate today the outrage provoked at the time by such ideas. But to Paget and his followers, this was part of their appeal. They were the accessories of intellectual dandies, worn like rare orchids or flamboyant waistcoats, *pour épater les bourgeois* as they walked down King's Parade. We relished the loathing we provoked among the grey state scholars from the Labour Club with their faith in Mao, Marx and Che Guevara.

Gordon's secretary left a message for me at Caversham to say that Paget would expect me for lunch in his rooms at Clare on Saturday. Denise stopped me in the passage and asked: 'How are you?' 'Fine.' Then I remembered. My cold! I told her that the early night seemed to have nipped it in the bud. 'So you'll be all right at the weekend?' She speaks as if we have arranged to play a game of squash. I say that I am going to lunch at Cambridge. 'But you'll be back in time?' A statement. Not a question. In time for what? *Don Giovanni*. I had forgotten. My mind is on other things.

Alison, too, senses that I am distracted. I explain that an opportunity has arisen which might lead me to take a long period of unpaid leave from Caversham or perhaps resign altogether. My enthusiasm does not infect her. She asks me to consider whether this opportunity might not be a device to avoid facing up to my problems just at the moment when the process that might lead to their resolution has reached a painful stage. I point out that the opportunity was presented to me: I did not seek it out. She explains that the unconscious often elicits the means of escape. It occurs to me once again that she is less anxious about my psychological well-being than about her fee. I say nothing but she reads my mind and asks, as I leave, for notice if I am to go away for any length of time so that she can alert those at the top of her waiting list. I suspect that the waiting list is a fiction, a marketing ploy.

As soon as I got back to my flat this evening, I opened the trunk at the bottom of my wardrobe containing my books and notes from my Cambridge days. Ruth would not allow me to put the books on the shelves. She said a large number of spines with Cyrillic titles would intimidate our guests; in reality, I suspect, she thought they would make visitors think that we were narrow specialists when the image she wanted to foster was of widespread cultivation – hence her hardback editions of novels that had won the Booker Prize. She took these with her when she left. I have not yet got round to filling the gaps left on the shelf.

From the trunk, I retrieved the arch files containing the notes I had taken when attending Paget's lectures. The metal fitting holding the paper had slightly rusted but the handwriting was legible and the paper itself was intact.

I was not taught by Paget. I studied modern languages. But in my final year Gordon and George persuaded me to attend his lectures. At that time, George was Paget's most loyal disciple and subsequently his most successful creation. Both Gordon and I, on our state grants, were too poor and too cautious to believe in ourselves as Nietszchean supermen. Nor could I easily cast off the values I had learned from my father, the man of God. It was one thing to prefer a free market to state planning, but another to accept the right of the strong to use the weak. Did it matter, Paget asked, if Michelangelo paid a fair wage to those who cut his marble from the quarries at Carrara? A rhetorical question from the podium to which one who did not see himself as a Michelangelo might yet have answered, 'Yes.' Even Gordon sometimes hesitated to accept the implications of all that Paget taught. He did not see himself as a Michelangelo either. But George did: if not Michelangelo, then a new Cesare Borgia for whom Machiavelli wrote *The Prince*. Inspired by Paget, George went into politics in pursuit of glory – glory for George and glory for Britain, he would make no distinction between the two. He accepted without question from Paget that Britain's decline after World War II came from the pusillanimity of our statesmen who, from a false sense of justice, surrendered our empire to native agitators and squandered the substance of the nation on the Welfare State. *A state must rise or fall, dominate or decline* – one of the phrases I underlined while attending Paget's lecture on the unification of Italy. His point: it was not the federation of the several states but the triumph of Piedmont over the rest, just as the unification of Germany represented the triumph of Prussia.

I was admitted into Paget's circle on the coat-tails of George and Gordon. They took me to dine with him in his rooms on two or three occasions. He questioned me closely about Soviet Russia. Did I think it was a nation on the way up or on the way down? I cited E. H. Carr's *What is History?* to support the theory that it was on the way up. 'Carr would say that. He's a fellow-traveller. He's over-impressed by their military power.' Paget then put forward the hypothesis that the mix of Slavic sloth and Communist contradictions would lead to a collapse of the Soviet economy 'in fifteen or twenty years' time'.

For a young man, at the age of twenty, it was exhilarating to be addressed on equal terms by someone known to have direct access to the centres of power. At that time, the Official Secrets Act was taken seriously:

Paget could never talk about what he had done during the war, let alone what role he continued to play in intelligence. It was said that he remained on the committee that supervised the intelligence services, and received calls in his rooms in Clare from the Prime Minister. It was also said that he acted as a talent spotter for MI6. That rumour I knew to be true.

## Saturday

A first-class return ticket to Cambridge arrives in the post this morning from 'the editor's office' at the *Gazette*. I had meant to drive. The talking timetable tells me over the telephone that there are now trains on the hour from King's Cross. Peruse this morning's papers to see if there is anything new on the Harding affair. There is not.

## Sunday

The human brain may be prodigious when compared to the same organ in other mammals, but it is hard pressed to assimilate and sift through all the information fed into it in the modern world. Yesterday's newspapers make a pile on one of my kitchen chairs. There are also the *Spectator*, the *Economist* and the *Times Literary Supplement*, which I take because they are indispensable but rarely find time to read. I listen to the news on the radio in the morning, and see the same stories illustrated on the television at night. What is the effect of this over-abundance of information? We all become anxious about everything – diesel fumes, interest rates, over-population – even though they are beyond our control.

Clearly, the most useful facility to develop in one's own mind would be one which discerns between those areas where one's action can affect the outcome and those areas where it cannot. But this is not always clear. And the involuntary intrusion of one preoccupation can sabotage the outcome of another.

Take orgasm and interest rates. In this particular instance, German interest rates and last night's orgasm. This is the sequence of events: lunch with Paget in Cambridge leaves certain ideas in my mind – ideas that could be described as significant, even momentous; return by train (in a first-class compartment) with these ideas 'turning' in my head; a change of trains at King's Cross on to the Underground (no first class) to Leicester Square station, from which a short walk down St Martin's Lane to the English National Opera, arriving there in good time to meet Denise at the arranged time of 7.15.

Why was I there? I ask the question now. I did not ask it then. So preoccupied was I by the issues raised by Paget over lunch that my mind was not on what I was doing. I was on autopilot: the kiss of greeting, the bustle in the foyer, the ordering of a glass of white wine and a whisky and soda for the interval. To say that I was impervious to my surroundings would be wrong: annoyance filtered through the fissures in my concentration. I would rather not have been there. Why? Complicated to analyse, let alone explain. To do with snobbery – the flush of excited anticipation on Denise's face as if a seat in the upper circle of the Coliseum was as grand as a box at Covent Garden.

Autopilot took me to supper after the opera with Denise at the nearby Café Pelican. Autopilot sustained conversation as we waited for grilled calves' liver and poached turbot. Autopilot led us to finish a bottle of red wine. Autopilot hailed a taxi that took us back to my flat in Fulham and, despite an aching head and exhausted body, autopilot threw us, naked and entwined, on to my bed. But though my body was obedient to the demands of the moment, my mind was less easy to command. History. Interest rates. The Knights of the Cross. Cleopatra's nose. Unquestionably, the costs of German unification had led the Bundesbank to set high interest rates, which in turn had obliged the Bank of England to do the same. But was our subsequent ejection from the European Exchange Rate Mechanism really a 'liberation' as Paget had suggested? And would a European Central Bank really be beyond any kind of democratic control? And if there was a conspiracy that would change the course of history, could one man alter the outcome by exposing it in the pages of the *Gazette*?

Here was I, after all, rising and falling like the melodies in Mozart's music, yet apparently intent upon endless reprise. How to bring the aria to an end? Had the wine numbed my senses? Or was it because my mind was on other things? I felt powerless to affect the outcome. Like a man waiting in the rain for a taxi, I began to lose faith that there would be one. How powerless is man in the face of history when even his own orgasm is beyond his command! Patiently man persists, and finally his faith is rewarded. The pace quickens and finally the long process of parturition comes to an end.

I awake to the sound of singing. Denise is up before me and gives a pretty rendering of a Gilbert and Sullivan ditty as she fries bacon and eggs. I stumble into the kitchen. She stands at the stove wearing one of my shirts. 'I thought the smell would get you out of bed.' A happy smile. It would seem she has either forgiven or forgotten last night's fiasco.

'But you haven't put it in your diary!' This was Denise after breakfast when I explained that I was going out to Sunday lunch. Of course, it was untrue. Had I received any invitation I would have turned it down. I wanted a clear day to digest yesterday's revelations but I could not do that until I had got rid of Denise.

She misunderstood my motive. Or pretended to. I was dressed. She still wore my shirt. She lingered. I looked at my watch. She yawned and stretched on the bed. I lamented my acceptance of an invitation to lunch, above all lunch *in Richmond*, which would mean leaving sooner rather than later. Denise was on the point of asking if she could come too but stepped back from the brink. Slowly, she got dressed. Then, when my back was turned, she went to my desk and leafed through my diary. 'But you haven't put it in your diary, and you write down everything else.'

'I forgot, but they rang yesterday to remind me.'

Did she believe me? Probably not. Yet she lingered. Not because she wanted to stay, but to prove to me and to herself that she had not come simply for sex.

'You seem preoccupied,' she said.

'I'm sorry.'

'What's on your mind?'

Murder. Conspiracy. The future of Europe. 'Nothing in particular.'

A kiss. A smile. She was gone.

Paget had scarcely changed. In most ways, he had not changed at all. This is probably because, as an undergraduate at Cambridge, he was already in my eyes an old man. He must have been around sixty then; now, over eighty with only the mummified tightness of his facial skin and a bleary look in his grey eyes to mark the passing of those fifteen years. I had knocked. He had called me in. I felt like a student coming for a tutorial. He greeted me as if a week rather than a decade had passed since we had last met. Did he remember our last encounter at the Garden House Hotel? The lunch when he had suggested that I might like to be put in touch with MI6. And my high-minded rejoinder: that I wanted to remain above the fray. If he did, he did not allude to it. He showed me a chair: low-slung, corduroy cushion, wooden arm-rest. I sat down. He filled a glass with bronze sherry. 'Will you drink that? Or would you rather something else?' I took the sherry. He filled a glass for himself and sat down in the arm-chair facing mine.

'What have you been up to these past few years?' I sensed that he knew already, but wanted to see how I would present my undistinguished career. Out it came. Smolensk, the Institute, the book, the cancelled contract, the broken marriage, ending at Caversham.

'So your Russian is up to scratch?'

'Yes.'

'And your German?'

'That too.'

He frowned, scrutinising me beneath his wrinkled brow. 'Could you, I wonder, speak German with a Russian accent?'

I laughed and reeled off a stanza of Rilke with a Muscovite lilt.

'Have you ever gone in for amateur dramatics?'

'Only here, at the Footlights.'

He nodded with what seemed to be satisfaction; but it was a sign of his age, I thought, that he could not contain his curiosity on these questions, which were as yet meaningless to me. I glanced around the room. The

Piranesi prints had not been moved or changed. On the mantel above the gas fire, a line of embossed invitations, most of them from the masters or bursars of other Cambridge colleges. Parochial. Complacent. Cambridge as the epicentre of the civilised world.

'I'm sorry,' Paget said. 'I'm putting the cart before the horse.'

I made a gesture to denote that this had caused no offence.

'You will realise that George's death ...' His voice trailed off. 'We were not only fond of George. We also had high hopes of what he might achieve.'

We? To what plurality did Paget refer?

'Gordon told me that he ran into you at George's funeral.'

'Yes.'

'Sadly, I was unable to attend.' A pause. Then: 'Had you seen him much lately?'

'No.'

'So you will not have known much more than you have read in the newspapers?'

'About what?'

'About George. What he was doing.'

'No.'

'Are you interested in politics?'

'Up to a point.'

Paget waited.

'Inevitably, because of my job, my attention has been focused on the Soviet Union.'

'Of course. But you will have read about the Maastricht treaty?'

'Yes.'

'And the divisions in the cabinet between those in favour of further integration with Continental Europe and those against?'

64

'The Europhiles and the Eurosceptics.'

'Precisely. And you will know that George was a leading Eurosceptic, even a Europhobe.'

'Yes.'

'And he was brought into the Government partly to appease the anti-European wing of the Party.'

'So it was said.'

'Less well understood were the reasons for giving him a post at the Ministry of Defence. The Government wants to cut defence spending. Eurosceptic MPs are among those most likely to object. But how could they object if it was being done by one of their own?'

'George?'

'George. And George did as he was told by the chief secretary to the Treasury, because if he did not someone else would.'

'Of course.'

From the way he spoke about George, Paget betrayed a close knowledge of George's thinking. How closely had they remained in touch? What role had he played in his former student's political career?

Besides overseeing the defence budget, Paget continued, George apparently had had a number of other duties, most of a nominal and humdrum kind. One was to oversee the administration of the British Army on the Rhine. Papers would pass over his desk for his authorisation that were of little intrinsic interest but, since the Scott Inquiry, ministers were careful not to sign papers without reading them first.

Around three months ago, George's curiosity was aroused by a report from his ministry's legal department about an accident on the German autobahn involving an armoured car from a base near Celle. A steering rod on a Saracen had snapped, leading it to lurch to the left and collide with an articulated lorry, pushing it through the concrete barrier and over the parapet of a bridge. The lorry driver and his companion were killed outright. The public prosecutor of Lower Saxony had wanted to prosecute the driver of the Saracen for dangerous driving: he appeared to doubt the story about the snapped drive-shaft because the German police had not been allowed to inspect the Saracen back at the base.

So far, nothing out of the ordinary. But two things in the report caught George's attention. First was the report of the young lieutenant called Brennan, who had been in command of the Saracen and, indeed, the convoy of five armoured cars. Uninjured in the accident, he had got into the second Saracen in the convoy and managed to barge through the fence enclosing the autobahn and reach the articulated lorry a good quarter of an hour before the arrival of the German police.

His principal objective was to aid the driver and his companion but both were dead. His secondary objective: to file a report. He therefore wrote down the make and number of the articulated lorry and entered the container, which had split open after the fall from the bridge. So had some of the crates that he found in the container. Their contents? Arms. Rifles, revolvers, submachine-guns, ammunition, grenades. All with Soviet markings.

This was noted not so much because of its intrinsic interest but because the value of the cargo would naturally affect the level of a likely claim. But here we come to the second anomaly: no claim was made. Neither was the initial intention of the public prosecutor of Lower Saxony pursued. Indeed, further details requested by our adjutant-general's office – for example, the name of the driver and his companion – were not provided by the Germans. Nor did any of their official communications refer to the contents of the container.

So far as the Ministry was concerned, all well and

good. The Germans' discretion had not just saved them embarrassment, it had saved them money. But George remained curious. What was this consignment of arms? Where was it going? He referred the question to MI6. At first they shared his interest, suspecting that the arms might have been bought for the IRA. Enquiries through normal channels to the German police and secret service produced a categorical denial that the container had contained arms.

Here, the plot thickens. Or, to be precise, it meanders and runs into the ground. George was called in by his minister and given a dressing-down. He had exceeded his authority in talking directly to MI6. He, the minister, had the matter in hand. The Government was satisfied with the Germans' explanation that the container had not contained arms or, if it had, that the arms had not been for the IRA or any other terrorist organisation of interest to HMG. The Federal Government had gone out of its way to save the UK from embarrassment. The least we could do in return was to let the matter drop. The file was to be closed.

At this point there is a knock on the door; not the door to George's office in Whitehall but to Paget's rooms in Clare. Enter two college servants with our lunch. Briskly, they lay two places on the table. A hot-plate is put on the sideboard, dishes on the hot-plate. They leave. Paget stands and shows me to the table. Smoked salmon and thin slivers of buttered brown bread. We sit and start eating. Paget continues his story.

The minister's intervention only serves to stimulate George's curiosity. In particular, it strikes him as strange that the Germans should deny that there was a cargo of arms. What possible motive could the young lieutenant have had in inventing this in his report? But if he did not invent it, then why were the Germans lying to HMG?

To satisfy his curiosity, George acted outside official channels and at his own expense. Patricia's brother Rudolf worked as an international lawyer in Zurich. At George's request, he hired a private detective and gave him the registration number of the truck. Within a fortnight, George had a report. The lorry had been hired, from a large transport company called Kaiserfracht based in Mannheim, by a small import–export company called Estergay, registered in Frankfurt. Estergay, it turned out, was a subsidiary of the conglomerate Bettelheim Krull, but there were one or two oddities in the transaction, some noticed by the detective, others by Rudolf.

First of all, the staff at Kaiserfracht had been struck by the youth and apparent inexperience of the two drivers sent by Estergay. They had valid licences to drive HGVs, but 'they did not seem like truck drivers. More like schoolteachers' (this from the detective's report, which had been passed from George to Paget and which Paget has now described to me).

Second (the point picked up by Rudolf), Estergay was a subsidiary company not of Bettelheim Krull as such but of Bettelheim Krull (Holdings), a company registered in Luxembourg. Since such a holding company is normally a device to avoid tax or to retain ownership of a public company in private hands, it was odd that it should have set up a small import–export company in Frankfurt.

At George's request, Rudolf had instructed his detective to pursue enquiries in Luxembourg. Who owned BK (Holdings)? Luxembourg's confidentiality laws made it difficult to find out. Difficult but not impossible. Ownership of BK (Holdings) was divided between a number of charitable trusts. Who controlled the charitable trusts?

Two families, one called Krull, the other von Willich, and a charitable confraternity called the Knights of the Cross. The founder of Bettelheim Krull in 1945 had been Gustav Krull; his daughter, Julia, had married Heinrich von Willich. All this could be discovered by perusing *Who's Who in Germany*. More arcane information: Heinrich von Willich was the current Grand Master (*Herrenmeister*) of the Knights of the Cross.

We were not to be interrupted. Paget, who in the old days had always been served at table by his scout, himself rose to take away the plates that had held the smoked salmon and lifted the silver domes from the dishes containing what was to follow: carrots, cabbage, potatoes, roast beef and Yorkshire pudding. The pudding was soggy, the beef now dry, but I was sufficiently intrigued by Paget's story to feel that the quality of the cooking was by the way, and the claret was good.

Who are the Knights of the Cross? I put this question to Paget who, apparently dismayed at the degeneration of the Yorkshire pudding, nevertheless crammed it into his mouth with a vengeful savagery, dribbling gravy down his chin.

The Knights of the Cross – *die Kreuzritter*. Originally, like the Sovereign Order of Malta or the Templars, a Crusading order; founded in Palestine in the early twelfth century but, after the fall of Jerusalem in 1187, driven back to Europe and used principally in Germany against the pagan Lithuanians, but also against the Cathars in Languedoc and the Moors in Spain. 'Brutal, high-minded members of the German nobility who converted the heathen at the point of the sword, and in return for saving his soul expropriated and enslaved him together with his wife and children.'

'And now?'

'Less straightforward.'

A quick tutorial on the orders of Crusading knights. The Templars: the most powerful, suppressed by the French King Philippe IV in 1307, dissolved by the Pope in 1312, their Grand Master Jacques de Molay accused of heresy and roasted to death over a slow fire. The Teutonic knights: conquered Prussia, became Protestant at the Reformation, took wives, became secular barons, their Grand Master the Duke of Brandenburg, later King of Prussia, finally Kaiser of the Germans. The Knights of Malta: after the fall of Acre, retire to Rhodes; then, when the Turks take Rhodes, fortify Malta. Remain there as an autonomous naval power fighting the Turks and the Barbary pirates until Malta is taken by the French after the Revolution. The Knights of Malta give up fighting and return to the charitable objectives of their original foundation. They remain a sovereign order; in reality, a fund-raising confraternity of Catholic aristocrats.

The Knights of the Cross: remained Catholic at the Reformation. Still a force against Wallenstein and the Swedes in the Thirty Years War. Marriage permitted in certain ranks in the eighteenth century and fighting members subsumed into a regiment of the Austro-Hungarian Empire. In Germany, the Knights remained an aristocratic confraternity keeping their distance from the Protestant court in Berlin. Though they were a predominantly German order, there were chancelleries throughout Europe, in South America and the United States. A freemasonry of influential Catholics. Dinners held once a year to enable the Knights to dress up in their robes and crosses, but their ostensible objectives now charitable: hospices, hospitals, doss-houses, soup-kitchens, as well as pious enterprises such as pilgrimages and financial help to religious orders.

*

A pause. My plate is empty. One can listen and eat but not talk and eat. Paget cuts the gristle off the edge of the slice of roast beef: trouble with his teeth? I wait while he eats. When he has finished, he stands to bring bowls from the sideboard containing apple pie and ice cream. The ice cream has mostly melted. We eat for a while in silence, then I put down my spoon. I am full. I can eat no more. But, like many old men, Paget has a good appetite. He eats all his apple pie and ice cream, then wipes his mouth with his napkin before he continues ...

In 1945, Paget had been attached to the Control Commission in the British zone in Germany. He had been put in charge of the denazification programme in Westphalia, and one of his tasks was to vet the displaced persons – the DPs. Germany was in chaos. Millions of Germans had been expelled from East Prussia, Silesia, Pomerania and the Sudetenland. Often they had left their homes at an hour's notice with virtually no possessions, and arrived in Germany as destitute refugees. Their plight was pitiful. Many were starving, but since most had been enthusiastic Nazis, they received little sympathy from the charitable agencies of the victorious allies. Instead, help was provided by an organisation now called Kreuzhilfe, originally Kreuzritterhilfe or 'Help from the Knights of the Cross'.

Paget attempted to enlist their help in finding Nazis among the DPs. In 1945, in the chaos caused by the influx of refugees, it was only too easy for prominent Nazis and war criminals to shed their old identities and adopt new ones. Paget's job had been to sniff them out but he had got little co-operation from the Knights. Like most of the Catholic upper classes, their fear of the Soviets was greater than their contempt for the Nazis. They also had a concept of 'sanctuary', which left the

71

worst war criminals to the judgement of God in the next world rather than before the Tribunal at Nuremberg in this one. They did not obstruct Paget but neither did they help him.

By 1947, when the problem of the refugees had been solved, and the Allies had handed back the government of Germany to the Germans, Kreuzhilfe was not dissolved but turned its attention instead to the plight of Catholics in Eastern Europe. As the climate of crisis grew in the late 1940s and 1950s with the declaration of a cold war between East and West, Kreuzhilfe raised funds to aid the persecuted Church behind the Iron Curtain. By the 1980s, its annual income was almost $100 million. Eighty people were employed at its headquarters outside Münster either raising money or spending it on printing bibles, restoring churches, building seminaries and reviving religious orders from Poland to Kazakhstan ...

## Monday

There comes a point when events in our life outpace our ability to record them. This is the fallacy behind a journal. I spent all of Sunday describing what happened on Saturday but only reached the end of lunch. True, my account was not chronological: the evening had preceded the afternoon. However, it leaves me with a choice this evening between describing my conversation with Denise at Caversham, with Alison in Cleveland Square or with Paget over coffee at Cambridge. I hesitate. I chew the end of my Bic. Paget triumphs over the women, suggesting that both amorous intrigues and psychological introspection are things men fall back on when they have nothing better to do. President Kennedy's *amours* were

72

said to have been concentrated into three-minute couplings between meetings in an antechamber to his office. Napoleon and Stalin had no time for either lovers or shrinks. We assume that such men were driven by a lust for power, but it is equally possible that their lust was in fact for distraction. It is often found that men and women die soon after retirement unless, like Cincinnatus, they are called out of retirement whereupon their vigour returns. What does this mean? That we die not of decrepitude but of boredom.

Ergo, I shall now follow the strand in my life that interests me most. To Alison's dismay, this is no longer my subconscious. I accept that my mother was cold, my father was weak, and as a result I became a passive, self-pitying, bullying husband, driving Ruth to leave me, accelerating the downward spiral in my self-esteem. But what is more likely to see it rise again? Further pregnant pauses on Alison's couch at a pound a minute? Or a minor role in the making of history? And Denise? She accelerates the downward spiral. Denise embodies the second best.

*A minor role in the making of history*. Is this really what is on offer? Gordon called me this morning to ask how the lunch with Paget had gone.

'Well.'

'Are you convinced?'

'More or less.'

'Are you free for dinner on Tuesday? We're having some people you might like to meet.'

Gordon seems to assume that I will take the assignment. It is something that no true journalist could refuse. But

73

am I a true journalist? If I could prove Paget's hypothesis, it would save George's reputation, changing him from a seedy embarrassment to a national hero. Both Gordon and Paget assume that I would want to save the posthumous reputation of our dead friend. I did not tell them about my elation upon hearing of his death.

Gordon also assumes that the element of danger is an inducement. He is used to dispatching those psychological misfits who like nothing better than to fly to Timbuktu wearing a flak jacket, and file their copy from a tin-can lavatory even as dysentery voids their bowels and bullets whistle overhead. He cannot conceive of a man preferring a quiet life.

And yet … Fame and fortune. To escape from Caversham, from Alison, from Denise. To show Ruth!

I see from the clock on the stove that it is already 10.25. The choice is between watching *Newsnight* or returning to Clare College, Cambridge.

I return to Clare. Saturday afternoon; lunch over; two men back in the arm-chairs; horizontal shafts of sunlight through lead-paned windows; small cups with the college crest filled with coffee from a white Thermos jug; the older smoking a pipe, the younger a cigar provided by the older; both faces red in patches from the consumption of claret.

The younger man: Let me see if I have understood what you have told me so far. George sees a memo mentioning an accident on the autobahn involving an articulated lorry and a British armoured car. It reveals that the lorry was carrying a consignment of arms. He enquires further about these arms and is told first that the

74

Germans deny that the lorry was carrying arms, and second that, even if it was, the fact is of no interest to Britain. On his own initiative, George hires a private detective, who discovers that the lorry had been hired by a company belonging to different trusts whose common denominator is a Catholic fraternity called the Knights of the Cross.

The older man: That is right.

The younger man: Did he find out why?

The older man: I think he did, and it cost him his life.

The younger man (puffing at his cigar): It sounds like a novel by John Buchan.

The older man (puffing at his pipe): *The Thirty-nine Steps*, but without the happy ending.

The younger man (to himself): And the role of Paget played by the Leslie Howard of *Pimpernel Smith*. (Aloud) I cannot understand why George, as a minister in the Ministry of Defence, did not simply leave the matter to MI6.

The older man: To understand that, you have to appreciate the deep rift among ministers on the question of Europe.

Paget explains. There are, roughly speaking, three groups in the cabinet: those in favour of a Federal Europe whom he calls the Federasts; those who want to pull out of Europe altogether, the Europhobes; and the middle group who want a free trade area but no political union, the Eurosceptics. George was firmly in the Europhobe camp, and was brought into the cabinet as a sop to the Europhobes in the Party. But, according to Paget, politicians have less direct influence on the running of government than the public supposes. They come and go from the different ministries and largely follow the advice of the permanent staff of their department. There is no necessary link – indeed no link at all – between the opinions of ministers and the opinions of their senior civil servants who, when it comes to Europe, are Federasts to a man.

Why? For a number of reasons. First, they belong to that generation which started out as young high-flyers in the Civil Service when Britain first joined the Common Market. They pinned their colours to the mast. They are still there. Second, they are bureaucrats and as bureaucrats they naturally warm to their fellow bureaucrats in Brussels. Some even believe that our complex modern societies will be unable to function effectively in the future if they are subject to the kind of democratic scrutiny that we are used to in the British Isles.

And then there is an inbuilt propensity to support a policy simply because it is there. For decades it has been a truism in Whitehall that it was a grave error for Britain to have remained aloof from Europe after the end of World War II. We preferred the Americans and our old empire, but the countries of the British Commonwealth fell into the hands of barmy black fanatics, and the Americans, though they may have an Anglophile élite, are instinctively isolationist and loathe the British. Europe seemed the only way to go. The decision was made to alter the course of the great ship of state and now, thirty years later, it is too late to change our mind.

Such is Paget's talent as a teacher, that he invariably persuades you of a position with which he himself profoundly disagrees. 'Is there not some validity,' I asked him, 'in that point of view?'

Paget's pipe had gone out. New shag. Another match. More blue smoke. 'Of course. And it is just the kind that appeals to the mentality of the civil servant. Add to the

political arguments the supposed economic advantages –
economies of scale in a home market even larger than
those of the Americans and the Japanese – and the case
seemed open and shut. We were irrevocably committed
to Europe and so our partners on the Continent were
struck off the list of PEs.'

'PEs?'

'Potential enemies. We were anyway stretched by
dealing with the Soviets, who devoted a large proportion
of their national resources to espionage. It was quite a
relief not to have to bother with the French or the
Germans. But it means that when the Germans reassure
us about a lorry-load of arms, we find that we are not in a
position to verify what they say.'

Paget talked, the even stream of words interrupted only
by the puffs at his pipe. The voice of learning, not
polemic; he was explaining, not persuading. The pipe.
The arm-chairs. The afternoon light. I might have been
an undergraduate sitting there fifty, even a hundred,
years ago. Here, nothing had changed. But there?

The unanswerable question. Has the German leopard
really changed its spots? Has a nation that had had no
experience of democracy established in fifty years what it
took Britain or the Netherlands several centuries to
evolve? Or did a people after its defeat put on a *semblance*
of democracy to appease and placate the victorious
powers?

Of course, constitutionally Germany is a democracy
and is likely to retain a democratic constitution: it is now
impossible to envisage the government of a European
nation without its citizens' consent. But, suggests Paget,
that is not the point in a Europe where decisions are
made by majority voting of the member states, weighting

77

according to population. This will give 70 million or so Germans a preponderance over 50 million or so Britons and a similar number of French. Add to the Germans the people of those countries within its orbit – Austria, Hungary, Poland, the Czech Republic – and enter into the equation the authoritarian traditions of Portugal, Spain, Greece and even France, and you will see that the ancient and deep-rooted democracies such as Britain, the Netherlands and the Scandinavian nations are a small minority among Europe's nation states.

Does it matter? Paget asked the question. I did not. 'I think it does,' he answered in reply to his own question, 'because many Germans still see themselves as an unfulfilled people which has hitherto been frustrated of its destiny but whose hour has now come.'

I said that I did not quite understand what he meant. He explained. People who belong to a nation, by and large, need a self-image that they can contemplate with some satisfaction. Here, we may recognise that Britain is now a minor power but we can look back with some pride on our history, and on what we have done for the development of civilisation around the world. The French, too, have the glories of Louis XIV and Napoleon; the Spanish and Portuguese, the whole continent of South America formed in their image and likeness; and the Italians, well, they can look back on the splendour of the Renaissance and the glory that was Rome.

The Germans, however, formed into a nation only in 1870, have felt that their moment has yet to come. All previous attempts at a major role on the stage of world history have failed. In 1918, a débâcle. In 1945, a catastrophe.

'And now? Third time lucky?'

'Without a doubt.'

'But are you suggesting that Chancellor Kohl envisages the European Union as a kind of fourth *Reich*?'

Paget temporised. 'The word *Reich* has unfortunate connotations. Can you name the first two?'

'The second was surely the German Empire proclaimed in Versailles in 1870?'

'Quite right. And the first?'

I shook my head.

'The Hohenstaufen in the Middle Ages – Otto I, but above all, Frederick Barbarossa. It was he who took the title of Holy Roman Emperor, claiming a notional sovereignty over all the territories of the former Roman Empire, those that is that belonged to the Western Empire and were spiritually subject to the Pope in Rome. Look at a map and compare the extent of Latin Christianity in the Middle Ages with the future European Union proposed by Chancellor Kohl – the present members, Poland, Hungary, the Czech Republic, Croatia and Slovenia, all Catholic states that have traditionally been within the German or Austrian sphere of influence. You will find they are largely the same. Greece is the odd man out.'

'But are you suggesting that Kohl is responsible for the murder of George?'

Paget hesitated. 'No. That's to say, I don't believe that anyone in the German Government ordered the assassination of George. But it is undoubtedly significant that the investigation of his death has not been pursued with the Germans' customary efficiency and dispatch.'

'But surely our government must have insisted ...'

'Of course. And officially, the case remains open. But the line taken by Whitehall seems to be that the truth can only be scandalous so the less known the better.'

'While it is possible that he might have been killed

because he was making enquiries into arms-smuggling by the Knights of the Cross?'

'Precisely.'

'Did no German newspaper mention the accident on the autobahn?'

'No. And that in itself is strange. Lieutenant Brennan's report states that two journalists reached the scene of the accident soon after the ambulance and the police. A crash involving the British Army on the Rhine was certainly topical and, according to Brennan, the cargo of arms was plain to see. There is no question but that the story was suppressed. Was it to save the British Government from embarrassment? Or the Knights of the Cross?'

I glanced at the clock on the mantel. If I was to meet Denise for the opera, I would soon have to leave. 'Do you know if George's last trip to Luxembourg had any bearing on his private investigation?'

'No, I don't. But I think that there is quite enough evidence to suggest that he may have been murdered, either for what he stood for or because of what he had found out about the Knights of the Cross. I am also convinced that neither the German Government nor the British Government want the truth to be known.'

'That makes it difficult for a journalist.'

Paget could see that I was preparing to leave. 'Using normal journalistic procedures, impossible.' He stood and went to a cupboard beneath the bookshelves. 'But with unconventional procedures ...' He crouched and took out a bulging Jiffy-bag. 'Here is some background material. When you have read it, let's meet again.'

I took the package.

'I have an idea about how this can be done. I've discussed it with Gordon. But there is no need for you to be bothered with the details until you have decided whether or not you want to go ahead.' He led me towards the door. 'Given what happened to George, I cannot pretend that we can be certain that no danger would be involved. But if you were to uncover what I suspect is there, then you would perform a considerable service both to your friend and to your country. Indeed, it is not an exaggeration to say that it could affect the future course of the history of the world.'

## Tuesday

After the tutorial, the student must sit down and collect his thoughts. Not easy after a hard day's work at Caversham: President Yeltsin's press conference; bluster over Bosnia. What can Yeltsin do? The US pays all the pipers, so the US calls the tunes.

Also, dinner in an hour's time with Gordon and Delia in Kensington. 8.15 for 8.30: so it states on the engraved card, sent *pour memoire*. What should I wear? In the old days, Gordon was never out of a jersey; but he lived then like me in a flat in North Kensington, not in a mansion on Argyll Road. One can never be sure what one should wear when dining out in London these days. There is a whole new fashion for smart but relaxed attire – cashmere blazers, open-neck shirts. Wear a grey suit at a dinner given by an actor or a film director, and you would be dismissed as a fogeyish dullard before you had opened your mouth. Wear anything but a suit to a dinner given, say, by John and Anne and you would be regarded as someone subversive and probably perverse. *Vive la différence*. In France, they mean the difference between the sexes. In England, they mean the differences between cliques and classes. I will play safe and wear a suit.

*

Why am I wasting time worrying about what to wear when major historical conundrums await my attention?

Paget's dossier. Item One: a number of cuttings to illustrate a pattern of accidents, scandals and even deaths that have befallen European journalists and politicians of the Europhobe and Eurosceptic persuasion. Coincidence or conspiracy? Hard to tell. If George was killed, was it because he was a Europhobe or because 'he knew too much'? Or were they killing two birds with one stone? They? Who are they? The Knights of the Cross? By implication, although I cannot remember whether Paget specifically said so.

Other items in the dossier …

## Wednesday

To continue where I left off yesterday, itemising the contents of the package given to me by Paget in Cambridge? Or describe last night's dinner party while it is fresh in my mind?

The list can wait. So – the dinner. First point to make: I was quite right to have decided to wear a suit. Gordon and all the other male guests were wearing suits, Gordon's navy-blue, double-breasted and, I suspect, tailor-made. The jacket had an azure lining. Quite a dandy, these days: a long way from the shapeless pullover.

It was a gathering of Europhobes. Algie Pascoe, MP, a rabid Little Englander; the more sagacious James Watts, junior minister at the Home Office; Billy Ashton, who resigned over the Maastricht treaty as government whip in the House of Lords; and Walter Bostock, a journalist and reputedly a novelist though I have never met anyone who has read any of his novels. The single woman, my date, was called Annette. She had been at Edinburgh University with Delia and now worked at Conservative Central Office. We quickly established a certain camaraderie: we were the only two singles, and had both known our host and hostess before they were quite so grand.

There were also, of course, the politicians' wives. I was placed between two of these: Pascoe's, an indulgent housewife who spoke little but smiled benignly at her husband's antics as if he was an unruly but favoured child; the other, Watts's wife, an assertive civil servant from the Department of Education, determined to convince me that she was a significant figure in her own right. Tedious. Those without children are bored by education. The conversation that interested me was taking place at the other end of the table. I listened to it with half an ear. Pascoe was saying, so far as I could make out, that the industry on the Continent had become hopelessly uncompetitive. Lavish social benefits for the workers added costs that made their products overpriced on the world's markets. Watts agreed. The objectives of British policy should be to retain access to the single market, but avoid political involvement of any kind. As he spoke, Pascoe's wife leaned over me to ask Delia about the stuffed aubergine on her plate. Stuffed with what? Could she have the recipe? Was it from Josceline Dimbleby or Delia Smith?

The other wives had fallen silent, as political wives so often do when their husbands are discussing great matters of state. The junior minister, Watts, had taken up a theme of Pascoe's – that the economies of Western Europe were finished, that the torch of economic progress had now been passed to the nations of the Pacific rim. Blah, blah, blah. As I listened to them, I was once again overcome by the anxiety I had felt when I had first heard that George was now a minister. Were these buffoons really the men who governed us? Did the destiny of the nation lie in their hands? The level of debate seemed no different from that of the Union at Cambridge, or even the Debating Society at school. The child is not father to the man. The child *is* the man – older but equally infantile.

Bostock, the journalist, now intervened. Almost certainly, he knew nothing about either politics or economics but he had seemed tipsy when he arrived and now was certainly drunk. 'Could anyone explain,' he slurped, waving his hand in the direction of Gordon, 'how it is that, if industry on the Continent is overburdened with social costs and Britain is now so lean and competitive, we still have a balance-of-payments deficit with Germany, and that despite a devaluation of twenty per cent?'

Silence. Then a cacophony of voices. Technical reasons. An historical imbalance. A temporary anomaly. New factors that had not as yet worked through to the statistics.

'And another bloody thing. All the British industries that do export seemed to be owned by the Japs, the Germans or the bloody Yanks.'

Gordon extemporised. It was true, certainly, that a number of Asian manufacturers had chosen to build factories here in Britain but that was precisely because our labour costs were so competitive when compared to those on the Continent.

'So we've become the fucking coolies of the Western world.'

'I wouldn't put it like that.'

Pascoe, as drunk as Bostock: 'I can see that you're one

84

of those journos who likes to run down Britain whenever you get the chance.'

'And you're one of those –'

'Gordon,' Delia interrupted, 'why don't we go upstairs for coffee?' We all stood and chivalrously waited for the women to leave the room before us. As she passed me, Annette caught my eye and winked. I was about to follow her but Gordon waited, resting his body against the dining-room table. He invited us to refill our glasses with port. Was he emulating the old-fashioned upper-class custom whereby the gentlemen remain behind to drink port and smoke cigars? We did not resume our seats. That would be going too far in London in the 1990s. But there was an implicit nostalgia in Gordon's dawdling, as if customs of this kind were part of our national heritage and should be revived.

Gordon did not offer me a cigar and I had brought none with me. This spoiled this later phase of the evening because the cigar I had smoked in Paget's rooms after lunch on Saturday had rekindled an enthusiasm which I now rarely indulged because of the expense. No doubt the expense was the reason why Gordon did not offer his guests cigars. A good Havana now costs around ten pounds. Nor did he have little silver bowls containing cigarettes that were once found on the dining tables of the upper classes. Perhaps that was for the sake of our health. Indeed, the only upper-class custom he seems to have adopted – that of the ladies withdrawing at the end of dinner – was, no doubt coincidentally, one that incurred no extra cost.

Not so, said Annette, to whom I made this observation when we finally 'joined the ladies', feeling encouraged to do so by her earlier wink. 'Not so, because it means that

85

the girl hired for the evening to cook and clear up stays longer and so is paid more.'

'Only if they pay her by the hour. What if she gets a flat fee?'

Annette agreed that if it was a flat fee my observation remained valid.

If only she had been attractive, but the unfortunate truth I had to admit to myself, as Bostock continued baiting the Europhobes, was that while she was clearly intelligent, obviously sympathetic and possibly amusing, she had even less sexual allure than Denise. Thus, while she would have been more *sortable*, as the French say, particularly in right-wing circles, she was less beddable, as the boors say, indeed not beddable at all. Had she ever been attractive? Perhaps, in the bloom of youth. Every dog has his day.

I now asked her, following the theme of my train of thought about faded bloom, whether men looked at her when they passed her in the street. She blushed. Used to questions on the economy or politics, she seemed at a loss as to how to reply. I realised that, without knowing what had led to the question, it might seem double-edged: if she said yes, it might suggest that she welcomed such glances; if she said no, it might be taken to imply that she was too plain to provoke them.

Which was, in a sense, what I wanted to find out. Was I typical or untypical in finding her unattractive? But, seeing her confusion and not having intended to confuse her, I backed up my question, before she had had time to formulate a reply, with a lot of blather about sexual harassment, feminism, and whether there were adequate laws to protect women. 'In America, apparently, a university lecturer is subject to dismissal if his eyes linger on one of his students for more than seven seconds at a time.'

She laughed. 'That's going too far.'

'It seems to me,' I said, returning to the street and my original question, 'that it must be offensive for a pretty woman to be appraised by every passing man, but perhaps even more offensive to be ignored.'

She laughed again. 'You must ask a pretty woman.'

'I thought I had.'

She gave me look which said: 'Thanks for the compliment. I know you don't mean it, but thanks all the same. You're an agreeable companion for a dinner party of this kind, and no doubt Delia hopes that we'll get off together, but I know that you don't find me attractive and, quite frankly, you don't attract me either, so the chances are that we will never see one another again.'

It is extraordinary how much women can express with a single look.

As we were leaving, Gordon took me aside. 'I had wanted you to talk to Jamie Watts. Never mind. Another time.' Then, 'You see how serious the situation is?'

'You mean …?'

'Europe. Yes. We must break the shackles now, before it is too late.'

'Indeed.'

'If we can show that George was a victim –' He stopped. Others came up to say goodbye. They left. Gordon turned back to me. 'Did Paget explain what he had in mind?'

'Not exactly.'

'It's quite ingenious.'

'He's given me some papers to look over.'

'Good. Of course, the staff at the *Gazette* are at your

disposal if there is any way they can help. And we must discuss terms. I know that you are doing this for George's sake, but there's no reason why you shouldn't be well rewarded.'

As I walked towards my Peugeot, I noticed the Europhobe Pascoe climb into a BMW, Watts into an Audi and Ashton into an enormous Mercedes. Only the Europhile Bostock had a British car, an old Rover. Annette waved goodbye as she drove off. In a Renault.

*Thursday*
_____

At lunch today, Denise brought her tray to my table. The presence of colleagues made an intimate conversation impossible but once again anyone intercepting her secretive glances would realise at once what was going on.

When I got up to go, she followed. In the corridor, she whispered: 'What are you doing this weekend?'

Alison, equally imperious. She ticked me off for not writing down my dreams. I told her that all my spare time is spent keeping my journal up to date. Without going into detail, I explained that there had been one or two dramatic developments in my professional life that I felt I should record, at least in outline.

'But a journal is only useful when compared with an account of your dreams. It charts your conscious mind; your dreams, your unconscious mind.'

'I can make no sense of my dreams.'

'That's my job.'

At a pound a minute!

She asked me how I felt about the diarist – viz. my conscious self.

'He's a bit of a wimp.'

'Meaning?'

'He lets himself be manipulated by women.'

She ignored my use of the plural and asked about Denise. 'You're clearly attracted to her.'

'On a primitive level.'

'Primitive?'

'Instinctive.'

'You feel that instincts are primitive?'

'Not always, but when they lead you to sleep with someone you despise ...'

'Why do you despise her?'

'Perhaps despise is too strong a word.'

'Yet you used it.'

'Yes.'

She waited.

'She is not someone whose mind I admire. I feel that I am sleeping with her *faute de mieux*.'

'Yet you share interests – literature, languages.'

'Her values, then.'

'Moral values?'

'Social values.'

'For example?'

I thought of dinner at the Taylors'. 'She would not fit in with some of my friends.'

'Why not?'

'They would find her uninteresting, even banal.'

'Would that matter?'

'Yes.'

'Why?'

'It would reflect on my judgement and ...'

'What?'

'Just because she satisfies my sexual urges seems no reason to impose her on others.'

I was avoiding a word. Alison sensed it. She gently directed the line of enquiry back to my childhood and asked about my parents' attitude to social class. My father? He was genuinely indifferent to social distinctions, and was delighted that I married a Jew. My mother? Ah. A different story. Her parents had been snobs who thought she had married beneath her station. She was determined that her children should sink no further. There had been cold arguments with my father as to which of his flock could be asked to dinner. And what would she think of Denise? That she was common. That is the word I have been avoiding. *Common*.

Was it possible, Alison suggested, that Denise was the farmer's daughter in the haystack? That my disdain for her came from a fear that my mother would disapprove? Yes, she would disapprove, but had I not braved her disapproval when I married Ruth? If my mother would loathe the aura of gentility that still surrounded Denise despite her university education, love of opera and emancipated sexual morals, she loathed still more the liberal culture of Hampstead and Belsize Park. Like insurance companies, she assessed people by their postal codes. NW1, NW3, NW11 inspired an instinctive revulsion. Xenophobia? Anti-Semitism? No, her disdain encompassed the English in boroughs like Camden and Islington who read the *Guardian* and made programmes for Channel Four Television about gays and lesbians. To her, liberalism and decadence went hand in hand, while patriotism incorporated honesty, decency, conservatism. Living in a vicarage enabled her to behave as if little had changed since the days of Jane Austen.

That I did not share my mother's prejudices seemed to me to be established beyond doubt by my choice of Ruth as a wife. Alison is not so sure. She suggests that the son who wants to escape from the maternal embrace may choose as his love object a woman as unlike his mother as he can find; but the choice, expressing a reaction against his mother, establishes only that the son is not free of her influence at all.

There is also the question of narcissism. Every young man, in searching for a 'princess', wants not only to elicit approval from his parents but also to enhance his self-esteem. When these two imperatives conflict, he may choose his 'princess', as it were, from a foreign land, in my case that foreign land being Belsize Park. Ruth may not have been the daughter of an English duke, but her father was an eminent academic. She had been to South Hampstead High School and Oxford University. She was beautiful and much courted within her own community by the likes of Joshua. She was a princess, whereas Denise ... Whomever she married, people would assume that he had married his secretary.

*Friday*

Am I a snob? How can I be a snob if I despise snobbery? Alison explains how it might be possible. The part of me still seeking to elicit affection through approbation from my mother inevitably espouses her social values; while the part of me that is free from her influence, has autonomous unsnobbish values that happen also to be my father's values or, for that matter, common sense. I feel relieved by this interpretation. It suggests that I am not *truly* a snob. At the same time, I wonder whether this diagnosis is wholly correct.

The point is this. We must live in our own skulls and in

our own skins. From brain and body comes self-consciousness, and from self-consciousness an identity. The identity each of us develops tends to be pleasing to its owner because life becomes intolerable if it is not. We look in a mirror. We want to be pleased with what we see. Of course, as any child observes, watching its mother prepare for a party, the face we make into the mirror bears little resemblance to the one we make when looking at others. Thus, our own idea of ourself may bear little resemblance to the persona we present to the outside world. We flatter ourselves because, if we do not, who will?

Identity and nationality. The second is a component part of the first. Who am I? An Englishman. I have a clear idea of what that means. The knowledge makes my heart beat faster when I think of the battles of Crécy or Trafalgar or El Alamein. But who is Ruth? She was not sure. A Briton? No one uses the word and to my mother there is no such thing. There are the English, the Scots, the Welsh, the Irish and foreigners. To my mother, Ruth was a foreigner. Her family had lived in London for three generations, so she was a third-generation foreigner. My mother was delighted when we were divorced. Ruth's mother was delighted too. So was her father. Only my father was sad.

But: this is the question which perplexes me. If our nationality is part of our identity, then so also, perhaps, is our social class. Particularly where that social class has a tribal cohesion. A shipworker on Tyneside is not just an Englishman, he is a Geordie, but to describe the Duke of Newcastle as a Geordie is patently absurd. So, too, a Liverpudlian is a Scouser but only if he belongs to the working class. This need for tribal identity applies

92

particularly to football – a puerile game, by any rational measure, but one that elicits powerful emotions from grown men. True, you will find intellectuals who 'support' one team or another, but this is a symptom, perhaps, of the bourgeois' confusion about his identity. He searches for a tribe to alleviate his sense of alienation.

Where is this leading? To the conclusion that deliberate enhancement of national or tribal characteristics dissipates the confusion and alienation of modern man. So it is right that, just as the National Trust or English Heritage conserve our national monuments, Gordon Taylor should re-enact the customs of the class to which he aspires by remaining behind with his male guests at the dining table while Delia withdraws with the women. And equally right that I should feel reluctant to get involved with a woman who keeps a rubber plant on the window-sill of her flat in Henley-upon-Thames and has a framed reproduction of Van Gogh's *Sunflowers* on the wall. But how can I convey this to Denise and Alison without appearing to be a snob?

## Saturday

Fate intervenes. Unknown to me, Denise has a sister living in Bristol. She is divorced and lives alone with her daughter and a cat. On Thursday, the cat was killed by a car. This brought on a fit of hysteria in the daughter which, together with the sight of the squashed cat, led the mother, Denise's sister, to a nervous collapse.

Denise told me this in a breathless whisper as we passed one another in the corridor at Caversham yesterday afternoon. The upshot: that she must go to Bristol for the weekend. She says she is sorry. I brush aside her apologies. She thanks me for being so understanding. Then, standing on tiptoe, she whispers into my ear: 'Don't worry. I'll make it up to you.'

It is typical of the middle classes to make such a fuss about a cat. The upper classes reserve such strong feelings for their dogs.

Denise's absence means that I have a free weekend to consider Gordon's letter, which arrived this morning, and read Paget's dossier before meeting him with Gordon.

The letter is on paper headed 'The Sunday Gazette'.

Dear Michael,

I am delighted that you have agreed to undertake the journalistic assignment we discussed which I have provisionally entitled 'The Harding Report'. Clearly, until you have conducted your further research, you will be unable to decide how best to tell the story; but on the understanding that you will submit an article suitable for the *Gazette* Review front, or the *Gazette* magazine, viz. one of at least 3,000 words, I am prepared to offer you a fee of £10,000 for first British serial rights, or £20,000 to include world syndication, half payable upon counter-signature of this letter, half on submission of the article. The *Gazette* will also reimburse any expenses you incur.

If you should decide to write a book based upon your research, then I feel it only fair that the *Gazette*, having made the initial outlay, should have first option on the serial rights of such a book, the price to be negotiated in good faith at a later date.

The *Gazette* would make no claims to participation in any other rights to the book.

There are two further points pertinent to this agreement. The offer in paragraph 1 is conditional upon your agreement with the *Gazette* as to the methods to be employed in your research; and your willingness to accept any person or persons proposed by the *Gazette* to assist you.

It is also understood that if the period required to conduct the research should be such that your present employment is terminated, then the *Gazette* undertakes to offer you a contract on terms at least as advantageous as those you presently enjoy.

If you are willing to accept this proposal under the above terms, please countersign the enclosed copy of this letter and return it to me.

Yours sincerely,

Gordon Taylor
Editor, *Sunday Gazette*

He does not specify the length of time required for my research. However, I am entitled to four weeks' holiday and on top of this I should be able to obtain a month's unpaid leave of absence. Eight weeks should be more than enough for whatever research Gordon has in mind. I can then write the article in the evenings and at weekends. £20,000! Almost a year's salary. And if I should lose my job with BBC Monitoring, a contract with the *Gazette*! This is an offer I can hardly refuse unless … What 'methods of research' do they have in mind? And what 'person or persons' do they want to assist me?

Paget's dossier.

(1) Photocopies of cuttings from a number of newspapers and magazines including *Die Bunte*, *Hello!* and the *Almanach de Gotha*.

(2) A book on the Knights of the Cross, published in 1985 in Frankfurt-am-Main. Lavishly illustrated. A PR job. Their charitable work throughout the world, largely through Kreuzhilfe. Photographs of Heinrich von Willich, the present Grand Master, at his castle at Zelden. Splendid robes. Dazzling decorations: the bejewelled cross of the Knight of Justice of the Most Venerable Order of the Knights of the Cross.

(3) A slim book, *Die Zukunft der Moderne Welt*, by Lothar von Willich, Cologne 1948. Who was this Lothar von Willich who ruminates after the war about the future of the modern world? A slim volume but, from the look of it, heavy reading.

(4) A history in German of the Crusading orders from the eleventh century to the present day.


*Sunday*

A day's reading has made me an authority on the family of Willich. German nobility. Land given by the Emperor Frederick Barbarossa to a Lothar von Willich. His brother, Kaspar, a Grand Master of the Knights of the Cross. Fights against the Saracens in Southern Italy and is at the side of Barbarossa in Asia Minor when he dies on crusade.

In the twelfth and thirteenth centuries, three arch-bishops of Cologne from the von Willichs, two of Münster, and five Grand Masters of the Knights of the Cross. In the sixteenth century, a Willich was sent by the Emperor Charles V to serve the Ban of the Empire on

Martin Luther after the Edict of Worms. Von Willichs, both as Knights of the Cross and in their own right as Catholic magnates, fought for the Catholic Emperor against the Protestant princes in Germany's wars of religion. Theirs was one of the 350 sovereign states recognised by the peace of Westphalia in 1648. Caught between the episcopal states of Osnabrück and Münster, it encompassed no more than 10 square miles around the town and fortress of Zelden.

In the seventeenth and eighteenth centuries, the von Willichs were zealots of the Counter-Reformation. There was another archbishop of Cologne, an archbishop of Treves, an archbishop of Salzburg – this at a time when archbishops were territorial princes in their own right. Half a dozen von Willichs became Jesuits: one was made the rector of Ingolstadt, others went as missionaries as far afield as Saskatchewan and Peking. And time and again, von Willichs pop up in the annals of the Knights of the Cross: Grand Masters, Commanders, Knights of Honour, Knights of Justice. When Napoleon created the Confederation of the Rhine, the von Willichs fled from Zelden to the court of their Wittelsbach cousins in Bavaria. At the Congress of Vienna, their principality went to Prussia but they retained the fortress and estates at Zelden.

Distinguished service in World War I. Albrecht von Willich, then a young lieutenant, was awarded the Iron Cross with Oak Leaves. He was killed in the last days of the war. His brother Kaspar, born in 1903, narrowly escaped the trenches. He was nevertheless commissioned in 1922 into the army of 100,000 men permitted by the treaty of Versailles. In 1939, he commanded a Panzer brigade, first in Poland, then in France, finally in Russia. He fought in Stalingrad but escaped the Soviet encirclement, returned to Berlin and survived the war.

Kaspar's wife, Ilse von Wied. Eighteen years younger than her husband. Date of marriage given as November 10, 1942 which cannot be right because this was before Kaspar flew out of Stalingrad.

Kaspar's son, Heinrich, the present Grand Master. A businessman? Director of the Dortmunder Bank and Bettelheim Krull. Chairman of Kreuzhilfe. At one time, mayor of Münster. Married to Julia Krull. Four children.

Little about the four children. Two sons, two daughters. Only Barbara, apparently called 'Babi', appears in the cuttings from *Die Bunte* and *Hello!*, and the gossip columns of *Bild Zeitung* and *Tagespiegel*. One of Munich's smart set, the *Chickseria*. The pictures in *Hello!* taken on the ramparts of Zelden. Tall, blonde, an unmistakable Teuton. A sour smile.

Kaspar's brother, Lothar von Willich, author of *The Future of Modern Europe*. A professor or lecturer at Heidelberg University. Subject? Philosophy, or the history of philosophy. Suspended by the Nazis. Reinstated at the end of the war. His predecessor ousted by the British Military Government.

Find it impossible to immerse myself in the turgid German of *Der Zukunft der Moderne Welt*. Vacuous phrases and the kind of empty, bombastic pontification favoured by German academics. 'Man seeks to apprehend the nature of the present epoch which is being born out of the womb of history.' I skim and get the gist. Only oblique references to Nazism. 'The last decades have suggested what life without Christ really is.'

What relevance can this possibly have to the death of George Harding? No question of my reading it from start to finish.

One of Lothar von Willich's pronouncements sticks in
my mind. Its emptiness creates a vacuum, which involuntarily I try to fill as I sit on the train to Reading. 'True
culture depends upon the ability of the human spirit both
to distinguish itself from and to stand out against the
natural order of things that surround it.' What is true
culture? The contrary to false culture. What is false
culture? Indeed, what is culture? I suspect that for
Germans the word has a meaning that Anglo-Saxons
cannot comprehend.

At Caversham, between bulletins, I look it up in *Webster's
New World Dictionary* in the Research and Information
Unit. Early definitions concern the cultivation of the soil
and the breeding of bacteria. It is only when I reach
definition 6 that I find what I want: 'the training and
refining of the mind, emotions, manners, taste, etc.'.
Definition 7: 'the result of this refinement of thought,
emotions, manners, taste, etc.'. Definition 8: 'the concepts, habits, skills, arts, instruments, institutions, etc., of
a given people in a given period, civilisation'.

I go to my work-station. In Moscow, Zhirinovsky is
giving a press conference. Here, clearly, is an uncultured
man. Yeltsin, too, is uncultured according to *Webster's*
definition of the word. The old Soviet Union had a
confused attitude towards culture. On the one hand they
revered it, and gave lavish subsidies to art and literature:
on the other, there was a cult of the proletarian. A certain
coarseness was a qualification for the post of a Party boss.

What has culture to do with class? In Germany and
Austria, the aristocrats were the patrons of the arts – the
Esterházys, the Habsburgs, the prince-bishops of Mainz

and Salzburg. So too were the burghers. Bach would not have been hired as *Kapellmeister* by a working men's club. But in England? What German academics like Lothar von Willich could not understand is the cult of Philistinism among the English upper class: the duke who cares more about his grouse moor than his Rubens.

Refinement of thought, emotions, manners: coffee drunk from a porcelain cup with a crooked little finger rather than a mug gripped by a fist filled with strong, sticky tea? Then Denise is cultured. But here is the paradox that perplexes me. It is precisely this aspect of Denise that I find repugnant, and only brute instinct that draws me to her. My human spirit unquestionably distinguishes between the natural order of things and the things that surround it, only to reject the things that surround it – opera, rubber plants, compassion for cats – and go for the natural order of things: dark, malodorous oblivion.

Marta Kusinski, one of my colleagues, hands me a message as I transcribe Zhirinovsky's raving. She glances at my transcript on the screen, then looks puzzled because I smile. She cannot see how I can find his rabid nationalism amusing. Her verdict on her compatriot Zhirinovsky: 'Uncultured.'

The message is from Gordon's secretary at the *Gazette*. Would I be free to have lunch with Gordon and Paget at the Garrick Club on Wednesday? Marta, having read the message and knowing my schedule, offers to swap shifts. When Zhirinovsky eventually finishes his tirade, I ring the *Gazette* and accept.

Lunch with Denise. She gives me a full account of the weekend spent counselling her sister and niece. Neither could forgive herself, apparently, for permitting a neighbour to throw the cat's corpse into the dustbin. They did not realise what had happened until the next morning when it was too late: the black bodybag containing the cat, empty cereal packets, coffee grounds, empty tins and cartons had already been removed by the refuse collectors. The best they could do was hold a memorial service in the back garden.

## Tuesday

I put to Alison, during yesterday's session, the conundrum about culture versus instinct. She disputes the premiss of Lothar von Willich. Far from distinguishing itself from, and standing out against, the natural order of things, the human spirit should seek to comprehend it so that it can flow with the tide. This in essence was the function of psychotherapy. The idea that spirit and nature, body and soul are inevitable adversaries comes from the Gnostic strains in the Christian tradition which even the Christian churches now disown.

This irritated me. I am always irritated when Alison leaves the confines of her discipline. What does she know about Gnostic strains in the Christian tradition? Probably something she picked up in religious studies at school. To punish her, I suggest that discussing such things with her means that I do not discuss them with Denise; that this course of psychotherapy, instead of helping me to form a mature bond with a woman, in fact prevents its development by siphoning off the conflicts and contradictions that we would otherwise have worked through.

This places Alison in a dilemma. She has decided that

Denise is a good thing, but she does not want to lose a client. She tells me, after pondering my question, that there is no reason why the questions I raise with her should not also come into my conversation with Denise.

'Should I tell her that I despise myself for sleeping with her?'

A pause. Then: 'No.'

## Wednesday

Lunch at the Garrick yesterday with Gordon and Paget. Their plan is so perilous and absurd that it took all my powers of self-control not to show exasperation. I have been led up the garden path although now, sitting at my kitchen table eating toasted cheese, I can see how the devious mind of a former intelligence officer could come up with a scheme of that kind.

I also realise that I was perhaps predisposed to reject what they suggested. I can think of no other reason for rising this morning at six thirty as usual, and setting off for Reading, only to remember the lunch when I got to Paddington Station and saw a copy of the *Daily Gazette*. This set up a sequence of associations: *Daily Gazette*, *Sunday Gazette*; *Sunday Gazette*, Gordon; Gordon, lunch. I went back to Fulham, made a fresh pot of coffee, read the paper, then skimmed through Paget's dossier once again before setting out for Leicester Square.

I have always liked London clubs. They seem to me to be an irreplaceable aspect of our uniquely English culture but I have never joined one largely because I have never felt that I could justify the expense of the annual subscription. If I worked in Bush House rather than at Caversham, it might make sense to belong to a club like

the Garrick, assuming, that is, that I could find someone
to put me up. Would Gordon? Ten years ago, I would
have said yes. Five years ago, no. Now? An academic
question, while I work at Caversham. In any case, I have
a sufficient number of acquaintances to satisfy my
appetite for these male preserves. Balzac wrote that only
a fool pays for a newspaper, a mistress or a country house
because a man can always use one belonging to some-
body else. The same could be said of a London club.

Gordon and Paget were waiting by the fire in the hall.
Out of his Cambridge context, Paget looked a little odd.
He was smaller than I had realised, and wore an old but
elegant grey pin-striped suit. Gordon took us upstairs to
the bar where I followed them in asking for a glass of dry
sherry. We talked about this and that. A man we had
known at Cambridge, now a barrister, talked to Gordon:
he did not appear to remember me. Paget, too, caught
the attention of one or two members – ex-pupils,
perhaps, or junior colleagues from his secret-service days.
  We went down to lunch at a table in the corner of one
of the rooms at the back of the club with large, oil-
painted portraits of actors and actresses on the walls.
There was some distance between ours and the next table
but Gordon, nevertheless, when we got down to business,
spoke in a quiet, conspiratorial tone of voice. Had I got
his letter?
  'Yes.'
  'Were the terms satisfactory?'
  'Yes, depending, of course ...'
  'Of course. You have to know what you're letting
yourself in for.' He turned to Paget.

Paget: There are three hypotheses. The first, accepted by
the Government, is that George took up with some

woman of the night in Luxembourg who, for some unknown reason, took him to Saarbrücken where they indulged in some kind of sado-masochistic orgy that ended up in the river Saar. The search continues for such a woman. Until now, she has not been found.

The second hypothesis, which is a variation on the first: that George was somehow seduced as part of a plan to discredit Europhobic politicians. The principal objective may have been a scandal. His death may not have been intended: as with the first hypothesis, it may have resulted from an orgy that went too far.

The third hypothesis: he was murdered. He was murdered not, or not just, because he was a Europhobic politician but because he was investigating the import of arms by the Knights of the Cross. This, to Paget, is the most likely explanation but it is not one that the governments of either Germany or Britain are willing to investigate.

He pauses as the waitress brings him toast and potted shrimps.

'Of one thing I'm certain,' says Paget, leaning forward and speaking in a subdued but emphatic tone of voice. 'There exists on the Continent a secret, well-organised network that has as its objective the creation of a powerful, centralised European state. This network is centred in Germany and there is evidence that it is controlled by the Knights of the Cross. It intends that this future Europe should be dominated by Germany and should promote and embody the dogmas and teachings of the Roman Catholic Church.'

Gordon looked to see how I had reacted to what Paget had said but, before I could continue, Paget turned to me and asked: 'Did you find time to read the book by Lothar von Willich?'

'Of course.'

'Didn't you find it revealing?'

'Yes, indeed, of ...' I hesitated as if searching for the right words.

Paget finished my sentence for me. 'Of Catholic ambitions for a political movement that would rise out of the ashes of Germany's defeat in World War II.'

'Which, in a sense, it did, with the triumph of the Christian Democrats.'

'But you must certainly have realised that the vision of Lothar von Willich was not confined to the rump state cobbled together from the Allied zones.'

'He talks of Europe as much as Germany.'

'To him, the two are the same.'

'In which case, yes, it is a programme for Catholics to assert themselves in the political sphere.'

'Did you catch his references to Fatima?'

'Fatima?'

'Incredible as it may seem to us as Englishmen, there is a widespread belief among Roman Catholics that the Virgin Mary appeared to three children in the Portuguese village of Fatima in 1917. She warned of catastrophes sent by God to chastise the world unless the world repents. She also told Lucia, the eldest of the three children, a secret which she was to repeat only to the Pope. It is said that on his accession Pope John XXIII emerged white and shaking from the room where he had read it. Papists love supernatural sensationalism of this kind. The point relevant to our venture, however, is this: the Virgin Mary told the children in Fatima that they must pray for the conversion of Russia. It was only through the conversion of Russia that the world could be saved.'

'But surely,' said Gordon, 'no one takes this kind of thing seriously – no one, that is, besides ignorant peasants, gullible children and uneducated old women.'

105

'On the contrary,' said Paget, 'the miraculous appearance of the Virgin Mary at Fatima is believed by the most sophisticated prelates and theologians in the Roman Catholic Church, as well as the bankers and businessmen who fund Kreuzhilfe, and the strange body of aristocrats who make up the Knights of the Cross. Who do they credit with the collapse of Communism in the Soviet Union? Reagan? Gorbachev? The contradictions inherent in a non-market economy? No. Our Lady of Fatima. Who saved the life of Pope John Paul II when he was shot by a Turk in St Peter's Square? The surgeon at the hospital? No, Our Lady of Fatima. The bullet today is on the altar at her shrine. It is she who will champion the forces of good as they engage with those of evil as we approach the millennium. Not God, or the Archangel Gabriel with his flaming sword, but Our Lady of Fatima. And what does she ask in return from her loyal adherents? The conversion of Russia!'

Even while Paget was speaking, with Gordon paying close attention to what he said, I was trying to remember whether it was here or at the Connaught that they served a celebrated bread-and-butter pudding. This was inspired by my disappointment with the plaice that I had chosen for my main course. Clearly, if I had not been paying some attention to what Paget was saying, I would not be able to record it here; but I could not as yet see what possible connection there could be between visions of the Virgin Mary and the murder of George, and, not seeing the connection, found it only too easy to be distracted by the question of bread-and-butter pudding.

Russia: its conversion to Catholicism promised by the Virgin Mary at Fatima as a task that would save the world. Step One: the ousting of the Soviets. Achieved, 1989–91. Step Two? This, he explained, was more problematic. After sixty-five years of indoctrination in an atheist ideology that had now failed, the Russian masses were ripe for conversion, and the Knights of the Cross, through their agency Kreuzhilfe, were more than ready to convert.

However, Russia under Yeltsin, although internationalist when it comes to loans from the World Bank, is wholly xenophobic when it comes to religion. The Orthodox prejudice against Latin Catholicism remains as strong as it has been for the past five hundred years. How, then, should the Knights proceed? Hitherto, the work of Kreuzhilfe had been in the Catholic countries of Eastern Europe – Poland, Hungary and Czechoslovakia. Access to the Soviet Union itself had been virtually impossible. However, there was a Trojan Horse. Lithuania. Alone among the Soviet Republics, Lithuania had a Catholic population that had remained in Lithuania until tens of thousands were sent by Stalin to the gulags in Siberia.

There was no bread-and-butter pudding. I ordered trifle instead and, to show that I was paying attention to what Paget was saying, I put a question. Did it matter, did he know, to the Virgin of Fatima whether Russia was converted to Catholicism or reconverted to the Orthodox faith?

Paget confessed that, since he was not privy to the detail of her revelation or in a position to put supplementary questions, he did not know. He did not imagine that Mormons or Baptists would be acceptable to her, but very possibly Orthodox conversions would do. The trouble was that the Orthodox Church in Russia was gravely compromised with the former regime. It was known that a number of its bishops were commissioned officers in the KGB. But the one thing the pro-Communist and anti-Communist bishops had in common was their loathing for the Church of Rome. The only help they were prepared to accept from Kreuzhilfe was hard currency, paid to the bishops with no strings attached.

Is this true? Paget is quite capable of making up such things to amuse an audience: on the other hand, I know from my own experience that in the former Soviet Union, truth is often stranger than fiction.

I sensed, as I ate my trifle, that we were getting to the point, and my intuition proved correct. Paget returned to the Lithuanians who had been deported to Siberia. Many had been released from the gulags in the 1960s and 1970s but had not been permitted to return to their native land. There had, therefore, grown up sizeable Lithuanian communities. These remained Catholic because among the deportees there had not only been priests but also bishops who in the gulags had secretly consecrated their successors. Quite cut off from Rome, and even from the Catholic Church in Lithuania, they were only now making contact with their co-religionists in the West.

I had finished my trifle. Gordon ordered coffee.

'What I suggest is this,' said Paget, turning for the first time to look directly at me. 'You should adopt the identity of a Russian priest. You arrive in Germany with another Russian from Siberia and go to Kreuzhilfe for help. You tell them of an isolated community of faithful Catholics in some remote corner of Siberia – on the river Amur on the border with China, say, or on the upper reaches of the Yenisei close to Mongolia, or perhaps the Kamchatka peninsula or the island of Sakhalin – there are half a dozen places that remain utterly remote and still completely cut off from the outside world. You talk to them about the spiritual hunger of the alienated, disillusioned masses; their ripeness for conversion; how the harvest is great, but the labourers are few. You need prayer-books, bibles, rosaries, and the funds to build a church. Kreuzhilfe will welcome you with open arms. They will embrace you and, while your request is being processed, look after you in Germany and as likely as not invite you to stay with the von Willichs in Zelden. And if there you can gain the confidence of any of the family, you will be in a unique position to discover what is going on.'

I felt slightly sick. Was it the trifle? Or the contraction of nerves in the pit of my stomach as my great journalistic assignment shrivelled before my eyes into an absurd pantomime, concocted by a senile *metteur en scène*? I turned to Gordon to see what terms he would use to tell Paget that his plan was absurd.

'Brilliant.' Gordon sat gazing at his former tutor with an expression of whole-hearted admiration. Describing this now, I suspect that the word 'brilliant' was for my consumption rather than Paget's since it seemed likely that the two had discussed the plan before. Take Gordon's letter: the offer was conditional upon my agreement as to the methods to be employed in my research, and my willingness to accept any person or persons proposed by the *Gazette* to assist me. He must have heard already what Paget had in mind and now was merely applauding the reprise.

Both turned to me. I searched for the word. Unworkable? Ridiculous? Preposterous? Absurd? No. I said: 'Ingenious.'

As I sit here picking at the chip in the Formica of my kitchen table, I accuse myself of gross cowardice in saying 'ingenious' rather than 'absurd'. There are points, however, that can be made in my defence.

(1) Ingenious is a less positive word than brilliant: it certainly did not commit me irrevocably to accept my role in the plan.

(2) It is difficult to reject out of hand a proposal made by a man who is paying for one's lunch.

(3) My reflex is always to temporise: invariably one regrets a decision made on the spur of the moment.

(4) At Cambridge I had tended to go along with whatever George and Gordon suggested.

None of these was the true reason, however, for leading them to believe that I would go along with what they proposed. The true reason, if I am honest with myself (and what point is there in a journal if one is not?), was that, as Paget was reaching the end of his exposition, I recognised a man who rose to leave a table at the far end of the room.

The man was Joshua, the future husband of my former wife. In a minute or so Joshua would pass the table and see me sitting with the editor of the *Sunday Gazette*. How would he report it to Ruth? How would it look? What expression would he see on Gordon Taylor's face? Triumph or disappointment? Satisfaction or frustration?

'Ingenious.' A look of delight came on to Gordon's face at the very moment when Joshua was passing. So pleased was he with my reaction that he leaned forward, patted my shoulder, and said: 'Good man.'

Joshua caught my eye. He nodded. I nodded. He passed on.

'Ingenious,' I said again, 'but –'

'Of course,' said Gordon. 'You would have to have help. No one would expect you to take this on alone.'

'I would need help, not least –'

'A Russian,' said Paget. 'There would have to be a genuine Russian to accompany you. That can be arranged.'

'And –'

'And the Russians would have to be ready to deal with any enquiries that Kreuzhilfe might make on their turf.'

'Of course,' said Paget. 'That, too, can be arranged.'

'I don't think that I'd be convincing as a priest,' I said.

'You would have to be briefed,' said Gordon.

'I don't speak a word of Lithuanian.'

'All the better,' said Paget. 'You are a Russian convert, ordained secretly by a Lithuanian bishop but now with a parish of native Russians.'

'Wouldn't my accent give me away?'

'To a Russian, perhaps, but not to a German.'

'Do they speak Russian?'

'At Kreuzhilfe? Yes. The von Willichs? I doubt it. But that doesn't matter. During the long nights in Siberia, you have taught yourself German.'

'And English?'

'No. Not English. You would speak it too well.'

Now Gordon raised an objection: describing it now, I wonder whether or not this, too, was not somehow rehearsed. 'Surely,' he asked Paget, 'some contact must already exist between these Catholic pockets in Siberia and the Lithuanian Church?'

'Yes.'

'Won't Kreuzhilfe then check the credentials of a priest who turns up out of the blue?'

'Of course. But my Russian friend can take care of that.'

'The General?'

'Precisely.' Paget frowned as if Gordon had been indiscreet in mentioning this Russian. That, too, may have been contrived.

Lay awake for an hour last night between approximately three and four in the morning. Left for work with a befuddled mind. Fortunately, no major stories at Caversham: business as usual for the Russian team.

Do anxieties wake one up? Or are they drawn into the void of the inactive mind? I had important things to consider. A major decision had to be made. Typically my mind skirted the important issue and tormented me with minor concerns such as changing the lock on my front door. Some months ago I had received a letter from my insurance company saying that cover was now conditional on a five-bar mortice lock being fitted to the door that separated my flat from the communal areas of the building. I had not yet had it changed. On any day I might return from work to find that my television, video-recorder and notebook computer – even some of the antique pieces of furniture given to me by my mother – had gone. There would be no compensation from the insurance company because there was no five-bar mortice lock fitted to the door.

Clearly, my mind was avoiding the prime anxiety – the one that had woken me up in the first place – and only after switching on the light, getting out of bed, going through to my desk in the living room and writing myself a memo to remind me to order a new lock, only then, back in bed and once more in the dark, did I remember that I was on course to go to Germany disguised as a Russian Roman Catholic priest.

I say 'on course' because, while I had not actually agreed to take on this hazardous assignment, I had not explicitly declined it. I knew that both Gordon and Paget had left the Garrick Club ninety per cent sure that I was 'on board'. This was Gordon's phrase: our general manager at Caversham uses it from time to time. It has a comforting ring to it. You jump off the quay into a boat; you become part of a crew. From any dispassionate analysis of the mission, however, 'keel-hauled' would seem a more accurate metaphor. Or, even more exact, walking the plank. After all, if the Knights of the Cross were ready to murder George, a minister of the Crown, they would not hesitate to kill me.

Denise, at Caversham: a gleam in her eye reminds me of her promise to make up to me this weekend what she had failed to deliver a week ago because of the death of her sister's cat. I feel unable to face it, perhaps because of my broken night, and on the spur of the moment tell her that my father has had a stroke.

It was Goebbels, I think, who said that the more audacious the lie, the more likely it is to be believed. For a moment Denise gave me a sceptical look, but the crumpled look of my facial skin after the sleepless night, taken with yesterday's unexpected and unexplained absence, appeared to convince her that what I said was true. Her expression changed from eager anticipation to consoling compassion. I backtracked a little, saying that the stroke was not serious, but that it meant I would have to go to Avelscombe this weekend.

I told Alison about my broken night. She did not seem particularly interested. If I had felt able to describe my principal anxiety then she might have had something to say, but I have picked up enough of Paget's MI6 ethos to realise that it would be hazardous to breathe a word about the German operation, even to Alison.

She asked what I had thought about as I tossed and turned on my bed between three and four in the morning. I told her about the lock. Now she pricked up her ears. Was I sure I *had* been awake? Quite sure. Why? Because a dream about an inadequate lock, and the fear that the things I treasured would be stolen, would be wholly consistent with my contradictory feelings for Denise. I was reluctant to let Denise into my life because I was afraid that, like Ruth, she would rob me of my self-esteem. By the end of our session, she had almost convinced me that it *had* been a dream after all. When I got home this evening, I had to go to my desk to see if there really was a letter from the insurance company. I found it in the file marked 'pending'.

I telephoned my parents just now to ask myself to Avelscombe for the weekend. My mother said, 'Of course, darling,' in her usual, indifferent tone of voice. She thinks it is vulgar to show emotion.

*Saturday*
___

Avelscombe. Whenever I come here, I ask myself why I do not come here more often. Particularly on a morning like this, with the winter sun shining horizontally through the long sash windows of the drawing room; the view of the lawn running down to the ha-ha, trees along the stream, forests on the horizon. And earlier: waking to the smell of coffee, the warm kitchen, bacon and egg; *The Times*; Mrs Hartley peeling potatoes in the scullery; my father in his study composing tomorrow's sermon; my mother out and about.

Apparently, Anne and John are staying at the Hall and have asked us over for supper tonight. Otherwise, an empty day. That is the joy of the country. Empty days.

I hear my father calling me. He suggests a walk.

On our walk, I asked my father what he thought about the supposed appearances of the Virgin Mary at Fatima. He hesitated for some time before giving an answer. The question, put as we left the rectory garden, was not answered until we had reached the summit of the hill that rose behind Avelscombe where we stopped to take in the view.

'I don't know. Why do you ask?'

My father has always been a man of few words. The brevity of his sermons is certainly one of the reasons for the substantial size of his congregation on Sundays. There are other factors: one neighbouring parish now has a female priest and another a bearded homosexual. Defections from these parishes gives my father a congregation of around twenty. The average attendance at the other two parishes is five.

'Apparently,' I said, 'the Virgin Mary appeared to some children in Fatima in 1917 to warn us that unless we repented the world would be destroyed by war. And one has to concede that we did come close to self-extinction. But now one is inclined to wonder whether the relative peace that exists today is thanks to the telling of millions upon millions of rosary beads that followed the warning of the Virgin of Fatima, or to the prosperity that has followed the triumph of capitalism and the success of the global market economy?'

My father nodded. 'Perhaps prayer produced the prosperity.'

I knew that he did not believe this, and he knew that I knew. We walked on for a while in silence. In his presence, I always feel immensely fond of my father. None of the resentment at his weakness that bubbles to the surface when I lie on Alison's couch intrudes into my conscious mind when we are face to face. I feel less affection towards my mother but that is not because of the way she treated me as a child but because it is not in her nature to elicit affection. She takes it as given that children love their parents and parents their children. If I were to say, 'Mother, I love you dearly,' she would probably answer, 'Don't be absurd.'

I am straying from the path taken by my father and me on our walk. 'Before the Reformation,' he said, 'there was great devotion to the Virgin Mary in England. The shrine of Our Lady at Walsingham was on a par with that of St James at Compostela. But the Reformers effectively erased it from the national consciousness and, of course, the Papists subsequently made things worse with their infallible dogmas of the Assumption and the Immaculate Conception.'

I have noticed in my father, and in other older people, that they often hide their opinions behind displays of erudition. I was unwilling to let him off the hook.

'Do you pray to the Virgin Mary?' I asked.

'To invoke her intercession, do you mean?'

'Yes. That kind of thing.'

Again, a long wait. Then: 'I have done, from time to time.'

'Not in a service?'

'No. There are always those who would object.'

'At Fatima,' I went on, 'one of the visionaries was shown the everlasting torment of souls in Hell.'

He nodded. 'So I remember.'

'Do you believe in such a place?'

He thought for a while as we walked as if it was a novel question that he had not considered for some time. 'Presumably,' he said eventually, 'if Christ died to save us, it must be from something unpleasant.'

'Eternal torment?'

'It is difficult to interpret the Gospel in any other way.'

'Have you ever come across anyone in the course of your life whom you felt deserved eternal torment?'

A long pause, then: 'Some of the things done by the Germans during the war could only have been done by evil people.'

'So some Germans may be damned, but no Englishmen?'

Again, a long pause before: 'No, I have known Englishmen, too, whose lives were dissolute and depraved.'

Dissolute. Depraved. Decadent. Debauched. Dishonoured. My poor father. He frequently uses such words that have lost their meaning. Things that are heinous sins to him are merely a matter of taste to my generation. Every suburban teenager routinely behaves in a way that would have horrified Moll Flanders and shamed Madame de Pompadour. They smoke pot as de Quincy smoked opium, and drink vodka as Oscar Wilde drank absinthe. You can only deprave where there is innocence: today television, glossy magazines and sex-education classes in schools ensure that all our children know the details of every perversion before they reach the age of twelve.

Innocence. Another word that has lost its meaning.

*Sunday*

Out of courtesy to my father, I go to church when I am staying at Avelscombe. I do not take communion, but I enjoy joining in the hymns, hearing his sermons and listening to Cranmer's mellifluous prose during the

117

readings from the Book of Common Prayer. Of course, I do not believe a word of it. I am astonished that anyone can.

The communion service in church this morning, and dinner last night with the Templetons at Avelscombe Hall, formed part of the same seamless garment of English country life. In the mellow candlelight of the Templetons' dining room, or in the chilly pews of the church this morning, I feel that I am immersed in the essence of England. Or, to put it another way, that this is what we mean by English *culture*. But even as I enjoy it, I realise that it is retreating before a new British culture that is either a sham version of Avelscombe lived out in the Home Counties by people like the Hardings, or the ever-encroaching culture of Pakistani corner-shops and tower-blocks filled with delinquent West Indians or third-generation Irish – unmarried scrubbers living off social security, topped up with a bonus for having an illegitimate child.

Until recently, Anne's father, Reggie Templeton, changed for dinner every night. He would put on black trousers with a satin stripe along the seam, a white shirt, a black bow-tie and a dark green velvet smoking jacket. Her mother, too, changed into a long dress, even when they were eating alone. Dinner was a solemn ritual. Candles were lit on the dining-room table. The cook served the food.

They gave up this custom only when they could no longer afford to employ a cook. Now on weekdays they eat supper in the kitchen, watching a small television on the kitchen dresser. They change only on Saturday nights when a local catering company called Scrummy Things sends a girl to serve a precooked dinner. The daily

118

polishes the candelabra. Avril Templeton fills the decanters from one of the few remaining bottles of her husband's vintage port.

I always enjoy dinner with the Templetons. Anne's father is now almost eighty and retains an exquisite modesty and old-fashioned charm. His task is to make a cocktail, itself something of a rarity in my generation. The gin, dry Martini and oil squeezed from the lemon rind are in such harmony that you feel you are drinking a small glass of ice-cold water from a mountain spring.

By the time you sit down at table, the gin has taken effect. You feel eloquent, amusing; you argue about the state of the nation and later, after the ladies have withdrawn, fill your glass with port, light a Havana cigar and listen to Reggie's reminiscences about his days in the Indian Army.

His tales are astonishing but not always in the way he intends. He served in Palestine during the Protectorate but seemed to have played polo rather than chase the Irgun. He remembered Caesarea well because it was there that his team beat the Yorkshire Hussars 17–7, and he had shot some snipe in the Jordan valley. Two of his closest friends had been killed when Begin, the future Prime Minister of Israel, had detonated a bomb in the King David Hotel.

John is embarrassed by his father-in-law: he thinks I think he is a Colonel Blimp. Yet there is more vulgarity in John's brand of jingoism than in Reggie's unreflective xenophobia. Reggie still, on occasions, refers to the Germans as 'the Boche' but he would never, like John, call them 'Krauts'. Reggie, of course, had the satisfaction of leading his Indian sepoys to victory over the Germans in World War II while John, one of the team that failed to prevent the takeover of his bank by a Frankfurt rival, had tasted the bitterness of defeat.

119

It always seemed to me magnanimous of the Frankfurt bank to let John keep his job. I have never been able to discover what particular talent, if any, John might possess. But that is true of many of my friends who work in the City. They earn large salaries and large bonuses, but what do they do? Anne once told me that John is very good with Arabs; perhaps that is why the Germans pay him £150,000 a year.

Anne was on good form. She is irritated by her mother as grown-up daughters so often are. There is friction, I think, over the way Anne brings up her children. She explained to me, *sotto voce*, how difficult it was to give them their supper in the kitchen at the same time as dinner was being prepared by the girl from Scrummy Things. Nor were her children used to being sent off to the nursery at seven. 'Mother always behaves as if we had not just a nanny but a nursemaid as well.' Anne does have an au pair girl but they left her in London.

Anne was pleased I was there. We are very old friends. In recent years, however, she has adopted a protective manner towards me, the other side of the coin to John's patronising tone. Clearly, in John's terms, I am a failure. My salary is puny. I have no wife, no country house, no Mercedes. I can tell that he regards me as a loser whom he only sees because of his wife.

Anne's solicitude is almost worse. She knows well enough that I have a dead-end job but tells others that it is 'hush-hush'. I play up to this ploy, leaving the impression with my fellow guests at her dinner parties that I am a high-powered analyst working for MI6, possibly licensed to kill. John later disabuses them of the misconception. 'He spends his time watching Moscow television. He wouldn't know the butt from the barrel of a Beretta, and if he was licensed to kill, he'd have killed his wife.' This was said in my presence. It was John's idea of a joke.

Last night, Reggie Templeton's cocktail, together with my long-frustrated desire to impress John and Anne, led me to confide to Anne that I might soon be sent on a tricky mission abroad. It slipped out when she asked me to go to a charity ball in six weeks' time, adding the no doubt kindly meant but somehow humiliating: 'Don't worry. We'll pay for the ticket.'

'I'd love to come if I'm in England.'

'Are you going abroad?'

'It's possible.'

'On holiday?'

'No. For work.' I spoke hesitantly as if I should not in fact be telling her as much as I did.

'Where will you go?'

'Here and there.'

'Spying?'

I shrugged. 'Let's call it ... research.'

'How intriguing.'

'I'm too old, really, for this cloak-and-dagger stuff.'

'You're not even forty.'

'I dare say, but danger's only fun for the young.'

'Danger?'

'Well ...'

'For God's sake, don't do anything risky.'

'One doesn't always have a choice.'

'You mean, they can order you to risk your life?'

'You know the score when you take on the job.'

'Even so.'

'And, in this case, there's a personal incentive that makes the risk worth taking.'

'What do you mean, a personal incentive?'

'I would very much like to know what happened to George.'

'George? It's to do with George?'

'There are grounds for thinking that he was murdered.'

'And you volunteered to find out?'

I placed my index finger over my lips to show that they were sealed. I had already said too much. I could say no more.

My father's sermon. He had composed it before we had gone on our walk, and yet it was on a theme relevant to our conversation. Slander. Detraction. Where did a Christian's duty lie when there seemed to be a conflict between truth and love? What should he say when evil presented itself as good? Depravity as tolerance? Rebellion as progress? Had not the Church become paralysed in the modern world by its reluctance, through a misplaced sense of charity, to call evil by its proper name?

Fortunately, most of those present were sufficiently familiar with their rector's bugbears and hobby-horses to get the drift of what he meant. 'Rebellion' was invariably a reference to women priests, 'depravity' to bearded homosexual vicars. The decision by the Synod of the Church of England to ordain women had astonished him. Although temperamentally somewhat austere, and certainly not inclined to prance around with thuribles and in fancy vestments, he had always belonged to the Catholic wing of the Anglican Church. He believed the Anglican communion was part of the wider, universal Church which, like the Orthodox Church in Russia, did not for historical reasons acknowledge the authority of the Pope.

The decision to ordain women distressed him first

because the Anglicans had made a unilateral decision on this momentous question; and second because it ignored all the arguments against the measure which he himself thought sound. A priest stood in for Christ; Christ was a man; therefore a priest must be a man.

It did not take much psychological insight to understand how his personal circumstances gave urgency to his theological opinions. His ministry was the only area of his life where he could not be bullied by his wife, my mother. In the rectory it might seem that God had made Adam to be the helpmate of Eve, rather than the other way round, but at the altar he was the one in charge and in the pulpit he could speak without interruption or contradiction.

Why did he not resign and join the Church of Rome? Left to himself, I dare say that he would have done, but if he was to resign the living, he would have to leave Avelscombe Rectory. Where would he live? What would he do? There would be a meagre pension and some compensation, but only enough to move to a bungalow or a terrace house.

For my mother, that would be the end of everything that made her life worthwhile – the elegant eighteenth-century rectory, dinner with the Templetons, her standing as the rector's wife. My father was a man of principle, but he had not the stomach to put his principles before my mother's contentment. He continued therefore to minister in a Church whose validity in his innermost conscience he now denied. A tragic, wasted life.

'Depraved', the other key word, referred in the context of his sermon to the neighbouring, bearded homosexual priest. This man also wore sandals, which some of his parishioners found hard to take, but the beard took on a greater significance because of Simon, the male companion with whom he lived. To a man like my father, whose carnal relations with my mother had almost certainly been of a straightforward kind, the image of what men did in the exchange of sexual pleasure was both baffling and abhorrent, and the yellowish thicket of the vicar's beard around his feverish pink lips and liverish tongue made the mouth seem like a sexual orifice unnaturally placed at the wrong end of his body. Each Sunday it drank the blood of Christ from the Holy Cup. This was a sin that cried to Heaven for vengeance.

I once explained this to Alison but under cross-examination was obliged to admit that my father had never actually expressed these thoughts to me. She concluded, as a result, that these were in fact *my* feelings about the bearded vicar, not his, and that they came from my own abhorrence of homosexuality, which in turn stemmed from a fear that I might be homosexual, something quite normal in a man with a weak father and dominating mother ...

*Quatsch!* Nonsense. Why do I use the German word? Am I already thinking in German? Is the mission I was going to turn down already under way in some corner of my brain? I say 'nonsense' because I do not have an abhorrence of homosexuals, only of bearded, sandalled, homosexual Anglican priests. Nor do I use the word depraved, or even know what it means. The mouth may have been evolved for the ingestion of food, and the tongue for the formulation of speech, but as Havelock Ellis noted, 'If the individual can find joy and inspiration in using his organs for ends they were not made for, he is following a course of action which, whether or not we choose to call it moral, is perfectly justifiable' – a sentiment with which Ruth and Denise would wholeheartedly agree.

124

9.00 p.m. Fulham. Kitchen table. Late. The vile return to London on a Sunday night. Paddington, which I shall see again in eight hours' time. Train half an hour late. Headache from reading Sunday newspapers in the ghastly, fluorescent light. All this on top of the sadness I feel at leaving home. Why? A longing to return to the womb. The security of childhood; but, also, Alison would tell me, the seedbed of our later neurosis.

Above all, pity for my parents. Why? Because the changes in their lifetime have left them baffled. Does this happen in every generation? The mutual incomprehension of old and young? My mother: trussed up by innumerable strands of convention; paralysed by inhibition, unable to break free; denied by her nature an imagination that would show her that life could be lived some other way. My father: the rug pulled out from beneath his feet by the ordination of women as priests; and the mass indifference to the beliefs to which he has devoted his life.

Why do I write 'mass indifference'? It is *my* indifference that baffles and demoralises him. The river of faith in Christ as the Son of God that has flowed for a thousand years through the Lathams runs into the sand in me. I have no faith, no wife, no progeny. A child of my time.

## Monday

Enter the Russian. Small, old, an amused and mischievous look on his face. Chain-smokes. A terrible wheeze. Impeccable English.

Paget left a message for me at Caversham. I telephoned him during my coffee break. He asked if I could dine with him tonight at the Special Forces Club in Herbert Crescent. Did not know whether or not Gordon would be able to be there. Fortunately, I had worn a suit to work: fifty minutes with Alison left no time to return to Fulham to change.

The porter at the Special Forces Club pointed to the room where Paget and the Russian were waiting for me. The Russian was introduced as Grigori Savchenko. Both the old men were drinking whisky. Paget ordered another round, and for me, gin and tonic. They were laughing; they had been reminiscing; two old rogues. Paget explained that they had first met in Berlin at the end of the war. Then in the 1970s Savchenko had turned up in London, as correspondent for *Moscow* magazine.

'We are old adversaries,' said Savchenko, patting Paget on the knee. 'But, even at the height of the Cold War, I like to think that we kept our sense of proportion and, above all, our sense of humour.' He drank his whisky undiluted in one swig, Russian style.

Paget turned to me. 'General Savchenko is willing to help us.'

'Unofficially, of course,' said Savchenko. 'We would, as it were, like to take out an option on the Russian rights to your article and as a down payment – since we have no dollars – we can arrange some of the back-up you may require.'

'A Russian companion,' Paget interposed.

'Indeed. I have already picked the man.'

We went through to the dining room. The old Russian, Savchenko, was clearly enjoying his evening out in this club for British spies. Like Paget, he was wearing an ancient but well-cut suit. Everything about him exuded Anglophilia. Only his high cheekbones gave him away as a Slav.

126

Why would this KGB veteran want to help us find out the truth about the death of a British minister? The explanation came when the conversation turned to the world situation. At once, Savchenko became more serious and talked with an impressive lucidity. The Russians feared the Germans. Twice within half a century the two countries had gone to war. The costs – tens of millions dead. Was there an inherent *Drang nach Osten* in the German psyche? A drive to expand to the east? Russia under the Soviets had relied upon two things to keep the Germans at bay. The first, superior armed forces. The second, a *cordon sanitaire* of pro-Soviet satellite states. The concept had been flawed. The cost of sustaining the Soviet defence forces had crippled the Soviet economy and deprived the Soviet people of a reasonable standard of living; and the satellite nations had inevitably been beguiled by the superior quality of life in the capitalist West. As a result, the strategy had been unsustainable; the Soviet system had collapsed; and Russia was now in a weaker position than at any time since the reign of Ivan the Terrible – a toothless tiger forced to abandon its allies like Serbia, its kith and kin in Latvia, and beleaguered even in its own outlying provinces such as Chechnya.

This weakness made Russia's relations with Germany problematic. In theory, all the strategic reasons for containing Germany remained in force: in practice, however, Russia's historic allies, France and Britain – the two nations that had joined her in the Triple Entente before World War I – were now inextricably linked to Germany in the European Union.

In practice, too, the Russian economy was totally dependent upon German largesse. Where both the Kaiser and Hitler had failed, the Deutschmark had succeeded. The states bordering Russia, like Poland,

Hungary and the Czech Republic – and even republics of the former Soviet Union like Ukraine, Belarus and the Baltic nations – had become wholly dependent upon the Germans for material aid.

What did this mean? That the official policy-makers in the Kremlin had no choice but to accept the German blueprint for the future development of Europe. But *un*officially, it was a different story. Unofficially, the policy was *reculer pour mieux sauter*. Imitate the Germans after the treaty of Versailles. The core defence industries must be kept going; the economy built up. With its enormous natural resources and well-educated work-force, there was no reason why Russia should not achieve enormous growth and in a decade or two return to its full weight as a world power.

'How do you imagine we feel,' asked Savchenko, looking me straight in the eyes, 'with the memory of our past suffering at the hands of the Germans, to contemplate a political colossus dominated by the Germans stretching from Lisbon to Brest Litovsk, from Tallinn to the Caucasus?'

The question was rhetorical. It required no answer but itself explained why the Russians were willing to help us to discover if the Germans murdered George. Anything and everything must be done to weaken and destabilise the European Union.

'Now tell me,' said Savchenko, suddenly speaking to me in Russian, 'do you think you can impersonate a Catholic priest?'

'I would rather play another role,' I replied.

'That would make your task more difficult. As a priest, you would have two advantages: first, because there are no Catholic priests in Russia no one has a preconception of what a Russian Catholic priest is like; second, only as a

128

priest will you gain the trust of the Knights in a short space of time.'

'Couldn't your colleague play the priest and me the layman?'

Savchenko laughed. 'When you meet him you will see why that would be out of the question.'

Did Paget understand Russian? Enough, at any rate, to reassure me about playing the role of a priest. 'Your father is a clergyman, after all. You must have picked up something from him. And I've lined up a defrocked priest to brief you. He lives in Cambridge – a Jesuit theologian who ran off with one of his students, a nun. I told him you were an actor who is to play a priest in a film. He said he'd be happy to help.'

## Wednesday

Dinner last night with Denise at the Grouse and Claret. Her 'treat' to cheer me up after my father's stroke, and make up for the weekend before last when she forsook me for her sister. Rich food. Long wait between courses. Difficult to find anything to say to her. My mind was on my mission. She was happy to do the talking, judging this the moment to introduce me to her parents – in conversation, if not in fact. Her father, the inspector of taxes, a tall, heavy man who picked at the hardened skin on the palms of his hands, taciturn, unfulfilled. Her mother, quiet, intelligent, also unfulfilled. Were they happily married? I did not put the question because I had no interest in the answer. Denise asked it and then answered it as best she could. Yes and no. Both were the first in their families to go to university, her father to Leeds, her mother to Edinburgh. They had met when working for the Inland Revenue in London but transferred to Yeovil when they had children. Houses there were cheaper.

Denise thinks that both parents had hoped for more out of life. A disadvantage of marrying young, Denise observed, was that a wife knew of her husband's youthful ambitions. And he knew she knew. She became a mirror that constantly reflected his failure to achieve them. No man is a hero to his valet – or his wife.

'So better not marry,' I said.

'No,' said Denise. 'Better marry later in life.'


## Thursday

A call on my answering machine from someone called Brian, suggesting a meeting at Cambridge some time this weekend. Who is this Brian?


## Friday

A message to ring Paget at Caversham. I call between bulletins. All is revealed. Brian is Stephen Bryan, the defrocked priest. I am to have lunch with him at his house tomorrow and be taught how to act the part of a Catholic priest.

Alison obtuse this evening. First, she was clearly put out when I reminded her that I would soon be going abroad, perhaps for as long as a couple of months. She asked again if she was to keep my slot open. I said I thought not. I felt that I was over the crisis that had first brought me to seek her help. I had got over Ruth and was in control of my feelings for Denise.

Ha! It took only a few probing questions for Alison to refute both these contentions. We went through Tuesday night: the dinner with Denise; my boredom as she described her parents; my unease when she talked of the advantages of marrying later in life; my annoyance when she suggested that I might like to keep a clean shirt at her flat. 'Clearly,' said Alison, 'you are far from being free of a fear of entrapment ...'

'It's not a fear of entrapment,' I said. 'I just don't want to marry Denise.'

'And you think that the idea of keeping a clean shirt at her flat and the suggestion that it is wiser to marry later in life mean that she wants to marry you?'

'Yes.'

'A clean shirt hardly commits you.'

'It's the thin end of the wedge. She'll then feel entitled to keep a nightdress in my house.'

'Would that upset you?'

'It's putting down a marker, like a tom-cat.'

A pause. Then: 'Is that how you see her? A tom-cat?'

'In this context.'

'Interesting.'

'Why?'

'It's the male of the species.'


*Saturday*


*Introibo ad altare Dei. Ad Deum qui laetificat juventutem meum.* I will go up to the altar of God. To God, the giver of youth and happiness. It was my father who insisted that I learn Latin at school. He said it would prove useful later in life. Little can he have imagined the uses to which I would put it.

*

The complication, Paget explained to me as he accompanied me in a taxi from the station to Bryan's house on the other side of Cambridge, is the total isolation of the Catholics in exile in Siberia. They knew nothing of Vatican II. All the liturgical changes had passed them by. That was why Bryan would be so useful. Paget briefed me on his CV. Born around 1930; parents of Irish origin but the family had been settled in Britain for several generations. Father a solicitor. Bryan educated by the Jesuits at Wimbledon. Entered the order aged eighteen. Studied classics at Campion Hall, Oxford. First-class degree in both Mods and Greats. Moved on to Rome. Theology at the Gregorian. Again, top marks. A brilliant student and teacher. He was their star. Swept up in the excitement of Vatican II: a zealous advocate of reform. Returned to London. Taught theology at Heythrop College. Fell in love with one of his students, a twenty-year-old nun. Resigned from the Jesuits. Laicised by Pope Paul VI. Got a job as a publisher, first in London, then in Cambridge. His wife took her degree and now teaches theology at the university. 'With any luck, she won't be there.'

A nondescript, semi-detached red-brick house. An untended front garden: the neighbours must feel that it lowers the tone. Paget rang the bell. We waited. The sound of raised voices. 'I forgot to mention,' Paget whispered, 'Stephen is fond of the odd drink.'

A fact evident from the complexion of the man who opened the door. 'Ah, David. And your friend. Come in, come in.' Paget hesitated. Had he meant to flee? We entered in time to see an adolescent boy in pyjamas retreat along the landing at the top of the stairs. 'Let's go straight through to the kitchen,' said Bryan. He was wearing a red apron over a navy-blue shirt and brown

132

corduroy trousers. I glanced through an open door into their front parlour: a cluttered desk in the window, the walls lined with books.

The kitchen was in the rear extension, misty with the steam from a saucepan; an aroma of cabbage or broccoli mingling with that of bacon fat; rind and dried egg yolk on the plates still on the table.

'Now ...' He reached for an open bottle of Bulgarian wine, filled three glasses and handed two of them to us. There was never a question of choice. 'Why don't you sit down at the table? Here.' He took away the breakfast plates. I did as he asked. Paget hesitated again, then followed suit. 'I thought there'd be no point in starting until we'd had some lunch.'

'Sadly, I can't stay for lunch,' said Paget quickly.

It was difficult to assess Bryan's age: if he was forty in the 1970s when he married the twenty-year-old nun, then he must now be over sixty. The puffy features of a drinker may make him seem older than he is. He sat down at the table and raised his glass. ' "Wine gladdens the soul." Cheers.'

We drank. I glanced at Paget. No reaction to the vile concoction. A secret agent's supreme control.

'Have you children?' Bryan asked me.

'No, I'm not married.'

'Of course not, no. You actors aren't usually the marrying sort. As you will see, we have been fruitful and have multiplied. They're lurking somewhere, two boys and a girl. They're very interested that you're an actor and want to know what you've been in.'

'I'm an unknown, I'm afraid. This is my first role in a film.'

'Never mind, never mind. It'll be something for them to look forward to, something to tell their friends.'

'I think,' said Paget, putting down his still filled glass, 'that it would be best if I made myself scarce.'

'As you wish, as you wish,' said Bryan, rising from the table.

'I'll see myself out,' said Paget, scuttling towards the door. Then he added: 'My love to Morag.'

Bryan sat down on the bench again. 'Where shall we begin?' he asked. 'Tell me about the role you are to play.'

'It's a complex one … I should have let you have a look at the script. I'm a Catholic priest, ordained secretly in a gulag, who has little knowledge of the changes made after Vatican II.'

'Then he would say the Tridentine mass.'

'So I should imagine.'

'I've my old missal. I can lend you that.' He leaned over me as he spoke to take the glass of wine left by Paget and empty it into his own.

'It would be useful,' I said, 'to know how he would say mass.'

'Almost certainly in Latin, with his back to the congregation. He would have a cultic view of his role.'

'Cultic?'

'He would see the mass as a mystical re-enactment of Christ's self-sacrifice on Calvary with himself acting *in persona Christi* …'

'Instead of …?'

'Now, the priest presides over a meeting of the People of God. He is, as it were, host and facilitator at the communal eucharistic meal.'

'Somewhat different.'

'Indeed.'

'What else?'

'He would be concerned for the salvation of individual souls.'

'Salvation from Hell?'

134

'Precisely. The fiery furnace.'

'Whereas now?'

'That was all dropped in the nineteen seventies. Now it is salvation from the powers of evil in *this* world – poverty, starvation, oppression.'

'Political oppression.'

'Yes. By sinful social structures.'

'Such as Communism?'

Bryan frowned. 'I was thinking more of military dictatorships in Latin America.'

'But surely to him socialism would be a sinful structure.'

'From the perspective of the gulag, perhaps, but that would only show that he was out of touch.'

'Socialism is not a sinful structure?'

'It aspires to the liberation of mankind. But his subjective viewpoint might make it difficult for him to see this. Nor would he be likely to appreciate the forms of tyranny and oppression endemic here in the West.'

'Such as?'

'Racism and the oppression of women.'

He rose, went to the oven and glanced in. 'Gammon? Is that OK?'

'Of course. It's very kind of you ...'

' "I was hungry and you fed me ..." ' He returned to the table and refilled our glasses. 'What else? He would almost certainly be unaware of developments in the ecumenical field. The very fact that he, a Russian, is Catholic rather than Orthodox suggests a preconciliar mindset.'

'He was converted by imprisoned Lithuanians.'

'Lithuanians! Worse than the Poles.'

'But surely the Pope is Polish?'

'That's just what I mean. He finds it difficult to accept that the old sectarian rivalries are a thing of the past.'

'Are the differences between Protestants and Catholics now resolved?'

'What differences?'

'Well, I seem to remember concepts like transubstantiation …'

'A matter of words. Mere semantics. What does it mean? That the bread changes into the body of Christ upon the words of consecration. But if Christ is God then Christ is already present in the bread because everything comes from God. God is all in all.'

At that moment, a woman came into the kitchen; early forties, dishevelled hair, wearing jeans and a large, loose cardigan. She met my eyes with a look of smouldering suspicion.

'Ah, Morag.' Bryan rose. 'This is Michael.' He filled a glass of wine for his wife. 'We were talking about transubstantiation.'

'Not a word I've heard for twenty years.'

'Stephen was explaining,' I said, 'that Catholics no longer make a distinction between their eucharist and that of other Christian denominations. If God is all in all, then He –'

'She,' she interrupted.

'She?'

'We use the feminine form for God in this household,' said Stephen.

'Is God a woman?'

'God has no gender,' said Morag quietly, 'but referring to her in the male gender is one of the methods that have been used to empower men and demean women.'

'I see.'

She turned to Bryan. 'Is lunch ready? If not, I have work to do.'

'It won't be a moment.' Bryan emptied his glass, then

rose to drain the broccoli and take the gammon and potatoes out of the oven.

Morag sat down facing me. 'You're an actor?' Strangely, for someone so scruffy, she exuded a sexual allure.

'Yes.'

Bryan laid five places on the table, then went to the door of the kitchen and shouted, 'Lunch.'

'They won't want lunch,' said Morag. 'They've just had breakfast.'

'They're always hungry,' said Bryan.

Three adolescent children loped into the room. The girl glanced at me for a moment and, failing to recognise a famous actor, snorted in disgust.

They sat down around the table. Bryan waited by the stove. Morag said grace. 'We give thee thanks, Almighty Mother, for the bounty that flows from thy munificent breast.'

All mumbled, 'Amen.' Without premeditation, I found myself judging that Morag, too, had a munificent breast. She caught my eye. She blushed.

'Juliana,' said Bryan to his daughter, 'why don't you move next to me so that our guest can sit next to your mother?'

'I always sit here.'

'Please …'

'Leave me alone.' Then she added, under her breath: 'Fucking patriarch.'

Bryan refilled his glass. Morag smiled.

Conversation at lunch was about sex. Apparently Catholics like the Bryans no longer regard it as a bad thing. God has made us what we are. Even nuns now 'rejoice' in their sexuality. Quite what is meant by 'rejoice' is left ambiguous. Has the hair shirt been replaced by the vibrator? Priestly celibacy will be abolished as soon as there is a new Pope. Morag explains that the Church's traditional strictures against sex were introduced by misogynistic Church fathers to denigrate and oppress women – 'the whole Eve thing'. Apparently, most theologians now concede that Christ slept with Mary Magdalene and that she was a leading figure in the early Church. Peter got the better of her in an early power struggle and, with the connivance of the misogynistic St Paul, made sure that her role was cut out of the gospels. St Paul's contempt for women and his horror of sex are obvious from his epistles. St Augustine is another villain: he denigrates sex in disgust at his own sexual excess. 'The truth is,' said Morag, 'that our sexuality is part of our humanity. Christ was truly human, therefore we must embrace our sexuality if we are to embrace Christ.'

As she says this, her eyes meet mine. I feel, in my imagination, the impress of her munificent breast as we embrace, and my hands entwined in her bedraggled hair.

'Michael is not married,' an anxious Bryan tells his wife. 'He's an actor. Not the marrying sort.' Does he want to persuade Morag that I am homosexual? A desperate remedy. I hear the voice of Denise whisper: 'She married too young.'

Amazed at Bryan's ability to drink so much poisonous Bulgarian wine. This cannot enhance his ability to satisfy his wife. Yet he remains sufficiently in control of himself to clear away the plates, serve up a sponge pudding, make coffee, load the dishwasher. Neither Morag nor the children lift a finger to help him.

With a last sultry look in my direction, Morag returns to her study. The children, too, slope off. Bryan leads me into the front room, which is apparently where he works.

It is dark and untidy. He turns on the light. He takes down a black, leather-bound book. 'This is the missal I had at school,' he said, as he handed it to me. 'Of course, a priest would also have a breviary but this will take you through the mass.'

First we robed, not literally, he had no vestments, but he explained about the alb, the girdle, the surplice. 'Pure theatre, really. It used to be thought that they were the robes worn by the Jewish high priests. In fact, they're the everyday clothes of the Romans in the third century. Before Constantine, the priest at the altar wore the same clothes as the man in the street. And I dare say your Russian will have met with some difficulty in getting canonically correct vestments.'

There was an empty mug on his desk that had once contained coffee. 'Let's call this the chalice. You come in carrying the chalice and a kind of purse containing a small towel, both covered with a kind of scarf that matches the vestments. You go up to the altar, put down the chalice, and you're off ...'

How will I be able to remember everything he told me? Fortunately, the missal has stage directions. When the priest confesses to the congregation that he has sinned exceedingly in thought, word and deed, 'through my fault, through my own fault, through my own most grievous fault', he strikes his breast three times. Every now and then, he bows low, or bows his head. I shall have to memorise all this. A Russian priest can hardly appear with an English missal.

When we reached the offertory, Bryan disappeared for a moment and returned with some cheese biscuits, a small jug of water, a wine-glass, a saucer, and an open bottle of the Bulgarian wine. 'More dignified,' he said, replacing the mug with the glass. The bottle of wine was not full nor the wine-glass clean: I suspected that he had

had a swig in the kitchen. He now poured some wine, and then a drop of water, into the glass, put a cheese biscuit on to the saucer and the offertory got under way. He raised up the wine-glass: 'We offer thee, Lord, the chalice of salvation ...' He assured me that the new mass was less long-winded. He rattled through the preface and we reached the consecration. 'You take the host into your hands, so' – he took hold of the cheese biscuit – 'and say ... and say ...' He hesitated. 'You had better say it.'

'What?'

'The words.'

I read from the missal. ' "On the day before he suffered death, He took bread ..." Do you mean this?'

'Yes. But your tone should be more ... reverential. "Lifting up His eyes to thee, God, his almighty father ..." ' Bryan's voice thickened. He stopped. I carried on. ' "And giving thanks to thee, He blessed it, broke it, and gave it to His disciples saying: Take, all of you, and eat it for this is my body." '

I stopped, pausing over the stage directions. ' "The bell is rung thrice as he genuflects and the priest shows the sacred host to the people." How does he do that?' I turned to Bryan and saw, to my embarrassment, that the poor old drunk was in tears.

'I'm sorry,' he said, choking, sobbing. 'It's been so long ... It brings back feelings ... memories ... When I was young ... it meant ...' He stopped, sniffled, and pulled himself together. 'The rest is straightforward.' He turned the pages. 'The *Pater Noster*. The *Agnus Dei*. The kiss of peace. The priest's communion. The communion of the people. Be prepared to put the host in their hands or on their tongues but, having been out of touch for so long, your parishioners would probably take it on the tongue. And no wine,' he said. 'That came in with Vatican II.' He took our chalice and drank the wine. Then: '*Ite, missa est.* Go, you are dismissed. Have another drink.'

I left. Not as abruptly as this suggests. He refilled the glass, obliged me to take it, poured wine into the dirty coffee mug for himself and, after a gulp, collapsed into an arm-chair while I sat on a stool. 'You must understand,' he said, his speech at last slurred, 'that life is not easy for a former priest because there is always something that remains from that time in your life – I was a priest, after all, until I was forty – something remains, something. The challenge. The audacity, the sense of the holy – all triumphalist nonsense, of course, but we felt it all the same. We were the heirs to the martyrs. Thomas More, John Fisher and, of course, our fellow Jesuits like Edmund Campion. An élite. The shock-troops of the Lord. And the mass, ah, that was *the sacrifice.* Time stood still, there at the altar – no – we stepped outside time into eternity, and there we were, *in persona Christi,* God dying as a man so that we men could become gods.'

'And women,' I said.

'Oh, God, yes. And women. What I meant to say was – humankind.'

*Sunday*

Mass at a nearby Catholic church at ten this morning. A Victorian building. Hideous hymns. Hideous prayers. Hideous congregation. Irish and Polish with a few blacks and one or two yuppies. The church full; the aroma of unwashed bodies. The priest stood behind the altar, facing the congregation. Easy to follow what he said and did. I slipped a 'Parish Mass Book' under my coat and took it home.

A long piece in the *Sunday Times* on the Harding affair. I started reading it with the fear that we might have been scooped, but it quickly became apparent that they have no new information. All is surmise. It is critical of Interpol and the German police, and hints at deliberate procrastination to cover up vice in the upper echelons of the EU bureaucracy.

The telephone rings. Fearing it is Denise, I let my answering-machine record the call. It is not Denise. It is the Russian, Savchenko. Would I please ring him. I wait for a quarter of an hour, then make the call, explaining that I had been out buying the Sunday papers. He tells me that the man who will accompany me to Germany has arrived in London, and asks if I can meet them this afternoon by the Round Pond in Kensington Gardens.

The telephone rings again. Now that I have a bona fide excuse not to meet her, I risk speaking to Denise and pick up the receiver. It is Gordon. Have I seen the article on George in the *Sunday Times*? I say I have. What did I think? Nothing new. Precisely, but it showed that the story was still live, so the sooner I proceed the better. I told him that I was to meet the Russians that afternoon. 'Good,' he said. 'Ring me tomorrow.' He gave me a number for his direct line.

Cold, windy, wet. Few people in Kensington Gardens. Most are foreigners, so Savchenko and the other Russian are not conspicuous. He is introduced to me as Nikolai: no surname is given. He is around my age, perhaps a little younger; tall, with a heavy frame. Thick hair, thick lips, a slightly pock-marked face. Handsome in a vulgar way. He wears twill trousers, a blazer over a pullover and an open-necked shirt.

It begins to spot with rain. Savchenko suggests that we

go to find shelter. We leave the park, cross the Bayswater Road, and go into the London Embassy Hotel. In the foyer, we order tea and coffee. The waiter is an Arab. In this part of London, there is not a native Englishman in sight.

Savchenko switches from English to Russian. He says that everything is now ready at his end. He has recruited some 'former specialists' to help me. Presumably from the KGB. A dossier has been prepared on who I am and how I came to be a Catholic priest. I express concern about being rumbled by the Apostolic Administrators in Russia. Savchenko reassures me. Any queries about my identity will be intercepted and dealt with. 'You have people in their offices?' I asked.

'I assure you,' said Savchenko, 'controlling the spread of foreign religions is a priority for the security services of the Russian Federation.'

Nikolai listens to all this with little apparent interest. He seems more engaged in the question of cakes. A waiter brings a selection on a trolley. Nikolai glances uneasily at Savchenko, then points to a large *tranche* of Black Forest gateau.

'You will fly to Moscow as Michael Latham,' said Savchenko, 'and then back to Frankfurt as Piotr Ugarov. Nikolai will be in Moscow to meet you; he will be going under the name of Nikolai Advetsev.'

'After we arrive in Frankfurt, how should we make contact with Kreuzhilfe?'

'You will be expected. Someone from Kreuzhilfe will meet you at the airport.'

'How can that be arranged?'

'They will have received a fax from the office of Monsignor Werth, the Apostolic Administrator of Siberia, asking them to assist you.'

'With what?'

143

'Rosaries, bibles, prayer-books, and money to build a church.'

Only now, at the mention of money, did Nikolai's attention leave the Black Forest gateau and flicker for a moment on the face of his boss, Savchenko.

'Where are we supposed to come from?'

'Komsomolsk-on-Amur.'

'A godforsaken place.'

'Precisely. And, until recently, a closed city. It is therefore quite plausible that you would have had no contact with the outside world.'

'I cannot believe,' I said, 'that Kreuzhilfe will donate money to two Russians who appear out of the blue.'

'The point is not to get the money. The point is to lodge a request that will take time to approve. If it was only a matter of rosaries and bibles, they might send you back on the next plane.'

'But how can you know,' I asked, 'that while we wait for their decision, we will get a chance to find out about the Knights of the Cross?'

'Kreuzhilfe will take care of you. That is what it is for. As to Schloss Zelden, and the von Willichs, that is something our friend in Cambridge said he would be able to arrange.'

## Monday

My month's unpaid leave of absence confirmed by my head of department this morning. A ticket to Moscow to be sent by the *Gazette*, together with some roubles and marks. Savchenko will arrange a visa. All that remains is to deal with my women, Alison and Denise.

I gave Alison notice this evening that Thursday's session

would be the last. I told her that I was going away for six weeks to Russia and that it seemed both selfish and senseless to keep my 'spot' open if there were others in greater need.

She thought about this for a moment, then said: 'Well, if you feel you need to, you can always ring me when you get back and I'll do what I can to fit you in.'

This touched me. Here was not the clipped professional trying to convince me that I was far from cured, but a woman who was sad to think that we would lose touch. I wondered if it was unethical to suggest meeting socially and decided that it probably was. For the time being, anyway. And what would we talk about, anyway? Me? For free?

Denise. Trickier. She knows that I am going away but not that I plan a break in more ways than one.

## Tuesday

A day off from Caversham. Go to Cambridge for further training in priestly ways by Bryan. No sign of his wife. I take him out to lunch. He never stops talking about his time in the Jesuits and the state of the Church. Useful background information. He gets through two bottles of wine.

At least I do not have to worry about what to wear. Paget called me this evening to say that the Russians would kit me out. He thinks it would be fatal if the Germans found me wearing socks from Marks & Spencer. My cover would be blown.

## Wednesday

Nikolai came to my flat this evening with my visa. He sat down and bored me to death on the subject of American cinema. He finished a half-filled bottle of vodka. He asked me if I found Julia Roberts too scrawny, or was this simply a Russian prejudice? I was not entirely sure whom he was talking about but thought it would be to set off on the wrong foot for me to say so. I therefore said yes, I did think she was scrawny, an answer that seemed to please him. He explained how Russians despised Turks but were also influenced by them and, as we all know, Turks like women to be fat. He, Nikolai, had been afraid that his distaste for the slim Ms Roberts had been a symptom of this Turkish influence. This was why he was so delighted that an Englishman felt the same.

Have I really got to spend six weeks with this oaf? After he left, I went to my desk to reread Gordon's letter and remind myself about the £20,000.

## Thursday

As if to allay my anxieties, a ticket arrived in this morning's post together with a cheque for £10,000. A note from Gordon's secretary says that she understands I will not need any marks or roubles.

Made a date with Denise today for Saturday night and, crassly, gave her to understand that I had something of significance to discuss. I could see at once that she thought I was preparing to propose. She smiled, sniffed, and bit her lower lip. If I had not moved on – we were in a corridor – she might have started to cry.

My plan is this. A good dinner in London. Energetic sex. Then break it to her that this is the end. Post-coitus, she will not believe that I mean what I say.

Practise saying mass at my kitchen table with Ritz crackers and Rioja wine. Should I feel ashamed of the subterfuge? If most Catholics no longer believe in transubstantion, then it is hardly sacrilege. Apparently the people at Kreuzhilfe are all traditionalists who do believe that the wafer of bread becomes the body of Christ; but, even if they do, why should I pander to their superstition? The 'gods' of Hottentots and Bushmen hang in our museums. If God does not exist, then He cannot be demeaned.

## Friday

My last day at Caversham, perhaps for ever. Because I am supposedly only taking a month's leave of absence, there are no farewell parties or heavy leave-taking with my colleagues. The story is that I am going to do some research for the European Bank in Moscow. 'Lucky sod,' said Tarnowski. Little does he know.

The problem of what to do with this journal. Unquestionably taking it on my travels will add to the risk of exposure, but I feel a great reluctance to leave it at home. These daily entries have been a more effective therapy than any of Alison's insights into my psychological condition. I go to my bookshelves and take down a fat Russian textbook from my days in Smolensk: *The Development of Secondary Education in the Soviet Far East*. With a Stanley knife, I cut out a rectangle between pages

150 and 375. My canvas-covered notebook fits neatly into its new case.

Last session with Alison. She gives a summary of her conclusions about my psychic condition. A weak father and overbearing mother are at the root of my troubles. I both fear dominating women yet cannot do without them. To keep them at a distance, and therefore myself in control, I detach myself as much as I can from the act of love. Indeed the act, for me, is not one of love, but of vengeance – punishing Denise for my suffering at the hands of my mother and Ruth.

I listen. I do not defend myself. My mind is on other things.

## Saturday

Final briefing from both Paget and Gordon over lunch at Orsino's restaurant in Portland Road. I express my anxiety about my ability to convince the Germans that I really am a Catholic priest. Paget reassures me. No one can have any preconceptions about a priest from Komsomolsk-on-Amur.

Gordon asks what I thought of Nikolai. I shrug and say that he did not seem particularly spiritual either. Gordon agrees. Again, Paget reassures us. Savchenko has said that Nikolai is very good at his job. His only role, says Gordon, is to give credibility to me. He knows the Russian side of things. It means I will not be caught out by any questions about Komsomolsk. 'Your role is to get material for the story. If it can't be done, it can't be done, and no one will hold it against you; but *there are reasons* ...' He paused, then repeated: 'There are good reasons for supposing that the Knights had something to do with George's death.'

The pause disturbed me. 'Do you know more than I know?' I asked him. 'Are there things you haven't told me?'

Gordon glanced at Paget.

'There are inevitably sources,' said Paget, 'whose identity must be protected. I have not told Gordon anything that I have not also told you, but you will remember from our first meeting how, when it comes to Europe, I mentioned factions within the Government, the Foreign Office and, of course, the security services, and if in the latter there was a faction that was sympathetic to our point of view, it might be prepared to divulge information but only to those it knew it could trust. It would be incumbent upon that man to keep those secrets because if they should inadvertently leak out then the very people we would want to keep in place would almost certainly lose their jobs.'

After lunch, we all walked down Portland Road to look for cabs on Holland Park Avenue. Paget took the first. 'Good luck,' he said, as if I were about to be parachuted over France. Gordon hailed the second: it was for me. 'You have your ticket, your passport, your visa?'

'Yes.'

'I'll keep my fingers crossed.' And he waved a hand with two crossed fingers as I drove off in the cab.

## Sunday

Denise asked about the Ritz crackers on a saucer and the half-filled glass of Rioja. She noticed them on the dresser in the kitchen just before she left. We were having a last cup of tea. Had I been entertaining? No. She laughed.

Why couldn't I tell the truth? 'No one,' she said, 'puts Ritz crackers on a saucer simply for their own consumption. And you are far too ... frugal to leave a half-filled glass of wine.' She picked up the glass and held it up to the window. 'No lipstick,' she said, 'but that means nothing these days.'

Her remarks were ostensibly humorous, but there was clearly a germ of genuine suspicion. All women prefer to believe that they are being replaced by a rival, rather than simply dropped.

'And you're going alone?'

'Of course.'

If she had left last night, as I had hoped, mildly intoxicated and sexually sated, none of these sour suspicions would have arisen. I was determined that our last night together should be memorable, and so it was, so memorable that we fell asleep entwined. I half woke an hour later; the lights were still on in the bedroom. 'Are you awake?'

'Mmm.'

'I meant to tell you earlier that when I get back from my holiday ...' She breathed steadily. Was she awake? '... I don't want to go on as your lover. I'd like to see you more as a friend.'

She sighed, turned her back to me and fell asleep again. I switched off the lights, lay awake thinking, then curled up beside her and finally I, too, fell asleep.

Had she heard what I had said? I think she had but felt that I did not mean it and, it has to be conceded, she had some reason for taking my words of rejection with a pinch of salt. What reason? That when I awoke the next morning and found a warm, soft body next to mine in my bed ... my actions belied my words.

Also, she probably remembered what I can now

confirm by looking back to earlier entries in my journal –
viz. that this kind of thing had happened before. So as we
sat on the floor of my living room amid the coffee cups
and Sunday papers she turned to me with a mocking
smile and said: 'What was it you said last night? You
want to end our affair?'

'Yes.'

'For any particular reasons?'

'I think it's unfair to you to go on.'

'Because?'

'I don't want to get married.'

'And I do?'

'Don't you?'

'Perhaps.'

'And this break … my leave of absence … seems a
good time to do it.'

'Unless absence makes the heart grow fonder.'

'That's a risk I shall have to take.'

'Is it just that you want to feel free to have a good time
with the girls in Moscow?'

'That is a factor.'

She nodded. 'And leave me free to go wild in Reading.'

'Perhaps to find someone more suitable.'

She started to cry. I tried to comfort her. She brushed
me off. And so on. The Sunday papers. Moody silences.
Short bursts of normal conversation. A walk in Battersea
Park. Back to chicken mayonnaise sandwiches. An epic
film on television. Then into the kitchen for the last cup
of tea: the half-filled wine-glass, the Ritz crackers,
suspicion.

As I held open the door of a taxi, she said: 'I can't bear to
think that I won't see you tomorrow at work.'

'You wouldn't see me anyway. I'm going on leave.'

'But I could have looked forward to your return. Now I shall dread it.' Then off in a cloud of diesel fumes.

At last. Liberated from mediocrity. New horizons beckon.

*Two*

## Tuesday

A *dacha* outside Moscow – a large wooden house surrounded by pine trees and a tall chain fence. No doubt a safe-house of the former KGB. It makes me wonder whether the help I am being given by the Russians is as unofficial as we were told. Yesterday, at Sheremetyevo airport, I was met off the plane by Nikolai, who then whisked me through Customs and Immigration with a wave of his hand. At the entrance, a black Volga hovered in the no-parking zone. I climbed in next to Savchenko, waiting for me on the rear seat. He greeted me with effusive friendliness and, as we set off, explained that he was taking me to a *dacha* rather than a hotel in Moscow because there it would be easier for me to learn my role without distraction.

The *dacha* is comfortable enough: I have my own bathroom. There is a caretaker with a wife who cooks. Soon after we arrived she served us with supper: salad, borscht, pork chops, potatoes, apple purée, beer. Nikolai wolfed it down while I picked at it, listening while Savchenko described my new identity.

I am Piotr Ugarov. My father, Yevgeni Ugarov, is Russian; my mother, Ada Jamontas, is Lithuanian. Her father had taught history at Kaunas University before the war. The whole family had been deported to Siberia in 1940; my mother had then been aged five. The gulag had been on the river Yama near Verkhoyansk, north of the Arctic Circle. My grandfather had died within a year, but my grandmother and mother had survived to be released under Khrushchev in 1953. Also released from the same gulag in the same batch was the Lithuanian bishop, Witus Lanskauskas. All were forbidden to return to Lithuania but permitted to reside further south in the town of Yakutsk. Here, a small community of Catholics formed around Bishop Lanskauskas, consisting mainly of fellow Lithuanians and exiled Poles. There were secret ordinations of priests and, when Bishop Lanskauskas felt his powers waning, the consecration of a bishop as his successor called Vyatautas Stoskus. Bishop Lanskauskas died in 1962.

By this time, my mother has married a young Russian engineer. He accepts his wife's religion. I am their only child. I grow up in this Catholic community in Yakutsk. An old Volga German, a former inmate of the gulags, teaches me German, a subject I also study at school. At the age of eighteen, I do my military service in the Army and then study civil engineering in Yakutsk; but already by this time I have a vocation to the priesthood and am secretly prepared for ordination by Bishop Stoskus.

At the age of twenty-six, on graduation, I am assigned a job in an engineering co-operative in Komsomolsk-on-Amur. Before I leave, I am ordained a priest. In Komsomolsk, I pursue my apostolate, secretly bringing lost sheep among the Lithuanians and Poles back to the fold. There are also convert Russians, such as Nikolai. By 1995, I have a parish of some 370 Catholics with twenty more Russians under instruction. I have registered as a legal entity and have even obtained a permit to build a church.

Is my story credible? Savchenko insists that it is. Because nuclear submarines were built at Komsomolsk, it had until recently been a closed city. This is why the

Apostolic Administrator has only now made contact with me or my flock. Savchenko assured me that any enquiries will be intercepted and answered as we would wish. There is even a site agreed with the city planners where the Komsomolsk Catholics can build their church.

After supper, Savchenko left in the Volga. Nikolai and I watched television for a while before going to bed.

At nine this morning a gloomy man appeared with a suitcase containing the kind of dreadful clothes that would be worn by a Russian engineer. I balked at the underpants – orange nylon jockeys – but Nikolai persuaded me that my British boxer shorts would give me away.

An hour later, Savchenko returned with a younger man who turned out to be a barber. He cut my hair short. At eleven, it was the turn of a photographer to take my picture for my Russian passport.

## Wednesday

It seems like a month since I left London. In fact, it is less than three days. Savchenko has not appeared today but Nikolai remains. I begin to like him better. Last night over supper he told me how his wife had left him for a mafiosi boss who has put a price on Nikolai's head. Because of this, he now never sees his son. I express incredulity that the Russian security service is unable to protect its own agents. Nikolai shrugs and says: 'It just shows how times have changed.'

A woman called Ludmilla came this morning to give me a language lesson. She said she was satisfied with my

Russian but I must work on a Siberian accent. She tells me to listen to Nikolai, who does it well. Will the Germans be sensitive to such inflections? Nikolai thinks that we may meet Russian expatriates who work for Kreuzhilfe and, while he can do most of the talking, there may be occasions when I shall have to join in the conversation. Ludmilla is to come again tomorrow.

A briefing this afternoon from a man from the Department of Religious Affairs. Although my isolation in Siberia will explain some areas of ignorance, he thinks I should know something about what is going on in the Orthodox Church. For example, I should know the name of Archbishop Chrysostom of Irkutsk. I should also be aware that there is a Byzantine-rite Catholic Church in the Ukraine, persecuted until Gorbachev and loathed by the Orthodox to this day. I should also know that the Orthodox Church in the Ukraine is split between an Autocephalos Church and one loyal to the Moscow Patriarchate.

When religion causes so much dissension, one wonders why anyone would want to revive it. My tutor from the Department agrees. Under the former Soviet regime, the Government did what they could to enlighten the population but religious belief persisted among many of the uneducated country people. There were also dissident Orthodox priests such as Alexander Men and Gleb Yakunin. Fortunately, the average Russian believer retained his suspicion of foreign religions, in particular Catholicism. They associated it with their traditional enemies, Poland and Lithuania.

Nikolai asked me at supper last night which nation I felt could furnish 'the best fuck in the world'. He said this in English, not Russian, let alone the Siberian Russian we have been speaking since we moved into the *dacha*. Presumably this was to spare the feelings of our taciturn housekeepers. I was slightly taken aback by his question and hesitated before giving an answer, as if running down a list in my memory like Leporello in *Don Giovanni*.

The list was short. Most of my foreign 'conquests' had been furtive and disagreeable: a French girl at a camping site when I was eighteen; a German girl who was attending a summer language school at Cambridge; and a one-night stand with my Russian room-mate's girlfriend in Smolensk – an incident of the utmost squalor which it still pains me to recall.

Fortunately, it turns out that Nikolai's question was merely a pretext for him to hold forth on his own predilections. Italians: too theatrical, simulated passion. French: elegant when dressed but short legs. English: silly, self-conscious (he apologised if this gave offence). Americans: too matter-of-fact.

'Russians?'

'Sluts.'

'That leaves Africans and Orientals.'

'Outside my experience.'

'And mine.'

'But you have forgotten the Germans.'

'I have little to go on.'

He put his fingers to his lips and gave them a smacking kiss. '*Prima*. First class. They are slow to start but, once they get going, it is … awesome. It is like riding a tiger!'

Is Nikolai hoping to get lucky with the nuns at Kreuzhilfe? Who knows? Perhaps they will turn out to be like Morag Bryan.

159

Ludmilla again all morning, this time to test me on my German. This is our biggest worry: that my English accent will give me away. She nods as I parody a Russian accent. 'Don't hold yourself back. Imagine you are acting.'

Imagine? I normally say the first thing that comes into my mind but have now adopted the ponderous speech of a deeply reflective and spiritual priest. This gives me time to prepare what I say and how I say it. Ludmilla seems delighted. 'A real little *starets*.'

Savchenko to lunch. Contact has been made with Germany. Kreuzhilfe await us. After lunch, he takes me into the room with the piano and asks if I would like to be armed. At first, I do not know what he means. He explains that Nikolai will be carrying a Beretta but, since I am not trained in the concealment of handguns, he thought it wiser if I remained unarmed. 'You can rest assured that, in any emergency, Nikolai will defend you.' I agree.

Next, he opens a large cardboard box. 'These are your props.' Savchenko has ransacked some kind of KGB museum for souvenirs of the gulags. There is a ragged set of vestments which, he claims, were used by Bishop Lanskauskas in the 1950s. Also, a rosary made of knotted string with a hand-hewn wooden cross.

Finally, he hands me a tiny, grimy prayer-book of hand-written prayers called '*Marija, gelbiki mus*' – 'Mary, Save Us.'

'But I don't read Lithuanian.'

'Don't worry. They won't expect you to. You inherited this from your mother. It will have them eating out of your hands.

'But for you, the most important piece of equipment is this.' As he speaks, he takes from his bag a slim tape-recorder and what looks like a button. The button turns out to be a minute microphone which, if worn under the collar of a shirt or behind the lapel of a jacket, will transmit to the tape-recorder placed in a pocket or strapped to my waist. He shows me how to conceal both the microphone and the tape-recorder. Both are new and made by the Japanese.

## Saturday

Is Nikolai licensed to kill? I awoke in the early hours of this morning in a panic, remembering that I had been told by Savchenko that he would be armed with a Beretta. In what circumstances could he use it? To defend himself and, 'rest assured', to defend me. But how could my life be at risk? Had Paget or Gordon ever suggested that this assignment might be dangerous? Perhaps they had. I could not remember. But, if the Knights of the Cross had murdered George, they would not hesitate to dispose of me. And I had no means of defending myself. I am not licensed to kill. Only to be killed.

## Sunday

Parsheim, near Münster, Westphalia, Germany.

I sit at a clean beech-wood table with tubular stainless-steel legs. A white lamp directs light on to my notebook. There is a bed, a chair, a wardrobe and a wash-basin. On the wall, a large crucifix and a framed photograph of John

Paul II. This is one of the guest rooms at the headquarters of the Kreuzhilfe organisation. We arrived here soon after midnight. It is now one in the morning. The carpet is scratchy. There is a basin in the corner of the room but the lavatory and shower are down the corridor. Is this meant to demonstrate frugality? Or to encourage guests to move on?

I must sleep, but before I do I must record: final intensive training at the *dacha*; driven to the airport this morning in the Volga with Nikolai and Savchenko; whisked through Customs and Passport Control; board a Lufthansa flight, tourist class. I am dressed as a civilian; only a small metal cross attached to a pin in my lapel suggests that I am a priest.

In the Airbus, squeezed between Nikolai and the window. The Russian underpants cut into my groin. Nikolai in seventh heaven: he is leaving the realm of the mafiosi hitmen for the land of the first-class fuck. Does Savchenko know of his sexual proclivities? I suspect he does. In the car on the way to the airport he reminded Nikolai that he was now a zealous Catholic and must behave as such. Nikolai: '*Konechno*.' Of course.

On the flight, Nikolai drinks and smokes. Because he smokes, we have been seated in the back five rows, reserved for nicotine-addicted pariahs. I read yesterday's *Frankfurter Allgemeine Zeitung* and today's *Moscow News*.

The German immigration officer scrutinises our visas and then peers at the list of *personae non gratae* on his VDU. Finally, with patent reluctance, he stamps our passports and lets us through. A woman customs officer glares contemptuously at my tatty Russian suitcase, then asks me to open it. She looks through my few belongings with unconcealed distaste until she comes across my vestments, my rosary, the prayer-book. She looks perplexed. 'I am a Catholic priest,' I say, in my worst German. She blushes, carefully rearranges my belongings and shuts the suitcase. 'I am sorry to have delayed you, Father.' Out of uniform, probably a conscientious Catholic. '*Pax vobiscum*,' I say. She blushes again and smiles.

Outside the customs hall stands a man holding a placard on which is written in large letters: KREUZHILFE. Next to him is a young woman. Nikolai goes up to them; I hang back. In a moment, they are upon me. 'Worters, Russian Department,' says the man, shaking my hand. He speaks in Russian. 'Welcome to Germany on behalf of Kreuzhilfe.'

'Father Piotr,' says the young woman, also in Russian, 'welcome, welcome.' She, too, takes my hand but rather than shake it, lifts it to her lips. As she kisses it, tears trickle on to my knuckles from her eyes.

My own eyes look modestly to the ground. 'Thank you, thank you.' I affect to be deeply moved.

Worters now seizes my suitcase and leads us out of the airport to the car park. The girl follows with Nikolai. Worters explains that he is the deputy director of the Russian Department at Parsheim. His main anxiety at this juncture seems to be that I will be offended because I have not been met by the director himself, Dr Kammer. He explains that Dr Kammer has a young family and that it is a principle of employment by Kreuzhilfe that fathers should spend time with their children. I nod with approval. 'Of course, of course.'

Nikolai and I are placed in the back of a large Opel. Herr Worters drives. The girl, who is called Fräulein Tischbein, sits next to Worters. I am behind her. She has a pretty neck and a pleasing profile, which she displays when she turns to talk to us, and also a delightful smile.

163

There is something artless about her. Perhaps she was a nun. I sense that Nikolai is smouldering. But how could he ever burst into flame? He will be surrounded by dedicated virgins.

We drive along the autobahn at 100 miles an hour, skirting the Taunus Mountains, traversing the Wester-wald and the Sauerland. What can I see? Only darkness, flashing lights. Finally, we reach Parsheim. A modern building. Bright light from luminous tubes set in the ceiling. Fräulein Tischbein takes her leave. Herr Worters shows us to our rooms. He says that he will return at six thirty the next morning to take me to the chapel.

## Monday

So far, so good. At six thirty, a bleary-eyed Worters appeared as promised and led me down corridors to a side entrance to the chapel. Then, an unpleasant surprise: waiting in the sacristy were two German priests, one of whom said in halting Russian that they would consider it an honour if they could concelebrate the mass. Bryan had not mentioned concelebration, but I assumed it meant what the word implied: that, somehow or other, we would say the mass together. Looking as much of an imbecile as I could manage, I vested and then followed them from the sacristy into the church. There, a further unpleasant surprise: twenty or thirty people were kneel-ing at the pews. The priests led me to the altar. I stood between the two of them, facing the congregation. I saw Nikolai slip in at the back of the church, an anxious look on his face. For a good thirty seconds, I was paralysed with panic. Then, in my best Russian-accented Latin, I set forth: *In nomine patris et filio et spiritu sancto ...*

The missal on the altar was in German. I paused as an acolyte removed it and returned a moment later with one in Latin. Further confusion because this missal was not of the old Tridentine rite. I followed it as best I could, but every now and then would say a prayer from the old mass, which the elder of the two priests seemed to remember but which left the younger one at sea. However, I could see even this confusion suited my purposes down to the ground. A flawless performance might have aroused their suspicions that I was not that oddity, a Catholic priest from Komsomolsk. No impostor would make such mistakes. When it came to the consecration, a hush descended that inspired me to speak with particular reverence and emotion. *Hoc est enim corpus meum.* Simultaneously, in a quieter tone, the two priests spoke the same words. We genuflected. Bells rang. I raised the host. Bells rang again.

On we went. Mumble, mumble. Then *Nobis quoque peccatoribus.* According to Bryan, the priest says this in a loud voice to wake the slumbering congregation for the *Pater Noster*, the *Agnus Dei*, the priest's communion, the people's communion. I dished it out. Some held out their hands to receive the host; others stuck out their tongues. Suddenly, there was Nikolai, his eyes shut, his mouth open, a protruding tongue. *Corpus Christi. Amen.* I placed the host on his tongue. He closed his mouth and opened his eyes. Not a smirk, not a twinkle. The KGB's finest. A real pro.

As I came out of the sacristy after mass, I was met by Frau Doktor Karsfeld, the director-general of Kreuzhilfe. She smiled as she shook my hand: a glint of the gold fillings that I had noticed when she came to communion. Were they paid for, I wondered, from charitable donations? Where did frugality end and extravagance begin?

Frau Doktor Karsfeld led me towards breakfast. The two German priests followed behind. It was a great honour for her to welcome me on behalf of Kreuzhilfe. She hoped that all the arrangements for our journey had been satisfactory. It was impossible to exaggerate the joy she and her colleagues had felt at the news of the Catholic community in Komsomolsk. It was without doubt an answer to their prayers to the Virgin of Fatima ...

She spoke in German while Herr Worters, in obsequious attendance, translated what she said into Russian. Finally Nikolai said: 'But Father Piotr understands German.'

'Yes,' I said, in my best Russified German. 'Especially if you are kind enough to speak slowly.'

The staff restaurant: modern, efficient, bright, clean. Each of us took a tray, then loaded it from the counter with a white porcelain pot and cup. The pot was placed under a machine, a button was pressed and, hey presto, the machine released exactly the right amount of coffee to fill the pot. Then on along the counter to pick up small pots of cream, white rolls or brown bread, slices of cheese and sausage, small plastic-encased portions of butter, honey and jam.

With my tray modestly laden, I followed Frau Doktor Karsfeld to a table by the window where we were joined by Herr Worters and an older man. He was introduced as Worters's boss, Dr Kammer, director of the Russian Department and family man. From the window we could see the glass and concrete wall of the east wing of the Kreuzhilfe headquarters; beyond that, open countryside.

The rolls were crisp on the outside; fluffy on the

inside. The coffee, fresh and fragrant. The essence of Germany. No compromise on detail. Simplicity. Frugality. But real coffee. In porcelain cups.

Frau Doktor Karsfeld was in her middle forties. She was neither ugly nor pretty, stern nor smiling. If her manner told me anything, it was that she was efficient and serious-minded. After a few friendly remarks about the Apostolic Administrator in Moscow, Monsignor Kondrusiewicz, she asked us to tell her more about our community in Komsomolsk. They had known, she said, about secret ordinations in the gulags, and even of the consecration of new bishops, but no one had imagined that the faith had spread beyond the communities of exiled Poles and Lithuanians.

'It has been impossible until now,' Nikolai responded, in a German less fluent than I had heard him speak before, 'to make contact with the outside world. Even when our activities were declared legitimate under Gorbachev, any number of ways were found to harass us. Komsomolsk was a centre for sensitive defence industries. The KGB had unlimited power to restrict our movements and communications. In a real sense, the whole city was like a gulag.'

'How appalling.'

'The Church thrives on the blood of its martyrs,' said Nikolai.

'Even so.'

'Moreover, just because of its size and isolation, Komsomolsk had not even the tradition of Orthodox Christianity. The only faith of the people was Leninism and, when that was discredited, there was nothing.'

'Indeed.'

'But "Man does not live on bread alone." There was real hunger among the people for spiritual truth.'

167

Dr Kammer turned to me. 'But how did you evangelise among the people?'

Panic. 'We reached them –' I began.

'Through reading groups,' Nikolai interrupted. 'Among the intelligentsia, these are popular. You read a book and then meet to discuss it. This was an excellent way to introduce ethical questions, and from these we moved on to issues of faith.'

'And why,' asked Dr Karsfeld, 'were these not suppressed by the authorities?'

Nikolai sighed. 'Because now even the former Party bosses who run Komsomolsk can see what happens when a community has no form of belief. Drunkenness, drug-addiction, an epidemic of crime. The young, in particular, are disillusioned, nihilistic. The isolation of Komsomolsk compounds their despair. Under the Soviets, air fares were subsidised: they could visit European Russia. Now, we must pay the market price for air tickets. Most are lucky if they can visit Moscow once in a lifetime. They therefore feel trapped in the empty vastness of Siberia. Why should they want to be good citizens? What's in it for them?'

Impressed by Nikolai's talent for improvisation, I now picked up his theme. 'We are quite aware,' I said, in a quieter voice, 'that the authorities have their own reasons now to encourage religion – they want our people to believe in right and wrong. But this seems no reason not to take advantage of the freedom this gives us to evangelise –'

'And build a church.' This was Nikolai.

'Of course,' said Dr Karsfeld. 'And, certainly, it is our dearest wish to help you in every way we can. Our grant-in-aid committee meets tomorrow. Your requests will head the agenda.'

Nikolai is now closeted with Dr Karsfeld and Herr Worters. They are working on our application. I am deemed too spiritual to be involved in the squalid details of finance. Fräulein Tischbein confided that we were being given special treatment: normally a request takes several weeks to prepare and must be lodged a month before the meeting of the committee. If, at this meeting, the finance committee agrees to consider the application ('which it most certainly will,' said Fräulein Tischbein), then it will be passed back to the relevant department for scrutinising and assessment. In this case, of course, it will go to the Russian Department headed by Dr Kammer and Herr Worters. They will report back to the finance committee at its next meeting in one month's time. It is then that a decision will be made on whether or not to authorise our request for aid.

I have not yet recorded the rest of yesterday's events. In the first half of the morning, Herr Worters took us on a tour of the Kreuzhilfe building and explained the way the charity worked. Money is collected through the fund-raising activities of national committees in the different countries of the First World. These national committees do not rely on Providence to bring in donations but employ salaried professionals. In the last fiscal year, $92 million was raised worldwide and sent to the headquarters of Kreuzhilfe at Parsheim.

It is here that all decisions are made on the merits of the many thousands of applications for aid. Now that Kreuzhilfe had extended its scope from Russia and Eastern Europe, there was hardly a corner of the world that had not benefited from its help. A bishop in East Africa could now reach his outlying parishes, thanks to a

Toyota Landcruiser provided by Kreuzhilfe; a seminary in Central America could provide textbooks for its seminarians. Churches in Belarus and the Ukraine, which had been used as barns or factories, were being restored with the help of funds from Kreuzhilfe. Bibles and breviaries were translated into every language and dialect known to the world, and were smuggled into Communist and Muslim countries where Christianity was forbidden. Clinics were built in Mexico, convents in Guatemala, seminaries in Eritrea; each project having been evaluated by the experts here in Parsheim.

From the large open-plan office came the hum of a score of computers. As we passed the different modules, the project managers would abandon their VDUs to tell us about the work of their particular department. As we moved on, Worters himself bombarded us with statistics, but behind the language that might have been used by any businessman was the assumption that it was thanks to the intercession of Our Lady of Fatima, not skilful fund-raising, that the money kept pouring in.

'And tell me,' I asked, 'what is the connection between Kreuzhilfe and the Knights of the Cross?'

Worters showed no surprise at my question. 'Kreuz-hilfe was founded by the Knights at the end of the last war and they are represented on our governing council. Also, in those countries where there are chapters of the Knights, such as Italy, Spain and France, the Knights themselves have projects which raise funds for Kreuzhilfe.'

When our tour reached Dr Kammer's office, Herr Worters took me aside and asked if it would be acceptable to furnish me with some new clothes. I managed to look confused, as if in my humility it had not occurred to me that my tawdry Russian attire should have come to anyone's attention. Worters interpreted this as a reluctance to accept a gift. 'I assure you,' he said, 'we have funds just for this because so many fathers such as yourself have been unable to wear the clothes of a priest. I am ashamed to say that there are even priests here in the West who *choose* to wear the same clothes as the laity, when the Holy Father has quite specifically stated that priests should dress as priests.'

'Indeed.'

'It would therefore honour us if you would permit me to take you to a clerical outfitters' in Münster who will provide you with the clothes that befit your calling.'

For a moment I did not reply but did my best to suggest an agonising dilemma. 'I am most grateful,' I said at last, 'and of course I would like to wear the costume of my calling. I only hesitate because my companion Nikolai, who has also suffered as a witness to the truth, has only the wretched clothes that we brought with us from Komsomolsk. I would feel it wrong if I –'

Worters stopped me with a wave of his hand. 'Please, Father Piotr. You have no need to worry. Of course, Nikolai too … that was always our intention. Nikolai, too, shall have a new suit of clothes.'

And so it was. Herr Worters and Fräulein Tischbein drove us the twelve kilometres into Münster and, while Herr Worters accompanied Nikolai to the Kaufhof, Fräulein Tischbein led me along the arcades of the Principalmarkt to the premises of Kummerly und Schlacht, clerical outfitters, who with admirable discretion provided me with an elegant black suit and a cassock; six white shirts, six cotton vests, six pairs of cotton boxer shorts, six pairs of black socks, two pairs of black leather shoes and half a dozen Roman collars.

Leaving my old Russian clothes to be delivered to Parsheim with the balance of my purchases, I set out into the streets of Münster wearing a black suit and a Roman collar. Liberated from the orange nylon jockeys into crisp white boxer shorts, my spirits soared. I smiled benignly at those we passed in the street, noticing that in return some smiled, some scowled, while others looked away in confusion.

We had some time to spare before meeting for lunch at the Ratskeller and Fräulein Tischbein suggested that we use it to visit the great squat cathedral. Here, purporting to be tremendously moved, I fell on to my knees before the altar. Fräulein Tischbein whispered in my ear that in fact the Blessed Sacrament was in a side altar, and that it would be better to pray there. We wove our way through the meandering file of tourists and found, as she had promised, a side altar with the notice 'only for prayer'. Here was the flickering red lamp signifying that the fine silver tabernacle contained the transubstantiated flesh of God.

I went down on my knees. Fräulein Tischbein did the same in the row behind. Like a Method actor, I did my best to 'live' my part by saying in my prayers what I felt a priest in my position might have said: Thank you, God, for a safe journey from Komsomolsk; guard my little flock while I am away; receive into Heaven the souls of my dear departed parents and the blessed Bishop Stoskus who had ordained me a priest. Thank you, O Lord, for all the decent, gullible Germans who are so generous with widows' mites; and preserve your handmaiden, Fräulein Tischbein, from the lecherous intentions of your servant Nikolai.

Was this enough? How long would a priest from Komsomolsk spend on his knees? Supposedly this was the first Catholic cathedral I had seen. I would be moved to tears. The pain in my knees from the hard wood on which I was kneeling went some way to bring them to my

eyes but this physical agony was not enough. I imagined
some kind of catastrophe. My father was dead! Nothing.
My mother was dead! Even less. My father, mother and
sister were all burned to death in a fire at Avelscombe.
My eyes remained dry. But what if nothing had been
insured? Little by little, self-pity began to well up in me.
No inheritance! I was trapped at Caversham with no one
in the world who loved me but Denise!

Now, with real tears trickling down my cheeks, I
judged it appropriate to rise and leave the chapel.
Fräulein Tischbein followed. We went out into the
Domplatz. Fräulein Tischbein, with an expression of
reverence, offered me a paper handkerchief that she had
taken from her bag.

I wiped the tears from my eyes. 'You cannot imagine
how it feels for me to pray freely in this great and ancient
cathedral.'

'Oh, but I can,' said Fräulein Tischbein. 'And God
grant that one day a cathedral like this will be built in
Komsomolsk.' She held out her hand to take back the
paper handkerchief: the relic of a saint!

At the Ratskeller we were reunited with Nikolai and
Herr Worters – Nikolai in a new blazer and grey
trousers, a pale blue shirt and bright striped tie. A
moment later, Dr Kammer and Dr Karsfeld joined us,
and Fräulein Tischbein discreetly disappeared. Clearly,
her rank in the hierarchy at Parsheim did not merit a
place at table in the Ratskeller.

It was an excellent lunch and gratifyingly German. So
much of Germany is now part of a ubiquitous Eurocul-
ture, encompassing the bland modernity of Scandinavian
design and the same jeans and blouson worn throughout
the world. The pedestrianised streets have the same
McDonald's and Burger King, *gelateria* and spaghetti

houses, doner kebabs, Chinese takeaways. The only traces of Teutonic gastronomy are found in the stalls selling sausages, or in the old-fashioned restaurants like the Ratskeller – a gloomy, vaulted cavern decorated with shields on the wall where buxom middle-aged women rushed hither and thither with huge mugs of beer and plates of heavy, fatty food.

Dr Karsfeld, with her prim, pursed lips, seemed out of place in this temple of guttural gastronomy. Dr Kammer appeared to take it in his stride, licking his lips every now and then in anticipation of the next dish. He led me through the menu and recommended a local speciality. I accepted. I even agreed, on his insistence, to drink half a litre of beer. I trust I gave the impression that I was astonished at such material plenty.

Nikolai asked Dr Karsfeld why the headquarters of Kreuzhilfe was in a suburb of Münster. 'Essentially, because at Parsheim there was a property belonging to our founder, Count Kaspar von Willich.' She pointed to one of the shields. 'There, that is the von Willich coat of arms. He donated Parsheim to Kreuzhilfe after the war. But also because Münster is a significant city for Catholics in Germany. It was here that the Catholic princes were based when they negotiated the treaty of Westphalia at the end of the Thirty Years War. And it was here in Münster that the great Bishop von Gallen preached against the killing of the mentally deficient by the Nazis.'

'One of the only instances,' said Herr Worters, 'of effective opposition to the Hitler regime.'

'You see,' said Dr Kammer, 'we, too, had our time of persecution.'

'Although, clearly, the Nazis and the Communists are not strictly comparable,' said Dr Karsfeld.

'No, indeed,' said Herr Worters. 'One was not sent to a camp simply because one was a Catholic as one was in Russia.'

'Unless you also happened to be a Jew,' I said.

A look of reproof from Nikolai, as if it was a mistake to mention this. Russians, on the whole, are indifferent to the fate of the Jews.

## Wednesday

A third night at Parsheim. I whispered to Nikolai as we passed in the corridor – he on his way to, I coming back from the shower – that we were getting nowhere in our investigation into the murder of George Harding. No one had mentioned Schloss Zelden. Nikolai counselled patience. He thinks that things will begin to happen after today's meeting of the finance committee.

And they do. In the most polite fashion, Nikolai and I were asked to be available should the committee want to question us about our application. At around twelve, the summons came. We were shown by Herr Worters into a large room where a dozen men and women sat around a large oval table. Two of them were the priests who had concelebrated my first mass at Parsheim.

They smiled as we entered; furtive smiles, followed by quick nervous glances towards the man at the head of the table. A sinister brute. He was aged between fifty and sixty; close-cropped grey hair; bushy eyebrows, which he used to hide the expression in his eyes.

He was courteous. He stood when we came in and invited us to sit down on the two chairs that had been placed at the other end of the table. When we were seated, he said some words of welcome, then proceeded in a brisk, matter-of-fact manner to go through our application for a grant. In some instances he seemed to think that we had been too modest: surely provision should be made to pay a full-time catechist as well as a parish administrator? But it was clear that he was leading up to some major misgiving, and eventually he spelled it out. 'If you will forgive me, I should like to be persuaded that two hundred and fifty thousand dollars is an appropriate sum for the construction of a church.'

Did I betray my astonishment? A quarter of a million dollars? I turned to Nikolai. He seemed unfazed by the question. 'Thank you, gentlemen, yes. I realise that to you here in Germany, such a sum will seem wholly inadequate to build a substantial Catholic church. But you will realise that in Russia, particularly in Siberia, foreign currency goes a long way. I have no doubt but that such a sum will result in a building worthy of the Catholic Church.'

There was a short silence. Dr Kammer cleared his throat. 'It is certainly true,' he said, 'that foreign currency goes a long way, and in fact the question was rather whether such a sum was not perhaps *more* than adequate for the task you have in mind?'

'We understand from what you tell us,' said Dr Karsfeld, 'that your parish at present numbers rather less than four hundred people.'

'Of course,' said Nikolai. 'And to provide for our present parish, a much smaller and cheaper church would do. But we must think of the future. We must also think of the effect on the gullible citizens of Komsomolsk when they see large and impressive churches being built by the Baptists and Pentecostalists while the Catholics remain with a mere chapel.'

'Are the Protestants planning to build churches?'

'Of course. With munificent funding from the United States.'

Dr Karsfeld once again cleared her throat and turned towards the heavy man at the end of the table. 'Herr Krull?'

Krull? This must be Gustav Krull, founder and chief executive of Bettelheim Krull, brother-in-law of Heinrich von Willich, Grand Master of the Knights of the Cross. 'You have done preliminary costings?' he asked Nikolai.

Did Nikolai realise who this was? I suspect not. His mind was on the $250,000. 'Yes, in so far as this can be done at a time of rapid inflation. Of one thing I am quite sure. For less than the sum we have requested, it would be difficult to build an impressive sanctuary for the Lord.'

Krull turned to me and, leaning forward, fixed me with a penetrating look. 'And are *you* convinced, Father,' he asked, 'that such a substantial and impressive sanctuary is the best way to draw Russians into the Catholic Church?'

'You will know already,' I said, in my humblest tone of voice, 'that traditionally the Russian believers have attached great importance to monasteries and churches. As Nikolai says, we know that in the near future the Protestant sects who are already active in Russia plan to build their own churches in cities like Komsomolsk. If, when this happens, the Catholics have no church, then it will be much more difficult to draw converts from the Russians. If, on the other hand, we can build a church on the site we have in mind, dedicated to Our Lady of Fatima, then its tower will be seen from far and wide as a beacon of hope for those lost in the secular desert on both sides of the river Amur.'

As we were escorted from the room by Herr Worters, I

sensed a general approval for what I had said. As Worters led us towards the staff restaurant, he said his impression had been that our presentation had gone particularly well. We took our trays and helped ourselves to what we wanted to eat, then made our way to a table by the window.

Suddenly, there was Krull, the great industrial magnate, standing in line with Dr Karsfeld and Dr Kammer. And, a moment later, at our table. 'May I join you?'

'Of course.' This was from Worters, who obsequiously gave up his place to the Kreuzhilfe dignitaries of higher rank.

Krull sat down, then turned to me. 'I trust you did not feel that you were subjected to too severe an interrogation?' He spoke slowly and in a simple German as if he was talking to a child.

I put on an expression of perplexity as if I did not understand the word *Verhör*. He rephrased his question. 'That our enquiries were not too strict, too severe.'

I shook my head, gravely. 'When you are distributing the donations of the faithful, you cannot be too careful. Think of the fate of Ananias and Sapphira in the Acts of the Apostles who perpetrated a fraud on the early Church.'

Krull looked puzzled.

'They pretended to donate the full proceeds of a property transaction but in fact held back a proportion for themselves and when confronted fell down dead.'

'Ah,' said Krull, 'I had forgotten that episode.'

'I only wish,' I went on, 'that the kind of order prevailed in my country that would enable us to do things there as they are done here. But, as you know, we have to live with both chaos and corruption.'

'Russia will recover,' said Krull. 'Of that I am sure. Think of Germany after both of the two world wars.'

'Indeed.'

'My own company is already involved in a number of joint ventures in the former Soviet Union. You already have some of the prerequisites for industrial growth – a trained workforce, plentiful raw materials. What you need now is a better infrastructure, and, of course, a banking system that works.'

I bowed my head as if it was beyond my competence to comment on such worldly calculations.

'It is my view,' said Nikolai, 'that to work for the prosperity of our people should be part and parcel of our spiritual endeavour.'

'Indeed,' said Dr Karsfeld. 'We must never forget the social teaching of the Church.'

'The trouble at present,' said Nikolai, 'is that the working people of Komsomolsk see some people grow rich on the proceeds of crime and corruption while others are not even paid their wages for an honest day's work.'

'A sin crying to heaven for vengeance,' said Dr Kammer.

'Let us pray,' I said, 'that with the spread of faith will also come an increase in the kind of honesty and integrity that fosters social and economic progress ...'

And so on. High-minded platitudes until our stomachs were filled. Then Krull rose to take his leave. 'Did Dr Karsfeld mention the possibility of a stay at Zelden?' he asked.

'Zelden?' I affected puzzlement.

'I had not brought it up as yet, Herr Krull,' muttered Dr Karsfeld. 'I thought the invitation should come from you.'

Krull turned to me. 'Zelden is a castle that belongs to my brother-in-law, Heinrich von Willich. It is about an hour's drive from Münster and it has the chapter house of the Knights of the Cross. It is the home of my mother-in-law, Ilse von Willich. She lives there all the year round but other members of the family visit from time to time. The Countess is no longer young, but she still has a most lively mind. She has expressly asked to meet you, and thinks that Zelden would be a more agreeable base for your stay in Germany than the guest-rooms here in Parsheim.'

'But would it not be imposing?' I asked.

Krull laughed. 'Far from it. It is a huge place. There are twenty-two bedrooms in the castle and more in the chapter house of the Knights of the Cross. The only disadvantage is that you and your friend would be left largely to your own resources. Of course, you would be fed – full board, as they say. You would also have to put up with some of the younger members of our family who tend to be there at this time of year. We could put a car at your disposal and, of course, some pocket money for any excursions you might like to make.' He turned to Dr Karsfeld: 'That's all possible, isn't it, from the hospitality account?'

'But of course.'

I looked at Nikolai, then back at Krull. 'We would both be delighted to accept the Countess's invitation.'

'Good,' said Krull. 'Then that's agreed.'

*Three*

*Thursday*

Schloss Zelden

Half an hour until lunch. I sit at a large baroque desk looking out over the ramparts towards the plains of Westphalia.

We were driven here this morning by Herr Worters in the Opel Omega. Fräulein Tischbein followed in a smaller Opel, which has been left in the castle courtyard for us to use as we please. Both had been here before but seemed nervous, nevertheless, as they pulled the ancient chain at the massive front door.

It was opened by a servant – a middle-aged woman wearing an apron – who, after taking our suitcases and laying them aside, led us across a dark, cavernous hall into a large drawing room whose windows gave wide views over the ramparts and let in the light.

There we waited, only Nikolai sufficiently at ease to sit down on one of the sofas. Four or five minutes later, the door opened and a slender old lady came in. She nodded in recognition to Worters and Fräulein Tischbein. Worters stepped forward and introduced us. 'Father Piotr Ugarov, Nikolai Advetsev, the Countess Ilse von Willich.'

The Countess held out a fragile hand. 'Father Piotr, this is a great honour and a great pleasure. I'm so pleased that you and your friend felt able to accept our hospitality here at Zelden.'

I took the hand with care and shook it gently. For a

moment, her eyes met mine: they were blue, with that greyish tinge that comes with old age, their expression incongruously alert, curious, even amused. I protested my gratitude. She dismissed it with a wave of her hand. 'As you will discover, we are not short of space here at Zelden, and in the kitchen they will be delighted to cook for more than one old lady, above all when one of the guests is a priest. My only worry is that you will be bored. There is a library, of course, which may interest you, and there are some pleasant walks in the woods around the castle. But as for company, well, I fear there will be only the family.' She turned to Worters. 'Adolf arrives this afternoon, I believe, and Babi tomorrow?'

Worters nodded. 'So I understand.'

'And, of course, there is Monika, my younger grand-daughter. She has been living here with me but just at present she is making a retreat with the Carmelites across the valley. I'm not quite sure when we can expect her home.'

Herr Worters and Fräulein Tischbein now took their leave and returned to Parsheim, leaving the keys of the small Opel with Nikolai. The Countess showed us to our rooms. We went up the wide, sweeping staircase from the gloomy hall, then along long dark corridors, the walls decorated with huntsmen's trophies – dusty antlers and the tusks of wild boar.

'Yours is called the Bishop's Room,' said the Countess, as she opened a heavy wooden door. 'It has always been used by visiting priests and bishops. Let me show you why.' With Nikolai behind me, I followed her into this large, light room, which must have been at the corner of the castle because there were windows on two different walls. There was a large, four-poster bed with twirling

184

pillars of polished mahogany and thick cream-coloured hangings, embroidered with brightly coloured foliage and birds. A satin-upholstered prie-dieu faced a fine ivory and ebony crucifix, and on the wall there were a number of paintings: one, a view of Rome that might have been by a pupil of Canaletto, or even Canaletto himself; another, a quite delightful Madonna and Child in the style of Cranach, slightly cruder, perhaps, but nevertheless a fine example of the North German school.

It was not, however, to these fine works of art that Ilse von Willich drew my attention but to a small door set into the wall between the two windows. It opened on to a stone spiral staircase set into the turret at the corner of the castle. 'That leads down to the chapel,' she said. 'You can either hear mass or say it without meeting the other guests although now, I am afraid, we are without a chaplain, so the only way to hear it, Father Piotr, is for you to say it yourself.'

3.00 p.m. It is apparently the custom at Zelden to retire to one's room after lunch. The lunch was good. Meatballs in a caper sauce, boiled potatoes, wet German salad. Countess Ilse explained that we were eating *Königsberger Klopse* which, as the name suggests, is a dish from Königsberg in East Prussia. 'That was my home,' she said sadly. 'Now it has gone, all except a few recipes and memories ...'

I asked her about the portraits on the walls of the dining room. 'Those are my husband's ancestors, or predecessors as Grand Masters of the Knights of the Cross. They were not always the same.'

'But now, your son ...'

'Yes. He is Grand Master. It has been hereditary in their family since the eighteenth century.'

*Their* family. *Königsberger Klopse*. She keeps her distance from the von Willichs. As we rose from the table, she took hold of my hand, drew me towards her and whispered: 'How extraordinary, that *he* knew you were coming. From Siberia! But he knows everything. He always did.' She put a finger to her lips to denote silence or a secret, then drifted out of the room.

Who does she mean? Herr Worters? Dr Kammer?

## Friday

I have just returned from a walk in the woods with Adolf von Willich. We stopped at a point with a fine view of the castle and the small town of Zelden beyond. The castle is huge, far larger than I had realised. There are three major buildings within the inner walls, each with mullioned windows and steep tiled roofs. One is the residence of the Grand Master, the home of the von Willichs. Another is the Commandery, in effect the barracks of the Knights with rooms above and stables below. The third is the Great Hall of the Knights of the Cross, the room where they meet in conclave and dine together once a year.

There are two towers topped with red-tiled pyramids and a third with a black slate onion dome and belfry belonging to a church, one side of which forms part of the tall, crenellated, medieval walls. These in turn are surrounded by more recent fortifications – low ramparts with geometric projections in the style of Vauban. The space between the old walls and the new ones has been landscaped into a formal garden. Beyond and below the fortress, like the dwellings of pygmies, are the houses of the village of Zelden; beyond the village, fields and forests, forests and fields.

'It's superb,' I said to Adolf. He shrugged.

Adolf arrived yesterday in time for supper. Medium height, brown hair, thin – aged twenty-six or -seven. A student of philosophy at Heidelberg. A self-satisfied manner: he speaks with his head raised as if addressing a well-filled auditorium, but that is almost certainly a pose. It was Adolf, after all, who suggested a walk.

'We are all attached to Zelden. We come here whenever we can. But our real home is in Frankfurt – that's where my father works. A perfectly ordinary suburban house. Only my grandmother lives at Zelden all the year round.'

'It is good of her to have strangers to stay.'

'She likes to meet people, and to see the castle used.'

'Do your parents come to Zelden?'

'At weekends. We expect them this evening. My sister Barbara, too, for rather longer.'

'Where does she live?'

'In Munich. My younger sister, Monika, is living here at Zelden.'

'What do they do?'

'Babi is an actress. Moni … I don't know. You should ask her. At present she is making a retreat in a convent. She thinks she may have a religious vocation.'

To my relief, Adolf did not seem interested in the Catholics of Komsomolsk. Indeed, his curiosity seemed confined to his family and himself. As we walked back down towards the castle, he described the exploits of the von Willichs from the Dark Ages to the present day. 'Mostly soldiers or priests. Only my great-uncle Lothar could be described as an intellectual. He was a professor at Heidelberg.'

'And an author, I believe.'

'Yes. He wrote a book calling for a united Europe, a popular notion at the time among Fascists and anti-Fascists alike.'

'Your great-uncle was not a Nazi?'

'No. People of our kind despised them. Perhaps you thought that I was named after the Führer? No, the name Adolf has been in our family for several centuries and we were not going to drop it because it was also given by an Austrian customs official to his ill-fated son.'

'Did your family suffer under the Nazis?'

'I am afraid that their scorn did not lead to any active opposition. The most we can boast of is the arrest of my grandfather after the plot to kill Hitler. He was lucky to escape with his life.'

I affected the kind of ignorance about German history that one might expect in a Russian priest. 'What plot to kill Hitler?'

'A staff officer, Count Claus Stauffenberg, put a briefcase containing a bomb under the table on which Hitler was studying maps of the Eastern Front. The bomb went off but Hitler survived.'

'And what was your grandfather's role in the plot?'

'No one quite knows. Possibly none. But he knew Stauffenberg and some of the others and that was quite enough for the Gestapo.'

We returned to the castle. A red Mercedes sports car was parked in the courtyard. 'Ah, good,' said Adolf. 'Babi's here.' We went up the steps into the Residence. 'They'll be in the salon,' Adolf said, crossing the hallway to the drawing room.

As we entered, I caught sight of Nikolai, standing by the fireplace with two women, one the old Countess, the other young. 'Father Piotr, good,' said Ilse von Willich. 'Come and meet my granddaughter, Babi.'

She had the same features as her brother Adolf. On occasions this can mean, if one has met the brother first, that the sister has a mannish quality that mars her attraction. Was this one of those occasions? I could see at once that she was beautiful yet felt equally immediately that she was not my type. A friend, perhaps, but nothing more, a friend, because she greeted me in a friendly manner: on her lips an almost ironic smile, from her blue eyes a look of amused curiosity. Or was it because she was not only elegant but somehow too social, too sophisticated? I estimated that she was four or five years younger than I was; in her early thirties, perhaps older, it was hard to tell. She was wearing close-fitting jeans, a dark green shirt and a Hermès-type scarf gathered at her throat by a gold toggle. Her blonde hair was held back by a couple of combs and her eyes were skilfully shaded. I remembered what Adolf had told me – that she was an actress – and reassured myself that perhaps the ironic falsity of her greeting was not inappropriate after all.

She, too, said, in a soft, drawling voice, how honoured she was to meet a priest from Siberia. 'I am quite captivated by the stories Nikolai has been telling me about your parish in Komsomolsk. It sounds even *romantic* – the great river Amur flowing past towards the wastes of Manchuria and the Sea of Japan ...' Actorish – but was it her performance or Nikolai's? I glanced at Nikolai. Inscrutable.

I retreated to my room soon after supper. The grandeur of the salon and dining room make it difficult to feel at ease. Playing the role of a priest adds to the stress; only when I am alone and writing this journal can I be myself.

189

Although ... I say I can be myself without a clear idea of who I now am. Is this the result of the Method acting technique? A month ago I was a Russian specialist at BBC Monitoring, *l'homme moyen foutu* with a faithless wife, an unloved mistress, problematic parents and a shrink. Then, suddenly, I became a high-powered, undercover investigative journalist, whose story was going to change the course of history. I tell myself that I remain such a man; but some of the qualities of my cover as a priest are beginning to encroach upon those of the reporter.

For example, I already feel at home in my room here at Zelden. It is simple but also grand. No doubt, all those von Willichs who were archbishops of Münster or Cologne could hardly be given a straw palliasse when they came to stay. There are a number of books – some ancient and leather-bound, others more recently published – and half a dozen *objets d'art*, among them an exquisite small bronze dating from the Renaissance portraying St George slaying the dragon. This desk by the window dates from the eighteenth century. It is a warm evening. The window is open. I look out over the ramparts to the wooded valley behind the castle. Above the skyline, the evening star; below it, a few electric lights appear in the dusk.

At seven this morning, I went through the secret door set into the wall in the corner of my room, and down the spiral stairs to the chapel. Before you reach the bottom there is a balcony overlooking the altar; then wider steps down to the sacristy. After vesting, I said mass. No one attended. I was quite alone at the high altar of the cold baroque chapel. What is odd is that I almost enjoyed it: rising early, taking a shower, putting on the vestments, reading through the mass. This is what I mean when I say that Method acting confuses one's sense of who one is. I did not even applaud my own performance; for a brief moment I felt that I *was* a priest.

It is only with an effort of will that I now remind myself that I am here to find out who murdered George. This effort is made after a short visit from Nikolai. He knocks on my door and, having entered, sits on a high-backed chair by the other window. 'Well?' He speaks quickly in Russian. Remembering the secret staircase, and imagining other Borgia-like devices, I make a gesture to suggest that it is not safe to talk. He nods and suggests a walk in the garden beneath the ramparts.

I follow him out of my room. We walk the length of one corridor, then turn into another. As we pass, Nikolai shows me his room. It is less grand than mine, but with a bathroom *en suite*. It has art-deco fittings. There must have been refurbishment of this part of the Residence in the 1920s.

Nikolai appears to have learned the layout of the castle. We take some back stairs down to a door that leads from the back of the castle into formal gardens. No one else is there. We walk along between the box hedges, our feet crunching on the gravel. 'Well?' he asks again, quietly, in Russian.

'So far, so good.'

'So far, fantastic.'

'You mean the daughter?'

'Amazing, don't you think?'

'Attractive, certainly …'

'And no Virgin Mary.'

'Possibly not.'

'This mission could turn out to be more fun than I had anticipated.'

'Don't forget,' I reminded him, 'that you're a zealous Catholic.'

Nikolai nodded. 'Sure. But even good Catholics have their moments of weakness.'

'Maybe, but it's important to keep our eye on the ball.'

11 p.m. The older von Willichs and the Krulls arrived in time for dinner, each couple in its own fat Mercedes. The Krulls were in the salon when I came down, Krull dressed in a green Alpine suit. He introduced me to his wife, Annaliese – elegant, dull – and then to his sister, Julia von Willich, a woman who must once have been as handsome as her daughter, Babi. Babi then appeared in the company of her father. She wore a skirt and a cashmere sweater. Nikolai's eyes, I noticed, went straight to her breasts, then travelled down to her fine, long legs. There is a real danger that his lechery will give us away.

Babi presented us to her father, Heinrich von Willich. Here at last was the Grand Master of the Knights of the Cross. He is a man of between fifty and sixty, greying hair, tall, distinguished, a comfortable but otherwise uninteresting face. An archetypal Rhineland business-man. It is difficult to accept that he is the descendant of Crusaders. He greeted us both with great warmth, welcoming us to Zelden.

He then turned to his mother, Ilse von Willich, and asked: 'Where is Moni?'

'At the convent. She will be back tomorrow morning.'

He nodded. 'Good.' He looked back at me, as if to ask me something, but then thought better of it, or forgot what it was.

Double doors are opened. Dinner is served. We pass through to the dining room. Two young women in aprons wait to bring us our food. A more formal matter than the simple supper we had last night with Adolf and

192

the old Countess. I sit between Ilse and Julia von Willich. Nikolai is on the other side of Ilse and draws most of her attention. I am therefore thrown back on the inhibited Julia von Willich, née Krull. Like a guide to a stately home, she tells me about the paintings that surround us – the portraits of former von Willichs robed as Grand Masters of the Knights of the Cross. Then, cutting into her monotonous lecture, comes the acerbic voice of her son Adolf. 'You have yet to see the Grand Hall of the Knights of the Cross, Father Piotr. There on the walls are the great axes and double-edged swords with which our ancestors slaughtered the enemies of the faith.'

'It is true,' said Julia von Willich, with an uncertain look at her son. 'There is a fine collection of arms in the Great Hall.'

'Do you think it incongruous, Father,' Adolf asked me, 'that in our ecumenical age we should still display such trophies of religious intolerance?'

There was a momentary hush at the table. The other conversations stopped. Heinrich von Willich and his brother-in-law, Gustav Krull, turned to listen to my answer.

'I would be proud of such ancestors,' I said.

'And of their weapons?'

I paused. They waited. 'I believe it is often forgotten that ours is a God of power and might, and that to show such qualities in the service of the true religion is in some sense a reflection of the divine.'

'But does it not contradict the command to love your enemy?'

'You can love your enemy, even as you fight him.'

Heinrich von Willich leaned forward. 'But what are you saying, Father? That it is legitimate to take up arms in defence of the faith?'

193

I cleared my throat. Nikolai was watching me intently. 'I understand that such a view is not shared by many in the West, but our distinctive experience in Russia gives us a particular perspective from which we would judge it more than legitimate to fight for our faith. Think of Russia before the Revolution of nineteen seventeen. Holy Russia. Virtually everyone was a believer. Then, after a generation, when power and might were in the hands of Satan, a spiritual wasteland, a nation of lost souls.'

'But surely,' said Babi, with an amused sneer, ' "the blood of the martyrs is the seed of the Church"?'

'A neat saying,' said Adolf, 'but is it true?'

'In Poland, yes,' said Heinrich von Willich.

'In Poland,' I said, choosing my words carefully, 'because of the close association of Catholicism with the spirit of the nation, the Communists were never able to embark upon a total persecution. In Lithuania, however, the Communists did so with murders and deportations, the closing of seminaries and churches. There, I fear, though the faith was kept alive among the peasants, the Church was dealt a blow from which it has yet to recover.'

'And in Russia?' Adolf repeated.

I smiled – a bashful, modest smile. 'Well, you see before you two seedlings, and in our community in Komsomolsk there are a few hundred more. But if I am truthful, I would have to agree with you, that until now the crop is hardly bountiful when you think of what was sown in Siberia by such copious amounts of martyrs' blood.

'It is legitimate to ask,' I went on, 'whether such a situation would exist if the Whites had defeated the Reds in our civil war.'

'Or if the Church would have survived had the Republicans beaten Franco in Spain,' said Adolf.

'But what does this mean,' asked Babi, 'except that most human beings are either cowards or opportunists?'

'And that to the victor,' said Adolf, 'go the spiritual spoils.'

We returned to the salon for coffee. I sensed at once a lighter atmosphere, as if I had passed through some rite of initiation. Gustav Krull, sitting down beside me on the sofa, said: 'You speak excellent German, Father – good, that is, not only in how you say it but also in what you say.'

Heinrich von Willich shifted his position in his chair to address me. 'Of course, what you say is quite irrefutable. But I should warn you, Father, that such views are out of fashion here in the West.'

'Not among Catholics, surely?'

'*Especially* among Catholics. Tolerance is everything.'

'I blame the Vatican Council,' said Adolf, 'and Paul VI, a weak Pope.'

Babi, standing with her back to the fireplace, looked at her father and asked: 'You don't think our people came to see the value of tolerance after what they went through under Hitler?'

'Perhaps ...'

Babi turned to me. 'A large number of German Catholics saw the last war as a crusade against Bolshevik atheism. My grandfather is a good example. But then it emerged that our crusading armies were simply the vanguard for Himmler's angels of death, murdering not only Jews and Russians but also the Catholic Poles – officers, professors, schoolteachers, priests. He was obliged to recognise that he was not fighting for God but the Devil.'

'Of course, of course,' said Heinrich. 'That was the tragedy of the whole officer corps.'

'A tragedy, too, I think for the Jews.' She spoke in an almost insolent tone.

'No one wants to deny that,' her father said quietly.

Now Nikolai moved in as *agent provocateur*. 'But didn't the Jews themselves set the example which the Nazis followed?'

Babi turned: 'What do you mean?'

'It is perhaps clearer to us in Russia than it is to you here in the West, but the Jews were prominent in those units of the NKVD that massacred kulaks, Catholics, bourgeois – anyone whom they deemed an enemy of the people.'

'But it is hardly comparable,' said Babi.

'Not in degree, perhaps,' said Nikolai. 'They were not as efficient as the Germans. But consider this. In Kurapati, outside Minsk, they have now exhumed the corpses of a quarter of a million people, all killed with a bullet in the back of the head. When did this happen? In the nineteen thirties, a good ten years before Hitler dreamed up his Final Solution. Who perpetrated these atrocities? The NKVD, many of them Jews.'

Impossible not to admire Nikolai's *chutzpah*, overcoming his own *esprit de corps*. But if he had hoped to elicit an anti-Semitic outburst from our German hosts, he failed. Indeed, I sensed at once a deep embarrassment at what he had said, and to retrieve the situation, I remarked, in my best priestly voice: 'There can never be any excuse for evil, even evil perpetrated in the course of a war. To fight is one thing. To murder is quite another.'

'Exactly,' said Heinrich von Willich, patently relieved by my intervention. 'Himmler liked to think of his SS as an élite order, modelled in some sense on the Knights of the Cross; but the Knights have a code of honour that makes it unthinkable to injure the innocent and the defenceless.'

Adolf opened his mouth as if to dispute what his father had said, but then appeared to think better of it and turned away.

*Saturday*

A small congregation for my mass this morning: Adolf and his parents, the two Krulls. No Ilse. No Babi. Nikolai served.

No Babi at breakfast either. Nikolai disconsolate. We go for a walk in the woods. The verdict, once again: 'So far so good.' We feel that we have established that we were on their side. We disagree about which of the von Willichs would be the most likely to tell us what we want to know. I put forward Adolf. He is something of a braggart and might well tell us simply to persuade us of his importance. Nikolai suggests Babi. She is patently irritated by Adolf, and out of sympathy with her father's ideas. I cast doubt on Nikolai's motives for targeting Babi. 'She is most unlikely to know anything about the murder of George.'

'I am not so sure.'

'You want to uncover more than her secrets.'

He laughs. 'Well, if that is on offer, it would be hard to reject it, although to tell the truth, Michael, she's not really my type. Too easy. Used goods.'

'Piotr,' I said.

'What?'

197

'My name isn't Michael. It's Piotr.'

Describing this now, I wonder why I bothered to put him right. Was I afraid that someone might overhear us as we walked in the woods? Since we spoke quickly in Russian it would be unlikely that any eavesdropper would understand what we said. If he did not, then what could the name Michael, even if intelligible, give away? No, it was not for the sake of security that I corrected him; it was for the sake of my understanding of myself.

None of the men were at lunch. Afterwards, Ilse von Willich asked Babi to show us parts of the castle we had not yet seen. 'Except the Great Hall. Leave that to Adolf.'

We walked along the ramparts, peered into dungeons, and ended up in the castle library – a most beautiful room a good three hundred feet long and half as wide with a painted ceiling, ornate rosewood panelling and a huge collection of ancient books. At a large baroque leather-topped desk at one end of the room sat a man in his early sixties, whom Babi introduced as Herr Grunberger, the librarian. He gave us an impromptu lecture on the library of Zelden but when he had finished listing the incunabula, Babi cut him short. 'He used to be a schoolteacher,' she whispered, as she led us away. 'He's the most terrible bore.'

'How many people are employed in the castle?' I asked.

She shrugged. 'I don't know. If you don't count the estate, two dozen or so. But they're not all paid for by us. Herr Grunberger, for example, works for the Knights of the Cross.'

'Is there an office here for the Knights?'

'No. That's in Frankfurt – a whole secretariat.'

'What does it do?'

'Oh, they have a finger in a number of pies. Charity work, of course, but also politics. They organised Father's campaign for the European Parliament.'

'He is a member?'

'Yes.'

'Do the Knights have a particular political point of view?'

'They want a Federal Europe.'

'And don't you?'

She thought for a moment, then said: 'You know, because of our past, many Germans are afraid of the future. We would rather not face it alone.'

After the tour, Babi asked if we play tennis. I decided on the spur of the moment that it would arouse suspicions if the priest from Komsomolsk turned out to be an accomplished sportsman. I therefore said I did not. Nikolai had no such inhibitions. He went off with Babi to find some shorts and gym shoes. I retired to my room.

Heinrich's nephew, Thomas Krull, was there for dinner. A nasty-looking specimen, aged in his early thirties, with duelling scars on his cheeks. Pleased with himself. Afraid of his father? Impatient with his grandmother and Uncle Heinrich. He lectured Nikolai on the subject of Western investment in the Russian Federation. His thesis: that the Russians would only prosper when they became more like the Germans and less like themselves. He said that Bettelheim Krull were building a paper-mill in Siberia. Perhaps they could build our church? The first person I have encountered at Zelden who looks capable of having murdered George.

*

In the salon, while waiting to go in to dinner, I looked at some silver-framed photographs on a small inlaid table by the sofa where I sat. One showed four children, two boys and two girls. Babi came up behind me and leaned down to look over my shoulders: a delicious warmth and scent. 'Can you tell which of us is which?' I pointed to the older girl. 'Is that you?'

'Yes.'

'Then that is your younger sister?'

'Yes.'

'And that is Adolf.'

'No, that's Adolf. The other's Otto, my older brother.'

'Will he be coming here to Zelden?'

'No. He died.'

Stilted conversation at dinner. The men all looked preoccupied. I wanted to know more about Otto von Willich. How did he die? When did he die? What did he do? I dared not ask. Instead, I listened to Julia von Willich tell me about her pilgrimages to different Marian shrines – Lourdes, Fatima, Medjugorje, Garabandal. I struggled to stifle a yawn.

As we rose to return to the salon, she said: 'Would you be able to say mass at nine tomorrow morning?'

'Of course.'

'There will be the family, and perhaps some of the staff – say twenty or thirty people. We usually go to the village. The Bishop won't allow the priest to say mass here in the chapel. He told Heinrich that such privileges are against the spirit of Vatican II. Of course, he is quite willing to say house masses for the peasants with much smaller congregations. It is simply because this is a castle and Heinrich is Grand Master of the Knights of the Cross.'

'Will you mind if I say mass in Latin?' I asked.

'Mind? Not at all. We prefer it. But could you preach in German? Then the servants will understand.'

Preach? The thought fills me with panic. What can I say? I look at my missal. Tomorrow's gospel tells the story of the Good Samaritan. Perhaps flatter my hosts by casting them in that role.

## Sunday

I am still trembling after an incident that nearly gave me away. It happened during mass this morning, which was attended by at least the two dozen promised by Julia von Willich. There was even Herr Grunberger at the organ. We sang the *Credo*, *Sanctus* and *Agnus Dei*.

It was a cloudy morning. For this reason, the chapel was dark and because it was dark I was unable to scrutinise the individual members of my congregation. They were simply there. My mind was on my lines, and also on my first homily, which went down well. It was usual, I said, for Christians to model themselves on the Good Samaritan as Christ intended, but listening to the story this morning I found it easier to see myself as the victim, robbed and abandoned by the side of the road.

What this meant, of course, was that the von Willichs were the Good Samaritans, with Zelden as it were the inn where we recoup our strength and tend our wounds. I sensed my audience's unspoken approval. They sang the *Credo* with gusto. I carried on. From the offertory to the consecration, I was like a repertory actor in a long-running play: I could have said my lines in my sleep. Nikolai, too, served with aplomb, presenting the cruets of wine and water at the right moment, and ringing the bell on time. I thought his pious expression a little exaggerated, but then he might have said the same about mine. On the whole, given who we were supposed to be, it was probably better to err on the side of the theatrical.

*Nobis quoque peccatoribus.* We moved past the priest's communion and came to the communion of the people. Nikolai went to the tabernacle to fetch the ciborium containing the hosts. Together we went to the altar rail where a number of communicants awaited me on their knees. According to Bryan, kneeling to receive communion was the sign of a preconciliar disposition. Liberal-minded Catholics formed a queue and stood erect. They also received the host in their hands and placed it in their mouths themselves. Only recalcitrant traditionalists opened their mouths to enable the priest to put the host on their tongues.

Here at Zelden the entire congregation received communion in this traditional fashion. As I moved along the line from right to left, they raised their heads, opened their mouths and stuck out their tongues. I did my best not to appear embarrassed, but I was not yet used to peering into the mouths of strangers. I felt more uncomfortable about this aspect of my imposture than any other. It was not that I had scruples about serving up a counterfeit eucharist, but peering into their mouths was different. Tongues and gums are unattractive parts of our body; and one opens wide at the dentist on the assumption that to him one orifice is indistinguishable from another. So, too, with priests. But not with bogus priests. I could not help noticing, for example, the unhealthy yellow colour of the tongue of Nikolai, my server, or the many gold fillings in the teeth of Heinrich von Willich.

Then I stopped. I had moved on down the line at the altar rail to the communicant kneeling next to Heinrich von Willich but then came to a halt. I could not move. Like many a saint, I was paralysed by a vision. There, kneeling in front of me, was an angel, a creature with soft blonde hair, light blue eyes, lips, nose, skin, all apparently human but suffused with a luminosity that at that moment seemed to emanate from another world. My thoughts were quite lucid. I remembered Saul on the road to Damascus. Was it remorse that triggered visions? Was I less sanguine than I had thought in deceiving these people about their eucharist? Had this angel been sent to chastise me?

The eyes of the angel closed, the mouth opened, and from it came a tongue. A tongue? Having forcibly become something of an expert on tongues, I am loath now to call by the same name this perfect pink protrusion. Or is this absurd? A tongue is a tongue and this was no more than that of someone healthy, someone young.

Then it withdrew between the two rows of small white teeth. The plump lips closed. The eyes opened and a look of puzzlement was directed towards me, the priest. What had gone wrong? Why did I hesitate? I came to my senses. I held up the host. *Corpus Christi*. The eyes closed again. *Amen*. The mouth opened. I laid the white wafer on the pink tongue. The mouth closed. I moved on to Herr Grunberger: a complete set of false teeth.

After mass, a lavish breakfast. There, among the mortals, stood the angel who, now that I could clearly discern a delicate bosom, was apparently not an angel but a girl.

I sit now at my baroque desk, looking out over the ramparts, chewing the end of my Bic. How can I describe her? Even features, large eyes, a slender figure, fair hair, each feature perfect and yet the whole somehow lovelier than the sum of its parts. It was not a face like Babi's that one might find smiling from the cover of *Hello!* or *Die Bunte*. She seemed either unaware of her great beauty or indifferent to it; both her expression and her demeanour suggested an unusual simplicity, even innocence. Yet she was not a child. She must be twenty-four or -five, and she moved around the dining-room with more assurance than either Babi, Julia or Ilse, making sure that everyone had what they wanted for breakfast. The buxom women in aprons who bustled in and out looked to her for their instructions; and it was she who told them to bring more coffee or another plate of sliced sausage.

And she smiled at me. It is painful to remember it, an hour later, because the smile had a curiosity, a modesty and a benevolence all in one that wholly winded me in its effect. Nikolai and I came last into the room; I had had to remove my vestments in the sacristy. When she saw us, she came towards us and, in the German fashion, held out her hand. 'Father Piotr, I am Monika. Please forgive me for being away when you first arrived.'

As she shook my hand, she gave a slight curtsy; then, with an equally sweet smile, she turned to Nikolai. 'It is such a privilege for us to have you to stay with us in Zelden.' Again, the handshake but apparently Nikolai did not merit a curtsy. 'Come and have some breakfast. You must both be hungry.'

'Ah, you have met Moni ...' This was Adolf as we passed him at table. 'Look to your laurels, Father Piotr, she is a saint in the making.'

'Adolf!' This was Julia von Willich.

I glanced at Monika: the trace of a frown on the brow of a sister who still does not like to be teased.

She sat next to me at table. 'You've been on retreat?'

'Yes.'

'Was it worthwhile?'

'Oh, yes. Away from all distraction, away from the world.'

'To some it might seem that Zelden itself is a haven from the distraction and the world.'

She blushed. 'Of course. You must think me spoiled.'

'I did not mean it that way.'

She lowered her voice. 'I would be most grateful if, some time later, I could talk to you about how *you* were called by God to be a priest.'

I thought of the lunch with Gordon and Paget in the Garrick and a smile came to my face. Fortunately, Monika was looking away, her eyes raised towards the window with its view of the convent across the valley. 'It seems to me,' she went on, 'that particularly in Russia, it must be even more difficult than it is here to decide between an active and a contemplative religious life.'

'Why particularly in Russia?'

'Well, as I've always understood it, there is a strong tradition of monasticism in the Orthodox Church. Penitential practices like fasting and, of course, prayer and the liturgy are thought more important than running soup-kitchens for the homeless or teaching peasants in the Third World how to dig Artesian wells.'

'That is certainly true, and while the Catholic tradition is distinct, I would say that in my parish of Komsomolsk there is a greater need at present for the spiritual than the corporal works of mercy.'

'And I think that is true of Germany, too. But so many Catholics think that only vocations to care for the sick or help the poor have any validity in the modern world. They don't see the point of prayer.'

'That is a symptom of feeble faith,' I said. 'Think of Our Lord's words to Martha and Mary. Mary, who sat at His feet while Martha prepared the food, "has chosen the better course".'

'And yet,' said Moni pensively, 'it is so beautiful in the convent, and so peaceful, that it seems too pleasant a way to share Our Lord's suffering on the Cross.'

A knock on my door. Nikolai enters. He suggests a walk.

We were joined by Babi, who took us on a path that skirted the woods beneath the castle and then rose on the other side of the ridge to pass behind the Carmelite convent.

'Will your sister become a nun?' I asked Babi.

'Quite possibly, unless someone dissuades her.'

'Would you disapprove?'

'Of course. It's a living death.'

'Don't you value prayer?'

She laughed. 'I used to pray as a child but my prayers were never answered.'

'Perhaps you should think of prayer less as a series of petitions and more as an everyday conversation with God.'

'I cannot imagine that God would be particularly interested in anything I had to say.'

'Are you not a believer?'

Again, she laughed. 'If you are a von Willich, you are a Catholic whether you like it or not. But I cannot pretend to be a particularly good one, and many of the Church's teachings seem patently absurd.'

'For example?'

'On birth control. And sex.'

'I understand this is a common stumbling block here in the West.'

Babi turned to Nikolai and, with a trace of amused impertinence, asked him: 'And in the East? Do *you* accept the Church's teaching on sex?'

The suave agent was not thrown. 'In my head and in my heart, but I am not exempt from weakness.'

'Then you're lucky to have Father Piotr on hand to forgive your sins.'

'Certainly, what is important is to repent,' I said, 'but that is difficult if you cannot see the sin.'

'I don't see what harm it does,' said Babi. 'It's such a quick and easy way to make people happy.'

Nikolai pursed his lips.

'Have you never been in love?' I asked.

'Ach, love. What is love? *Egoisme à deux*. Sex is more honest without it.'

I shook my head. 'It seems extraordinary ...' I let my voice tail off.

'What?'

'That you should hold these views.'

'Because of who I am?'

'Yes.'

'Study our history, Father, and you will see that most of those who pretend to serve the Church in fact use it to pursue their own interests.'

'How is it in the interests of the Knights to help us poor Catholics in Komsomolsk?'

She laughed. 'Listen to my cousin Thomas about his plans for investment in Siberia. Then think back to the conquistadores and see how conversion and exploitation went hand in hand.'


*Monday*

---

The Krulls and the older von Willichs returned to Frankfurt last night. At supper: Ilse, Babi and Moni; Adolf, Nikolai, me. Pea soup with bits of sausage floating in it; brown bread; slices of cheese.

207

*

Only Moni at mass this morning. Nikolai oversleeps. I serve myself. Moni kneels for communion. A particular expression. As she raises her head, her eyes close like those of a china doll. White host. Pink tongue. Silence. Intimacy. The mass ends. I retreat into the sacristy. When I emerge, she is gone. Ten minutes later, we meet again at breakfast. Now she feels at liberty to smile.

That particular look as she came to communion. Respect? Love? Awe? No, veneration. An emotion unique to humans? One cannot imagine such an expression on the face of a dog or a baboon. Unique to those who believe in God? Or is this the look on the face of an art-lover as he looks at a painting by Vermeer or Cézanne?

After breakfast, I go to the library in search of a book. Those in the main shelves are from the seventeenth and eighteenth centuries, printed in Latin or Gothic script, leather-bound. Some are accounts of military campaigns; others Counter-Reformation polemic. Volume upon volume of the chronicles of the Knights of the Cross.

A discreet cough behind me. I turn. It is Herr Grunberger. He offers his help. I ask if the chronicles are kept up to date. Of course. But the most recent volumes are kept in the adjoining room, which is also Herr Grunberger's office. He leads the way. I follow. 'But I do not think you would find them particularly interesting,' he says. 'They are just records of their conclaves and appointments.'

We pass into a large room lined with books from the nineteenth and twentieth centuries. Herr Grunberger has a desk in a cubby-hole at the far end. He shows me the chronicles that have been published this century: volume upon volume, all beautifully bound.

'Of more interest, it seems to me,' he says, 'are the personal writings of some of the Knights.'

'Are they published?'

'Some, yes. Others not. It is part of my job to assemble and catalogue the records.'

'For a book?'

'Perhaps.' Grunberger offered me a chair and then sat down behind his desk: he appeared glad of some distraction. 'But the Knights and, of course, the von Willichs are naturally sensitive about what would be revealed.'

'Are there skeletons in the cupboard?'

Grunberger shrugged. 'Inevitably, all Germans have skeletons in their cupboards, many millions of skeletons. That is the problem. For example, we have here in the archive all the letters exchanged between Count Kaspar and Countess Ilse from the moment they became engaged, many of them historically significant because he was already fighting on the Eastern Front. Do you know their story? No? It is most romantic, but also terrible. She was Prussian, from a Junker family. They met in Berlin, fell in love and became engaged. All highly unsuitable, in their circle, because it was unheard of for a von Willich to marry a Protestant. Happily, the Countess Ilse agreed to become a Catholic. She was very young, seventeen or so. But Germany was already at war and Count Kaspar, commanding a regiment of Panzer Grenadiers, was in the vanguard of Operation Barbarossa. From the evidence of the early letters, it is clear that he was enthusiastic about the war. He talks of a crusade against atheistic Bolshevism and there are, alas, some anti-Semitic references which, though normal enough for someone of his class at the time, now seem, in retrospect, unfortunate, to say the least.'

'Was he a Nazi?'

'No. Quite the contrary. However, he believed that the German cause was just. But what you see from the letters, as the war progresses, is the way the scales slowly fell from the Grand Master's eyes. He was profoundly shocked by the Führer's order to the Army to execute all captured Soviet commissars. We know that Count Kaspar told Field Marshal von Brauchitsch that obedience to such an order was impossible for a Knight of the Cross, and it seems that von Brauchitsch told him to ignore it, as indeed did a number of officers. However, it seems clear that he also came across some of the activities behind the lines of the Einsatzgruppen and, later, Himmler's SS. This profoundly upset him: reading between the lines of his letters to the Countess, he came to realise that instead of fighting for God, he was allied to the forces of Evil.'

'What did he do?'

'What *could* he do? By this time Kaspar von Willich was with the Sixth Army under Field Marshal von Paulus in Stalingrad. The letters now become extraordinarily poignant. He longs for his betrothed to become his wife. Should he ask for leave? No. He feels that it would be dishonourable to leave his men, even for a week. Instead, they agree upon a proxy wedding: his brother Lothar, the academic, marries Countess Ilse in his place. That was on the tenth of November nineteen forty-two. On the nineteenth, the Russians launched their offensive on Paulus's flank. By the twenty-second, the Sixth Army was encircled. A quarter of a million German soldiers were trapped. The Luftwaffe attempted to supply them, but inexorably the Russians tightened their grip. Then, on the twenty-fifth of January, a week or so before Paulus surrendered, Kaspar von Willich suddenly appeared in Berlin. He had escaped on one of the last planes to leave Stalingrad.'

'Is it known why?'

Grunberger shook his head. 'It has never been satisfactorily explained. Given the Grand Master's vow never to desert his men, it seems inconceivable that he would have left simply to save his own skin. Did Hitler order him back? If so, why? Or – the more plausible explanation – did those officers already planning to kill Hitler and take power persuade Kaspar von Willich that he had a higher duty and arrange for his return? Certainly, the Gestapo thought so. After the failure of Stauffenberg's bomb to kill Hitler, and the collapse of the coup, Kaspar von Willich was arrested and held in Berlin's Plotzensee prison. Then, inexplicably, he was released. Many of his friends, against whom there was no more evidence of complicity in the plot than there was against him, were tortured, tried and hanged. What saved Count Kaspar? Again, there is no wholly convincing theory. It may have been clear to the Gestapo that he was not in the front line of the conspiracy. It is also possible that he was protected by his position as the Grand Master of the Knights of the Cross. Hitler and Himmler may have feared that his execution would have lost them the loyalty of Catholic officers. Remember, too, that Hitler was a romantic and may have wanted to preserve this symbol of Germany's heroic past. Whatever the reason, Kaspar von Willich was released and spent the remaining months of the war in Zelden.'

'Clearly, God was with him,' I said.

'To escape first from Stalingrad, then from the Plotzensee prison? Yes, clearly God was with him. But his troubles were not over. When the British Army reached Zelden, they requisitioned the castle and placed Kaspar von Willich under arrest.'

'On what charge?'

'I don't think that there was one. Simply, suspicion of complicity in waging a war of aggression.'

'But if he had conspired against Hitler?'

'That was no help. The Allied Control Commission was actually antipathetic towards the twentieth of July conspirators. They saw them as the relics of the Junker class who had only turned against Hitler because he was losing the war. Many of those men who had risked their lives to oppose Hitler were regarded as traitors by their fellow-Germans, and as reactionary militarists by the Allies.'

'What happened to Ilse von Willich?'

'She and the baby Heinrich moved to Parsheim. And after two months or so, after protests from Knights of the Cross all over the world, as well as Cardinal Frings and von Galen, and Konrad Adenauer in Cologne, Kaspar von Willich was released and permitted to live with his wife at Parsheim. It was then that the Knights set up Kreuzhilfe and, when political activities were once again allowed, Kaspar von Willich became a founding member of the Christian Democratic Union in Westphalia, and was elected to the first Bundestag in nineteen fifty-two.'

'Did they have no more children?'

Grunberger twitched. 'No. I have to say – of course, I have not yet had time to look through all the papers, many of which are of an intimate nature ... indeed, I wonder if Countess Ilse is aware of what is in the archives, her personal diaries of the period, for example – but from what I have seen I have concluded, sadly, that the marriage that started in such romantic circumstances was not a success. One can imagine ... But it is not proper to enquire too closely, certainly not while the Countess Ilse is still living.'

'Are you a Knight of the Cross?' I asked Grunberger. He laughed. 'Good heavens, no. To be a Knight of the highest rank, you have to have sixteen quarterings on your coat of arms, or other proofs of noble lineage on your father's side going back for at least three centuries. To be a Knight of a lower rank, it is a matter of four quarterings and two centuries. I, alas, have no claims to nobility of any kind. And even if I had, the pension of a schoolmaster could hardly provide for the donations that the Knights are required to make for their charitable work.'

'You were a schoolteacher?'

'Yes, in Münster. But I was always interested in local history and had made a particular study of the Knights. The Countess Ilse, and Count Heinrich, were kind enough to let me pursue my research here in the library, and when I retired, the Knights, thanks to Count Heinrich, offered to employ me as archivist, a position that is modestly paid but of unique fascination and also of great privilege because, as you will have realised, the von Willichs are a most open family, not a bit snobbish.'

'Indeed.'

'Of course, you as a priest have a particular standing. As Countess Monika likes to remind us, a priest is higher than the angels and so must be considered at least an equal of a Knight of the Cross.'

It was difficult to tell just how much irony there was in Herr Grunberger's remark. 'I get the impression,' I said, 'that perhaps not all the members of the family are quite as pious as Monika.'

'No, she is a little saint, determined, I think, to enter the convent although she has such a cheerful disposition that it might seem a waste to shut her away. But she also talks of going to Calcutta to join Mother Teresa's Sisters of Charity. Whatever she does, it will be dramatic and uncompromising. She is determined to give herself wholly to God.'

'And Countess Barbara?'

Again, Grunberger twitched. 'Quite different. One has to admit, I am afraid, that she is given over to ... How can I describe it? The fashionable world. She is amusing, intelligent – she likes to tease – but not, I am afraid, chaste. Her name is often in the gossip columns, always linked with that of a different man.'

'Does she bring these men here to Zelden?'

'No. She is very fond of her family, and proud of them too. She would not want to embarrass them.'

'Is she a good actress?'

'I have never seen her act.'

'Is she successful?'

Grunberger shrugged. 'I am told that she has appeared in plays in Munich and Berlin, mostly avant-garde productions, and has been commended in some reviews. But, of course, the magazines and newspapers are more interested in her as a socialite: it is good copy to have a picture of the Grand Master's daughter leaving a party at four in the morning a little the worse for wear.'

'Adolf?'

'Clever, I think, and serious-minded but a little too much with his head in the air. He is a student and it is difficult to see him as anything else – quite different from his cousin Thomas, for example, who is already in a responsible position in Bettelheim Krull. It is hard for Adolf, of course, because he grew up in the shadow of his brother. He takes his faith seriously, and it used to be thought that he might become a priest, but since the death of Otto ...'

'How did he die?'

'A road accident. A tragedy for the whole family.'

'When was this?'

'A year or so ago. He was a most outstanding young man. Able, intelligent, pious, even heroic.'

214

'In what way heroic?'

Grunberger scratched his cheek while he considered an answer to my question. 'I think I mean that while Count Adolf expresses his conviction largely through conversation, Count Otto did so through actions.'

'What kind of actions?'

'He organised various charitable endeavours.'

'He worked with Kreuzhilfe?'

'No, projects of his own. Among our youth, for example. The delinquents in Rostock, Leipzig and Dresden. He wanted to divert their energies from evil into doing good.'

'In what way?'

'Through youth clubs, I believe. I am not entirely sure. But I have had conversations with Count Otto when he was in Zelden. He liked intelligent conversation.'

'I am sure. It seems to me that the family are most fortunate to have a man of your calibre on their doorstep, as it were.'

Grunberger shifted in his chair. 'I am just a retired schoolteacher, but I like to think that I know as much as any man or woman about the Knights of the Cross, and Count Otto liked to make use of my learning. He was proud of his ancestors and most conscious that one day he would become the Grand Master. He said he wanted to adapt the original charism of the order for the particular conditions of the modern world.'

'But surely, in a sense, that is done by Kreuzhilfe?'

'Yes, of course. But Count Otto felt that after the fall of Communism Kreuzhilfe had become little more than a fund-raising organisation for the Catholic Church in the former Soviet empire. "Grunberger," he would say – he would always call me that, simply "Grunberger" – "Grunberger, are we not devoting our resources to removing the mote from the eye of our neighbours in Eastern Europe while failing to notice the beam in our own? Have we not lost our sense of who we are, here in Europe? What has happened to our Christian culture? What are we now but the inhabitants of a polyglot, pluralist trading area with no faith, no principles, no sense of who we are or what we are for?" You may have heard of the arson attacks on immigrants in Rostock. Count Otto was as appalled as we all are but not at all surprised. "It is not a protest against immigration, Grunberger. It is the youth of Germany showing us their despair." '

I probed further. Had Otto founded an organisation? Did he have political affiliations or ambitions? Grunberger did not seem to know. 'You see, Count Otto was always eager to pick my brain rather than have me pick his. He would ask me about earlier Grand Masters and what I had discovered in the archive. He was particularly interested in his grandfather, Count Kaspar – his change of heart at Stalingrad, the crusader becoming a conspirator, his imprisonment first by the Gestapo, then the British, the private melancholy and public triumph.'

'Did his father, Count Heinrich, share his opinions?'

'That I could not say. The present Grand Master is always courteous but he rarely finds himself here in the library and does not seem to share his son's interest in the past. He is, as you know, a director of Bettelheim Krull, and a member of the European Parliament. I do not imagine that his ideas diverge significantly from those of Chancellor Kohl.'

I had had enough of Grunberger and rose to go. 'Any time you would like further information,' he said, 'please do not hesitate to ask me. I am here most mornings. And, of course, you may study the archive.' He waved his hands towards the shelves and the filing cabinets. 'The library is here to be used.'

I thanked him and left. I went down the wide, shallow staircase to the hall. From the window on the landing there was a view of the garden where a man and a woman sat on a stone bench, their faces concealed by trellis and roses. Only when I reached the hall did I see that it was Monika and Nikolai engaged in earnest conversation.

## Tuesday

Ilse von Willich sends an invitation via Babi at breakfast to join her for tea in her apartment at four this afternoon. Difficult to remember that she is the same person as the young bride described by Grunberger. But this is always the case with old women. And it is hardest on those who were once beautiful. Plain women get used to the disappointed look in the predatory male early in their lives. It is only with age that the beautiful notice men's waning interest. As they enter a room, eyes turn to their daughters. Or, in the case of Ilse von Willich, to their granddaughters. Yet many years of their lives lie ahead of them. The same minds in withered bodies.

After breakfast, Adolf, Nikolai, Babi and Moni play tennis. I pass them in the hall as they set forth. Both girls in shorts. Babi's legs are long but rough from too much sun. Moni's as long and without blemish. Would she expose her limbs like this if she knew that it provoked such fierce desire?

A knock on my door just now. I put away my journal in a drawer. I shout, 'Come in.' It is Moni. To my horror, I feel myself blush. She no longer wears shorts but a skirt.

217

'I do not wish to disturb you,' she says, 'but I have to drive to Osnabrück this morning and I thought you might like to come with me. If we have time, we could also look at Tecklenburg.'

We are to meet in the hall in a quarter of an hour. My inordinate excitement at this invitation obliges me to accept what I have until now tried to deny: that I have fallen in love with Monika von Willich. Why have I tried to deny it? Because it is wholly irrational and unsuitable, not just in the particular circumstances of my presence at Zelden but in the broader context of my life. What can a middle-aged agnostic have in common with a twenty-five-year-old postulant nun? How can my cynicism ever be matched to her high-minded ideals? I am complexity; she is simplicity. I am disillusion; she is hope. Should she ever discover what I really believe, she would shy away in horror; and if I were true to myself, and not playing a priest, I would reject her narrow, priggish pietism out of hand.

Yet unquestionably my heart quickened just now when she entered my room. My eyes followed her every movement and gesture. Is it simply her beauty, or does passion exaggerate the perfection of her figure and face? Now, as I write, I try to think of some flaw in her appearance which, like a root growing on a cliff-face, can save my fall into the abyss. I can think of none. I conjure up only her long legs, her slender hips, her slight bosom, her lovely face – all of which might in themselves satisfy the lecher, but for the lover are merely the attributes of an enchanting being. It is not just her soft lips that draw him but their warm smile; not just the large blue eyes but their cheerful twinkle. Of course, the lips that smile can also kiss, but such a kiss would be so momentous and

218

exquisite that just to imagine it is almost more than I can bear. How sweet her innocence when I compare it to the knowing carnality of Ruth and Denise. All I can say today is this: in Monika's presence, my life is a delight; in her absence, it is drab. What more is love than that?


3 p.m. An hour or so before Ilse's tea party, time to describe this morning's excursion.

'Your sister seems close to your grandmother,' I said to Moni, as we stopped at the traffic lights in the centre of the village of Zelden.

She smiled. 'Yes. I suspect that Oma would like to have led a life like Babi's, at least when she was young.'

'I cannot imagine her as an actress.'

'She is more of an actress than she seems.'

'How do you mean?'

'Well, the widow of a Grand Master is a role that has been cast upon her. It is not one that she would have chosen.'

'What role would she have preferred?'

Moni pondered this question as she waited at a T-junction to turn on to the main road. The movement of her leg on the clutch had led the hem of her skirt to slip back above her knee. I could not avoid surreptitious glances at her leg as she changed gear. Fine blonde hairs. No lurking tarantula. I imagined laying my lips on the tendon beneath her knee.

'She would like to have had more fun,' she said at last.

'She is not pious?'

'No. In fact, I sometimes wonder whether she really believes.'

'Do you talk to her about such things?'

'From time to time. She used to warn me against marrying young, which suggests, doesn't it, that she would rather have waited?'

219

'But I was told that she married by proxy when your grandfather was on the Eastern Front.'

'That's just the point. She thought she was marrying the dashing officer she had met in Berlin, but when he returned from Stalingrad he was a different man.'

'Inevitably.'

'And they were difficult times. It was not that she went hungry: she was either here at Zelden or at the house in Parsheim, and she was infinitely luckier than those who were driven out of their homes further east. But there was the anxiety when my grandfather was arrested, first by the Nazis, then by the British.'

'That was absurd?'

'No.' She shook her head, a serious expression now on her face. 'He cannot escape all responsibility for the terrible suffering inflicted on your people – the twenty million dead.'

'But surely he only killed other soldiers in combat?'

'How can we be sure? Might he not have been in command of the soldiers who hanged Nikolai's grandfather as a suspected partisan, or those who raped his grandmother in front of her daughter? And the evil effects of such evil deeds carrying down from generation to generation – Nikolai's mother, traumatised by this childhood experience, ending her days in a mental hospital; his father, after losing his wife, killing himself with drink; and poor Nikolai, at the age of eleven, sent to an orphanage in Komsomolsk. The loneliness of his childhood. His desolation until he found God.'

It took me a moment to absorb this *curriculum vitae* of my Russian friend. 'Yes,' I said eventually. 'Undoubtedly many suffered. But it was not the fault of your grandfather, and certainly subsequent generations should not feel themselves to blame.'

'Does it not say in the Bible that the sins of the fathers are punished in the sons unto the sixth generation?'

'In the Old Testament. Not in the New.'

'But surely we can atone for the sins of others, not just for our own?'

'Certainly.'

'We can pray for the souls in purgatory, and offer up our own privations and suffering to mitigate the punishment for their sins?'

'Of course.'

'It must therefore be only right to do what one can to atone for the sins of one's own people, particularly one's own flesh and blood.'

Osnabrück. A cathedral, a number of churches, the 'peace chamber' in the Town Hall where the Protestant princes signed the treaty of Westphalia in 1648. The end of the pretence that Christendom would ever again be of a like mind.

Tecklenburg. The ramparts of a demolished castle. Fine views. Pretty, half-timbered houses. After a stroll, we sat down in a café in the central square. I drank coffee, Monika hot chocolate. Her pink tongue protruded to lick the residue from her lips. Her knee was concealed beneath the table. I was so happy to be alone with her that I wanted that moment to be eternal.

My mood declined as we drove back to Zelden. My spirits had soared because Moni had chosen me to accompany her on this excursion. Now I realised that this was to be able to talk to me about Nikolai. She seems to have been greatly affected by his preposterous yarns. She told me that he had trained as a microbiologist, passing out first in his year, but his excellent prospects were

221

blighted when he became a Catholic. 'To give up a career that would have led to the Academy of Sciences, and work as a school janitor for seven years! All for God!'

'He is certainly courageous,' I said. 'There are many in our community who hope that Our Lord will call him to become a priest.'

'But surely he has told you how he feels God has called him to a *lay* apostolate?'

'Of course, but all the same ...'

'He believes that people in Siberia are so estranged from the Christian tradition that they regard celibates as somehow perverted, or at any rate weird.'

'Some, perhaps.'

'And for that reason it is far better for Catholics to evangelise as married couples.'

'There is also the argument that celibacy demonstrates a priest's commitment to a supernatural life,' I said, with a modest lowering of my eyes.

'Of course.' She blushed at the suggestion that she had denigrated my chaste way of life. 'But, as Nikolai points out, the Russians – even those who are atheists or agnostic – are unconsciously attuned to the Byzantine tradition which permits priests to marry.'

'Orthodox monks do not marry.'

'I know. But Nikolai says that the concept of monasticism is very difficult for the modern Russian to understand. But why am *I* telling you this? I know that you have talked about this with Nikolai a thousand times and, as his spiritual director, have advised him to find a suitable wife.'

A suitable wife! What is Nikolai up to? Why has he invented a tragic past? It is one thing to play a role with conviction, as I like to think I do that of a Catholic priest.

But why say that I have advised him to marry? Where does he expect to find a wife?

## Wednesday

Yesterday's tea with the Countess Ilse turned out to be coffee and cheesecake. Babi takes me and Nikolai to her grandmother's private apartment on the second floor of the south-east corner of the Residence. A charming small drawing room with a low ceiling, rococo mirror, Italian paintings, more silver-framed photographs of her children and grandchildren. Ilse pours coffee from a silver pot into white porcelain cups and hands me a slice of feathery cheesecake on a white porcelain plate. Long fingers: straight bones crossed by dark blood-veins show beneath the brown parchment skin. Grey hair, tied back in a bun. Delicately made-up face.

Having delivered us, Babi wanders restlessly around the room. Her grandmother: 'Babi, please, come and sit down.' She turns to us. 'Babi gets bored at Zelden.' Babi does not contradict her. Ilse smiles at the two Russians. 'I hope *you* are not bored?'

'No, indeed, we are so fortunate ...' Etc.

'For us,' says the old lady, 'the war was the worst – for boredom, that is. We now know – so Heinrich tells me – that Speer wanted to put us women to work, to replace the men who had gone off to fight. This is what the English did, after all. And how we would have loved it, having something to do. But Hitler would not hear of it. He kept us in the home. I was here at Zelden. No men. Only Lothar, on occasions, and he was a terrible bore.'

'Did Lothar not fight?' asked Babi.

'He had some medical disability. Flat feet, I think.' She turned back to us. 'That was my brother-in-law, the

223

professor. Very academic. Always ready with a lofty theory to explain this, that or anything. Impossible to fault him because it was impossible to follow what he said.'

'Adolf takes after him,' said Babi.

'And who takes after you?' I asked the Countess.

Ilse smiled at her granddaughter. 'Why, Babi, of course.'

Babi smiled back.

'And does your son take after his father?'

'Heinrich? Ach! Their lives were so different. How can one tell?'

Babi now fixed me with a precise look: mocking, even cruel. 'As you must appreciate, Father Piotr, being born into such a strong tradition is rather like being poured into a mould. I do not believe that my father ever had a chance to choose his shape.'

'But you chose your shape,' said Ilse.

Babi sniffed. 'To rebel is not to choose. It is simply to turn the coin.'

'What you suggest,' said Nikolai, in his best ponderous, prayerful voice, 'leaves little room for either Free Will or the Grace of God.'

'I have yet to come across either,' said Babi.

'But surely there are moments,' I said, 'when we are faced with a moral choice.'

'Do you think so?' She gave me a penetrating look; then lowered her eyes, as she so often did, her glance cascading down like water in the fountain in the rampart gardens. 'In my experience,' she said, 'most people float with the current. They never stop to think or choose.'

'In Komsomolsk,' said Nikolai, 'we Catholics are obliged to swim against the current.'

'Against the main current, perhaps,' said Babi, 'but

there are the eddies of your subconscious. Perhaps your father was unsatisfactory so you find a better father through your belief in God.'

'Of course, in part, we are all influenced by experiences whose effect we do not wholly understand ...'

'Which makes nonsense of the whole notion of sin.'

'Why so?'

'Because the Church said nothing against Hitler's invasion of Russia but consigns to Hell the wretched girl who sleeps with her lover to get the affection she never had as a child in her home.'

Was this a self-portrait? I could hardly ask. 'Fortunately,' I said, 'it is not me but Christ Jesus who will judge the living and the dead.'

'An easy way,' said Babi, 'to avoid responsibility for the suffering caused by the Church's formulations that have nothing to say about the most monstrous atrocities and a great deal about the most trivial sexual sins.'

It was odd to have to counter the kind of arguments that I had used against my own father. 'I gather that such ideas are common here in the West,' I said quietly, 'even among Catholics. But our particular experience in Russia has taught us that most of us are powerless as individuals to affect the monstrous atrocities you talk about, even as a general, or a bishop and even as a Pope; whereas chastity is something that even the most powerless can present as an offering to God.'

'On the assumption that God wants it.'

'Your sister Moni would feel that he does.'

Babi snorted. 'It's a form of anorexia.'

'What?'

'Moni's fear of sex.'

'She does not seem neurotic to me,' I said, 'but, rather, someone open to the Grace of God.'

Ilse von Willich refilled our cups with coffee. 'You are so intolerant,' she said to Babi. 'You will not permit people to be different.'

'But even you are appalled, Oma, to think of Moni immuring herself in a convent for the rest of her life.'

'She has yet to make up her mind,' said Ilse.

'I understand,' said Nikolai, 'that she has yet to choose between a contemplative and an active calling.'

'Whatever she chooses,' said Babi, 'it will be a symptom of neurosis.'

'So the only fulfilled life is one spent among the *demi-monde* in Schwabing?' This rejoinder escaped me before I had had time to consider what I was saying. It was a mistake.

'Ah, Father,' said Babi, the mocking look back on her face. 'So you know about *demi-mondes* and about Schwabing? Komsomolsk cannot be as isolated as we suppose.'

I blushed. 'It was described to me by Herr Grunberger.'

'Yes, he likes to gossip about the family. Well, at least in Schwabing one can choose one's own way of life.'

Babi became silent and, when her grandmother started twittering on about this and that, she stood once again and started to move restlessly around the room. Why this animus against me? Because I am a priest? Clearly, priests personify a moral code which, even in those who have rejected it, can give rise to a sense of guilt. No one likes to feel guilty, particularly about something they have decided is not wrong. Like sex. We do not only feel guilty about sex: we feel guilty about hungry children in Africa. But while it is possible to deal with this guilt with donations to charities, it is not so easy to kill our guilt about sex. Why do we continue to feel involuntary post-coital remorse? Father Piotr would argue that guilt is the spiritual equivalent of pain. It alerts us to a moral malfunction. The better the sex, the greater the guilt. That is, sex outside marriage. Or even in marriage. With Ruth, at times, I felt appalled. By the pleasure. By the joy. It seemed that nature would exact a *quid quo pro*. It would have done, in the normal course of events. Children. But we cheated nature. Then nature cheated us.

## Friday

A fair gathering for mass. Monika tells me at breakfast that this is because it is the first Friday of the month. I still look puzzled. 'Don't you know about this in Russia? It's a devotion to the Virgin Mary. To hear mass on the first Friday of every month.'

'Of course.' I pretend that it has just slipped my mind. But how could one forget something like that? It would have been less compromising to have feigned ignorance altogether. Fortunately, Moni is too pure to let suspicions enter her mind.

After breakfast, a walk in the woods with Nikolai. Are we getting anywhere? We compare notes. What do we know? I summarise what I have learned from Grunberger. Otto von Willich with his cousin Thomas Krull started some kind of organisation which recruited delinquent skinheads. This probably incorporates a faction among the younger Knights of the Cross. It is presumably the same organisation that imported small-arms from Riga. It seems likely that the ideology of this organisation is xenophobic. German. European. Christian. Catholic. It also seems likely that Adolf's ideas are not dissimilar to those of his brother. But it is a

227

speculative leap from these few facts to Paget's hypothesis that this organisation is responsible for the murder of George.

'We must be patient,' says Nikolai. 'We may learn something more tomorrow at the dinner following the conclave of the Knights of the Cross.'

'And if we do not?'

'I am sure patience will pay off.'

'It is easy for you to say that.'

'What do you mean?'

'It is most disagreeable to have to pretend to be a priest.'

'It goes against the grain for me to act the holy fool, day after day. But I am sure the key to the mystery is here. They know more than they let on. Sooner or later, one of them will let something out. Babi – did you notice yesterday? She is under some kind of psychological pressure. And Adolf: he so loves the sound of his own voice that sooner or later he'll say something that he shouldn't, simply for the sake of saying it.'

'And Monika?'

'No. I cannot believe that she would be involved in anything touching on politics and crime.'

We walked on for a while in silence. Then, after covering another quarter of a mile of the path through the woods, Nikolai stopped, turned to me, and asked: 'Michael. You have been around a bit, haven't you?'

'I don't quite know what you mean.'

'With women, with girls?'

'I've known one or two.'

'Then tell me, can you deflower a virgin while wearing a condom?'

'I don't see why not.'

'Won't it rupture?'

'They're fairly strong, these days.'

228

We walked on. Nikolai seemed relieved. 'You see, in Russia it's been so difficult to get hold of condoms, and harder still to come across virgins.'

'Someone has to be the first.'

'Of course. And, of course, I've had that honour a number of times. But never, it so happens, when in possession of a condom.'

'So how did you make sure the girls did not become pregnant?'

He shrugged. 'That was their business. They could always have an abortion. In Russia, it's routine.'

'So I understand.'

'While here in the West, as I understand it, there are girls who are reluctant to have abortions.'

'One or two.'

'But they have the pill.'

'Of course. Unless ...'

'What?'

'They are strict Catholics.'

'They think it sinful?'

'Indeed. But they also think it sinful to make love unless one is married, and prepared to have a child.'

'They would not permit the use of a condom?'

'Most certainly not.'

'So the question of whether or not it would rupture would not arise?'

'No, except ...'

'What?'

'A real innocent might not realise that her lover was using a condom.'

'If he was discreet.'

'Precisely.'

Nikolai nodded. We walked a little further in silence. 'Why this curiosity about condoms?' I asked.

'Oh, for no reason. You know how it is. When one is idle, idle thoughts come into one's head.'

Disturbed by this conversation with Nikolai. What leads him to think about the seduction of virgins? Does he have a virgin in mind? One of the maidservants? Certainly not Monika. The purity of her expression as she came to take communion this morning was a welcome antidote to Nikolai's crude concupiscence.

Yet if I am honest with myself I have to admit that Nikolai's feelings are easier to understand. I remained baffled by Monika's reverence. What does she venerate in the wafer? What does she think goes on at the mass? It is similar in many ways to the communion service conducted by my father, which I attended most Sundays as a child. But apparently to Moni, the mass is something more.

After lunch, I go up to the library. Grunberger is not there: it is the weekend. In the annexe I find a section on religion and take out a *Catholic Encyclopaedia* and a book published in the 1930s called *The Spirit of Catholicism*.

After two hours' reading, I sit, stare into the air and chew the end of the pencil with which I have been making notes. I try to grasp what is at the core of Catholicism – the *sine qua non* of religious belief. God. Jesus, the Son of God. Wafer, the flesh of Jesus who submits to an unpleasant death as the scapegoat for our sins.

But even if God exists, why love Him with the emotion so evident in Moni's face? Why be bothered with Him one way or the other? He can go His way, I shall go mine. The same applies to Jesus. The values He promotes so clearly go against our instincts that no reasonable person can be expected to adopt them. Poverty? Chastity? Obedience? Instinct drives us to pursue money, sex and freedom. Jesus also tells us that we must love others, however obnoxious and however little those others love us back. Absurd. A religion for losers. It favours the weak over the strong. This is wholly contrary to nature which encourages the survival of the fittest. Try telling a fox in a chicken coop, 'Thou shalt not kill.'

Of course, the fox need not worry about an after-life. Man with his overgrown brain can imagine not only the death of his body, but also postulate a continuing existence thereafter. What if death is only a transition from one form of existence to another? And what if this second phase of our existence is longer than the first? What if it is *everlasting*?

This is the bottom line of Christian belief. There is life after death. There is no end. No oblivion. We live for ever. Either in peace or in torment, depending upon the judgement of God. That may not be a good enough reason to love Him, but it makes it advisable to treat Him with respect. 'The beginning of wisdom is fear of the Lord.'


## Saturday

I leave my room at midday and come down to find a commotion in the hall. The older von Willichs and the Krulls have arrived with a number of guests. Thomas Krull sees me and asks after Nikolai. 'I have bought him a dinner suit for tonight.'

Tonight? The annual dinner of the Knights of the Cross. I questioned Babi about it yesterday. 'It may amuse you,' was all she said. Apparently, my black suit and clerical collar are correct for a priest. The Knights will wear tail-coats and white bow-ties. 'Do women attend?' I asked Babi.

'Yes. The Dames of the Cross.'

'Are you a Dame of the Cross?'

'Of course. So is Moni.'

I see Moni talking to a blond beast – that is, a tall young German with blue eyes and fair hair. This provokes a painful spasm of jealousy. She catches my eye, calls me over and introduces me to Ignaz-Balthasar von Ostwall-Stubenkammer-Schussenreid, or some such name, as long as my arm. He clicks his heels and bows his head. 'Father, this is an honour ...' And so on.

Ignaz-Balthasar takes his leave. Moni gives me one of her gentle looks. 'Have you a moment?'

We go into the garden.

'Tonight, at the Knights' dinner ... You must realise that it is only one aspect of their activities.' I nodded. 'Many of those you will see tonight in their robes and decorations are also to be found running soup-kitchens, or nursing the sick on pilgrimage to Lourdes.'

'I quite believe it.'

'I would not want you to think that we are simply snobs.'

'It's all so far from our experience in Komsomolsk,' I said.

'Of course. And, to me, that is what makes you and Nikolai so appealing. You are unencumbered by tradition, like the first Christians.'

'Tradition has its advantages. It gives you a sense of who you are.'

She turned and smiled at me. 'But surely you know who you are.'

'Up to a point.'

'That must be the joy of being a priest. You know you

232

have been chosen. You are wholly committed to God, and you are in the hands of God. You need never look back or even sideways.'

Her proximity. Her smile. 'You must not presume,' I said, 'that those with religious vocations are never tested.'

'No, of course.'

'Satan wants to ensnare precisely those who are close to God.'

'Yes.' She lowered her head, giving me a chance to glance at the nape of her neck. Then she looked up and for a moment her eyes met mine with an odd happy-sad expression that I had never seen in them before. 'But fortunately Satan is often inept,' she said. 'He tests us in such a clumsy fashion.'

'How do you mean?'

'Well, if he wanted to frustrate a religious vocation, for example, he should have a young man fall in love with an eligible girl instead of with a married woman.'

'To choose the eligible girl would hardly be evil.'

'Unless God wants the young man as a priest.'

'Then surely God would make it plain.'

'Precisely. By permitting Satan to rouse a love that was unmistakably wrong.'

Babi appears in the garden. An odd look at her sister: quizzical, cautionary. I look back at Moni and catch the last signs of a blush. Babi takes me by the arm: 'Come, you are summoned to the salon to meet the Archbishop.'

As I climb the stairs, flanked by the two sisters, Babi reassures me that I have no need to be nervous: among those in the Archbishop's entourage is a Russian-speaking priest. Fortunately, when I meet him, he is talking to Nikolai and so is predisposed to accept that I, too, am Russian. Moreover, his knowledge of the language is not as good as he imagines. He is eager to use it. I am only required to give monosyllabic replies.

I kneel to kiss the ring of the Archbishop. He grips my hand, raises me, embraces me. A kind old man who darts occasional crafty glances in my direction. I tremble inwardly. Perhaps he has magical powers of discernment. He asks about Bishop Stoskus. I repeat my story. Finally, I take from my pocket the miniature prayer-book written by Lithuanian Catholics in one of the gulags. As the Archbishop examines it, tears come into his venerable eyes. 'How they suffered, how they suffered ...'

Midnight. By and large, we British are unrivalled when it comes to ceremonial, but I am obliged to acknowledge that the Knights of the Cross as they processed into their Great Hall this evening provided a glittering spectacle. The Great Hall itself is more magnificent than would be imagined from its fortress-like exterior: a huge room with a painted ceiling and superb baroque ornamentation. In the hall below where we all assembled there was displayed a superb collection of weapons – maces, pikes, swords, suits of armour, and shields emblazoned with coats of arms.

The clergy and the Dames of the Cross were invited to take their places at table before the Knights processed into the room. We were taken up the wide oak staircase, dark portraits of former Grand Masters looking down at us from the walls. In the Great Hall, there was a long T-shaped table with an inscribed name on a card at each place. I had no sooner found mine than there was a fanfare of trumpets from an orchestra in the gallery above. The fanfare led into a triumphal march as the Knights themselves processed up the stairs and into the Great Hall, the youngest first, those of the highest rank in the rear. The most junior of the knights – Adolf, Thomas and Ignaz-Balthasar – already seemed extraordinarily dashing in their tail-coats with a sash and a cross; but as the higher ranks appeared at the entrance, they displayed their magnificent attire: dark blue robes, white sashes, two or even three decorations, but pride of place going to the Cross of the order, of white enamel encased in gold, hanging from a bejewelled crown which itself dangled from a deep red ribbon.

At the end of the procession came the Grand Master himself, Heinrich von Willich, wearing a scarlet tunic embroidered with gold thread, gold epaulettes, a stupendous collection of decorations and, in his hand, an ostrich-plumed hat.

We all remained standing until the Grand Master had taken his place at table, the Archbishop to his right, a Dame to his left who, together with the other women, appeared singularly drab beside the colourful Knights. The Archbishop said grace, after which a hundred gruff voices said, 'Amen.'

With Nikolai, I was seated at the high table – the top of the T – next to a Dame of a certain age who spoke to me slowly in German, as if she was a governess and I was a backward child. She asked if there were any Knights of the Cross in Russia. I said that as far as I knew there were not. She then spoke with some bitterness against the Knights in America who required no proofs of nobility. 'Really, what is the point, if it is simply a matter of money?'

On my left there was a young priest who was part of the Archbishop's entourage. He had the look of a clerical bureaucrat with close-cropped hair and tinted glasses. He asked about my life in Komsomolsk. What contact did I have with my bishop? How close was I to another priest?

Did we run a school? 'In many ways, it must be easier starting from scratch in a wholly agnostic society. Here in Germany, the Church carries the burden of its history which may be colourful' – he nodded towards the Knights of the Cross – 'but is not of much relevance to the modern world. After all, how can one possibly justify an organisation like this that demands proofs of nobility for admission? Yet here I am, and here is the Archbishop!'

'He must see some value in what they do.'

'Their charitable work? Yes, of course. But he also approves of them because they are wholly orthodox, loyal to the Pope.'

'Are not all Catholics loyal to the Pope?' I asked, in a *faux-naïf* manner.

He laughed. 'Good Heavens, Father, have you never heard of Hans Kung? The truth is that a good half of the Catholics here in Germany are, in fact, Protestants: they make up their own minds on questions of right and wrong, even on theological questions of a complex kind.'

'They reject the authority of the Church?'

'Since the Nazis, it is considered a virtue to reject authority of any kind.'

'We find the same sort of thing in Russia, following Communism.'

'And can we blame them?'

I 'knitted my brow', pretending to consider this question with a seriousness that I am sure my neighbour at table had not intended. The role I was developing for Father Piotr was of someone earnest, literal, short on a sense of humour. 'You can blame them, I think, for bundling all sources of authority together – Hitler, Stalin, the Pope.'

'Quite so.' I think that my companion was not in the

236

mood for serious conversation. He emptied his glass of Gewürztraminer as soon it was filled – understandably, because it was an unusually fragrant and delicious wine of which I myself might have drunk more if I had not felt that I had to keep my wits about me. On the far side of the hall, I could see Babi and Moni, both in long dresses, both wearing the sashes of the Dames of the Cross. Both outshone the peacock Knights adorned with glittering crosses and decorations. Left alone by my neighbours, I was able to meditate on the different qualities of the Grand Master's two daughters. Clearly, Babi was out to beguile: her body, which sat so naturally in a yellow shot-silk dress, inclined casually towards the Knight on her left, her curled hair cascading over her bare shoulders while her animated face, prepared with the highest degree of skill, laughed and teased and flattered and charmed: I could see it all without hearing a word of what she said.

How different was my Monika, her face showing no vestige of make-up, her hair straight and unadorned. Her shoulders were also bare, but they were like those of a child in a swimsuit. No guile, no flirtation. She is patently uncomfortable in her long blue dress.

I watched her listening to the young man who sat next to her. Then, suddenly, she turned away from him to look around the room, at the same time playing with a bread roll with her left hand. Her glance lingered for a moment on Nikolai, then moved on and stopped on me. Our eyes met. She smiled. I did the same. She blushed, or so it seemed from fifty feet. She blushed, and looked away.

There were a number of speeches. First the Grand Master, Heinrich von Willich, welcoming his fellow

Knights of the Cross; then the Archbishop, a predictable homily, praising the Knights for their good works; and finally an address by a strange-looking man – Albrecht Franz von Sittendorf zu Glanz und Treibichdorn (or some such name). My companion, the priestly bureaucrat, told me in an undertone that he was the Chancellor of the Knights of the Cross, second in command to the Grand Master.

He was not large, and was unusually dark – swarthy, with black hair and deep shadows under his eyes. Age? Around sixty; but lean, even wiry. 'The time has come …' That was his favourite phrase. But for what? He spoke of Germany, but more often of Europe, of Christendom, then of Europe once again. He gave the impression that they were all one and the same thing. *The time had come* to shed the illusion that all was well with the world. Europe now faced a greater threat than at any time since the Turks had laid siege to Vienna. Islam was once again on the march; not now with armies of janissaries but with an insidious fifth column of immigrants and guest workers who, in collusion with unprincipled capitalists, had already occupied large parts of our great European cities – Marseille, Bradford, Berlin. In the name of toleration and racial justice, they demanded equal rights, and so we had permitted them to build mosques and schools. Why, even in Rome, the capital of Christendom, there was now a mosque to rival the basilica of St Peter's, paid for from the coffers of the Saudi King. But did they, the Muslims, extend the same toleration to Christians in their lands? Quite to the contrary. In Saudi Arabia, only Islam was permitted. Priests were excluded; the mass was forbidden. Christians were persecuted in Libya, Algeria, the Sudan, even in Egypt. How did our governments react? What was done to protect the interests of the

Church? Nothing! Not so much as a diplomatic protest. Why? Because our governments and media were in the hands of degenerate atheists, immoral materialists, utilitarian sceptics – men and women eager to promote the nonsensical egalitarianism of the atheist enlightenment, socialism, feminism, so-called racial justice and human rights. Comrades in arms. Fellow Knights of the Cross. Where is our modern St Louis? Where a Richard Coeur de Lion? Are we to desert the cause for which so many of our ancestors fought and died? Have we not shown, by our support for our fellow Catholics in Croatia, that where there is the will, battles can be won? Should that not encourage us to believe that, with a new crusade, we can also win the war? And should not the first campaign be to secure, in our European heartland, a Christian nation worthy of its past and confident of its future? Remember our motto, fellow Knights of the Cross, which is also our vow: 'For my honour, for my Church, for my God!'

Resounding cheers. 'Mad as a hatter,' whispered the bureaucrat priest in my ear. 'He says the same sort of thing every year.'

'Did you understand what he said?' asked the governessy Dame on my other side. 'He's my cousin, you know, on the Habsburg side. His mother is the sister of my brother Talman.'

'Indeed.'

'He should have mentioned Israel, don't you think? There, too, you know, the Jews persecute the Christians. They want to drive us out of Jerusalem and the Holy Land. But, because of the past, no one dares criticise them. They blackmail us with the Holocaust just as the Saudis do with oil.'

I looked towards Monika. Her head was bowed: I could not see the expression on her face. Babi? She exchanged a glance with her brother Adolf; then Adolf with Thomas; then Thomas with the blond Ignaz-Balthasar. Their eyes were bright with elation. So were those of all the younger Knights. The applause continued. Knives and forks were banged on the tables. Long live the Knights of the Cross! Hurrah!

## Sunday

I must have drunk more of the Gewürztraminer than I realised because after falling into a drunken slumber I awoke with a start an hour or two later. At first, I assumed that it was because the effect of the wine had worn off. I lay on my back in the dark, waiting to sleep again. Only slowly did I realise that I could hear the sound of voices, as if people were talking in the corridor outside my door. I sat up and listened. The voices were faint; I could not make out what was being said. I switched on my bedside lamp and looked at my clock. It was three in the morning. I crept to the door of my room. Silence. The voices were not coming from the corridor but from somewhere behind me. I turned and went to the concealed entrance that led down to the chapel. This was the source of the sound. I opened the door and in bare feet crept down the stairs to the balcony that overlooked the altar. The lights had been switched on in the chapel. On the steps of the altar sat Thomas Krull, facing twenty or thirty of the younger Knights seated in the pews. All still wore their robes as Knights of the Cross. Beside him stood Adolf von Willich holding a Bible. One by one, the others were coming forward to lay

240

their right hand on the Bible. As each did so, he said: 'In the name of Almighty God, I make this holy vow.' What vow? I had come in at the tail end of some ceremony.

Not wanting to be seen, I stepped back into the shadows and waited on the stairs. The last Knight returned to his pew. Then Thomas stepped forward and placed his hand on the Bible. 'I, too, swear this holy vow. May God make me worthy of your election, and give me the courage of my cousin Otto von Willich.' To which a chorus of bass voices said: 'Amen.' Then came the sound of shuffling feet. They left the chapel. The lights went out.

I groped my way back up the spiral staircase to my room. My feet were freezing. I curled up under my bedclothes and eventually went back to sleep.

### Monday

An exceptionally beautiful morning. From my window I can hear the birds singing in the garden below. I am tempted to join them, or to go for a walk in the woods; but I am also happy here in my room, sitting at my desk, breathing in the warm, scented air from the open window.

I am still turning over in my mind the events of yesterday and the day before. What were they up to in the chapel? Clearly, some extra occult ceremony of the younger Knights. Was Thomas their leader? Had it been Otto? And what had he meant by the courage of his cousin Otto? Or had it all been a dream?

Later that morning, they had all reappeared in the chapel

241

to attend High Mass said by the Archbishop, the concluding ceremony of the annual conclave of the Knights of the Cross. The venerable old prelate preached a homily that went some way to counter the rabid harangue of their Chancellor the night before. He reminded them that, in the time of their ancestors, violence was the only means available to resolve social conflicts, but that today we had learned from 'tragic experience' that the use of violence, even for the noblest ends, is self-defeating. It was now the duty of every Catholic to serve Christ, the Prince of Peace.

From where I sat by the altar, with four other priests who were concelebrating the mass, I could see the faces of the congregation, the Knights and Dames of the Cross. The older, Heinrich von Willich in particular, nodded in agreement at what was said by the Archbishop; but on the brows of the younger Knights there was a dissident frown. None felt disposed, or so it seemed, to 'turn the other cheek'.

But how much of their rhetoric is sabre-rattling and how much the ideology of a political movement? I feel I must come up with some convincing hypothesis for my article for the *Sunday Gazette*. I look back through the notes I made after talking with Paget in Cambridge and try to match the known facts with what I have seen. The armoured car; the accident; the small-arms shipped from Riga in a truck hired in the name of a subsidiary of Bettelheim Krull by two young men 'who did not seem like truck-drivers, more like schoolteachers'.

Could it be that one of them was Otto von Willich? Suddenly, a piece of the jigsaw slips into place on the board. The road accident that killed Otto was the collision with the British armoured car. It was Otto who drove the truck from Riga. Why had I not seen this before?

Even as I consider it, this hypothesis makes more and more sense. Otto, at the head of the younger Knights of the Cross, recruits disaffected German youths into some kind of political organisation dedicated to the establishment of some kind of European Fourth Reich. Did they plan to fire-bomb Muslim immigrants? And assassinate those who opposed them? From the rhetoric of the Chancellor on Saturday night, there can be no doubt that some of them believe in their right to use violence in pursuit of their objectives. Most of the mass murderers in history have felt that God was on their side.

Did they kill George? Did they discover that he was on the point of exposing them by naming the man who had been driving the truck? Certainly, Heinrich von Willich would have had little difficulty in persuading the German authorities to withhold the identity of his son: Heinrich was a leading Christian Democrat, a prominent member of the European Parliament at Strasbourg, a crony of Chancellor Kohl. George Harding, however, was outside the Germans' control. Nothing would have served his interests better than to expose as a racist and urban terrorist the eldest son of a prominent Federalist and the Grand Master of the Knights of the Cross.

How could they have discovered that George was on to them? Someone may have noticed the detective's enquiries, and perhaps frightened him into revealing his client's name. It would not have been difficult to discover that he was acting on the instructions of the brother-in-law of George Harding.

The picture begins to grow clearer, but it is still largely speculation. I must have confirmation for my article. I shall need something on tape. From Babi or Moni?

Almost certainly, both are ignorant of what their brothers were up to. Adolf might let it out, or Grunberger – if he knows.

I was able to place myself next to Adolf at lunch. 'It seemed to me,' I said, after a few preliminary remarks about Saturday's dinner, 'that there was a divergence of view between the Chancellor and the Archbishop over the strategy that should be followed by the Knights of the Cross.'

'Pah! Yes. Monsignor Blasburg is an old woman. So are all the bishops. He is sound enough himself, but he is in the hands of the liberals. They expend their energies on baiting the Pope, giving communion to divorcees and calling for women to be made priests. Meanwhile, the enemy advances. People leave the Church in droves, and who can blame them? Why should they pay extra tax to belong to a benevolent association led by a group of social workers in cassocks?'

'In cassocks?' said Babi. 'All the priests I know wear collars and ties.'

'You are unfair,' said Moni, facing us at the other side of the table. 'Monsignor Blasburg is a holy man. Didn't you feel that, Father Piotr?'

My principal impression of the Archbishop had been formed during the twenty minutes Nikolai and I had spent alone in his presence. It had been of a defensive, apologetic and unfortunate man. He almost wept when we presented him with our 'relic' of Bishop Lanskauskas – the threadbare, patchwork vestments from the gulag – and when we talked of the present day he lapped up Nikolai's account of our difficulties in Komsomolsk like a thirsty dog, and appeared actually to envy us our privations. 'Ah, if you knew, my dear children, how far we have come here in the West from the life of the Gospel. Pity the poor bishop who must govern a thousand priests, each with his own opinion, deal with delegations of hysterical feminists, answer to the Vatican for the writings of the theologians teaching in the Catholic universities in his diocese, and counsel the virtue of poverty while apportioning a budget of many millions of marks.'

We had made the appropriate rejoinder: Nikolai was particularly convincing in his sympathy for the Archbishop's woes. 'How much more insidious,' he had said, 'the temptations in a prosperous society such as yours, for truly, as the Apostle Paul said, "Money is the root of all evil." '

'Unless put to good use,' said the Archbishop, rising to convey that our chat was coming to an end. 'I have heard of your request for funds from Kreuzhilfe to build a church in Komsomolsk, and I should like you to know that I have made my own view clear that I can think of no worthier cause.'

As Nikolai left the room, the Archbishop had taken hold of my arm to hold me back. 'I have been asked, dear Father, if I would authorise you to hear confessions while you are here in my diocese, a request to which I am happy to agree. They have no chaplain resident here at Zelden, and I know that there have been differences between the family and the parish priest. It also refreshes the troubled conscience to be counselled by someone new, someone unknown, and any chance we have to encourage this sacrament, so woefully neglected in the West, must be taken, don't you think?'

'Certainly.' This was my answer to Monika's asking whether or not I had found the Archbishop a holy man.

245

She gave a triumphant smile at her brother. 'There. You see?'

'One can be holy and wrong-headed,' said Adolf.

'I get the impression,' I said, 'that it is not easy to be a bishop in Western Europe today.'

'You are more perceptive than some who live here.' Again, Monika's look seemed to challenge her brother.

Adolf yawned.

## Tuesday

After lunch today, Adolf took me aside and asked me if I would like to smoke a cigar. 'A real Havana, Father. My friend Helmuth von Gebsattel left a box as a house gift for Zelden.' He led me into the garden. 'And it's an innocent enough pleasure, surely? Something permitted, even for a priest?'

Pretending first that I had never previously smoked a cigar, I then acted out a charade of being reluctantly persuaded to accept one out of politeness; to take the Havana and let Adolf show me how to clip off its end, then light it with a match and draw the thick smoke into my mouth. I even coughed and spluttered as one might expect in a novice.

We sat on two wicker chaise-longues on a terrace looking out over the battlements towards the town. The huge cigar made Adolf seem like an adolescent aping an adult, and his manner lacked its usual confident bluster. 'It's not easy, Father,' he said, his eyes peering through the smoke towards the horizon, 'to be left with those two sisters.'

'Left?'

'By Otto. They both looked up to him as the older brother. They treated me as something of a joke.'

'Not Moni, surely?'

'Particularly Moni. She's the closest to me in age.'

'All brothers and sisters bicker from time to time.'

'I know. But the arguments Otto would have with Babi were somehow grown-up arguments about real things.'

'They can't have seen eye to eye on many issues.'

Adolf hesitated before he answered. 'Oddly enough, though they were quite different in temperament, they got on extraordinarily well. In fact, Otto was probably the only person whom Babi really loved.'

'I had gained the impression,' I said, 'that like Mary Magdalene, Barbara had perhaps loved too many rather than too few.'

'She has had lovers but I don't think she ever loved them, certainly not in the way she loved Otto.' He stopped, drew on his cigar, and when he spoke again went off at a different tangent. 'You may not realise, Father, seeing us here at Zelden, that just as it is not easy to be a bishop in the modern world, it is also difficult being a von Willich or, for that matter, a German. We carry a heavy burden from our past.'

'No one should feel guilt for things they did not do.'

He laughed. 'If only the whole world was so forgiving.'

'We no longer hold the Jews accountable for the crucifixion of Christ.'

'But it has taken us nineteen hundred years to forgive them, and it will take another nineteen hundred years for the world to forgive the Germans for Auschwitz.'

'Christ commanded us to forgive.'

'But not the God of the Old Testament. The Jews demand an eye for an eye and a tooth for a tooth, and believe that the sins of the fathers should be visited on the children unto the sixth generation.'

'An Auschwitz for Germans?'

'Hardly practicable. But a cultural incarceration.'

247

'I don't understand.'

'We have been made the pariahs of history. No attempt is made to distinguish between the different strands in the German tradition. Bismarck is tarred with the same brush as Hitler.'

'Is that,' I asked, 'why you want a united Europe?'

'Of course. We cannot live with our national past so we cannot envisage a national future. We must change the parameters of the nation and, as it were, dilute the German poison with the antidotes of the British and French.'

'Is that the only reason?'

'No.' He paused to puff out more smoke. 'I should like an influence commensurate to its worth. The new world order should not be left to the United States.'

'Can it be done?'

'As the English say, "Where there is a will there is a way." '

'But it is precisely the English, as I understand it, who do not share your vision.'

'They will have to join us in the end. They have nowhere else to go.'

## Wednesday

Rereading my notes on yesterday's conversation with Adolf, particularly his remarks about the Germans' predicament after Auschwitz, I could not silence a sneering voice within me saying, 'Poor little Krauts' – a voice that in due course took on the specific timbre and tone of a young woman educated at South Hampstead High School and New College, Oxford; the voice, in other words, of my wife Ruth. It was Ruth who was mocking the confessions of this German Knight.

In this, Adolf is right: if I am sure of anything, it is that Ruth will never forgive the Germans for trying to exterminate her people. There are certainly specifics: her great-grandmother and two great-aunts died in the camps; but the anger she might justifiably feel at this cruel fact is not restricted to Hitler, Himmler, Heydrich, Bormann, Stangl and other perpetrators with names unknown. Instead, her antipathy extends to anything German, from Wagner's operas to the last slice of pumpernickel. It is not consistent. She rode in her father's BMW, used her mother's Miele washing-machine and ate food from our Bosch fridge. She maintained that her principles were compatible with her desire for a Mercedes because 'Nowadays they're made by Turks.'

Her Teutonophobia was selective, and also irrational because Ruth scarcely thought of herself as a Jew. She was, after all, an atheist: how could there be a chosen people if there was no one to do the choosing? She thought of herself as British – secular, enlightened, rational. She was embarrassed by the pastrami and gefilte fish that her parents sometimes served for lunch. And the pumpernickel. 'How can you eat pumpernickel?'

Her parents, born in Germany, had kept their taste for the culture of their early youth. They liked pumpernickel, sausage, sauerkraut, Bach, Bruckner, even Wagner. They, too, felt angry about Auschwitz but they did not blame the Germans alone. 'Didn't you know,' my father-in-law once said, 'that by nineteen forty-five fewer than half of those in the Waffen SS were ethnic Germans?' He had been talking to his daughter, but the remarks were aimed at me. No use reminding him that my father was not a Hauptsturmführer in the SS Panzerdivision 'Totenkopf', but a Church of England rector: Samuel Mayer disliked Christians, especially

249

Catholics, whom he felt had prepared the ground for the Nazis and then tacitly condoned their attempt to exterminate the Jews. How else could you explain the silence of the Pope? Hitler, Himmler, Heydrich all sprang from a Catholic culture. Croatia, Lithuania, Slovakia all joined enthusiastically in the Nazi pogroms.

No use naming those Christians who had opposed the Nazis and lost their lives, such as Pastor Niemöller, Dietrich Bonhoeffer or Bernhard Lichtenberg, because they were few and the killers many. Nor could I persuade him that the anti-Semitic Franciscans in Herzegovina should be distinguished from the Rector of Avelscombe. To my father-in-law, the human race was divided between Jews and gentiles. Hitler was a gentile. I was a gentile. Ruth was a Jew.

Ruth ridiculed her parents' anxieties. 'They always feel uneasy outside Hampstead.' She was emancipated, her judgements formed by reason alone. Her dislike of anything German was based on facts, not prejudice. Germans were pedantic, humourless, unstylish, dull. 'All work and no play makes Hans a crashing bore.' She had none of her parents' blanket prejudice against gentiles: she had married one, after all.

But then one day, when she thought she might be pregnant, this plain-sailing ship hit a rock. We lay in bed one Sunday morning discussing names, then schools, then godparents and the christening.

'What christening?'

'But surely he will be christened?'

'She most certainly will not.'

'You can't have godparents without a christening.'

'Yes, you can.'

'It would upset my parents if he wasn't christened.'

'It would upset mine if she was.'

'It's part of our culture.'

'Crap.'

'I agreed not to marry in a church. You owe me.'

'It's our life, Michael, not theirs.'

'So he won't be circumcised?'

'Of course she'll … he'll be circumcised.'

'For what reason?'

'All boys are circumcised.'

'I'm not circumcised.'

'You would be if you'd been born in America.'

'No one in Europe is circumcised unless he's a Muslim or a Jew.'

'Is that what you're afraid of? That he might be mistaken for a Jew?'

Sigh: 'There is no medical justification for inflicting a painful mutilation on a newborn child.'

'Crap. There's less chance of disease.'

'And more chance of sexual malfunction.'

'Such as?'

'The foreskin is there to protect the penis: without one, it grows insensitive, so middle-aged men who are circumcised wait for ever for an orgasm.'

'And young men who *aren't* circumcised come too soon.'

What would Alison have made of this dispute about circumcision? Why did I never mention it in therapy? And why do I recall it now, sitting in Schloss Zelden, meditating on the unhappy history of the Germans and the Jews? Details are revealing. For example, looking back at the last page of this journal, I see that I have recorded Ruth saying: 'It's our life, Michael, not theirs.' The significant word here is my name, 'Michael'. In Britain, the interpolation of an interlocutor's name is uncommon among the educated classes: it is usually heard from the mouths of working-class criminals in a tight spot. They think it gives credence to some preposterous lie. In the United States, on the other hand, such an interpolation is ubiquitous and is consequently heard frequently from the mouths of actors and actresses in American films.

It is from these films, rather than from our working-class criminals, that Ruth picked up the habit. She used to insist upon seeing every film that Hollywood served up on the screen. She usually had to drag me along: I hated to feel, as I invariably did, that I had been suckered by Hollywood hype; that a small slice of my hard-earned income was going into the pockets of cynical moguls. So many of the films were the same: excitable policemen of Italian extraction confronting excitable criminals of Italian extraction; foul language, violence, extravagant stunts.

What I came slowly to realise was that the American movie, for Ruth, was the source of her identity; that all her talk of being British was, as she would put it, crap. Ruth had become what one might call a 'universal American', someone who bears only a passing resemblance to an actual American – say, a schoolteacher in Cleveland, Ohio – but who wears jeans and feels at home in downtown Los Angeles or New York. Is this because these are Jewish cities? No. There are more Irish or Hispanics. But the Jews colour the culture: they have made the urban seaboard of America their own.

I once put this to Ruth. 'You're pathetic,' she said. 'You're always trying to make me feel foreign, just to bolster your own self-esteem.' After which she smiled and we made love: in those days, sex – even uncircumcised sex – meant more to us both than ideas.

## Thursday

A morning in the library. Grunberger shows me around
the von Willich archive. Letters and diaries of the von
Willichs are open for my inspection. I start with the
letters of Albrecht von Willich, Kaspar's older brother.
Painful depictions of life in the trenches. Extraordinarily
pure and idealistic, despite the slaughter. He was killed
on 18 September 1917, near Brimont in northern France.

## Friday

At lunch, Adolf asked us if we would like to accompany
his grandmother and his two sisters on a visit to the
Carmelite convent this afternoon. He explained that the
von Willichs, as the founders, have an hereditary right to
enter even the enclosed parts of the convent. 'You can
imagine what some of our ancestors made of that
privilege,' he said, with a wink at Nikolai. I caught
Monika's eye. She blushed.

'But the privilege has not been used for several
centuries,' Adolf went on. 'This afternoon we will be
received in the guest house by the Reverend Mother,
who is most impatient to meet our Russian priest.'

We set out at three to walk through the woods to the
convent across the valley. Ilse von Willich led the way,
accompanied by Adolf; Nikolai and Monika followed. I
brought up the rear with Babi. We talked about this and
that. I wanted to catch up with Monika but Babi held

253

back. Eventually, when they were out of earshot, she said: 'Tell me, Father, is your friend trustworthy?'

For a moment, I was baffled. What friend? Then I realised that she meant Nikolai. 'What do you mean, trustworthy?'

'Can I trust him with my sister?'

I walked on in silence, pondering this question. Fortunately, people expect such pauses from priests: wisdom comes from unhurried reflection; we wait for God's counsel rather than saying the first thing that comes into our heads. In this case, I especially needed time to think. Babi's question obliged me to face the disagreeable truth that, until now, I had been reluctant to acknowledge: that Nikolai was taken with Monika and almost certainly had designs on her of a doubtful kind. I could see this. Babi could see it too. But if I encouraged her suspicions then it might cast doubt on Nikolai's role as a pious Catholic from Komsomolsk. His flirtation could put our mission in jeopardy; even our lives might be at risk.

'I cannot imagine,' I said at last, 'that Nikolai would behave dishonourably towards Monika, but it is possible that he may have become fond of her. She is, after all, both virtuous and kind.'

'Is he married?'

'No.'

'That seems strange when he is hardly young, and clearly a man who is drawn to women.'

'He was married, but his wife died.'

'Did they have children?'

'She died in childbirth. The medical facilities in Komsomolsk, as you may realise, are quite primitive.'

'Poor Nikolai.'

'It was some years ago.'

'He seems to have made a good recovery.'

'What do you mean?'

She paused. 'Let me put it this way, Father. You are unquestionably what one would expect in a priest, but your friend Nikolai does not strike me as a pious type.'

'You can see into his soul?'

'Yes. Through his eyes.'

'And what do you see?'

'Someone lecherous and materialistic.'

I waited, and then said 'more in sorrow than in anger': 'I think you misjudge him.'

'I have considerable experience of men,' said Babi, 'and your friend Nikolai, I think, of women.'

'How can you tell?'

'By the way he looked at me when we first met.'

'He was sizing you up?'

'Yes.'

'And you were found wanting? I find that hard to believe.'

'Thank you for the compliment, Father. I was found wanting only, I think, when my sister appeared ...'

'If what you say is true, it would seem that you and Nikolai have more in common than Nikolai and Monika.'

'That's what makes us of no interest to one another. We're two of a kind.'

'Surely a marriage of true minds —'

'The fun is in the seduction, Father. The thrill of the chase.'

I shook my head sadly. 'All this is so far outside my experience.'

'But you listen to sinners in the confessional, Father. Do they never tell you that love without a challenge is somewhat banal?'

'Russians are simple people.'

'Nikolai does not seem a simple person. He appears to know exactly what he is up to.'

'And what is that?'

'Seducing my sister.'

I had no need to simulate agitation. 'But surely Monika is incapable of being seduced?'

Babi smiled. 'By conventional means, certainly. She has turned down a dozen of Germany's most eligible bachelors with holy scorn. But as you must know, Father Piotr, one should never underestimate the wiles of the Devil.'

'Indeed, no.'

'And where one approach fails, another may succeed in capturing the heart, such as compassion with a dash of guilt.'

'I don't understand.'

'Then let me explain.' Babi was silent for a moment, as if considering carefully the words she should use. 'Take the case of a German girl who, aged nineteen, goes to the Free University in Berlin. There she meets an American student who is Jewish. He tells her that his grandparents died in Auschwitz. Her grandparents, of course, fought for Hitler during the war. The past weighs heavily on both the German girl and the American. He makes little distinction between the German Army and Himmler's SS. However, rather than being repelled by the German race, the American is strongly drawn to the female of the species, particularly one with blonde hair and long legs. He wants to sleep with the girl. She does not want to sleep with him, but eventually she decides that *it is the least thing she can do* to make up for the Germans' monstrous crimes.'

'But that is ridiculous.'

Babi flushed. 'Easy for you to say that, Father. Men can be remarkably persistent, and women easily confused. The girl in my story came to feel that to refuse the

American student would be taken by him to mean that she was prejudiced against Jews.'

'Did he accuse her of that?'

'Oh, yes.'

'And was she?'

'Prejudiced? How could she know? He was the first Jew she had ever met. There were things about him that she did not like. She found him physically unattractive but she went to bed with him all the same, just to prove to him and herself that she was not prejudiced.'

'Did she grow to love him?'

'Oh …' She waved her hand dismissively. 'You know how it is with girls at that age. She persuaded herself that if she was sleeping with him, it must mean that she loved him, until she found out that he was doing the rounds of her blonde-haired, long-legged German friends.'

'Was she upset?'

Babi shrugged. 'Not especially. At least she had proved to him and to herself that she was not anti-Semitic. But then others came along who had to be persuaded.'

'She had affairs with other Jewish students?'

'Yes. With two or three of his American friends.'

'It is pernicious,' I said, 'to feel obliged to sleep with someone one does not love.'

'And there is an ironic twist to her story,' said Babi. 'She subsequently discovered that none of them was in fact a Jew, but they had learned that pretending to be Jewish was a fail-safe method of getting young German girls into bed.'

I shook my head in disbelief. 'It sounds to me as if she was somewhat unprepared for the realities of life.'

'She had had a sheltered upbringing and, in any case, for a number of reasons, had no very high estimate of herself. But with a girl of a different kind, with an equally sheltered upbringing – a girl who was pious and prized purity, it would be devastating if she was ever to be used in the same way.'

'You mean Monika?'

'I mean Monika.'

'If she truly prizes purity, she will not be open to seduction.'

We turned a corner in the woods and saw, sitting on a log, Monika and Nikolai in earnest conversation.

'Perhaps he will ask her to marry him,' said Babi.

'That is impossible,' I said.

'Why?'

'Because ... because he could not support her, nor could she endure life in Komsomolsk.'

'But it is precisely that life that would appeal to her,' said Babi. 'She is determined to do something dramatic for God.'

'You must dissuade her.'

'You are the one in the confidence of the Almighty.'

'But I am not in the confidence of Monika.'

'But you are, more than you think, because of your position as a priest.'

'She has never confided in me.'

'Not as yet. But who do you think asked the Archbishop to permit you to hear confessions?'

'Not Monika, surely.'

'Of course. Although there are other members of the family who may take advantage of your stay at Zelden.'

'One need only confess,' I said quickly, 'if there is some serious sin on one's conscience.'

'Perhaps there is, Father Piotr, perhaps there is.'

We reached the gatehouse of the convent. Adolf rang the bell. We waited. Silence. Then a small spy-hole set in the door, which itself was set into the heavy wooden gates, opened and a voice asked: 'Yes?'

258

'It is me, Sister,' said Monika. 'I am here with my grandmother and our friends. Reverend Mother is expecting us.'

Bolts were drawn back. The door was opened. A nun in a full habit stood back to let us in. Her head was lowered; her face hidden by her cowl.

Moni led the way along the cool, clean corridors to the parlour, a large room with whitewashed walls and portraits of earlier superiors. Here we were joined by the Reverend Mother; the nun who had opened the gate brought in a tray with a pot of coffee and a plate of petit fours. A gesture from the Reverend Mother dismissed her; another led Monika to pour out the coffee and offer us the petit fours. Moni's manner was proprietorial, as if she already felt she belonged to the community. Every now and then she glanced towards the Reverend Mother for a sign of approval, which was given by the older woman with a smile.

Our conversation was formal. I asked about the convent – its history, the size of the community – while the Reverend Mother put questions to Nikolai and me in return, questions that were intelligent and to the point. How likely was the conversion of Russia? Could Orthodox suspicion of the Roman Catholics ever be allayed? I answered as best I could, pretending to a degree of *naïveté* and ignorance. ' "For God, nothing is impossible." ' As I spoke, I began to fear that the powerful intuition of this contemplative might see through my disguise. I stumbled over my German to cover the inadequacy of my answers, and what doubts she might have felt were overcome when I took out the grubby little Lithuanian prayer-book from the gulag, 'Mary Save Us', and showed her the rosary made of knotted string. 'Ah, the suffering, the suffering …' And so on.

Babi and her grandmother looked bored. Moni listened intently, her eyes first on the Reverend Mother, then on me, then on the Reverend Mother again, as if ours was a historic encounter that she must remember for the sake of posterity. She seemed determined that each of us should approve of the other to validate her love for the convent and her esteem for me. And this we did. I had no reason to doubt that here was a wise and holy woman, or she to doubt that I was a Russian priest.

It was Nikolai who was ill at ease and, at that point in our conversation ('Ah, the suffering, the suffering'), suddenly said, in an unusually vehement tone of voice: 'Yet we must also ask ourselves why it was that the great mass of the Russian people did so little to defend their Church.'

'It does seem surprising,' said Moni, 'when the Russians were supposedly so holy.'

'I believe we can ascribe it,' said Nikolai, 'to the monastic tradition.'

The Reverend Mother looked perplexed. 'But that was so strong in the Orthodox religion.'

'Precisely. The principal witness to the truths of the Gospel was to be found behind the high walls of the monastic foundations. It was remote from the everyday life of ordinary people, particularly the urban proletariat, which became easy prey for the apostles of the new Bolshevik religion.'

'That is undoubtedly true,' I muttered, wondering what Nikolai was up to.

'What is important,' said Nikolai, 'is not to make the same mistake again. It is precisely this same urban proletariat, now comprising the bulk of the Russian population, that is left without faith or hope. And while, no doubt, the prayers said in beautiful old monasteries and convents have their value, it is my firm conviction that the need now, in Russia, is to emulate the Apostles after Pentecost. We must evangelise among the people – in the market-place, in the factory, in the home.'

I glanced at the Reverend Mother, then at Moni. If the older woman felt rebuked by Nikolai's scornful reference to a beautiful old monastery, she did not show it. It was principally Monika who seemed confused. 'And yet prayer can be so powerful,' she said.

'Invincible,' said Nikolai. 'But you can pray at the lathe in a noisy factory as well as among beautiful woods and hills, and you can pray through your actions as well as your words, visiting lonely old people isolated in their high-rise flats, or old drunks who live on the streets. One good deed undertaken by one of Komsomolsk's Catholics is like a stone thrown into water – the ripples reach to the far corners of the pond. But while the harvest is plentiful, the labourers are few.'

The Reverend Mother now took us to the convent's chapel – a fine example of baroque architecture, like the chapel at Zelden, which in any other mood I might have admired. But somehow, after Nikolai's diatribe, the painted putti and writhing plaster saints seemed sensuous and indulgent, high art, perhaps, but nothing to do with religion. The Reverend Mother was polite, pointing out architectural features of interest and telling about the convent's history, but she said no more than necessary and seemed relieved when she saw us out through the gate.

On our walk back through the woods, Nikolai and I drew ahead of the Countess and her two granddaughters. 'What did you mean by that outburst?' I whispered in Russian.

'Outburst? What outburst?'

261

'Denigrating the contemplative life in that way.'

'I was making conversation, that was all.'

'You could have chosen to say something less provocative. Monika was quite upset.'

'So much the better.'

'Why do you say that?'

'Because it would be quite absurd for a girl like that to bury herself alive behind those walls.'

'That may be so but it is not part of our mission to determine the future of Monika von Willich.'

'We must use whatever methods we can to gain the confidence of any member of the family.'

'If anything, it seems to me that you will have lost their confidence by what you said.'

'Quite to the contrary. The old Countess and Babi agreed.'

'But Monika was offended.'

'So it might have seemed, but at a certain level I believe that she, too, was pleased.'

## Saturday

Another morning spent looking through the archives, which, thanks to the diligence of Grunberger, are remarkably complete. There are, for example, as Grunberger had promised, the diaries of both Kaspar and Ilse von Willich. When they became engaged in 1941, they knew they would be immediately separated by the war. Each therefore promised the other to keep a record of daily life. Kaspar's entries are inevitably hurried; his Panzer regiment was in the vanguard of the army invading Russia. But the tone is exultant. The Bolsheviks scatter before his tanks. The German motherland is triumphant. Ilse's diary is simple and dull. Pages and pages of trivia in a neat, methodical hand. Hard to think of her as the same person as the scatty old lady of yesterday's walk.

Grunberger has cross-referenced the diaries and their correspondence so that their letters can be read in the right place. Ilse's are as dull as her diary, Kaspar's at first jaunty: war is wonderful when you are winning and the weather is fine. He discusses plans for their future when the war comes to an end. Then, little by little, a note of caution creeps in. Perhaps the end is not as imminent as he has supposed. Also, oblique references to horror; to things 'it is hard even for a soldier to witness and endure'. Clearly, the contrast between the harshness of his own experience and the banality of his fiancée's preoccupations sometimes irk him: 'Really, Ilse, you should not complain if the worst of your mother's privations is having to shell her own peas.'

Ilse complains in her diary of this rebuke. 'What do German men expect? They confine their women to the home and then are bored by our domestic preoccupations.' She decides to do some kind of war work in Berlin but her parents are against it. Kaspar, too, sends a veto from the Eastern Front. The working woman is an alien idea, at once Bolshevik and American.

Slowly but inexorably, their future recedes. Both become tormented, Kaspar by the horror of war, Ilse by the boredom of life on her parents' estate. Kaspar is posted to the headquarters of the South-east Front at Vinitsa in the Ukraine. Ilse asks if he cannot get leave so that they can marry. His sense of honour will not permit it. It will not even permit him to remain behind the lines. A Knight of the Cross, above all the Grand Master, must be in the thick of battle. He volunteers for active service and is sent to join the Sixth Army at Stalingrad.

It is only now that Kaspar von Willich suggests a proxy

wedding. Ilse agrees, and wears a white dress and veil for the ceremony in Münster Cathedral. She is now Countess von Willich, but this changes nothing. Had she imagined that tying the bond would remove her frustration? It was not the wedding but the honeymoon that she craved; a week with her warrior husband in a double bed.

On 19 November 1942 the Russians counter-attack. Three days later, they have encircled the German army in Stalingrad. Kaspar, mired in blood and mud, has no inkling of the young woman's yearning. His diary is now reduced to brief outlines of the day-to-day military operations. They rarely refer to Ilse, and when they do, it is only to note how his memories of home have become peripheral and unreal.

Then he returns – that mysterious and unexplained recall to Berlin that gained him a place on one of the last planes to escape the Soviet encirclement. Ilse is incredulous when she gets the news; joy is jotted down in a quite untypical scrawl. She rushes to Berlin. They are reunited in her parents' flat. No need for a further ceremony. They are legally man and wife. The long-postponed wedding night can now take place. They dine at the Adlon. Later Ilse notes in her diary: 'I should have realised at once how much he had changed. He could not eat the rich food. He said his stomach had grown used to a diet of dry biscuits and tinned meat.'

Were his other carnal appetites also diminished? They had the flat in Charlottenburg to themselves, but Ilse's only comments are brief and chaste. 'We spent our first night together as man and wife.' Then: 'Kaspar tormented by the plight of his men. He says that without a direct order from the Führer he would not have left them.'

It is not difficult to imagine the feelings of a bride who is told by her husband that he would rather be back in a bivouac in Stalingrad than with her in a bed in Berlin. For the next few months she 'plays house' in Charlottenburg, and catches up with those friends who are living in Berlin. Kaspar rises early and works late. He anaesthetises his guilt with hard work. But what is that work? Why was he recalled? The most plausible theory, which also applies to his surviving the 20 July plot, is that Hitler felt that, as Grand Master, he should be preserved.

Ilse, in her diary, does not speculate: indeed, after the rapturous scrawl of those entries when she was anticipating her union with her husband, the writing becomes neat again and the entries banal. She is glad to have escaped from her parents and the country, and is eventually permitted by Kaspar to work as a clerical assistant in the Foreign Office. But her preoccupations remain social and domestic, with reference to bombing raids when they occur. When Kaspar is mentioned, it is with a certain detachment. Even when he is arrested over the 20 July plot, her diary shows no particular anxiety or anguish. 'If they suspect him it is only because they suspect anyone who knew Stauffenberg and the others. They will soon realise that K. would be quite incapable of breaking his oath of loyalty to the Führer.'

Why did Ilse continue to keep a diary? It is clear, by this time, that Kaspar von Willich no longer read what she wrote or kept a journal of his own. She seemed to do so partly because she was methodical – recording the events of each day had become a habit – and partly because she could confide in her notebook what she could not say to anyone else. If a real friendship had grown up with her husband, perhaps the diary entries would have stopped. Because it did not, she continued to address through her diary the handsome hero she had earlier seen off to the war.

She was loyal to Kaspar. When he was in prison, she lobbied their influential friends to make sure he was well treated. There was some urgency to her pleading because she was now pregnant. After Kaspar's release by the Gestapo, they left Berlin and returned to Zelden. There she did what she could to run a household that the war had deprived of most of its staff. Her son Heinrich was born at Zelden, an event described in her diary with no emotion or expression of joy. Indeed, flipping back through the pages, it seems as if the pregnancy itself had come as a surprise: she first alludes to it only six months or so before the baby is born, and then to say: 'Doctor Drecher thinks that I may be pregnant. I tell him that it is most unlikely.' Unlikely or not, it was true.

They wait at Zelden for the war to end. Ilse, the conscientious wife, takes pride in ensuring that there is always food on the table, but this relative abundance in a starving country exacerbates Kaspar's remorse. 'He eats little. His mind is in Russia with his men.' Some days later: 'I suggest fetching a bottle of wine from the cellar to celebrate K.'s birthday: he frowns and forbids it. "How can we carouse while our soldiers die?" A pity because there are so many bottles that are already past their best.'

Gloomy, silent meals, except when Kaspar's brother Lothar comes to stay. 'Lothar ignores K.'s protests: three bottles of Burgundy from the cellar. They stay up discussing what is to become of Germany after the war. I am permitted to listen but K. is not pleased if I join in. Is it because I am a woman or from a Protestant family? I am not sure. Both think that it is the Catholics who will have to pick up the pieces.'

In April 1945, the Germans surrender. Zelden is requisitioned by the British Army and the von Willichs move to

266

their estate at Parsheim. A cook and a nursemaid go with them. Kaspar's mood improves. He goes in and out of Münster where he meets with Lothar, other lay Catholics and the Archbishop.

But now there appears, for the first time, in Ilse's diary 'the Englishman', or, in the first entry, 'a young English officer with a driver', who asks for Kaspar von Willich. 'Most polite. He speaks good German. I offered him mint tea, which was all we had. He accepted and made compliments about the house and little Heinrich. Before he left he said there were questions he had to ask Kaspar.' The Englishman leaves. The next day, Ilse learns that he has been detained in Münster by the British military police.

The entries in Ilse's diary now become brief and broken, but with Grunberger's annotations it is possible to put together a narrative that goes like this. The English officer returns (she refers to him only and always as 'Der Engländer' or 'Der E.'). He tells her that she, too, must answer some questions (Grunberger: 'This refers to the 130 questions contained in the *Fragebogen* to be completed by those under investigation by the denazification commission'). He tells her that she should realise that truthful answers could help her husband. 'Why should he need help?' 'There are matters that need to be clarified.' He asks her if Kaspar told her why he was recalled from Stalingrad. 'No.' He then asks her about his friends – whether he knew Stauffenberg, Beck, Trott, Moltke and, particularly, Henning von Treschkow. She concedes that some were his friends. 'Did your husband ever discuss the plot to assassinate Hitler?' 'Afterwards, of course.' 'Before?' 'How could he? He did not know.' The young Englishman writes down her answers. Then: 'From the files now in my possession, Countess, it is clear that he knew about the conspiracy only too well.' 'He was a conspirator?' 'After a fashion.' Ilse does not understand. The Englishman smiles, a cold smile. 'Your husband, Kaspar von Willich, received a personal command from the Führer to return to Berlin. This was made at the request of Himmler. He suspected disaffection in the officer corps. Your husband, as Grand Master, would be a valuable recruit for any conspiracy.' 'Do you mean he knew about Stauffenberg's plan?' 'Not the time or the place, but even before the event he was in a position to pass names to the SS.'

Ilse von Willich is incredulous. She refuses to believe what she is told. But the Englishman taps the file on his knee. 'It is all here, in this file which we have recovered from the headquarters of the Gestapo.'

(Note by Grunberger: 'It seems unlikely that this file contained anything more than the London *Times*. It was the policy of the British Foreign Office to denigrate the martyrs of 20 July, portraying them as reactionary militarists in the Junker mould. They gave minimal recognition to their widows and children, and withheld evidence that would have helped Ernst von Weizsacker when the Americans put him on trial. Clearly, the political division of the Control Commission followed the same policy, and this led to the arrest of the Grand Master. Possibly, the Labour Government in Britain wished to discredit the emerging Christian Democrat grouping in their zone. It would seem that the young officer questioning the Countess used this policy to pursue an agenda of his own.')

Ilse von Willich is wholly confused by what she has been told. She cannot conceive that her husband would be capable of such dishonour. But, then, like every German officer, he had taken an oath to obey the Führer, so possibly his sense of honour had dictated obedience to a direct *Führerbefehl*. She recalled his unhappiness on his return from Stalingrad; the symptoms of an inner torment, perhaps a conflict of loyalty. There was also the riddle of his arrest after 20 July and subsequent release.

But … She turns to the Englishman. 'This must never be known.' 'It will not only be known,' says the Englishman, 'but will form the bases of charges.' 'But you will be dishonouring the Grand Master of the Knights of the Cross.' 'So much the better.' She pleads. Does he not appreciate the unique standing of the Grand Master? He is, in a sense, the leader of Germany's lay Catholics. His influence in a new Germany could be enormous, and it would almost certainly be for the good. He had never been a Nazi; he had loathed the Nazis. If, by any chance, he had spoken to the Gestapo, it was only because of his oath of obedience to Hitler.

She senses that she is getting nowhere. She expresses astonishment in her diary that someone so young could be so cold. (Grunberger: 'Why does she think the Grand Master's fate is in the hands of this one young officer? Undoubtedly, this was what he led her to understand.') She now makes a personal plea. Think of the honour of the family, the future of her son. 'Think of the shame it will bring to the name of Willich.' The Englishman laughs. 'Isn't shame what it deserves?'

Yet he lingers and Ilse must have sensed that he had some trade-off in mind. She was still young, unquestionably beautiful – twenty-two or so – and far healthier than most of the German population. Had she sensed his interest? 'Save him the shame, I beg you,' she pleads, 'save him the shame.' The English officer looks at her face, then her body. 'What are you suggesting, Countess? That shame is a commodity that can be traded?' 'It is my duty to my husband to do anything I can.' Did she say this to the Englishman, or merely write it in her diary to justify what follows? 'But what can you do?' asks the

Englishman. 'That is for you to say.' His eyes look at her again as if she was a heifer at the market. 'A beautiful young woman is herself a commodity,' he says. 'Dishonour for dishonour. Shame for shame. Why not?' (Note by Grunberger: 'This was almost certainly always the officer's intention.')

The bargain is struck. The next day, the cook and nursemaid are told to take the baby Heinrich to the village of Parsheim. The English officer's driver remains with the jeep. There takes place the first of several encounters. Fraternisation with the conquered enemy is forbidden; the Englishman is running a considerable risk; yet his visits continue and it becomes clear from the diary entries that Ilse's sense of degradation is soon replaced by an insatiable passion. Does he become more affectionate or was she in masochistic thrall to his coldness and perversity? Whatever the cause, after a month she writes:

'Oh, God, how I dread him going. I beg him to do what he can to delay Kaspar's return.'

## Monday

I returned to the library this morning to find Grunberger at his desk. He offers me a chair. I tell him that I was there on Saturday, looking through the archive.

'Yes, I noticed that someone had been reading Countess Ilse's diaries.'

'As you told me earlier, it seems quite extraordinary that she permits them to be read.'

'It is quite probable,' said Grunberger, 'that the Countess has forgotten that she kept such a diary, or that she placed it in the archive – and should she remember, she may have little recollection of what she wrote in it so many years ago.'

'The most dramatic implications, as I understand it, are that her husband, Count Kaspar, betrayed his friends in the officer corps after the failure of the July plot.'

'Indeed. But no one now would give credence to such a charge.'

'How can they be sure?'

'Because no evidence has appeared from any other source. Even if the Englishman had a file, which I doubt, and even if he destroyed it in return for ... as it were, as his part of the bargain, it seems unlikely that such information would not have been known to his superiors in the British Control Commission, or that it would not have emerged from other files in other hands. The Soviets, after all, occupied the centre of Berlin. They would hardly have hesitated to use any material in their possession against Count Kaspar, who became a prominent Christian Democratic politician at the height of the Cold War.'

'Then why was Countess Ilse so ready to believe it?'

Grunberger raised his eyebrows. 'Here, Reverend Father, we can only revert to a measure of speculative psychology. There is no doubt that the Count returned from Stalingrad in a state of depression. As a result of this, or even for other reasons, the physical aspect of their married life was a disappointment to the Countess who was, after all, young and healthy, and who had waited for so long. Enter the English officer. He, too, was young and, we may presume, good-looking. Also a conqueror, after all. May we suppose an immediate attraction? But neither could simply fall into the arms of the other. The Countess, after all, had been raised to observe the highest standards of propriety. Only a higher duty could persuade her to abandon them; only the sense that by giving herself to another man she was not betraying her husband but saving him.'

'And the Englishman? Why should he go through the same charade?'

'Because he, too, had mixed feelings. Remember the anger felt against the Germans at this time, just when the full horror of the concentration camps came to be known. He hates his former enemies, but he is attracted to this slim young woman. Fraternisation is forbidden, there can be no candlelit dinners, but a cold indulgence – that is something different. The rape of a Sabine woman. The spoils of war. He can both punish his enemy and satisfy his desire.'

'A desire, it seems, she came to share.'

'So it would seem. There is no question but that the Countess Ilse came to love her Englishman. They continued to see one another long after the end of the war.'

'Have you been able to identify the Englishman?'

'Not for certain.' Grunberger leaned forward to open a drawer in his desk from which he took a list of names printed on faded paper. 'There were a number of lieutenants serving with the political division of the British Control Commission, but none were posted to Münster as such.' He handed me the list. 'I hope to visit London shortly because last year, under the fifty-year rule, many of the official documents covering the denazification process became available to scholars. But this would be only to confirm what I learned from other sources.'

'What was that?'

Grunberger took on an expression of great self-satisfaction. 'Although the Countess's journal ends with the arrival of the Englishman, she continued to keep an appointments diary, and I noticed that every year, in the second week in June, she always spent a week on her own in a spa of some kind – sometimes Baden-Baden, later

272

Bad Ems, and finally, after 1953, Bad Reichenhall. Purporting to be a scholar doing some postgraduate research, I was able to examine the guest registers of the hotels where she stayed and always, every year, there is an English fellow guest.'

'And who was that?'

'The third name on your list. Lieutenant Paget.'

*Tuesday*

When you consider an old lady, it is hard to believe that she was once young – timid, trembling, yearning, besotted with love, weak with desire. I watched the Countess Ilse at lunch today, eating greedily with clacking false teeth, snapping at the maid, her face a mask of rouge and powder, creased and wrinkled with age. She was sitting, as she usually did, at the far end of the table with Babi at her side. Only now does it occur to me that she has shown no signs of piety and no interest in our Siberian venture. Yet our stay at Zelden was at her personal invitation. Was she put up to it by Paget? I cannot escape a growing feeling that I have been not just deceived but used.

Certainly, Paget had told me there were things he could not tell me, sources he could not reveal. But does this mean that the old lady has always known who I am? If so, might she not tell Babi? And Babi, Adolf? And Adolf, Thomas? With the end result that I will accidentally 'fall' from the ramparts of Zelden, and Nikolai choke on a Westphalian sausage? By what right did Paget entrust my life to the discretion of his faded mistress? What senile intrigue has been concocted between them?

I look down the table. Babi smiles. No sign in her eyes that she knows I am a fraud. The same is true of Adolf, who drones on beside me about the need to reform the political structures of the European Community. Further down the table, Monika. I cannot see her face. It is turned towards Nikolai. He is listening intently to what she says.

Should I warn Nikolai? After lunch, I suggest a walk in the woods. I wait until we are a safe distance from the gates of the castle before talking to him. But before I open my mouth to tell him what I have discovered from the files, Nikolai puts a question to me.

'Michael, you are a man of the world?' He speaks softly, in Russian.

'Whatever that may mean.'

'You understand women.'

'Less and less.'

'Western women.'

'Women are women.'

'Then tell me, do you think they now expect, as a matter of course, oral sex?'

'I have no idea.'

'You see, we Russians are fairly unsophisticated people who take their pleasure more or less in traditional ways, but now we see videos from Hollywood and in almost all of them the man and woman go in for oral sex – *To Die For*, *Casino*, *Mighty Aphrodite* ...'

'It certainly seems common.'

'Some Russians find it difficult to understand because it seems unhygienic, but I tell them that Americans are always taking showers.'

'That may be a factor.'

'But I have a friend who offers another explanation. He says that because of the Jewish influence in the United States, most of the men are circumcised. This leaves them with an unconscious anxiety about their mutilated penis. My friend believes that the blow-job is in fact a ritual reassurance of the American male.'

'Once one admits the possibility of subconscious motives, anything is possible.'

'The question is this. What would be the expectations of a West European woman?'

'They tend to follow Hollywood fashions.'

'Even though circumcision is less common than in the United States?'

'It is hard to say.'

'And what about oral sex performed by a man on a woman?'

'Clearly, your friend's theory would not explain it since only in Africa is there female circumcision.'

'Could it be the influence of American lesbians who wish to make the penis redundant?'

'That may be the case.'

'So a Western woman would probably expect it?'

'Some, perhaps.'

'They might even prefer it.'

'It no doubt depends upon their previous experience.'

'And a virgin? What would she expect?'

'I don't know,' I said sharply. 'It is not a question I have had to address.'

Nikolai sighed. 'What must be done, must be done, I suppose.' He walked on in silence, a fatuous smile on his lips.


So exasperated was I by this conversation, that I omitted to tell Nikolai about the link between Paget and the Countess. If he had himself brought anything up, I might have mentioned it; but he did not. Indeed, it is increasingly apparent that Nikolai has little interest in our mission. Either he is bad at his job, or the Russians have never seriously entertained a conspiracy of the kind

Paget and Gordon suggested. When you think that historically the Knights of the Cross led the vanguard of Western encroachment on the soil of Holy Russia from the Baltic States, you would think that there would be some anxiety that they might do it again. But all Nikolai seems to think about is sex.

No doubt he is frustrated by this period of enforced celibacy and has some plan to bring it to an end. But who is the mistress he has in mind? Babi thinks it is Monika, but she is not aware of the feelings I sense Monika has for me. The idea that she might marry Nikolai is quite preposterous. She would rather die than surrender her virginity to such an oaf.


## Thursday

It is late at night. Monika has just left. I dreaded her coming, yet her coming has at least shown me what is going on.

At her request, after supper, I held the service of Benediction. My father had occasionally conducted this, almost in secret, for the highest of high Anglicans in his flock. The low-church Protestants see it as a form of idolatry: the consecrated host is placed in a monstrance and worshipped as God. Memories of childhood gave me some idea of what to do. There was also the missal. The monstrance at Zelden was made of beaten gold, a magnificent piece of Renaissance art. One could revere that with sincerity, if nothing else.

Besides Moni, Adolf and one or two servants were in the congregation, but when I came out of the sacristy into the gloomy church, only Moni remained. She rose as

I approached her and asked if I would hear her confession.

'Of course.' I said this casually, but was glad of the poor light to hide my embarrassment and confusion. I returned to the sacristy for my stole, and came back expecting to find her kneeling at the baroque confessional. Instead she stood at the foot of the stairs leading to my room. 'Would it be all right to go to your room?' she asked. 'There are things that it would be difficult to discuss through a grille.'

I led the way up the stairs. In any other circumstances, the idea of a man leading a beautiful girl up a secret staircase to his room late at night would have had dubious implications, but such is Monika's innocence, and her trust in a priest, that the possibility of impropriety did not cross her mind.

We entered the room. I closed the door. She went at once and knelt at the prie-dieu facing the crucifix on the wall. I sat on a chair, the stole around my neck; at the sight of her fair hair flowing over her straight back in the fading evening light, my whole body ached with longing.

From my breviary, I said the opening prayers in Latin and then waited for her to speak. She began with some trivial sins – uncharitable thoughts, moments of sloth, instances of greed – then, having got these off her chest, she asked if she might get up off the prie-dieu and sit down.

I pointed to a tall, upholstered chair by the window with lion's claw feet. 'Why don't you sit there?'

She did as I suggested but remained perched on the edge of the seat. 'You will remember,' she said, 'that when you first came here to Zelden, I was at the convent making a retreat under the spiritual direction of Father Ignatius. For some time, I had felt that God wanted me to join the community and devote my life to Him as a

277

Carmelite sister. During this retreat, I was to make my final discernment. And I did. I came back to Zelden with my mind made up. I was to enter the convent as a postulant in two months' time.'

Now, for the first time, she glanced at me, then looked away out of the window, over the ramparts and beyond. 'But when I returned, it was to find you and Nikolai, and to encounter in the flesh two men who embodied all the suffering and the heroism of the persecuted Church. Until then, I had prayed for you, and had heard stories about all that you endured, but never before had I actually encountered any Catholics from Russia. And all at once, after hearing about life in Komsomolsk, the idea of spending my life in a beautiful baroque convent across the valley from my childhood home seemed too easy. I accepted the value of prayer and self-denial, but the more I listened to Nikolai the more I came to realise the great need for people to carry the Word of God where it has not been heard for generations. I came to envy you both your arduous work.'

She stopped, sighed, and turned to look back into the room. 'Then Nikolai suggested that I should share it – this life as an evangelist of the tundra. He said I should join him in the great task of the conversion of Siberia as his wife.'

'As his wife?'

'I am sure you know this, Father. He would hardly have made such a suggestion without discussing it with you first.'

'I had some intimation that he had something of this kind in mind.'

'Of course, he did not put it as baldly as that. He also said that he had come to love me, and to realise that God intended me to share his life.'

'And what was your reaction to this proposal?'

'I said that I needed time to think.'

'What were your feelings for Nikolai?'

There was a long silence. She glanced at me and the evening light was just sufficient for me to see a look of apprehension in her huge blue eyes. 'My feelings for him ... for Nikolai ... were confused because until that moment I had been quite certain that God did not want me to marry, and so I had never permitted myself to think of a man in that way.'

'But you must have had suitors?'

She gave a snort. 'Yes, but they were all snobs and bores and spiritual mediocrities, young men who liked the idea of marrying the daughter of the Grand Master, that's all.'

'And perhaps someone beautiful, too.'

'That is by the way.'

'But a factor, too, perhaps, in explaining Nikolai's intentions?'

She frowned. 'Did he say so to you?'

'I cannot divulge what he has told me in the confessional, but I can say that Nikolai has always had an eye for beautiful women.'

'But that was not the reason, I am sure, for his proposing marriage. He made it so clear that it was my faith that impressed him, and made him feel that God had chosen me as his partner in a pioneering, evangelising life. But, of course, as you say, I could tell that he also saw me as a woman. He was attentive – you must have noticed – and little by little I too began to think of him in that way.'

'As a lover?'

'As a husband. Not sinfully, I think, as yet, but one cannot consider marriage, can one, Father, without thinking ahead to what marriage entails?'

'As Our Lord himself said, it is the joining of two

279

bodies. "Therefore shall a man leave father and mother and cleave together as one person with his wife." '

'Cleave, yes, I had to think about that, and it is perhaps here that sin crept in because, in imagining what it would be like to share a bed with Nikolai, certain feelings were aroused which I had hardly felt before. Odd, turbulent feelings, a mixture of attraction and revulsion, for sometimes Nikolai seems pleasing but at other times he seems – I don't know – somehow gross.'

'What you must surely decide is whether or not you love him.'

'Of course. But it is not easy. Because there are feelings like respect and esteem which contribute to love and, of course, the attraction of the challenge of a life in Komsomolsk, that almost persuade me that I *do* love him, or *could* love him, and almost certainly in the end *would* love him, were it not for ... something else.'

'What else?'

The light had faded further. I could not now see her face, nor Monika mine. Only this obscurity, I think, enabled her to go on. 'I told you,' she said, 'that the idea of marriage aroused feelings in me that I had scarcely felt before – emotions, of course, but also sensations, even desires. What I had discovered by the time of the Knights' annual dinner was that once they are in one's mind, it is not easy to control them. It was not that I lusted after any of the younger Knights, but I found that I looked at them with a new kind of curiosity. I understood for the first time what passed through Babi's mind, and perhaps God permitted this to humble me because I have in the past been so contemptuous of the way she has behaved.

'None of the Knights particularly appealed to me: the only question in my mind was whether I should marry

280

Nikolai. Time was short. I realised that I would have to come to a decision. Nikolai was so impetuous, so pressing, and when we went to the convent, as you will remember, seemed to present his case so convincingly before the Reverend Mother for an active lay ministry in the outside world.'

'I do remember.'

'We even discussed whether we should ask you to marry us here at Zelden or wait until we reached Komsomolsk. I was on the point of agreeing to all he proposed when two nights ago I was confused by a profound and powerful dream – one of those dreams which are so vivid that when you awake they seem more real than your waking life.'

'What was the dream?'

'I was with a man, Father, a man I truly loved and truly desired, and I awoke weeping with the rapture I felt in both body and soul.'

'And that man was not Nikolai?'

'No, Father, it was you.'

The light in the room had finally faded. I turned in my chair to reach out and switch on the lamp on the table beside me. I glanced at Monika. She blinked at the electric light. One or two tears trickled down her cheeks. Her eyes avoided mine.

'There is no sin in a dream,' I said.

'I know, Father. I realise that. But because it was so vivid, it lingers on.'

'And has it affected your feelings for Nikolai?'

'Yes. It has made it clear that I do not love him.'

'Have you told him this?'

'No. Because even though I do not love him, I believe that perhaps I should marry him all the same.'

I sat in silence, wondering what I should say. Again, the words of St Paul to the Romans, so beloved of my father, came back to me: 'I fail to carry out the things I want to do, and I find myself doing the very things I hate.' I longed to do a single, simple thing – to take three paces across the room and lift into my arms a woman I knew I loved, and whom I now knew loved me. My investigation for the *Sunday Gazette* into the Knights of the Cross seemed wholly trivial compared to my present strong and certain feelings. I would happily have abandoned my mission simply to be able to take hold of Monika's pale hand and press it to my lips.

But I had a stole around my neck; I wore a black suit and Roman collar. To her I was a Catholic priest; and however powerful her dream, however confident I might be of her unrecognised love, I could not anticipate how she would react if I was suddenly to confess to my deceit.

And there was something beyond caution which held me back. The black suit, the clerical collar, the stole over my shoulders were the costume and props for my role; but it was a role that had somehow taken hold of me and left me at a loss for any words but those that would be spoken by a priest. Either I had to seize her and bombard her with impetuous kisses, or talk to her with the calm and detachment of a pastor; and since the first course of action was as yet too hazardous, the second was all that remained. 'You must thank God, dear Monika,' I heard myself saying, 'for your good and humble confession, and you must pray to him and to our Blessed Lady for help and guidance. Do not torment yourself with remorse for sins that are not sins. God permits the Devil to test us by putting all kinds of temptations in our paths. And if the Devil chooses to do so in your case, it is because he knows that yours is a soul of rare value that he would dearly love to bring to perdition. Temptations are not sins. They are there to enable us to show our love for God in resisting them. But never underestimate the Devil. Temptations to improper affections are clear; temptations to the sin of pride are often less clear. Bear that in mind as you continue in your efforts to discern your true vocation, deciding whether God is really calling you to work in Siberia with Nikolai, or whether He does not have something less dramatic in mind for you closer to home.'

She knelt at her chair. I gave her as penance one of the Glorious Mysteries of the Holy Rosary to be said in front of the Blessed Sacrament. She then said her act of contrition and I forgave her her sins. *Ego te absolvo* ... She then stood and went towards the door. 'Thank you, Father.'

'Please pray for me.'

'Of course.' For a moment, our eyes met. What was her expression. Gratitude? Relief? Or disappointment? The light was too poor. I could not tell. The door closed behind her. I had missed the moment. The opportunity was gone.

*Friday*

She was at mass this morning. At communion, her lovely face was raised to receive the morsel of the flesh of the Messiah, the Bread of Life. How can I ever tell her that from my hands it is no more than a wafer? Even if she loved me, could she ever forgive me for having so blasphemously deceived her? That is my conundrum. She cannot permit herself to love me because I am a priest, but if she was to discover that I was not a priest ...

283

At breakfast, after mass, she talked cheerfully to us all as if yesterday's confession had cleared the air. She teased Adolf with affection, and chatted to Nikolai with an easy familiarity. Nikolai hovers over her in a way that fills me with disgust.

The other members of the family will arrive this evening for the weekend.

## Saturday

After supper last night, Heinrich von Willich invited Nikolai and me into the small study next to the salon. When we were seated, he told us that he had some good news. The grant allocation committee of Kreuzhilfe had met that afternoon and had approved the recommendation of the Russian section that a grant of $250,000 be made forthwith to pay for a Catholic church and parish centre in Komsomolsk-on-Amur.

This information filled me with dismay. It meant that the moment of my parting from Monika was now imminent with nothing resolved. Nikolai, whatever his feelings, was more controlled. 'Thanks be to God,' he said, before lowering his head as if in silent prayer.

'Now that the grant has been authorised,' said the Grand Master, 'the funds can be released whenever you choose. But you will appreciate that it is not advisable to linger with such a large sum in cash.'

'Of course,' said Nikolai. 'We entirely understand.'

'You are happy to let the people at Parsheim make the arrangements for your departure?'

'Of course.'

Nikolai left the study ahead of me; I hesitated for a

moment, blocking the path of the Grand Master. 'Is the grant to be paid in cash?'

'In US dollars, as Nikolai suggested.'

'Is this usual?'

'Didn't Nikolai explain?'

'He likes to spare me worldly concerns.'

'He pointed out to us something which, alas, those in Kreuzhilfe already knew only too well. If the grant was paid in the form of a cheque or a money order, it would have to be lodged with a Russian bank. The banks in Russia are now controlled by the Mafia. It is highly probable that the money would disappear. Even if it did not, there would also be extortionate charges, and "taxes" of one kind or another levied by the central government in Moscow and the local government in Komsomolsk. In Nikolai's opinion, you would be fortunate to see a fraction of the original sum.'

'I can quite believe it.'

'He also points out that only with hard currency in cash will you be able to buy the site, receive planning permission and obtain building materials, all still in the gift of the Mafia and nomenclatura.'

'That is undoubtedly true.'

Heinrich von Willich patted me on the shoulder. 'You are most fortunate, Father, in having such a practical man to help you with your holy mission.'

Nikolai was waiting for me on the stairs. 'Come, Father,' he whispered, 'it is time for me to make my confession too.'

We went to my room. 'So what did she say, my little angel? Will she marry me or not?'

For a moment I could not answer, so possessed was I by revulsion and rage. If I had given way to my first

285

impulse, I would have run at Nikolai to strangle him but an inner voice reminded me that not only did he possess a Beretta but he was, no doubt, trained in unarmed combat – a man who had killed before and might kill again.

Finally, spluttering, I said: 'What can have possessed you to propose to Monika?'

He laughed. 'The same as possesses you, I think.'

'My feelings for her are honourable and sincere.'

He laughed again. 'We both want to fuck her. Let the best man win.'

Again, I groped for words. 'But you are married.'

'So are you.'

'I am divorced.'

He shrugged. 'A formality.'

'I would devote my life to her happiness.'

'You are a romantic. I am a realist.'

'And how does the realist predict her reaction when she discovers the truth?'

'After a couple of weeks, I don't think she'll care.'

'Such is your talent as a lover ...'

He gave a modest smile.

'First you must make her your wife.'

'Of course. That has been clear from the start.'

'And where do you intend to marry her?'

'Here at Zelden. Or wherever suits you.'

'Suits *me*?'

'Of course. We have to be married by a priest.'

'You presume a little too much.'

'We can negotiate later when we have the money.'

Again, I was impelled to hit him but was deterred by his powerful physique. I tried a different tack. 'It seems to me, Nikolai, that you have completely forgotten the primary purpose of our mission.'

He looked perplexed. 'What was that?'

'To find out the truth about the Knights of the Cross.'

'Ah, yes. The political conspiracy to found a Fourth Reich.'

'You speak as if it is all a joke.'

'Not a joke. A fantasy of your friend Professor Paget and your right-wing press.'

'You forget,' I said to Nikolai, 'that the body of George Harding was found floating in the Saar.'

'I do not forget it. He was undoubtedly murdered.'

'By whom?'

'As I understand it, you have been studying the von Willich archives.'

'That's right.'

'Look for the name of Count Kaspar's batman during World War II.'

'What is the significance of that?'

'You'll see.'

Anger prevents me from sleeping. I sit here at my desk, writing by the light of a single electric lamp. It is a quarter to three in the morning. Anger at whom? Nikolai. Savchenko. Paget. And perhaps Gordon, too. All have deceived me but I have yet to plumb the depths of their deception.

But my more acute fury is directed at Nikolai. He plans to marry Monika bigamously and then debauch her, safe in the knowledge that back in Russia he will be beyond the law. And perhaps he is right. Perhaps, once she has surrendered her precious virginity, her honour and integrity will go by the board. Such is the power of nature. She will cleave to this virile brute.

Is Nikolai the new Russian? Is this what *Homo post-*

*sovieticus* has become? No morals. No principles. An unscrupulous drive to indulge his appetites without the constraints of any morality? And yet, whispers Father Piotr, has he not learned the cult of indulgence from Western man? Is there such a difference between his designs on Monika and mine?

My position is impossible. If I expose him, I expose myself. The choice then would be between prosecution for fraud by the German police or, if there is substance in our suspicions, a nasty death at the hands of the young Knights of the Cross.

And Monika? For the first time in my life, I have come across perfection. I love her wholly and will love her for ever. And I have every reason to believe that involuntarily, despite my calling, she loves me in return. Yet I cannot declare my love. Even a look or a gesture would give me away. I am obliged to watch as the odious Russian seeks to persuade her that he is the one she should marry.

*Sunday*
---

High Mass in the chapel. The entire household attends. For the first time since the start of my imposture, some of the prayers begin to make sense. 'With the pure in heart, I will wash my hands clean … Lord, never count this soul for lost with the wicked, this life among the bloodthirsty; hands ever stained with guilt, palms ever itching for a bribe …'

When I came to the consecration, I could hardly bring myself to say the words because there before me in the front pew was Monika, her eyes fervent as never before.

Now that I know that she loves me, it is painful to continue to deceive her. It is the same at communion: Heinrich and Julia von Willich, Adolf, the cook, two of the maids, Thomas Krull, and then Monika – her closed eyes, her white teeth, her pink tongue. Next to her, the odious orifice of Nikolai. As I placed the host on the tip of his tongue, I remembered his gun.

The archives. I retrace my steps through the World War II diaries of Kaspar von Willich, looking for the name of his batman. There are references to a 'Franz' who accompanied him on the last plane out of Stalingrad, and was permitted to remain with him during the last months of the war when he was confined here at Zelden.

At midday, Grunberger walks in. 'Interesting,' I said, 'that a place was found for the batman when Count Kaspar returned from the Eastern Front to Berlin.'

'This was still the German Army,' said Grunberger. 'An officer could not be expected to polish his own boots.'

'What happened to him, I wonder.'

'To Franz Ziegler?'

'Yes.'

'After the war, he returned to his birthplace where the Grand Master bought him a small hotel.'

'And where was that?'

'In the Saarland. To be precise, Saarbrücken.'

After lunch, Heinrich von Willich tells us that on Wednesday morning Dr Kammer and Herr Worters will come to Zelden with the full grant in US Treasury notes. They will then drive us straight to Frankfurt airport, where we will board the 1600 Lufthansa flight to

289

Moscow. Monika listens as her father outlines these arrangements: no particular expression on her face. Thomas Krull, on the other side of the table, studies Nikolai's face for his reaction. Nikolai meekly bows his head: 'God be praised.' I say: 'After all your kindness, it will be hard for us to leave Zelden.' As I speak, I glance at Monika. She blushes and looks away.

## Monday

After supper this evening, Adolf invites me to join him in the garden to smoke another of his Havana cigars. We sit on the slatted wooden chairs by the fountain, the rich aroma of the smouldering tobacco mingling with the fragrance of the plants in the balmy evening air.

'We shall miss you when you are gone,' said Adolf.

'Less, I think, than we shall miss you.'

'You may not realise it, but you have made a great impression on my sisters – on all of us, of course, but particularly on them.'

'It is kind of you to say so.'

'I cannot see Monika going into the convent. She now sees her vocation out there in the wider world.' He waved towards the horizon, a ragged line against the evening sky. 'And even Babi ...' He laughed. 'She says that for the first time she has met a priest who is *convincing*. I am not quite sure what she means by that.'

'I would thank God if I felt I had done anything to bring her back into the Church,' I said.

'In a sense, she never left it. It is quite impossible, if you are one of our family, to get away from the Catholic Church. But you may have persuaded her to take it more seriously which, as you probably realise, would mean quite a change to her way of life.'

I puffed at my cigar. 'The longer I live,' I said, 'and the more I know of the human condition, the happier I am that it is God and not man who judges the morality of our actions.'

'Only God can see into our hearts, but surely man can judge whether or not we keep the commandments.'

'In theory, yes. But in practice, a combination of sophistry and circumstances can lead a man to break a commandment as fundamental as "Thou shalt not kill".'

Adolf drew on his cigar. 'Do you mean during a war?'

'Or a revolution. Or a counter-revolution. But particularly during a war. It has been fascinating, for example, to study your grandfather's wartime letters and diaries in the archives here in Zelden.'

'Which is more than I have done.'

'He is an interesting figure.'

'He lived through interesting times.'

'Whereas your father – correct me if I am wrong – has suffered less from self-doubt about his role as Grand Master than either his father or his elder son.'

'His generation saw their main task in the rebuilding of Germany and the German economy, and the Knights' mission in terms of raising money for those in need.'

'For which many in Eastern Europe are profoundly grateful.'

'Indeed. But then the pendulum swings again with the next generation.'

'With you?'

'Above all, with my brother Otto. He thought that raising money was not enough.'

I waited for a moment, then said: 'I understand that Otto was killed in an accident.'

'Yes. On the autobahn, together with one of his friends.'

'A collision with an armoured car from the British Army.'

Adolf shot me an uneasy glance. 'Is that in the archives?'

'And that the lorry he was driving contained arms.'

Now Adolf's face clouded over. 'If Grunberger told you that, he had no business to do so. These are family secrets.'

'I am a priest.'

Adolf shook his head. 'Of course. I'm sorry. It's just that, well, his death was not just a tragedy for the family but the manner of his dying could be so easily misunderstood.'

'I have to admit that it left me curious, only in so far as I would like to understand him and his idea of the mission of the Knights of the Cross.'

Adolf frowned, sighed, then leaned forward and said in a low voice: 'The arms had been bought in Riga and were on their way to the Sudan.'

'To the Sudan?'

'Yes. Via Marseille and Eritrea. You see, there was a group among the younger Knights, led by Otto and Thomas, who saw the world we live in in almost apocalyptic terms. They saw the forces of evil assaulting Christ's Church from both within and without – from within, under the guise of reform, ecumenicism leading to indifferentism undermining the faith of Catholics in their unique mission, and externally, a pitiless struggle between Christianity and Islam. And in this struggle – an armed struggle – it was our Church that was in retreat. Whether in North Africa, Nigeria, East Timor, the Balkans or Sudan – everywhere, oppression and persecution of Catholics passes without protest, goes unopposed.'

'Otto's aim was to change this?'

'Yes. He thought Kreuzhilfe's charitable work was all very well, but that it was absurd that its resources should go to countries like Poland and Lithuania where the battle was already won. Meanwhile, in Bosnia, units of fanatic Muslims from Algeria and Iran were fighting to establish an Islamic state in the heart of Europe. It was the duty of the Knights to fight back.'

'Did he actually fight?'

Adolf laughed. 'No. He had done his time in the Army, as we all have, but by nature he was very gentle – not a military type at all. There were one or two who volunteered to fight alongside the Croats but at that stage the Croats did not need men so much as arms and ammunition, which we were able to provide.'

'The Knights armed the Catholic Croatians?'

'At the start it was the Knights and a few sympathisers. Later the Federal government took a hand, and the Americans.'

'And in the Sudan?'

'That was Otto's private project, known only to the family and a small group of the younger Knights. Papa knew about it but did not approve.'

'And what did he think about the British?'

Adolf looked puzzled. 'The British? Why should he think about them?'

'I don't know. I just thought that since the collision was with a British armoured car –'

'If he had not been killed, then I am sure he would have had some thoughts about the British but before then he did not think about them one way or the other.'

'So the collision was a genuine accident?'

Adolf hesitated. He looked down at his cigar. It had gone out. 'No,' he said softly. 'Otto was betrayed. But that aspect of the story is even more complicated and must remain secret, even from a priest.'

The mystery is solved. The ruse I once thought so hare-brained has borne fruit. Schloss Zelden has given up its secrets, just as Paget predicted. George Harding was murdered. I have the confession of the murderer on tape.

It is cooler now – I have just closed my window – but after supper it was so warm that I took my breviary out into the gardens beneath the ramparts and sat down to read the office on the stone bench that surrounds the fountain. I listened to the sounds of the bubbling water and breathed in the scented evening air. It was a moment of great contentment: I now enjoyed reciting the psalms, litanies and prayers.

I could hear voices of others elsewhere in the garden, and I was prepared to be interrupted by Adolf or Nikolai, but it was Babi who appeared from behind the box hedge: Babi on her own.

'Am I disturbing you?'

'No.' I closed my breviary.

'I would like to talk to you.'

'And I to you.'

'About Moni and Nikolai?'

'Yes.'

'She seems determined to marry him.'

'I know. But does she love him?'

'No. If she did, she almost certainly *wouldn't* marry him. She is determined to do something heroic for God and God alone.' As she said this, she picked at the cellophane of an unopened packet of cigarettes.

'In a sense that is commendable,' I said.

'And in a sense perverse.'

I sighed. 'The best thing might be for you to tell your parents what's going on.'

'Oh, they know. Moni has told them.'

'Will they permit the marriage?'

Babi laughed as she pulled a long cigarette out of the packet. 'They are far too frightened of Moni to tell her what and what not to do. Her righteousness makes her invincible: she is so sure she has a direct line to God.'

'But they cannot want her to live in Siberia?'

Babi shrugged, lit her cigarette with a silver lighter, then used it to point across the valley towards the convent. 'They had grown used to the idea that she would disappear there.'

'Perhaps if I talked to them.'

'Better talk to Moni. She respects you more than she respects them.'

'I have done so. I have tried.'

'If you can't dissuade her, then no one can.'

I hesitated. 'I still have a card up my sleeve which I can play if I have to.'

'A knave?'

'More like a joker. But it will take the trick.'

If Babi was curious, she did not show it: this suggested that she had not cornered me in the garden simply to talk about her sister. She sat on an old wooden chair, her feet resting on the stone surround to the fountain. Behind her was the bright red sky, her face cast into shadow by the setting sun.

'There's something else I wanted to discuss before you go,' she said, drawing on her cigarette. I said nothing, but reached into the pocket of my jacket to switch on the tape. She thought for a moment, then said: 'I suppose what I have in mind is a kind of confession, but I can't face kneeling at a grille and I've forgotten all the prayers ...'

'They aren't necessary.'

She laughed. 'You see, I want to have my cake and eat

it. I'm not really a Catholic, but there are things I have done …'

'As far as I am concerned, whatever you may say will be protected by the seal of the confessional.'

'And in a day or two's time, you will be on the other side of the world.'

'Precisely.'

'Though that isn't the *only* reason for choosing you to hear my confession, Father Piotr. It's also because you seem so calm and detached and … holy.'

'It is God who forgives your sins, not the priest.'

'I know. And I am still enough of a Catholic to believe that He *will* forgive my sins if only I can bring myself to feel sorry.'

'Is that difficult?'

She shrugged. 'Most of them – the sins of the flesh, that is – meant so little to me that I find it hard to feel anything as strong as remorse.'

'They may have meant more to God than they did to you.'

'Yes. And I am sorry for that, though why God should be so easily offended, I don't know.'

Nor, indeed, did I: but it was not Michael Latham who was hearing Babi's confession, it was Father Piotr, and by now Father Piotr had taken on not just a life but ideas of his own. 'Perhaps,' I said, 'we do not stop to think what we are *really* doing when we make love to a man or a woman.'

'What do you mean?'

'We may be motivated by an emotional impulse, which we call love, or by physical desire, but the end result is not just emotional fulfilment or sensual pleasure. It is also the potential creation of another person, a new life, a being that will live for ever.'

She shrugged. 'In essence, yes, that is the biological reality.'

'Which for a rabbit or a cat has no more significance than bringing another rabbit or cat into the world, but with us creates a being with an immortal soul. In other words, the act that appears, on the face of it, so animal is in reality the most divine.'

'Few think of sex in that way.'

'Of course. We only notice our feelings for the other person. But one could say that the *making* of a life is, in its way, as momentous as the *taking* of a life, and sometimes with the taking of a life it is just the same. The murderer does not ponder the existential significance of his action; he simply indulges his hatred just as the lover indulges his desire.'

Even in the pink light of the sunset, I could see that Babi had turned pale. 'But murder is surely a more serious sin?'

'Murder, certainly, is irrevocable but, then, so is the conception of a child. We can discern between serious and trivial sins, but among serious sins we cannot be sure which causes the greatest offence to God. Of course murder is wrong, but in Russia today innumerable murders are committed by men who are driven by drink to kill and by despair to drink – characters straight out of novels by Gogol or Dostoevsky.'

'So you can feel sorry for a murderer?'

'He, too, can be a victim.'

'He is not damned?'

'No one is irredeemable. Christ died for the sins of all.'

Babi sat for a while in silence, then moved her feet from the stone bench to the ground, leaned forward and whispered: 'I have killed someone, Father. That is the sin I wanted to confess.'

I waited for a moment, then asked: 'And are you sorry?'

She hesitated. 'Yes.'

'Why?'

'Because if there is a Hell, I would rather not go there, certainly not for killing *him*.'

'You still think of your victim with hatred?'

'I try not to think of him at all, but when I do I find it hard to suppress the feelings that led me to do what I did.'

'Was he an unfaithful lover?'

She laughed, and took a fresh cigarette from the packet. 'If I had killed all of those there would be a trail of corpses.'

'So what did he do?'

'He betrayed me. He betrayed us all.'

'In what way?'

She lit her cigarette. 'To you, Father Piotr, it must seem that, beside me, the black sheep of the family, the Willichs are paragons of virtue and pillars of the Church. But every family has some skeletons in the cupboard, and we are no exception.'

'Are you referring to the last war?'

'Oh, the war. No.' She shook her head. 'Those skeletons are not in the cupboard. They're rattling around the world.'

'So what is the skeleton in the cupboard?'

'My grandmother had a lover. He was the British officer sent to investigate my grandfather's case.'

'And did your grandfather know about the affair?'

'I once asked Oma. She said she didn't know. Nothing was ever said. Questions were never asked. But every year she would go to some spa or other for a week or two, and there she would meet her lover. He was her cure.'

'For what?'

298

'An unhappy marriage. Their sex-life was clearly disastrous. Had that been otherwise, well, successful sex covers a multitude of sins. But without that to bring them together, their inherent differences drove them apart. She was not born a Catholic. She came from a Protestant Prussian Junker family. What she held against Hitler was not just the evil but also the vulgarity of what he did to the Slavs and the Jews – and what she could not forgive her husband and the entire officer corps of the Germany Army was the way in which they had acquiesced in this vulgarity, themselves irrevocably dishonouring the whole Prussian tradition. If that tradition had survived – if the Germans had not been thrown out of Silesia and East Prussia, and if the Junker estates, including her parents', had not been expropriated by the Communists – then the Junker class might have redeemed itself, but it was given no chance. The Prussian gentry, where it still existed, lived in small flats in Munich and Frankfurt. One of my earliest memories is of Oma saying: "My Germany no longer exists." For her, it expired in ignominy in nineteen forty-five.'

'Was her affair with the Englishman a form of revenge?'

'Without a doubt – a way of punishing my grandfather but also, it has to be said, of punishing herself. After all, honour had meant everything to her and by continuing to see the Englishman, she chose dishonour.'

'She must have loved him.'

'Of course. And they had many things in common. Music, literature, good food, good wine. But, above all, they shared one great passion – a hatred of Germany. That seems to have been their strongest bond.'

'But how could your grandmother hate a country when her husband and son were pillars of the state?'

'Because it was not her state – not Prussia. To her,

West Germany – the Federal Republic – was the horrible concoction of vulgar Rhinelanders and gross Bavarians.'

'Do you think your grandfather realised how she felt?'

'They never communicated.'

'And your father?'

'He never took her seriously. He would just laugh.'

'And you?'

'Oh, I always loved Oma. She was sweet to me when I was young. I think she had an idea of how I would turn out.'

'A black sheep?'

'And a Prussian. I, too, rebelled against my parents' idea of West German respectability.'

'Did you share her hatred of Germany?'

Babi hesitated before she answered. 'You know, Father, most Germans born since the war half hate Germany. In that, my grandmother is right. We are a nation irredeemably dishonoured. That is why we would rather think of ourselves as European. But then again, there is so much that is good in Germany, such a unique contribution to the culture of Europe and of the world. And we Germans have worked so hard to change, and we have succeeded in a way that no nation has succeeded before. Today's Germans are far more like the French or the Dutch or even the British than they are like the Germans before the war.'

'So you don't hate Germany?'

'No. I love Europe, and Germany is part of Europe. In that, all four of us were agreed.'

'You, Monika, Adolf and Otto?'

'Yes. But I have to concede that the boys thought about these things more than Moni and me. If I had taken it all more seriously, then I might have realised ...' Her voice tailed off.

'Realised what?'

She lit another cigarette before she spoke. 'A year or so ago, Oma told me that she wanted me to meet an Englishman – a friend of *her* Englishman – whom she had invited to stay. At first I assumed that this was just another of her attempts to marry me off. I soon discovered that he was already married. He also turned out to be a politician – in fact a minister of some kind. He went from time to time to Luxembourg and Strasbourg, and Oma told me she thought it would interest him to meet Father and see Zelden.

'As soon as I saw him, I knew that we were two of a kind. It was not love at first sight, but sexual attraction plus ... Plus what? I don't know.' She drew on her cigarette as she considered. 'I am a Piscean. So was he. I know it is superstitious to pay attention to that kind of thing, but I have often found that I get on really well with my fellow Pisceans, although we never fall in love. It is just a rapport, with or without sex, depending upon the physical type.'

'And what was his physical type?'

'Too good to be true. Thick black hair, a handsome, fleshy face, a deep voice, loud and bombastic, a caricature of John Bull, always in a pin-striped suit. Only the bowler hat was missing. He was also quite transparent. He made no bones about what he wanted, whether in terms of sex or information. An unashamed egoist. I could not imagine him blinking unless there was something in it for him. So what was he doing at Zelden? It seemed highly unlikely that he was here to pay his respects to the ageing mistress of his English friend. Yet that was what he told me, after Oma had gone to bed and we sat together drinking whisky in the salon. I said I did not believe him. He backtracked and admitted that he had really come to Zelden because he had heard about me. I did not believe that either, but if it was a form of flirtation, that was fine by me. I offered to show him round the castle. The tour ended in my bed.

'That was the first of a number of encounters with my Englishman, not just that weekend but at odd times and places where we met from time to time. He had to be careful: a sex scandal at that moment would be certain to end his career. I was quite happy to keep it secret: I had had enough stories about my love-life in the papers. If he was in Luxembourg or Strasbourg, we would go to a small hotel in Saarbrücken run by the son of my grandfather's batman. I could rely on him to be wholly discreet. It was a simple hotel, almost squalid, but we both liked that. What do you call it? *Nostalgie de la boue?*

'He was sexually perverse. Does that shock you, Father? No, you must have heard people confess such things before – perhaps worse. He liked me to put on my riding breeches and boots and beat his naked body with my whip. I would tie his hands to the bedstead and prod his body with my heated curling tongs. Childish? But I enjoyed it, too, making his body squirm.

'By the start of this summer, we had met around half a dozen times. For me, it meant long drives in my Mercedes but the intrigue made it worthwhile. I would pick him up in Luxembourg or Strasbourg and drive to Saarbrücken; and the next morning or even the same night, back again to his hotel. Why? I don't know. I suppose that in some way I loved him. But I had no illusions about his feelings for me. I knew quite well that he did not love me. I had never retracted my first judgement that he would do nothing without a reason, but I assumed that a woman who would appear when it suited him and give him the kind of sex he enjoyed was reason enough.'

'Did you not feel humiliated, being used in that way?'

'Of course. But I liked that, playing the role of a

whore.' She drew again on her cigarette. 'He was not the only one who was perverse.'

'But there must have been times …'

'When we weren't in bed? Of course. Driving down the autobahn in the Mercedes, or sometimes eating in cheap restaurants, we would talk and laugh and even argue about this and that. He was curious about the Knights of the Cross and my family. I told him about Moni and Adolf and, of course, Otto. In fact, I boasted about Otto's work among the Ossi skinheads, and the risks he ran in gun-running for the Catholics in Croatia and Sudan.'

'You knew about that?'

'Yes. I was close to Otto. He never condemned the way I lived, and sometimes he would ask me to help him on odd missions. He would use my flat in Munich for meetings with mysterious foreigners. He trusted me completely and I was enormously grateful to him for letting me help him. It somehow seemed that his courage and goodness made up for my sluttish self-indulgence – his good deeds made up for my sins.'

'What did your Englishman make of the gun-running?'

'He was interested because he was a minister in the British Ministry of Defence. He warned me that Otto would be in real danger from Islamic networks operating in Europe. Sooner or later, they would discover what Otto was up to, and when they did, they would kill him. This upset me. I cried. To console me, George said that he might be able to arrange some form of protection from the British secret service, but he would need to know precisely when Otto was next buying arms in Riga.

'This seemed extraordinarily kind – for George to use his official position to protect the illegal activities of the brother of his mistress. My spirits rose. Perhaps he loved me more than he cared to admit. It also gave me a chance to do something for Otto. I took up his offer. I found out from Otto when he was next going to Riga, and passed on the information to my English friend.'

Babi stopped talking. I thought she had paused to think but then saw that she was quietly crying. I passed her a paper handkerchief. She took it, wiped her eyes, sniffed, and went on. 'Otto was killed. So was his friend Florian. There was a collision, not with any Arabs but with a British armoured car. The police did not think it was an accident but, because of the arms in the container and because of Otto, it was thought best to cover the whole thing up. But they did not know about George.'

'Did you tell them?'

'He called me the day after the accident to say he was sorry. Since it had not been reported in the papers, that meant he knew from his own sources. He said that the collision was a genuine accident. He would like to pretend that he had sent the armoured cars to protect Otto, but in fact they were on a routine exercise: it was a coincidence that they had been on the autobahn at that time.

'I did not believe him. I knew he was lying because of his tone of voice. He did not sound sorry. He sounded annoyed. He asked why the accident had not been reported in the German papers. I told him that my father had enough influence to prevent it. Do you know what he said then? *"How bloody corrupt!"* '

'What does that mean?' Babi had said this in English: I pretended not to understand.

She gave a rough translation. 'The point is this, Father. He could not conceal his irritation that details of the accident had been kept out of the press. And he used it as a pretext for ending our affair. "Think what a journalist would make of it if we were ever seen together. It's not worth the risk."

'That, too, seemed unconvincing. As long as it was not known that Otto had been involved in the accident, then my identity did not matter. The risk was no more than before. Also, he spoke like a businessman ending some joint venture, not a lover ending an affair. That made me suspicious.'

'Suspicious of what?'

'I didn't know. The coincidence of the armoured car and Otto's lorry being on the same stretch of motorway at the same time seemed unlikely, given that Otto's itinerary was known to the British Ministry of Defence. It seemed to point to George's intervention. But if George had engineered the accident, what could have been his motive? Why should he want Otto dead? What particularly tormented me was the thought that I was somehow responsible for the death of my brother. I longed to be told that I was being fanciful, but there was no one in whom I could confide. None of the family knew of my affair with George, except possibly Oma. Nor did I dare disclose it. Thomas and a number of the young Knights were quite sure that the accident had been staged, probably as a favour by the British to the Saudis or the Sultan of Oman.

'Those were terrible days, Father. The grief of the whole family was dreadful to see. Otto had gone. Monika was going into a convent. All my parents were left with was Adolf and me. My own sadness was redoubled by my sense of remorse – the terrible fear that I was responsible for Otto's death. The uncertainty tormented me. I decided I must confront George and find out.

'How could it be done? If I telephoned him, I would not be put through. Should I fly to London? I did not

305

know where he worked or where he lived. Then I read in the *Frankfurter Allgemeine* that on the twelfth of March there was to be an important meeting of the junior ministers of defence of the European Union in Luxembourg. George's name was given as the representative of the United Kingdom. On the morning of the twelfth I drove to Saarbrücken and checked into Ziegler's little hotel. He always gave me the same room, discreetly tucked away at the back of the building with a balcony overlooking the river. After lunch, I changed into one of my most elegant outfits and drove in my Mercedes to Luxembourg. I suspected that George, if he remained for the night, would stay at the Europa Hotel because we had met there a number of times before. I waited at the bar and, sure enough, at around ten he emerged from the restaurant with one of his civil servants. He saw me. Our eyes met. I smiled. He got rid of his aide and came to join me. Ten minutes later we were in the Mercedes on our way to Saarbrücken. I assured him that he would be back in the Europa by seven the next morning.

'I do not think for a moment that he thought our meeting was as coincidental as I had pretended: such is the vanity of men, Father, he almost certainly assumed that I craved his sexual attentions. Of course, this was what I wanted him to believe and, when we reached Saarbrücken, we surpassed ourselves – a real orgy. Cognac, a little cocaine and a lot of sex.

'Afterwards, we fell asleep. About an hour later, I woke up to see George, naked, staggering back from the bathroom. He went to the open window and looked out on to the balcony. I got off the bed and stood behind him. "Tell me about the accident on the autobahn." He grunted: "They outsmarted us on that one." "How?" "Keeping it from the press." "You wanted them to know?" "Of course. It was staged for the tabloids!" "But two men were killed." "The only good Germans are dead Germans." "But one was my brother!"

'George turned. He was so drunk that, until that moment, I am sure he had quite forgotten that I was Otto's sister or even a German. Now his bleary eyes focused on me and a look of disdain came on to his face. "He was your brother? So what? You're only a whore."

'I pushed him. He staggered backwards out on to the balcony. I followed and pushed him again, over the wooden railing into the river. He said: "What the devil —" and then there was a splash. I watched for a moment as he floundered. He was too drunk to swim. He disappeared into the darkness. I knew he would drown and I was delighted. That, Father, is my sin.'

I sighed. It was a deep sigh — one of those exhalations that come with the relaxation not just of the lungs but of the whole body. Beneath my cassock I could feel the warm shape of my tape-recorder and the words of Christ on the Cross came to mind: 'It is finished.'

Babi, who sat there in front of me — tears, tousled hair, cigarette after cigarette — must have felt that I was sighing in despair at the wickedness of the world because she now looked at me uneasily and whispered: 'I know I should not have done it, Father. Even I realise that it is always wrong to kill.'

'Of course,' I said, 'of course. It is wrong to kill.' I was temporising, still caught up in the thought that had produced my sigh, the thought that the riddle was now solved, my assignment was over; that I could now pack up and go home. But then the sight of that unhappy Magdalene in the evening light, looking all the more lovely in her distress, reminded me that to her I was not an investigative journalist working for the *Gazette* but a Catholic priest with the power to absolve even the most heinous sin.

'And *for that reason* I am sorry,' said Babi.

'What reason?'

'The reason that it is wrong to kill, although I cannot help feeling glad that he is dead and that he deserved to die.'

The moment had come for a priestly homily. 'As Our Lord himself said, those who live by the sword must expect to die by the sword, and that is as true for your brother Otto as it is for your lover George. But their motivation was quite different, and while your brother died as a true crusader, this Englishman, it seems to me, fell victim to his own political passions and intrigues. This is not to excuse what you did, but your outrage was in a sense a reflection of the nobility of your brother's cause which allows an element of mitigation ...'

'Can it be forgiven?'

'Any sin can be forgiven when there is repentance, even a minimal form of repentance that comes simply from fear of eternal punishment in Hell. And it seems to me that your repentance, though it may be imperfect, is enough to merit God's forgiveness. You may not regret what you did to the Englishman, but you regret what you did to God.

'However, to gain absolution, you must also be sorry for your other sins and determine to turn away from a life of self-indulgence to one that conforms to the teachings of the Church. Do not hesitate to ask God to help you. What we may not be able to do for ourselves, can be done by Him ...'

And so on. I gave Babi a hefty penance – all fifteen

decades of the rosary – murder is murder, after all; after which she made a rudimentary act of contrition, words remembered from her childhood. Then I absolved her from her sins. *Ego te absolvo.* Again, those powerful words which, once they were spoken, and once my hand was lowered from giving a blessing, brought almost palpable relief to the troubled spirit of Barbara von Willich.

## Wednesday

Babi at mass this morning. Took communion. The new leaf? Also Adolf, Nikolai and Monika. For a moment, as I held up the host, Moni seemed to look at me with an expression that was at once curious and sad. Then her eyes closed, her mouth opened, out came her tongue. *Corpus Christi. Amen.*

Again, from the other side of the breakfast table, a look from Moni that is hard to interpret. Does she sense that I love her? Does she also realise that she loves me? Does that look mean: 'What are you waiting for? Carry me off!' The Aboriginal challenge of woman to man, even when the man is a Catholic priest? Or is she merely puzzled by *my* look? Do I inadvertently betray my feelings? I lean forward to take another slice of *Landbrot* and two slices of sausage.

I now sit in my room, wondering what to do. As things stand, I leave Zelden tomorrow with Nikolai, a quarter of a million dollars and a tape which proves that George was killed by Barbara von Willich. We fly to Moscow and disappear. I return to London, write my story for the *Gazette*, and earn twenty thousand pounds. But what is my story? Babi killed George but what was her motive?

309

Revenge for the death of her brother. Why was George responsible for the death of Otto von Willich? Because he was drawn into a plot by a crazed old don at Cambridge to present gun-running by German sympathisers with Sudanese Christians as a Euro-Fascist plot.

I could see how all this could add up to an entertaining piece in the *Sunday Gazette* but would Gordon print it? His Eurosceptic martyr, George Harding, could not come out of it looking anything but absurd. It also seems likely that he was always a co-conspirator with Paget and George. He sent me to get proof that George's death could be ascribed to the Knights of the Cross. That I had done. But the link I had established was not of the kind he had in mind.

And would Babi be arrested? And charged with murder? As I think about it, I realise that I will never write the story. Why? Because I loathed George? Because I like Babi? Because she is Moni's sister? Or because I find it difficult to envisage breaking the vows of a priest?

I am laughing. My handwriting is almost illegible because as I write this I laugh at the total absurdity of my predicament: an atheist trapped in the role of a priest, unable to declare his love to a woman who loves him but is considering marriage to another man! This is the issue I have been avoiding, far more important and urgent than anything else. I conjure up the image of her with Nikolai, enduring his loathsome caresses. Enduring? Perhaps enjoying ...

I stop laughing. I also stop writing to pace around the room. I am now back at my desk. What can I do? Respond to that look at mass and across the breakfast table? Declare my passion. 'I am a priest but I love you and I know that you love me, not Nikolai. I am the one you must marry ...' Even as I imagine saying this, I see her faint at the scandal. Monika von Willich would never sleep with a priest.

'I am not a priest ...' That might be worse. All those white wafers on her pink tongue: counterfeit morsels of the Body of Christ. No spiritual nutrition. Divine calorie-free. And my absolution? A fraud. And would she feel the same passion for an English journalist spying on her family as for a priest from Komsomolsk?

A knock on my door. Perhaps it is her.

It was Adolf asking me to come down to his father's study. The people from Parsheim have arrived.

3 p.m. Catastrophe. My worst premonitions are fulfilled. But I must start at the beginning ...

I went down with Adolf to the salon. There, much shaking of hands as Dr Karsfeld, Dr Kammer and Herr Worters congratulated Nikolai and me on the favourable decision of the grant-allocating committee. Dr Kammer raised a grey Samsonite briefcase in his right hand and said: 'The means to build your church!' Nikolai: 'God be praised.'

The Grand Master summoned us into his study. The six of us sat down. Herr Worters took from his leather briefcase a fat pile of documents, which both Nikolai and I were to sign. Nikolai caused some embarrassment by preparing to sign the documents without reading them. Dr Kammer raised a hand to stop him: it was most important that we should know what we were signing. 'But I cannot imagine,' said Nikolai, 'that there would be any clause to which we might object.'

'Even so,' said Dr Karsfeld, 'there are certain commitments to accounting procedures and that kind of thing.'

'Of course.' To make up for this misjudgement, Nikolai now started to scrutinise the documents clause by clause. I pretended to do the same. Nikolai did far better than I. He questioned certain clauses about building standards in the construction of the church that would be impossible to enforce in Komsomolsk, and another about 'the employment policies of the contractor being consistent with the Social Teaching of the Catholic Church'. Dr Kammer happily struck them out. By midday, the contract was agreed but apparently the actual signing is to wait for some kind of ceremony later today.

'Now, I am afraid,' said Dr Kammer, 'you must go through the somewhat onerous process of counting the money.' He picked up the case and laid it on the low marble-topped table in front of the sofa on which Nikolai and I were sitting. Taking a key from his pocket, he then opened it to reveal tightly packed bundles of dollar bills.

'We counted it at the bank,' said Herr Worters, 'but it would be improper for you to sign a receipt unless you had counted it too.'

Nikolai had learned his lesson. 'Indeed.'

'Of course,' said Dr Karsfeld, with an unexpected smile, 'no one wishes to suggest that Herr Worters or Dr Kammer have helped themselves to the odd thousand dollars.' There was some feeble laughter. 'But with such a large sum of money, things must be done by the book.'

'Perhaps it is not necessary for Father Piotr to count the money?' asked Nikolai.

'I am quite happy to assist,' I said, 'and witness such munificence.'

The counting started. All watched as Nikolai took the bundles out of the case and, having verified that they contained the amount specified on the bands which held them together, placed them in a pile on the table. Only

Heinrich von Willich attended to some other papers that demanded his attention on his desk. The pile of dollars grew in to a tower. Finally, the counting was completed. 'Two hundred and fifty thousand dollars,' said Nikolai. 'God be praised.'

He signed the receipt. 'And surely Father Piotr should sign as well.' He passed the receipt along the table. I appended a Cyrillic scrawl. Nikolai packed the banknotes back into the case with a relish that I think I was the only one to detect.

'It would be best to leave it here until your departure,' said Heinrich von Willich, rising from his desk.

'Of course,' said Nikolai, handing the briefcase to the Grand Master, again with a reluctance imperceptible to our German friends. The Grand Master put it in a baroque cupboard at the back of his study, which he then locked with a small key.

'God willing,' said Nikolai, 'you will all come to Komsomolsk in a year or eighteen months to see your generous donation transformed into a magnificent church.'

As we passed in to lunch, Dr Karsfeld told me that she and her colleagues were staying at Zelden for the night. The ceremony at which we will sign the contracts is to be at five this afternoon. There will be a photographer, some reporters and one or two distinguished guests. In the dining room, Dr Kammer and Herr Worters waited nervously by the table as if ready to be told that they were not to eat here but in the servants' quarters. I counted the number of places. There was one too few. Julia von Willich invited us to sit down. It was Monika who was missing.

Next. After lunch, Heinrich von Willich came up beside

me and asked if I would be kind enough to return for a moment to his study. Julia von Willich came in behind me and closed the door. The Grand Master had an expression at once weary and resigned.

'Father Piotr,' he said, 'you probably know that your companion Nikolai has asked to marry our daughter Monika, and wants her to return with him to Russia tomorrow.'

I nodded. 'Yes.'

'As you can imagine, this proposal came as a shock to us, particularly since only a month ago Monika had told us that she was going to enter the Carmelite convent.'

'Indeed.'

'When Monika first told us about Nikolai's proposal, it not only came as a shock, but I have to say that we were both somewhat surprised to discover that she was considering accepting it and going off to live in Siberia.'

'We should not have been surprised,' said Julia von Willich.

'No, we should not have been surprised because we always knew that Monika was pious and idealistic –'

'Stubborn and wilful,' put in the mother, 'ever since she was a child.'

'Clearly, the idea of evangelising the tundra appealed to these qualities, and last night she told us that she had decided to accept Nikolai's offer of marriage and leave with him tomorrow for Moscow.'

'We tried to dissuade her,' said Julia von Willich.

'Yes, we tried to dissuade her, but to no avail,' said the Grand Master sadly. 'Once her mind is made up, there is nothing anyone can do.' He sighed. 'And so, in an attempt to make a virtue out of a necessity, as it were, we feel that if she must marry, then she should marry here at Zelden, and we would therefore be most grateful if you,

314

Father Piotr, would perform the ceremony tomorrow morning in the chapel before you leave.'

I swallowed, hesitated, played for time. 'Are there no civil formalities to be observed?' I asked. 'Forms to be filled in? Banns to be read? Licences to be obtained?'

'In so far as they are necessary, these things have been arranged. There may have to be some kind of civil ceremony at the German Embassy in Moscow. But for us it is the sacrament that matters.'

'Of course.'

'If you could marry them during your morning mass, then we could have a wedding breakfast before you leave.'

'As you like.'

'Monika herself particularly wants *you* to perform the ceremony, though I understand that, like us, you have expressed some reservations.'

'Indeed. I am not sure she quite understands what life is like in Komsomolsk.'

The Grand Master shrugged. 'I am sure she does not, but I fear that the worse you make it sound, the more determined she will be to go.'

'Where is she now?'

'At the convent, telling the Mother Superior of her decision, and preparing herself for the sacrament tomorrow.'

'One daughter will not marry,' said Julia von Willich, 'and the other goes off with a Russian to the ends of the earth!' She raised her hands in a gesture of despair.

Once again, the sense that I have been betrayed. I sit here in my room, keeping a pedantic account of the day's events, seething with anger that *she* should not have told me that the decision was made. And Nikolai? A smug look this morning, but I thought that was because of the money.

A plan of action. What matters most? That I save her from Nikolai. That I win her for myself. What must I do to attain these objectives? Declare my love. Tell all. But when? Nikolai may marry her in Zelden but he will not have an opportunity to exercise his conjugal rights before they reach Moscow. But in Moscow, we are both at the mercy of Nikolai and General Savchenko. Tell her in Germany before we go? Then we are at the mercy of the Germans and the Knights of the Cross. 'Make haste, O God, to deliver me; make haste to help me, O Lord.'

10 p.m. I await her. She said she would come.

She returned from the convent in time for the signing ceremony in the salon. The von Willichs, Thomas Krull, Grunberger, the three from Parsheim; a monsignor from the office of the Archbishop; one or two local journalists; a photographer; and half a dozen others, some of them Kreuzhilfe donors.

I affect modesty in an attempt to avoid being photographed, but to no avail. Nikolai seems unconcerned. We line up with Dr Karsfeld on one side and the Grand Master on the other. Nikolai poses, pen poised over the documents. He signs. I follow. Applause. Many shake my hand. 'Congratulations.' 'God be praised.' I find myself looking into the grey eyes of the old Countess. She holds out her frail, bony hand to shake mine. No particular look in her eyes: clearly she, too, has been used by Paget. She has no idea of what is going on.

Heinrich von Willich makes a speech; then Dr Karsfeld. Nikolai replies – so pure, so modest, so grateful. He has them eating out of the palm of his hand.

When he finishes, all applaud and Monika, who stands beside him, spontaneously takes hold of his arm.

I seethe with jealousy and resentment. How could she betray her true feelings and marry a man she does not love? The maidservants appear with glasses of *Sekt* on a tray. Heinrich von Willich proposes a toast. 'To the Catholics of Komsomolsk!' Next come canapés. I have to talk about our mission to a journalist, then to the Monsignor, then to a donor. Suddenly, I find myself next to Monika. She makes as if to move away. Before she can do so, I say: 'I gather you have made up your mind to marry Nikolai.'

She blushes. 'Yes. And you have kindly agreed to perform the ceremony.'

'It is customary for the priest to give the bride some preparation.'

'Of course.'

'Come to my room for a brief talk after supper.'

'Very well.'

She said she would come. I await her.

## *Thursday*

1 a.m. The die is cast. I write this on a thick piece of writing paper embossed with the von Willich coat of arms. There is also the simple address: 'Schloss Zelden, Westfalen'. I write because it is the only way to analyse what has just happened, what I have done.

Supper followed the signing – more than supper, a decent dinner. Nikolai and I were the guests of honour. There were more speeches, toasts and an announcement by Heinrich von Willich that his daughter, Monika, was to go to Komsomolsk the next day as Nikolai's wife. He even made a joke at Dr Karsfeld's expense: 'I did not realise that the aid given by Kreuzhilfe to the Church in Russia would include our daughter.' Julia von Willich did not laugh. Her expression: sour and serious. Monika looked at Nikolai and smiled. She was settling into her role.

At ten, the party broke up. I looked towards Monika: she nodded to signify that she remembered her promise to come to my room. Would she bring Nikolai? That was my principal anxiety as I waited. At around a quarter to eleven came the knock on the door. She was alone.

She came in cautiously, even reluctantly, as if she had far rather not be there. For the first time I could see how the jaw that I so longed to smother with kisses could set in a stubborn expression. The look in her eyes was guarded as if she was prepared for dissuasion and was determined to resist it.

'Is this your idea or theirs?' she asked, crossing the room to the chair on which she had sat when she made her confession.

'Whose?'

'My parents.'

'No. They seem … resigned.'

She turned and looked at me fiercely. 'Never before have I been more certain that what I am doing is the will of God.'

How lovely she looked when she was defiant. Her long, strong body beneath the thin silk of her flowery summer dress was taut as if, like her ancestors, she might have to seize a sword to defend her cause.

'Why don't you sit down?' My tone was kindly – priest-like. Even now I was finding it difficult to shed the role.

She did, on the same chair as before, but her body remained ready to spring up again at any moment.

'If I am to marry you,' I began, 'I must be sure that you both conform to the canonical requirements for a valid marriage.'

She laughed. 'Well, I haven't been married before.'

'I realise that. My only doubts are as to whether your decision is voluntary.'

She looked puzzled. 'Who might be forcing me to marry Nikolai?'

'No one as such, but perhaps undue pressure is being put on you by ... Nikolai himself?'

She did not reject this notion out of hand. 'He is ardent,' she said, 'and quite sure that God wants me to be his wife.' Then she added: 'As am I, of course.'

'But you are not so ardent?'

She did not answer.

'You do not love him,' I said.

'That will come,' she whispered, 'and –' She did not go on.

'How can God want you to marry a man you do not love?'

'We are marrying,' she said, 'because it is the best way, probably the only way, for me to join him in Komsomolsk. If we were living in a different era – of St Francis of Assisi and St Clare, for example, or St Francis de Sales and St Jeanne Françoise de Chantal – then it might be different. But I am quite sure that Nikolai is right that it would only be practicable in Russia today if I were to go there as his wife.'

'But being a wife involves certain obligations.'

She blushed. 'I realise that.'

'A wife must share a bed with her husband.'

'Of course.'

'Do you find him attractive?'

She looked down. 'That, too, will come with time.'

'You can contemplate it without repugnance?'

She looked up at me, now angry. 'Haven't I explained already that God has made it clear, crystal clear, that I am not destined to belong to a man I might love?'

'The dream?'

'Yes, the dream.'

'Because I was that man?'

'Because that man was a priest.'

'And if I were to tell you ...'

'What?'

'That I love you more than life itself.'

She gave a cry and shrank back in her chair. I jumped forward, took hold of a pale hand, and knelt at her feet. *How can I pretend any longer? From the first moment I set eyes on you, I loved you. There has never been a moment in your presence that is not beauty, nor a moment without you that is not drab and empty. And when I think of you with that loathsome, lecherous hypocrite, who only wants to debauch you and then abandon you ...*

I looked up. Her face was pale. She looked astonished, but also curious. 'So you also speak English, Father Piotr?'

English? In the stress of my protestation of love, I had reverted to my native tongue. 'Yes, English. I am English.'

'You're not Russian?'

'No. And, God forgive me, I am not a priest.'

There. It was done. I plunged my face into her lap, clinging to her two cold hands. I was sobbing and mumbling, 'God forgive me, God forgive me.' Monika was ominously quiet. She did not remove her hands from mine and I was determined to remain as long as I could

320

in this delicious proximity to her body – possibly the first and last time that I would touch her slender legs.

She withdrew one hand and, with it, stroked my hair. If this was to calm me, it had the intended effect. I stopped sobbing and looked up into her face. Her eyes looked down on me with an expression that was infinitely sad. 'You are not a priest?' she whispered.

I shook my head.

'And you are not Russian?'

'No.'

'And Nikolai?'

'He is a Russian, but not a Catholic.'

'Are there no Catholics in Komsomolsk?'

I shrugged. 'I don't know. I have never been there. Nor has he.'

She was silent. Then: 'But why did he want to marry me?'

'Why do you think?'

'But I would have found out, after a week or a month.'

'A week or a month would have been quite enough.'

'He would have left me?'

'He already has a wife.'

Again, a silence as she considered what I had told her. 'But why did he come here? What did he want?'

I shrugged. 'The money.'

'And you?'

I got to my feet and went to the window. In the dark beyond the ramparts, the lights of the village houses.

'Was it also the money?'

'No!' I said this indignantly, as if she had no right to suggest it.

'Then why?'

What could I say? How could I explain? I looked down on to my desk. My eye fell on *The Development of Secondary Education in the Soviet Far East*, the hiding-place

321

for my journal. And at the same time another phrase from St Paul, used by my father in his sermons, came into my head: 'And the truth shall set you free!' The truth. I crossed to the desk, opened the textbook, took out the notebook and thrust it at Monika. 'Do you read English?'

'Of course.'

'It's all here. Take it. Read it. Then decide. My life is in your hands.'

With a certain caution, she got up from her chair, took the notebook and, with a look of mixed bafflement and curiosity, said: 'Very well.'

*Tout comprendre, c'est tout pardonner.* To understand everything is to forgive everything. Not St Paul but Madame de Staël. How much longer must I wait to find out if this is true? Was it a stroke of folly or of genius to give her my journal? How else could I explain what brought me to Zelden as a Russian priest?

My hopes are pinned on that hand that quite unbidden withdrew itself from mine and stroked my head. She did not reject me. She comforted me. I am sure she loves me. If she loves me, she will forgive me. *Tout comprendre, c'est tout pardonner.*

5.30 a.m. All is not forgiven. All is lost.

She came into my room without knocking, an angry ghost. I had fallen asleep in my chair, and awoke to see her staring down at me. As soon as she saw I was conscious, she thrust the notebook back at me. 'Please take this back.'

'Have you read it?'

'Of course.'

'And?'

322

'It is vile.'

She turned to leave. I jumped to my feet and took hold of her arm. 'It proves I love you.'

She turned and looked at me with a look of chilling disdain. 'Many men have loved me, although never before, I think, a divorced journalist from the BBC.'

'It was no real marriage. It could be annulled.'

'What would be the point for someone who does not believe in God, let alone the Church? And what of this other woman you seduced? It seems to me that between you and the odious Nikolai there is little to choose.'

Denise! Only now did I recall that there were certain passages in this journal that had nothing to do with my coming to Zelden. 'Please sit down and let me explain.'

She hesitated, then, with great reluctance, returned to the chair with lion's claw feet. 'How can you explain? Your depravity, your neurosis, your mediocrity, your self-pity are all recounted with no shame or remorse. But all that is nothing when compared to the iniquity of your behaviour here. To pretend to be a priest! To say a blasphemous mass and give us all counterfeit communion, and then to encourage us to confess our sins. To *record* the sins of poor Babi so that now she will be sent to prison ...'

'Never!' I crossed to my desk and took out the tape that contained Babi's confession. 'Here. It is yours. No one will ever know.'

She took the cassette, clutched it in her hand and muttered: 'That is something.'

'It is only the beginning. The man there' – I pointed to the notebook – 'is dead and gone. I agree he was vile. He was mediocre. But that was because he had had no vision of purity and heroism to inspire him. What is such a man like that to do? It was only after I met you that I knew what it was to love and, dare I say it, to be loved.'

323

'Don't presume –'

'Don't deny it. I was your lover not just in a dream.'

She blushed. 'There were moments, yes – but I could hardly help myself – yes, I was in love. But it was not with you, Mr Latham, it was with Father Piotr, a Russian priest. I was ashamed. I dared not confess it. I thought it was God's way of showing me that I was not meant to enjoy human happiness of that kind. The most I could hope for was to remain near him by marrying Nikolai and going to Komsomolsk. That was the sacrifice I was ready to make for Father Piotr – a loveless marriage in a foreign land.'

I knelt once again and took hold of her hands. 'But now God has shown his mercy. Nothing need keep us apart.'

She drew back her hands, moved back her chair and got to her feet. 'Us?' She drew herself up to her full height and, even in her exhaustion, pointed to the notebook on my desk with a fierce and terrifying disdain. 'Do you really imagine that the daughter of the Grand Master of the Knights of the Cross could marry a middle-class mediocrity like *him*?'

'I love you,' I said hoarsely. It was all I could say.

'And all I feel for you, Mr Latham, is pity.' She turned towards the door.

Again I grabbed her arm. 'Forgive me!'

She looked at me. The expression of contempt had gone. Once again she seemed sad. 'If a life of prayer and penance can work miracles, yes, I shall forgive you. And may Almighty God do the same.' Gently, she removed her arm from my grasp, left the room and closed the door.

I sat dumbfounded, my head in my hands. Then I heard a sound from the far corner of the room. I ran to the

324

concealed door leading on to the staircase that led down to the chapel. It was ajar. I opened it and listened. The sound of footsteps on the stairs below. Someone had been eavesdropping and must have heard everything that had been said.

7 a.m. I wait. For the police or the Knights of the Cross. No one comes. The castle is silent. What can I do but continue as if nothing has happened? I shall go down to say mass.

8 a.m. I come to the altar from the vestry and find a large congregation, all dressed for a wedding. Heinrich von Willich steps up to the lectern. 'My dear friends, for various reasons, the wedding we planned for this morning will not take place.'

Monika is not present. Neither is Nikolai. The entire family come to take communion, including Babi, the people from Parsheim and the castle staff. One of the maids has been crying; she is red around the eyes.

What should I do now? Go down to breakfast. Act as if nothing has happened.

9.30 a.m. The table laden for the wedding breakfast. Heinrich von Willich commands us all to enjoy it, despite the fact that there has been no wedding. From his bonhomie and the happy expression on Julia von Willich's face, the broken engagement is for them a cause for celebration. Monika appears and sits pale-faced between her parents. Obvious that she has had a poor night's sleep. She avoids my eyes.

I sit between Babi and Dr Karsfeld. There is one empty place. 'Where's the bridegroom?' asks Heinrich von Willich. Adolf and Herr Worters go off to find him.

Babi, to me: 'Do you know what happened? Why did they call it off?'

'Your sister changed her mind.'

'Back to the convent?'

'So it seems.'

'I never thought she would go through with it.'

'Why not?'

Babi shrugs. 'She is so clearly a dedicated virgin, a bride of Christ.'

'Babi,' I whisper, 'whatever may happen in the future, you must never worry about what you told me.'

She looks puzzled. 'How do you mean? Whatever may happen?'

At that moment, Adolf returns and says, as much to me as to his father: 'Nikolai's room is empty. There are no clothes and no suitcase. And the Opel has gone.'

Herr Worters comes up beside him. 'So has the briefcase. The cupboard has been forced open. The money has gone.'

Confusion. We all rise from the table without the usual formality of saying grace. Dr Karsfeld turns to me: 'What can have happened?'

I shake my head. 'Perhaps he was so upset about the wedding that he could not face us all this morning and decided to make his own way to the airport.' I move towards the door. 'Or he may simply … I shall go and see.'

From the corner of my eye, I see Heinrich and Julia von Willich talking to Dr Kammer, and next to them Moni whispering in Babi's ear. I take advantage of the confusion to slip away to my room.

I write the above in this journal as I await my fate. Now I sit looking out of the window towards the village of

Zelden, cursing Nikolai, cursing myself. There is a knock on the door ...

*Four*

*Friday*

London. Dusk. I sit once again at my kitchen table, this journal open on the yellow Formica. The windows light up in the houses that back on to our block. Before the curtains are drawn, I catch glimpses of unknown neighbours and, should they care to look, they can see me. The inhabitants of a city live in goldfish bowls; the externals of their lives are easily observed. But the inner life remains hidden, even to oneself.

To continue where I left off. I was in my room at Schloss Zelden. There was a knock on the door. I called, '*Herein*.' It was not Thomas Krull or even the police. It was Adolf. He was carrying a grey suit, a shirt, a tie. 'You must quickly change,' he said, 'and then you must go.'

He looked away while I exchanged my priest's cassock for the clothes of a civilian, affecting to study the Flemish painting of the Virgin Mary. The clothes fitted quite well. They could not have been Adolf's. Perhaps they had been Otto's.

'I'm ready.'

He turned and saw that I was dressed. 'Good. Follow me.' I snatched up this journal and put it in my black briefcase; he seemed uninterested in what I took with me but was intent only that we should make haste. He led me through the door through which Nikolai had learned that the game was up, and down the spiral staircase to the chapel. It was empty but we could hear shouted words echoing from the corridors within the castle: I could not make out what they were. We went into the vestry where

Adolf opened one of the huge wardrobes that once housed the priest's vestments. The back of it opened on to another, narrower spiral staircase smelling of damp and mildew.

We went down. It was dark but he had a torch to light his way. I stumbled down after him, down and down, round and round. He stopped. He told me to hold the torch and shine it on two bolts. 'It's been years since anyone's been down here.' He grunted with the physical exertion, but in the end the bolts shifted. The door creaked open. Bright daylight shone in.

We had come out through this small postern gate on to the steep wooded bank beneath the ramparts. 'It would be better,' said Adolf, 'if we were not seen from the castle.' Half crouching behind the different bushes and trees, he clambered down towards the road that led down from the castle. We emerged from this undergrowth twenty metres from Babi's red Mercedes. It moved forward and stopped. Babi was driving. Adolf opened the door to the seat beside her. 'This is where I must leave you.'

'Thank you.'

He smiled thinly. 'This is for the best. *Adieu.*' He did not say *auf Wiedersehen* – until we see each other again – but that courtly, old-fashioned form of leave-taking, 'to God', *adieu.*

I climbed in beside Babi. Adolf shut the door. Babi drove off down the hill. We passed through the lower gate and turned on to the road towards Münster.

'We thought it would be best,' said Babi, 'if you followed the example of your friend Nikolai and disappeared.'

'I had no right to expect your help.'

'Don't you have an expression in English – *tit for tat*? You gave back the tape.'

'Babi, you must understand that –'

'What?' Her face had an expression of half-suppressed amusement.

'You are an actress. Perhaps you can understand, that sometimes, when one is acting, the role overwhelms one's actual persona, and while one is on stage one becomes in a sense the person one plays.'

'Certainly, you deserve an Oscar …'

'That is not what I meant.'

'No, I know.' She looked at me briefly, then back at the road. 'Whether or not you were a priest, it was good to talk to someone about certain matters, someone I feel I can trust and will never see again.'

'You can trust me, I swear it. No one will ever know what happened to George Harding.'

'So justice will never be done?'

'So far as I am concerned, justice has been done.'

We drove on for a moment in silence. Then Babi said: 'As I understand it, you, too, fell in love with my sister?'

'Yes.'

Babi laughed. 'She is *la belle dame sans merci*, responsible for many a broken heart.'

'She also fell in love, but it was with Piotr, the Russian priest, not me.'

'So she has learned what it is like to fall in love, but of course with someone inaccessible. She will never give herself to a mortal man.'

We drove into Münster and stopped by the railway station. There Babi bought me a ticket to London. 'You must change in Cologne on to the train to Brussels, and in Brussels on to the Eurostar. Can you manage that?'

'Of course.'

She smiled. 'There, you see. I still think of you as a helpless Russian priest.'

'Babi …'

333

She put her fingers to my lips. '*Tit for tat.*'

'All the same.'

'Take care.' She embraced me. 'We must both try to avoid getting into any further scrapes.' She opened her handbag and took out an envelope. 'And this is from Moni. To be read on the train.'

> Michael. I do not want you to misunderstand what I said to you this morning. It is not because of your social origins that I could never marry you. It is because you have no faith. Without faith, we are all mediocre. You will be for ever in my prayers.
> Monika W.

This note lies in front of me on my kitchen table. The thick paper with the embossed address 'Schloss Zelden, Westfalen' is the same as that on which I wrote that scrap of this journal while she had this notebook in her room. It is the only tangible evidence that I was ever at Zelden. How quickly recent reality can seem like a dream. How quickly, too, familiar surroundings draw us back into our everyday life.

On the trains carrying me across northern Europe, I had time to read and reread Monika's note. Since Babi had bought me a first-class ticket, I did so in some comfort. On the first leg of my journey, I sat in the corner seat of an empty compartment, looking out at the flat landscape of Westphalia, then at the letter, back to the landscape, again the letter. I analysed every phrase. By the time I reached Cologne I had decided that what she wrote in her letter was a lie. It *was* because of my social origins that she could never marry me. Would my prospects have been better if I had been the son of a duke, listed in the *Almanach de Gotha*? Probably not. Only the Son of

334

God was good enough for a daughter of the Grand Master of the Knights of the Cross.

By the time I reached Brussels, I had ceased to love her; by which I mean, that the image and memory of Moni no longer provoked the emotions that I had felt at Zelden. I had loved an angel, a vision of innocence; now, as with Lucifer, pride had led to her fall.

The telephone rings. Jane. She invites me to Sunday lunch.

## Saturday

The papers filled with trivia. Nothing about the murdered minister. The story is as dead as George.

My preoccupation with my feelings for Monika distracts me from other matters. What am I do about my commission from the *Sunday Gazette*? What am I to say to Gordon? Or to Paget. My mission was successful. I found out who killed George. But I shall keep my word to Babi. The world will never know.

Without Babi, is there a story? Yes. That George and Paget arranged the accident on the autobahn that led to the death of Otto von Willich. Was Gordon part of the conspiracy? Did he think that George was killed by Knights in revenge? Did they hope that Nikolai and I would uncover the evidence? For what purpose? To suggest sinister forces at work in Germany. Renascent nationalism. Neo-Fascism. Papist triumphalism. To frighten the British out of Europe. To feed the tabloids.

335

When we return from abroad, people ask about our travels but their curiosity is feigned. So it was with Jane.

'How was Russia?'

'Interesting.'

'You seem to have changed.'

'In what way?'

'You're more ... subdued.'

I shy away from my sister's scrutiny. She will not let me escape.

'Ruth got married while you were away. Someone sent me a cutting from the *Jewish Chronicle*. I kept it for you.'

'Thank you.'

A short pause, then: 'It's time you found another wife.'


Return mildly drunk from Mark's claret. Write the above. Jump up to answer the telephone. It is not the telephone but a burglar alarm in the street below. The sound is quite dissimilar. Why did I imagine it was the telephone? Am I expecting a call?

Watch television. An old film. When it ends, to the kitchen to make some supper. Scrambled egg. Why, when I once prized solitude, am I now reluctant to be alone? Because alone I cannot escape from the sense of my own stupidity. How can a man fall in love so instantly with someone he hardly knows? And out of love with the same speed.

Despised and rejected. By Monika and Ruth. I sit raging at these perfidious women. How could Ruth prefer Joshua, and Monika the life of a nun? Would Alison provide the answer? Parents. Childhood. I already know what her explanation would be.


And Father Piotr? He was a simpleton but, given that he

came from Siberia, one could hardly expect much sophistication. Yet he gave some sound advice to Babi. What would he say to me?

## Monday

Back to work. Some penetrating questions from my colleagues about conditions in Russia, which I answer as best I can. My excuse for not knowing more: I had been given a narrow remit by the European Bank.

I see Denise in the staff restaurant. To be precise, she sees me where I am sitting with Bill, duty editor for the day. She holds a laden tray. There are empty places at our table. But she does not sit down.

'How was your trip?' she asks me in a bored tone of voice.

'Fine.'

She moves on and sits down with Jerry Fermor and Pavel Kravchek. I know she finds Jerry dull and Pavel obnoxious, yet she now appears wholly engaged by their conversation. Not a glance in my direction.

During the afternoon break, I call Gordon on his private line.

'You're back?'

'Yes.'

'How was it?'

'Interesting.'

'When can you file your copy?'

'We ought to talk about it first.'

'Very well, if you think it necessary. I'll hand you over to Josephine.'

Josephine fixes a date. Thursday. The bar at the Connaught at 7 p.m.

Walking back to my work-station, I see Denise approaching along the corridor. What expression should I put on my face? She is better prepared than I am. No break in her pace. A cold nod as she walks on.

A strong impulse on my way home to resume my visits to Alison. I should like to have discussed Denise. Is her detachment feigned? Or has she ceased to love me just as abruptly as I ceased to love Monika? It seems that I have been down-graded from lover to mere colleague, not to a good friend.

I feel offended by the idea that she has changed her feelings for me with such ease. My case with Monika seems to me quite different. I had no physical relationship with Monika. We scarcely knew each other and, in the event, neither of us was quite what we assumed the other to be. I was not a priest. She was not an angel. In other words, we both loved an illusion. Such love can be more powerful than a love that is rooted in reality. But it is more superficial.

What does this say about love? That it is an introspective emotion, an impetuous demand of the psyche that settles on the beloved for purposes of its own. Better to settle for a companion of the opposite sex to end our solitude and satisfy our desires. Sex and friendship, not the weakling's constant quest for a boost to his self-esteem. A man is a man, a woman a woman. However much we embroider the elemental encounter with sentiment, we are part of nature. The lion lies down with the lioness, not with the lamb. The voice of Father Piotr whispers: 'Be grateful for what you have got.'

338

A message on my answering machine from Paget. He is in London this evening and suggests a drink or dinner at the Special Forces Club. The message was recorded at four in the afternoon. I replay it at six. Because I no longer visit Alison, I get back earlier in the evening.

I had wanted to see Gordon before Paget. Indeed, I had wondered whether it was necessary to see Paget at all. Sooner or later, it would be unavoidable so I decide I might as well see him now. I call the club and ask the porter to tell Paget that I will meet him there at eight.

Paget is old. How much of what he has done can I ascribe to senility? How much to boredom? How much to pride? He was wearing the same pin-striped suit as always, but there was a stain on the waistcoat: perhaps jam from a teacake eaten that afternoon.

'Tell me,' he said in a whisper, after we had been served with sherry. 'Tell me, how did you get on?'

I gave him a steady look which, if he had been more perceptive, would have told him that I 'knew all'. But he still looked at me with an expression of reptilian curiosity. 'Was it the Knights? Did they kill George?'

I shook my head. 'No. I fear it was much as the Government supposed. A sordid sexual encounter. Drugs. Alcohol. He simply fell into the Saar.'

A look of fury crossed Paget's face. 'It cannot have been as simple as that.'

Again, the look I returned, had he been able to read it, might have told him that it was not. But he was preoccupied with his own certainties. 'How did you find out it wasn't the Knights? How can you be sure?'

'Let me begin from the beginning,' I said.

'Of course.'

'First of all, you can be well pleased with your plan. It worked to perfection.'

'They accepted you as a priest?'

'Without hesitation.'

'Excellent. And what about Savchenko's man?'

'Better than we could have hoped. In Russia, we had all the back-up we needed. They must have their people in the office of the Apostolic Administrator. When we reached Frankfurt, we were expected.'

'Well, of course,' said Paget, as if this was hardly surprising. 'The KGB was the only institution in the old Soviet Union that worked.'

'My companion Nikolai was invaluable in lending credibility to my role.'

'As we predicted.'

'But it became clear as we proceeded that he had an agenda of his own.'

Paget leaned forward. 'What do you mean?'

'He showed less interest in the possibility of a political conspiracy than in a large sum of money to build a church in Komsomolsk.'

'To build a church?'

'A quarter of a million dollars in cash.'

'And did they provide it?'

'Yes.'

'And where is it?'

I shrugged. 'In a Swiss bank account, or perhaps in Moscow.'

Paget sat back in his arm-chair. 'Ah, Savchenko ... I should have known. He was always as cunning as a fox.'

'It was presumably what they always had in mind.'

'Perhaps.' Paget stood to lead me through to dinner. He seemed less upset by the swindle than I had expected. 'Of course, they are short of foreign currency and he may have envisaged something of the kind as a fee for services rendered.'

'He had no fear of the threat to Russian security of a European Fourth Reich?'

'I cannot believe,' Paget said as we sat down at table, 'that everything he said when we met here before was bogus.'

I took my place facing him. 'I can believe it only too well. In fact, I cannot escape the sense that I have just returned from a journey in a balloon held up by hot air from various sources.'

Paget gave me an uneasy look, then lowered his eyes to the menu. 'Do you like grouse?'

I followed his choice on the menu. I was not interested in what I ate.

'To continue ...' I said, after the waiter had taken our order.

'Oh, yes, by all means, continue.'

'A priest, as you predicted, elicits confidences from all sorts of different people.'

'Indeed.'

'And there was an archive at Schloss Zelden with documents and diaries.'

'Whose diaries?

'Ilse von Willich's, for example.'

Paget turned as if to see if the waiter was bringing the smoked salmon that was to precede the grouse. 'Ilse von Willich.' He repeated the name when he faced me once again. 'The name is familiar.'

'More than the name, I think.'

He now looked me in the eye. 'You would have made a good intelligence officer. You should have accepted my offer all those years ago.'

'It would certainly have made more sense when we had real enemies instead of imagined ones.'

341

'Don't underestimate imagination,' said Paget. 'It can see into the future.'

'And invent conspiracies where there are none.'

'Better safe than sorry.' His eyes followed the plate of smoked salmon as it was placed before him. Then, after eating a few mouthfuls: 'At least you discovered that there was no conspiracy by the Knights of the Cross. Or so I assume.'

'There is a conspiracy of a kind, but I think you knew that already.'

'You mean?'

'The guns.'

'Ah, the guns. Yes. Bought in Riga.'

'By Otto von Willich and some of the younger Knights to arm the Christian forces in the Sudan.'

'And before that in Croatia, so I believe.'

'But not to arm some Federalist militia in Europe.'

'That was always improbable.'

'Yet it is what you suggested.'

'One must consider every eventuality. You would have learned that if you had joined us.'

'Did you persuade George to believe it? Or was he the one who saw the potential?'

'The potential?'

'Fodder for the tabloids.'

Paget sighed. Was it at the thought of his dead friend, or because he had finished his smoked salmon? I could not tell. 'I had high hopes of George, but he had weaknesses.'

'That does not answer my question.'

'George knew what he was doing.'

'Did he know what *you* were doing?'

'Our aims were identical.'

'To frighten the British?'

Paget sighed again. The waiter removed our plates.

342

'You were never one of my students, were you? Of course not. You studied languages. You see, politics, which is history in the making, never follows a straight course. Even a government with a solid majority is at the mercy of public opinion. This is true of dictatorships as well as democracies. Even Hitler took great pains to keep the German people on side. He was extraordinarily fortunate in Goebbels – we all admired his skill. "If you must tell a lie," he said, "tell a big one. It is more likely to be believed."'

'And you followed his example?'

'During the war? Of course. We controlled the dissemination of information as closely as he did.'

'And now?'

'Now, of course, it is more complicated. There is no censorship. No Ministry of Information. But there are any number of gullible journalists and editors desperate for a story.'

'So you feed them falsehoods?'

The grouse arrived. Paget tackled his at once. Was he hungry or simply eager to get rid of me as soon as he could? At first I thought he had forgotten my question, but after a couple of mouthfuls of the dead bird's breast, he laid down his knife and fork and said: 'Falsehoods? That is too strong a word. You feed them images and let the readers form their own impression. The story is forgotten but the impression remains.'

'And this was behind the accident on the autobahn? The crates of Kalashnikovs were to create an impression?'

'Yes.'

'That the Germans were up to something sinister?'

'Of a nation not to be trusted.'

'But Otto von Willich was hardly the German nation.'

'No, but imagine what could have been made of his

343

father's position in the Christian Democrat Party, and the sinister fraternity of the Knights of the Cross.'

'Did Ilse von Willich know what you had in mind?'

For the first time, a shadow of self-doubt crossed Paget's face. But he at once recovered his self-assurance. 'You must understand that Ilse von Willich was a Prussian. To her, her homeland – her *Heimat* – ceased to exist after the war. Then, with reunification, the chance arose to restore it. The old landed families had reason to believe that their estates would be returned. Kohl refused. He said that Gorbachev had only permitted reunification on condition that the Junkers should not be reinstated. This was denied by Gorbachev. It was Kohl and the bourgeois West Germans who wanted to deny the Prussian landowners their rights.'

'Was that why she helped you?'

'She hardly helped me. She told me what her grandson was up to, and invited George to stay at Zelden. And, later, you and the Russian. That was all.'

'How did she feel about the death of Otto?'

'She knew that was not intended.'

'But to you it was a price worth paying?'

Paget shrugged. 'Ours is a dangerous business. So was his.'

'And – let me be clear – you sent me to Germany to find out if George had been killed by the Knights in revenge.'

'It seemed likely.'

'I was to expose them as his assassins?'

'The murderers of a British minister. Yes. Which would create an even greater impression than the gun-running.'

For a while we both ate our grouse in silence. Eventually, I put down my knife and fork and said: 'Why do you hate the Germans?'

He frowned: the disappointed tutor. 'I thought I had explained the danger they posed before you left.'

'You said they wanted to dominate the European Union and create a Fourth Reich, which would succeed where the others have failed. But it seems to me that quite the contrary is true. They are quite as horrified as we are by what happened under Hitler, and must live with the knowledge that it was their parents and grandparents who were to blame. They do not look upon a European Union as a way to increase their power but as a means to diminish it and make it impossible for them to perpetrate such evils again. They have learned perhaps better than we have the lesson of recent history. They have changed. They are now more like us, the British, than they are like their former selves.'

Paget did not argue against what I was saying, but every now and then muttered, 'No, no,' or 'I beg to differ,' as he fumbled with the leg-bone of his grouse. At first I was annoyed that he would not come out and fight. What, in fact, did he know of modern Germany outside the spas where he kept his annual trysts with Ilse? By what right did he meddle in our national affairs?

But then I thought of his age, and his past. He had fought against Hitler. His formidable brain had helped bring about a victory that was as clearly a triumph of good over evil as the world had ever seen. Was it not only to be expected that he should regard our future in Europe with dismay?

We finished our grouse. Paget asked if I would like anything more. I said that I had eaten enough. He wiped his mouth with his napkin. A few breadcrumbs remained on the stubble left on his upper lip by clumsy shaving; and, as he stood up, I saw that some bread sauce had fallen on his waistcoat next to the stain left by the jam.

'What about some coffee?'

'I'm afraid I have to get back.'

Paget seemed relieved. 'You'll see Gordon?'

'On Thursday.'

'He'll be disappointed.'

'I dare say.'

Paget accompanied me into the hall.

'She must have been very beautiful,' I said.

'Ilse? Could you still see that? Yes. She was lovely.'

'And her two granddaughters,' I began. He was not listening. His bleary eyes were looking back into the past.

## Wednesday

Denise still loves me. This is the significance I give to a toss of her head. The scene: the staff restaurant at Caversham. The time: lunch-time today. I sit at one table. She sits at another. I look in her direction. She avoids my eye. Then she throws back her head as if her hair is in her eyes. But her hair is not in her eyes. It is a gesture of exasperation. Stop harassing me. Leave me alone. Why does she mind me looking at her? Because it reopens the wound. Again, the voice of Father Piotr whispers: 'Be grateful for what you have got.'

I cross to her table. Denise looks up with angry eyes. I mean to suggest a drink after work but am frightened off by her expression. I mumble something inconsequential and go back to my work-station. As I leave at six she intercepts me.

'What did you want to say?'

'What about a drink?'

She snorts and walks away.

Gordon was late for our meeting at the Connaught. I had already finished a whisky and soda that I had ordered on my arrival and eaten half the olives and all the potato chips. He asked for a glass of Perrier water. I ordered a second whisky and soda.

I told Gordon the whole story – as much of it, at any rate, as was consistent with Father Piotr's priestly vows. I began with the war: Count Kaspar, his disappointed wife, the young officer in British intelligence, their life-time liaison, the trysts in German spas. 'So she was the mysterious mistress?' Was he pretending to be ignorant? At this stage I could not tell. I told him about Otto, the grandson, running arms from Riga to the Sudan. Ilse tells Paget. Paget tells George. A plot is hatched to expose him – fodder for the tabloids.

There is a change in the colour of Gordon's complexion. One might have ascribed it to his drink if his drink had not been carbonated water. I continue. The accident on the autobahn. Crates of Kalashnikovs plain for all to see. But it never reaches the tabloids. The influence of the von Willichs is sufficient to cover it up.

'So they took their revenge on George?'

'How could they have known George was behind it?'

Gordon nodded. How indeed. 'So who killed him?'

I shrugged. 'It would seem that he was with a woman. They were both drunk. He fell into the river.'

'Who was the woman?'

'I don't know.'

Gordon sat silently for a moment. Then: 'What happened to the Russian?'

I told him about Nikolai and the money. 'I suspect that from the start they had plans of their own.'

'Yet you couldn't have done it without them.'

'No.'

'What's that you're drinking?'

'Whisky and soda.'

He summoned the waiter and ordered two more glasses, one for me and one for himself. 'You have discovered a lot,' he said, 'but it hardly adds up to a story.'

'Certainly not in the *Sunday Gazette*.'

'Would you take it elsewhere?'

I did not answer his question directly. 'I should like to know,' I said, 'how much of all this you knew already.'

Gordon's eyes flickered: his face went darker still. 'There were a number of rumours and suppositions ...'

'You knew what Paget and George were up to?'

'More or less.'

'You wanted to feed the tabloids?'

'I wanted to feed the *Sunday Gazette*.'

'You knew it was all an invention?'

'What was an invention?'

'The conspiracy to form a Fourth Reich by the Knights of the Cross.'

Gordon looked at me, his brow creased with the well-known look of perplexity. 'Caversham,' he said, 'is a long way from Fleet Street.'

'What do you mean?'

'Newspaper journalism, these days, is not about imparting news. That is done better and faster by television.'

'So what is its function?'

'To entertain its readers by telling a story, a never-ending story, the soap opera of our national life.'

'I don't understand.'

'We live in a complicated and confusing world. The Empire has gone. The Cold War is over. The British people want to know who they are and where they are

348

going. It is our job to tell them. So we do so by telling a story with weekly episodes, a story that enlightens them with statistics and amuses them with scandals but, above all, a story that enables them to see themselves as noble, heroic and good. But good only exists in contrast to evil. There has to be an enemy.'

'And if there is no enemy?'

'You have to invent one. During World War II, we had the Nazis. Then we had the Communists. But now the Soviet empire has collapsed.'

'So you bring back the Germans?'

He shrugged. '*Faute de mieux*. The Germans, the French, the Commission, all those descendants of Napoleon and Hitler who failed to defeat the British with their armies, and are now conspiring to destroy our liberty and independence by other means.'

'But you must know that's nonsense?'

'Why is it nonsense?'

'Because the principal guarantor of a nation's liberty and independence is its ability to defend itself, and we surrendered that to the Americans when we joined NATO after the war.'

'The Americans are different.'

'Why?'

'They were our allies against the Germans. And they speak English.'

I shook my head with incredulity. 'It is difficult for me to accept that you mean what you say.'

Gordon leaned forward. 'You don't understand,' he said. 'What I believe is irrelevant. What matters is the paper's circulation. We are in a battle to the death with our rivals, and must use every weapon in our armoury to defeat them. What would happen, do you imagine, if the paper took the line you suggest? Pro-Europe? Pro-

German? Look at the papers that do. Their circulation drops. Their profits fall. And their editors lose their jobs.'

## Friday

Awoke feeling depressed: ascribe it to yesterday's conversation with Gordon. We parted amicably enough. I am to keep my £10,000 advance on the condition that I do not write anything for any other paper based on my researches at Zelden. What depressed me on reflection was not this practical outcome, but the discovery of Gordon's formula for journalistic success. Cultivate nostalgia and xenophobia. Foster illusion and self-deception. For the sake of his proprietor's profits, encourage the people to live in the past.

At lunch, I look for Denise. She is not there. Her day off? Discuss Europe with Bill. He thinks my pessimism is wrong. Naturally, the politicians at Westminster will fight to retain their power, and newspapers will cultivate xenophobia; but sooner or later the people will realise that it is precisely the politicians who have debauched our currency, and reduced Britain from the top of the European league to near the bottom. 'In the end, given the choice between being governed by a buffoon like the late George Harding and an efficient bureaucrat in Brussels, they will choose the bureaucrat.'

## Saturday

I take an early train to Henley. Buy a large bunch of flowers. Walk through the town as if to the cemetery but end up at Denise's flat. Ring the bell. She opens the door. Looks at me with an expression I can only describe as one

350

of despair. 'Oh, Christ, Michael ... All right. Come in.'

Reconciliation. Spend the whole day in Henley. A walk along the Thames. Fate favours me: a cancellation at the Manoir aux Quat' Saisons. Drive there in Denise's Honda Civic. Back to her flat. Reconciliation confirmed. She lies weeping afterwards. Joy or sorrow? In such circumstances, better not to enquire. I ask: 'Are you free next weekend?'

'Of course I'm free. I'm free every fucking weekend.'
'Unless there's a death in the family.'
'A death in the family?'
'Your sister's cat.'
She laughed, then sniffed. 'What had you in mind?'
'I'd like you to meet my parents.'
She looked at me oddly. 'Very well.'


## Sunday

Reading the Sunday papers reminds me of the cutting that Jane gave me describing Ruth and Joshua's wedding. I go to my dressing table and remove it from my wallet, then study it sitting in the arm-chair by the window. A bald announcement of the fact together with a list of guests at the reception. Also, a picture of the bride and bridegroom. I dip the black-and-white photograph into my mind like a litmus paper to see if it shows a trace of residual love or jealousy. A faint trace. Not the actual emotions but the memory of them.

I think of Ruth's black locks, then Monika's white-golden tresses. Blend the two, and you have Denise's brown shoulder-length hair. How strange it is that, though half the people in the world are women and half men, it is so

351

difficult to find someone of the opposite sex to satisfy the yearning of the spirit and the flesh. Piotr would say, I think, that this is because we are created man and woman, not men and women. 'And the two shall cleave together and become one flesh.'

I write a note to Ruth to say that I hope she will be happy. Try to phrase it so that she will not think I am being ironic. Go out to post it before Denise arrives from Henley with the ingredients of our Sunday lunch.

## Monday

Woke this morning with a vivid image in my mind of the breadcrumbs on Paget's whiskers and the bread sauce on his waistcoat. What is to be done in old age? Our faculties wither so long before we die. Paget distracts himself by living in the past, but what if there is a future? Life after death.

Eat the remains of Sunday lunch for supper: reheated chicken fricassée. Salad and rice.

## Tuesday

Indigestion last night from the peppers in the chicken fricassée.

I telephone my mother and ask if I can come down for the weekend.

'Of course, darling.'
'And can I bring a friend?'
'By all means. Is it anyone we know?'
'No. She's called Denise.'

'Will she be happy in the red room? Jane's coming down with the children.'

'More than happy.'

'And you'll have to go in one of the attics.'

'That'll be fine.'

The telephone rings. It is Alison. She says it is marked in her diary that I might resume my visits to her next week. I reply that this will not be necessary. 'I am cured.'

A pause. Then: 'Well, remember I'm here if you need me.'

I thank her and ring off.


*Wednesday*

Called into his office by Bill. He tells me he is taking a job at Bush House and suggests I apply for his job. He would back me. I simulate gratitude, but my mind is still pondering the question: when we are old is there a future or only a past?

A film in Henley with Denise: then supper at an Indian restaurant. I stay the night.


*Thursday*

A message from my mother on my answering machine. 'We've been asked to dinner by the Templetons. I told them about your friend.' My mother. Jane. Anne. The Templetons. In at the deep end.

*Friday*

---

I warn Denise about dinner at the Templetons. 'Smart?' I
shrug. 'Up to a point.'

*Saturday*

---

Avelscombe. Mrs Hartley has pneumonia. This put my
mother into a rage. She has as much compassion for a
sick servant as for a broken vacuum cleaner. Denise steps
into the breach and offers to peel the potatoes. I leave her
just now in the scullery. Jane stops me on the landing.
'She's awfully nice.' Mark comes out of their bedroom
with the obnoxious Toby tugging at his sleeve. 'West
Country?'
 'What?'
 'Her accent.'
 Jane scowls at her husband and goes down the stairs
with the whining Clarissa.
 'Yeovil.'
 'I thought it was somewhere like that.'

Roast chicken, roast potatoes and cabbage for lunch. My
mother's mood much improved. 'So unpretentious ...'
she murmurs. Presumably this refers to Denise. Coffee in
the drawing room. She passes round the Bendicks
Bittermints that Denise brought as a house gift.

My mother and Jane suggest a trip to the garden centre.
'Something to do with the children.' Jane insists that
Denise goes with them. Denise looks to me for guidance.
I shrug. 'Why not?' It leaves no room for me in the car.
Mark goes to his room to work. My father goes to his

study to prepare tomorrow's sermon. I retire to my attic to write in this journal.

Midnight. I kiss Denise goodnight outside her room, then go up the stairs to my attic.

Dinner at the Templetons passed off without incident. Denise elegantly dressed in a blue skirt and cashmere jersey. Reggie Templeton all over her with his old-world charm. I sit next to Anne.

'What happened?' she whispers.

'Where?'

'On your mission.'

'What mission?'

'To find out what happened to George.'

I hesitate, as if considering how much I could tell her. 'The official story stands. It was an orgy that got out of hand.'

'But unofficially?'

I put my finger to my lips: I could say no more.

Anne nodded towards Denise. 'And is she ...?'

'She works for the same outfit.'

'She seems awfully nice.'

'And unpretentious.' I repeated my mother's phrase.

'Yes. Unpretentious. Quite a relief, after Ruth.'

The ladies withdraw. The gentlemen smoke cigars and pass around the port. As we leave, John, drunk, takes me aside to say: 'I like the look of your friend. I bet she's bloody good in bed.'

At church this morning, I found myself going to the altar to take communion. I did so on impulse, without knowing why. Perhaps it was just curiosity – to be on the receiving end after so many weeks of giving it out. My father showed no surprise He handed me the morsel of bread. I took it and ate it without quite knowing what it was.

After the service, my father and I went for a walk. We followed our usual route up the hill behind the house. It had rained earlier but now the sun shone through gaps in the clouds and the view was clear.

He did not mention my going to communion. I wanted to know what expression I had on my face. Curiosity? Or was there a trace of reverence? It seemed improper to ask.

He asked about Denise. I told him that she was a colleague at Caversham, a monitor on the French desk.

'Your mother seems to like her.'

'I assumed she wouldn't.'

'Why shouldn't she?'

'Because of her class.'

'Yes, well, there was a time … but now, I think, even your mother understands that such things don't matter much.'

We walked on for a while, then he said: 'I'm glad you've found someone at last. As God says in the Book of Genesis, "It is not good for man to be alone." '

I told him about my travels and I found myself describing my meeting with Father Piotr, a Russian Catholic priest.

'A native Russian?'

'Yes.'

'That's surely a rarity.'

'His mother was Lithuanian, deported by Stalin to Siberia.'

'And they kept their faith?'

'Yes. He was ordained by a bishop consecrated in a gulag.'

'I believe that the Russians are by nature a spiritual people.'

'More than the British, certainly.'

'I should like to have met him.'

'Yes. You would have liked him. Perhaps, one day, you will.'


## Monday

At lunch today, at Caversham, Denise said how miserable she felt leaving the train at Reading last night and returning alone to her empty flat. If I had kept a suit and a clean shirt in her wardrobe, I could have gone with her; or if she had had some clothes in my flat, she could have come on to London. The upshot of this discussion on logistics was an agreement that we should try living together. Denise said she would rather move to Fulham than have me move to Henley, despite its proximity to Caversham. 'I hate my horrid flat, and you've got such beautiful things.' We agreed that she would drive up tomorrow in her Honda with some of her belongings and I would clear some drawers and wardrobes tonight.

This means I shall no longer be able to sit at my kitchen table keeping this journal. I look back at the first entry. I wanted a woman. Now I have one. My daily introspection ceases. I will put this black canvas-covered notebook back between the covers of *The Development of Secondary*

*Education in the Soviet Far East* where it will remain hidden among the unwanted Russian textbooks on my bookshelves until someone can be bothered to throw them out.

All Orion/Phoenix titles are available at your local bookshop or from the following address:

Littlehampton Book Services
Cash Sales Department L
14 Eldon Way, Lineside Industrial Estate
Littlehampton
West Sussex BN17 7HE
*telephone* 01903 721596, *facsimile* 01903 730914

Payment can either be made by credit card (Visa and Mastercard accepted) or by sending a cheque or postal order made payable to *Littlehampton Book Services.*
DO NOT SEND CASH OR CURRENCY.

**Please add the following to cover postage and packing**

*UK and BFPO:*
£1.50 for the first book, and 50P for each additional book to a maximum of £3.50

*Overseas and Eire:*
£2.50 for the first book plus £1.00 for the second book and 50p for each additional book ordered

-----------------------------------------------------------------------

BLOCK CAPITALS PLEASE

*name of cardholder* ..................... ...... .    *delivery address*
                      ...... ...... ..............    *(if different from cardholder)*

*address of cardholder* ..................... ...    ..........................................

........................................             ..........................................

........................................             ..........................................

........................................             ..........................................

      *postcode* .......................                     *postcode* ..........................

[ ]  I enclose my remittance for  £...........................

[ ]  please debit my Mastercard/Visa (delete as appropriate)

    card number  [ ][ ][ ][ ][ ][ ][ ][ ][ ][ ][ ][ ][ ][ ][ ][ ]

    expiry date  [ ][ ][ ][ ]

      signature  ...............................................................

            *prices and availability are subject to change without notice*